Wakefield Press

# Incredible Floridas

Stephen Orr is the author of six previous novels – *Attempts to Draw Jesus* (runner-up *The Australian*/Vogel's Literary Award 2000), *Hill of Grace*, *Dissonance*, *Time's Long Ruin* (basis for the opera *Innocence*), *One Boy Missing* and *The Hands* – as well as a collection of short stories, *Datsunland*. Stephen has an abiding interest in the dynamics of families and communities, as well as the plight of isolated individuals. He has been nominated for several major Australian literary awards, and works part-time as a teacher in Adelaide.

**Praise for *One Boy Missing***

'Stephen Orr's detective is sunnier than Kurt Wallander, but his talkative characters and bitter realism stands comparison with Henning Mankell. He's a sincere storyteller with a flinty eye for the landscape and the sadness that drives good stories forward.' – *Weekend Press*

**Praise for *Dissonance***

'Stephen Orr writes a story with great tension and momentum. The emotional and psychological layers of *Dissonance* prompt us to ponder the deep nature of familial relationships ...' – *Good Reading*

'Orr brings us a cast of characters that are wholly believable. The first hundred pages alone would make a fine novella. As it stands, the entire novel is an accomplished work.' – *InDaily*

'This is an intelligent, beautifully-wrought novel. Its finely nuanced characters intrigue and move because of the complexity of their motivations and identities.' – *Australian Book Review*

'Orr is a no-nonsense, vivid storyteller. He punches out exchanges between his characters in a pragmatic way that transmits jealousy and heartbreak without sentiment.' – *Australian*

**Praise for *Time's Long Ruin***

'*Time's Long Ruin* is Orr's eloquent, unusual, bold but responsible retelling of a veritable urban nightmare that still haunts the Australian imagination.' – *Sydney Morning Herald*

'The writing is accomplished, the imagery beautifully evocative ... despite the distressing subject matter at its core, this is a deeply affectionate novel.' – *Age*

'It is Orr's cleaving of the ordinary to the unspeakable that gives the novel its potency and brings it within the margins of the Australian Gothic.' – *Big Issue*

'Every now and again, you open a book that is so richly evocative, so poignant and haunting that the characters leach into your subconscious and you are caught in an intricately spun web of emotion, scent and feeling.' – *Sunday Tasmanian*

By the same author

*Attempts to Draw Jesus*
*Hill of Grace*
*Time's Long Ruin*
*Dissonance*
*One Boy Missing*
*The Hands*
*Datsunland*

# Incredible
# FLORIDAS

## STEPHEN ORR

**Wakefield**
**Press**

Wakefield Press
16 Rose Street
Mile End
South Australia 5031
wakefieldpress.com.au

First published 2017

Cover designed by Liz Nicholson, designBITE
Edited by Emily Hart, Wakefield Press
Typeset by Michael Deves, Wakefield Press

ISBN 978 1 74305 507 6

A catalogue record for this
book is available from the
National Library of Australia

CORIOLE
McLAREN VALE

I have struck, do you realize, Incredible Floridas, where mingle
with flowers the eyes of panthers in human skins!

'The Drunken Boat'
Arthur Rimbaud


The earth became a dream; I myself had become an inward being,
and I walked in an inward world. Everything outside me faded to
obscurity, and all I had understood now was unintelligible. I fell
away from the surface, down into the depths, which I recognised
then to be all that was good.

*The Walk*
Robert Walser

# 1962

Roland Griffin couldn't stomach horses, classical music or chat about what was best for cleaning shoes. But Sam would pop in, take the transistor from the work bench, and fiddle until he found Moonee Valley; correct weights and prices for a win or place. He'd sit and watch Roland paint, sketch, or just look at a blank canvas. On those days he'd say, 'What yer gonna paint?'

'Haven't decided.'

'What about a still life? I could go pick a few oranges.'

'Na, did that once, didn't like it.'

A red-brown canvas with vaguely cubist fruit; an embarrassment from the early days, stacked with a dozen others behind the timber pile in his shed-cum-studio. It was corrugated iron, painted brown, green, leftover beige from the sleep-out. Hot-in-summer, cold-in-winter, cracked and crumbling concrete. He'd covered the oil stains with an old rug and set up his easels and canvases, an armchair and a table for his brushes and paints. The Dodge sat in the sun, or rain, while Roland painted, listened to the third from Randwick, as old Sam from next door rolled cigarettes. There was still a workbench, and tools, a knife grinder and a tea chest full of walnuts and almonds (which Sam'd sometimes start cracking) – but mostly, it was Roland's studio.

'Cezanne, they sell his pictures for millions.'

'Well, that'd be nice,' Roland would reply.

'That'll be you one day.'

'Yeah, maybe, Sam.'

Roland wanted to tell Sam he was doing okay, that his name had got around, that his shed had hosted directors from several state and overseas galleries. But he knew Sam wouldn't understand. To people like Sam, unless you were Cezanne, painting was a hobby. Something a man did after work, if he was that way inclined.

'Why they always standin' in a desert?' Sam would ask of Roland's figures.

'Just are.'

'And they're always lookin' at yer, like they think you're stupid.'

Sam would eventually tire of asking questions, light a cigarette.

But there was no Sam today, and no desert, either. Roland sat in his painting chair, his don't-get-comfortable chair, and looked at his canvas. He'd managed some jungle, a river, a boy in a boat with a bag of wheat, a bale of cotton and a look of amazement. Tigers, panthers, and in the background, a collection of natives wearing war paints. Submerged rocks, and the boat taking on water. But the boy didn't seem to care. Whatever he was seeing held him transfixed.

The boy had Hal's nose, but Roland was careful to avoid letting the lines add up to Hal. He was just a typical child. A boy. No one in particular.

Roland thought about the boy's shirt. Plain or stripes? Even this was too much of a decision. Perhaps he shouldn't work for a few weeks, or months, even years. Maybe it was reason enough to stop altogether. Get a job up the Murray? But here he was, sitting on his chair, drawing mental lines before actual ones.

Roland Griffin was only forty-two, but he had the face of a sixty-year-old. Receding hair, a cast-iron forehead with single wrinkle-as-horizon, heavy eyes (that might've had more to do with his horror week), a strong Scot nose and a chin that stuck out slightly further than his wife, Ena, liked.

Roland stood, walked through the shed doors and stopped in the carport. He leaned over his car and felt the grille, the fender, crushed, the paint crumbling. Wondered whether it would need fixing. The radiator had survived, and the wheel was still turning. So it was just cosmetic. Ena had already insisted they fix it, but she'd get used to it. Cars couldn't stay new forever.

He opened the door and sat in the driver's seat. He'd powdered the carpet and seat covers with baby talc, but the smell of beer was winning.

'See, that's why you have accidents,' Ena had said, but he'd explained that he'd only had a sip as he drove. 'I wasn't even tipsy.'

He got out and crossed the cracked drive to where soil had turned to sand. He put his bare foot in it, moved his toes through it, and remembered sitting beside his tent, one shoe on, one off, paper on a folder in his lap, the smell of Hal's beans drifting over from the campfire. A few marks, another horizon, a hill, and Hal, in his short shorts, body painted, stealing old King's thunder as he danced his propitiatory dances, interrupting the Pukamani when it had reached its loudest moment. But no one stopped dancing, or said anything about the white boy. The same boy, at the wheel of their Dodge, driving into the scrub, headed for a truck that was headed for them, the red letters on its side: DANGER HIGH EXPLOSIVES.

Roland flattened the sand with his foot and returned to the shed.

The breeze was coming in. He could hear Ena inside clattering through the drawers. He studied his canvas and wondered whether to continue. Jungles, adventures, were so old-fashioned. His friend, James Bailey, had explained how they'd both been left behind. This Warhol character in New York, with a dozen soup cans. Not even painted, but copied. There was always the chance people would tire of his work: small towns, deserted pubs, half-castes addressing the viewer. But it was all he knew. It was a big investment (his whole life) if it was going to come to nothing.

Roland was walking into a barber shop in Darwin. Hal was beside him. Lionel Mill welcomed them. He took Hal by the shoulder and sat him in the leather seat. Roland watched Hal's eyes as he attempted to work out the backwards letters on Mill's front window: CIVILITY, SERVICE AND LONG ODDS. Mill himself never stopped talking. He knew they weren't local.

'Travelling?'

'Yep,' Hal replied. 'Right around the top.'

Roland could remember all of this. It wasn't so long ago. And yet he counted the years: 56, 57, 58, 59, 60, 61, 62.

He stretched back, looked up. The iron roof was supported by wooden struts and crossbeams. His good eye passed across the central support; the one he avoided looking at. He'd dropped a mental plumbline; the imaginary weight dangled just to the left of his easel. He wondered, for the hundredth time, if Hal had chosen this spot for the message it might send. But his son wasn't like that. Simple, practical, no-nonsense; just got on and did a thing. There was nothing *Ada and Elsie* about him. His life was a nail that had to be knocked in.

Yes, he guessed. It's best being alone. As much as possible. He had cried, but stopped. The physical act had exhausted him, and itself. Now, it was just the worst sort of self-pleasure.

He watched a shadow moving across the far wall. The window had cracked but you couldn't tell from the dusty light. He waited for the dark patch to touch the edge of a rake. Another day gone, and wasted.

He heard Ena calling.

'Griff!'

There was a cup of tea every morning and afternoon. Whoever was handy, sitting around the table, sifting through the penny-jar of conversation. But it didn't matter. As long as the water was hot and the tea strong, the milk cold, chipped china with the strainer rattling in the lip, soft biscuits that had to be eaten because what else would you do with them. A cosy that Shirley had knitted. All of these things set out on the table like some Japanese ritual.

It was always the same. Tea sipped, a few words about the Christmas puddings hanging in Mary's laundry, all gone mouldy. 'I'll just have to start again,' she'd say. Mary, sister of Sam, mother of Shirley and her fortunate, unfortunate life, the trio of survivors washed up next door to the Griffins.

Mary shuffled into Ena's kitchen at ten-thirty. Always ten-thirty. Shirley followed a few steps behind and, without speaking, picked up the kettle, filled it, lit the stove and put it on to boil. Ena barely acknowledged them. It was as though her family extended out the back door, across the drive, through the arch and past Sam's sleep-out.

Mary placed seven biscuits on a plate, took a bite from one and put it back down. That would be hers. Then the kettle was boiling nicely and Ena was at the back door, one hand in her apron pocket, calling to Roland. 'Griff, you comin'?'

Mary was wearing her apron too. Her pockets were full of brown leaves from where she picked lemons, popped them in, and returned to the house like a cow that had missed the milking.

The women stood in Ena's kitchen looking out of the window that didn't let in enough light. She'd asked Griff to do something about it. He had the tools and the wood, and there was a glazier at the end of the road, but he didn't really have the will. It still worked. It still let in light. So, he'd just say, 'I'll get to it, dreckly,' and Ena would think, Bullshit. Typical Griff: always off with the fairies, sitting on the toilet sketching old men in pubs.

The dining room was all table. There wasn't enough space to get around the sides. Ena had suggested they cut it down but Roland wouldn't hear of it. 'It's an antique. You can't take a saw to an antique.'

'But you can barely move.'

Like Shirley now, adjusting chairs to get to the teapot. She filled it from the kettle, returned to the kitchen and came back with the lid and cosy. Sitting beside Mary, she waited for the brew to draw. 'They got that pole sitting at Brighton,' she said, one hand half-hiding the butterfly rash that spread from her neck, across her chin, to her face.

'What's that?' Ena asked, coming in.

'They sit on top of a big pole, in a box, for a week.'

'Why?'

'Just do.'

'How do they go to the toilet?'

'Dunno. Just saw the picture in the paper. Maybe they got a bucket.'

Mary sniffed the cut flowers and said to Ena, 'Them roses are strong.'

'Rotten leaves, from the gutter,' Ena explained, but Mary already knew, had seen Griff up his ladder, flicking the leaves to the ground, gathering them and spreading them around his rugosas. She saw everything from her window, or in transit to the letterbox. That was life: a succession of moments, other people's, overlooked, -seen or -heard to a soundtrack of scratchings droned down her lamb-mint hallway.

Silence. As the tea took its time, and they fell into their own thoughts. There were other things to say: the Pope ill, Menzies off overseas again, sniffing out the new queen, Weet-Bix on special. News seemed out of place, still. But Mary felt the silence more, the inference that it was quiet for a reason.

'Griff coping?' she asked.

Ena shrugged. 'I suppose. You never know with him.' And what she really meant: with a man. They were all shopfront and no eggs. The door was locked, and they were always out the back doing something else.

'It'll take time,' Mary said.

'Yes.'

Mary thought of other things to talk about: the Thebby school closing, but that involved kids, and it was best to avoid that. The murder of a woman at Belton, but that led to courts, and gaol, and hangings. So, in the end, there was less than usual to discuss. But you had to keep talking; if you didn't you started thinking, and wanting reasons for things that didn't have or need reasons.

'Griff!' Ena called.

Mary started pouring the tea and settling each cup in its saucer. 'Sonia 'round?'

'Sonia!'

'Coming,' a voice replied.

'Everyone's coming,' Ena said. 'Always coming.' She wished people would just do what they said.

Sonia came into the room. 'Hi, Mary, Shirley.'

'Mornin', darls.'

Shirley just smiled, lowering her head.

The Griffins' daughter sat down and said, 'You want me to come shopping with you today, Mum?'

'No, just need a cabbage. Go get yer father, will yer?'

Sonia did as she was asked. She went out to the shed (she knew there was no point calling) and looked in. 'Dad, cuppa.'

'Said I was coming.'

'Come on, that can wait.'

Roland listened to his daughter. He knew she knew better than him, or Ena, or anyone. She'd topped her Leaving Honours, and university degree. She'd got a good job and moved in with her best friend. He wondered how he'd managed to contribute to such a good girl. Maybe she'd just managed to overcome anything he'd given her.

He stood and followed her in and they settled around the table. He said, 'Where's Sam?' and Mary replied, 'The stables.'

'Late in the day for that?'

'Tim's got him exercising them. Think they were going to the beach.'

Roland wondered why Sam hadn't asked him. Perhaps he'd thought he wouldn't be up to it, or that he'd run out of things to say, or was best left alone. Maybe he'd guessed he was better off with the women, for now.

Mary was thinking, Quiet, isn't it? But she couldn't say this. Instead, she asked Roland, 'What you workin' on?'

Roland knew she didn't really care, but it was a neutral question. 'Not working.'

'Another desert, perhaps? You've done a few of them, eh?'

'They're easy to paint.'

Sonia was reading her father's face. 'You can get lost in a desert, can't you, Dad?'

'There's a bit of that goes on,' Mary said, like a seagull stealing a chip from a man's hand. 'That family, in the desert, that was terrible.' And then she realised even this would lead back to Hal.

'Those immigrants?' Ena asked.

'Yes.'

'What immigrants?' Sonia said.

Mary leaned forward, determined. 'This fella from England. He tried to drive his family from Marree to Queensland. Had no idea.'

'What happened?'

'They got bogged. Tried to walk back to Marree. Three days in the heat. Two little boys and his wife, and the radiator was full of water.'

'Terrible,' Ena said.

'They reckon they coulda burned the tyres,' Mary continued. 'They woulda been seen. But I suppose you mightn't think of that, especially if you'd just come from Kent.'

There was silence again, and in the silence, agreement: never leave your car, tell someone where you're going, don't get bogged.

Mary knew there was lots of meat left on the bone. The family, the daughter they'd left behind in town, the visit she'd received from the police as she was ironing her husband's shirts. But it was a tragedy, and someone's kids were dead, so she'd have to let it go.

Then Roland said, 'They found footprints, where the father had walked in circles, hundreds of times. He must have gone mad.'

No one wanted to buy into it.

'Imagine that … lookin' at his wife and kids.'

'Is that who yer painting?' Mary asked.

'No.'

Mary felt the weight: the three of them, and their grief. She was still expecting tears. That's how it had been. Since Roland has discovered him, since the ambulance and hospital and the first night they'd all sat in the lounge staring at the telly. The following day, when sleep alternated with rambling treks around the yard. She'd busied herself cooking casseroles. Sam had helped her take them in, warm them in the oven, and clear them away, uneaten, as they all sat staring at the ground. 'I done a coupla banana cakes,' she said.

'You keep 'em,' Ena replied.

Roland liked banana cake, but he wasn't going to argue with his wife.

'I still can't understand,' Sonia said. 'If he hada said something.'

'You don't, do you?' Ena said.

We all know why, Mary thought. Now we've just got to wait, and drink tea.

From her window, Mary could see Hal walking up the drive in his school uniform, satchel in one hand and brown paper bag in the other. She knew it contained his pants. It did every day. Within half an hour they'd be washed and hung on the line. And one day, she remembered, he came home at one in the afternoon, when his parents were out. Sam saw him and called, 'Home early?'

'Half-day.'

'Really? It wasn't a half-day today.'

'It was.'

'Maybe I can take you back. They're gonna miss you.'

At which point Hal dashed up the drive, down the road, off to God knows where.

Roland finished his tea and Mary poured another. She was taken by the way words ebbed, then flowed in a reflux of conversation. She guessed that humans were just full of puff. Try not talking for one minute, she'd say to Hal, and he'd try and try, but he never could. Grinning, his mouth full of words, the alphabet spaghetti spewing onto her apron. Hal, who had always teased Shirley, but then always apologised, like it was a misunderstood joke.

'I can smell him,' Sonia said. On his pillow, and sheets, as she slept away the days since he'd left them, but her, especially.

No one had a response. People had a smell. But that would go, quickly – quicker than any other part of him. So, Sonia guessed, she'd just have to lie on his bed for as long as possible. Breathing deeply. Remembering every stupid comment, every lifted eyebrow, every flick of hair from his eyes.

For Roland it wasn't so much the smell as the seeing. Hal was still sitting on the floor in his shed – on the rug, on his gristly knees, painting a jungle and river on a piece of old cardboard. He was biting his lip, looking up for approval, working on the wobbly horizon.

Roland asked, 'What about some trees?'

'No.'

'You gotta have trees for a jungle.'

'You don't have trees.'

'I like people.'

'I like them too.'

The paint had splattered onto his knees, and legs, and shorts. 'Your mum's gonna kill you.'

And Hal smiled at Roland and thought, Not me. You. You're the adult.

The last of the tea was drunk, and water bills discussed. They still had to be paid. Mary said, 'There's no point watering the lawn in summer. You end up paying for it.' But of course she did, or at least made Sam do it. She wasn't going to be the first to let the street down. 'Sam wants to rip up the lot and concrete it.'

'You can't do that,' Ena said.

'That woman round the corner, she did, and she painted the bastard green. Fancy that? Like we wouldn't notice.'

Roland was determined to buy the cabbage. Sonia wanted to go with him. Walking along a street was a simple task, a sort of meditation, and he liked to do it alone. But things were different now. He sensed he had to open up to others.

'How you feelin'?' Sonia asked, as they set off.

'How about you?'

She smiled. No, you, she was saying with her eyes.

'I was wondering who else we need to contact,' he said instead.

'What's it matter?'

'You don't want people finding out in the paper.'

'You're gonna put it in the paper?'

He thought about it. 'No, I suppose not.'

Mr Ireland's front yard was carpet grass, cut low, perfect. Roland never saw him out watering. Green grass just came to Mr Ireland, apparently.

'I was wondering if I should tell Alice,' Roland continued.

'Why?'

'Of all the people … she was the one I thought would get him through.'

Sonia knew this was true. For a while Alice had become her brother's fifth limb. She was the only one (outside the family) who understood him, knew what to ignore and consider, when to stand up to him and when to back off. 'She's probably got her own life. Some other fella.'

'Maybe not.'

Sonia thought about it. Even Dr Neri hadn't understood him. No one at Glenside, for all their diplomas and degrees. 'Would you know where to contact her?'

'Didn't she live in Westerly?'

'No, that was Rose.'

So Alice would have to wait. She and Hal had spent two years together – weekly flicks, Coke and sandwiches on the Garden lawns, long days filled with the kids they'd make, the house they'd build, the lamb shanks they'd cook.

'Say something.'

They walked, coins rattling in pockets.

Roland shook his head. 'What's to say? It happened, you deal with it.'

'*You deal with it?*'

'Yes, you do. Your grandfather, fifty years at the chemical works. Falls into a vat of sulphuric acid. Eight weeks lying in bed. I was six years old and I can still remember the smell of his flesh. *You deal with it.*'

'But he got better.'

'Exactly.'

'Hal won't.'

He glared at her. What a stupid thing to say.

The footpath was uneven. Mrs Ireland had tripped on it and done something to her knee, so Mr Ireland had phoned the city manager, but nothing had happened. That's how it was these days. Now the residents of Burleigh Avenue, Pennington, unclogged the leaves from the street gutters and mowed the verges themselves.

'I'm concerned,' Sonia said.

'Worry about your mother.' He walked faster to get the cabbage over and done with. He wished she hadn't come.

'It's just … you were the one found him.'

'Men in the war saw that every day.'

'Not their own sons.'

He was quiet.

'You haven't told me about it.'

'Christ! I got the shears and cut the rope. He dropped into my arms.'

And Roland was there, again.

'He was heavy.'

Roland was laying the heavy body on the old rug, pushing over his easel, straightening and examining his son, as though this moment was always going to arrive. He was feeling his neck for a pulse, somehow surprised by the whiskers. Adjusting his head, although it just kept dropping onto the rug. 'I don't need to be reminded.'

'You can't pretend it didn't happen.'

Roland focused on another neighbour's clivias, but the thought persisted. Him calling out, 'Ena!' The click of the back door, and her running into the shed, as though she, too, knew what she was going to see. 'What do I do?'

She was kneeling beside her son, but she could only look at Roland. 'What do I do?'

'Blow into his mouth.'

Neither of them did. There was no point. They just dropped, sat on their bums, and she started screaming, and soon Mary and Sam were standing in the doorway. Sam didn't need to be told. He turned and headed back to his house, and the phone they'd just installed.

As they walked, Roland said, 'Everyone's got their own way.'

Sonia couldn't agree. You had to talk about it, even if it was painful. You had to have a ceremony and let people look and cry and remember and sing and get drunk and go home with a head full of anger.

They approached the front door of the shop and Mrs Ireland came out with a few things in a string bag. She covered the shock of the moment with a smile. 'Morning, Griff,' she said. 'How are you, Sonia?'

A plain, string-bag sort of how-are-you.

'Good, thanks, Mrs Ireland.'

'How's mum?'

'Well, you can come see her.'

This wasn't the answer Mrs Ireland wanted to hear. She stiffened at the commitment. 'I was going to wait.'

'No, she'd like it.'

'It's only been a couple of days.'

'She's just got the four walls, and us.'

'Right. And how are you, Griff?'

He just wanted to get the cabbage. 'Getting there.'

'We all worry about our children, don't we?'

'Yes.'

'After a certain point, there's little you can do. I mean, it's their life.' She realised this might sound wrong.

'Yes.' Roland didn't want to make it any easier for her. Then she'd start talking about her Alvis and her polio and the six weeks in the iron lung and all the kiddies in the kiddies' hospital, dying of terrible diseases. As the cabbage went unbought.

'Well, give Ena my best,' she said.

I take it you're not coming then, Sonia thought.

Mrs Ireland was gone, down the road, a week's worth of cordial pulling on her arm.

'Old cow,' Sonia whispered.

'Come on.'

They went in to trays of over-ripe tomatoes and bruised peaches, half and quarter watermelons and pumpkins that waited around for weeks until someone got desperate enough. Roland couldn't see how they'd come from a market. Maybe a collection of backyards associated with the little Balt who sat, all day, behind a counter tackling crosswords. Roland had always wanted to tell him to come out, arrange his fruit, restock the shelves, price some of the groceries and at least *pretend* he wanted to stay in business.

He found a tin of Elastoplast, Lifesavers and the cabbage and placed them on the counter as Sonia examined bunches of wilting carnations, wondering if they might do any good.

They started home. John Carey, watering his lawn, scampered behind his house. He'd left his hose running and hadn't gathered his dogs in time.

Fair enough, Roland thought. Carey was a man of few words, happy to chew over a drought or wheat prices, but as for death … He wasn't a Hallmark man, although his wife, who was about half his size, was a volunteer visitor at the repatriation hospital. 'G'day, John,' Roland called, as they walked past, and a faint voice came from the side: 'Is that you, Griff?'

They continued. '"Patrons must not bring bottles, dogs or peanuts into the theatre",' Roland said.

Sonia just waited for the story.

'It was up on the screen – the open-air theatre in Darwin. I thought it was beautiful. Hal had a laugh, too.'

It was Mitzi Gaynor in *South Pacific*. They'd hated every minute, but there wasn't a lot of choice. Still, there was a breeze, and they could hear the sea. The locals (in gloves and hats for their big night out) sat creaking and farting as the songs went on and on. A few people had smuggled in grog, and this was shared along the rows. Then the breeze dropped and half the audience went home, sweating. By the time the nurses started washing their hair, Hal and Roland had had enough too.

Wandering through the deserted town, Roland had asked, 'What next?'

'How about a swim?'

So they'd walked to the beach and stood looking north to Sorong until Roland said, 'Well?'

Hal had stripped down to his underpants as Roland looked away. Sixteen was an uncomfortable age. The boy had become part-man but the man was still mostly boy. Hal had walked to the water and tested it with a toe.

'I wouldn't,' a voice had said.

They'd turned and noticed an old man, shirtless, sorting through his lures.

'Them jellyfish are bad today.'

Hal had got dressed and they'd returned to their car and driven back to their camp.

When Roland had finished telling Sonia this story she smiled. She guessed her father had softened and realised she'd gone about it the wrong way. There was too much water to navigate to get to Roland Griffin.

'I ended up squirting him down with a hose,' Roland said.

'No shower?'

'Na. Every coupla nights, if there was a motel. But it was damn hot. Dunno how anyone can live there.'

'I bet Hal was grizzling?'

'Not much. There was no use complaining. The weather's no one's fault.'

They turned down the drive and found Charlie Bass, from number eighty-two, sitting at the milkie's table with Shirley, two children at his side. Sonia said, 'How are you, Charlie?'

'Fine and dandy,' he replied, as he always did, often invoking his blood cancer, and the way, one day, it just went away under the curing hand of God. Retired tailor Charlie always wore his beige suit (with a carnation) and his bow tie, white socks and polished shoes. Charlie, the Jehovah's Witness, with his belief in the End and his two prop grandkids, as Roland called them. The girl in a pink dress, with her own little Bible, and a boy, a year or so older, with long shorts and high socks. Neither child spoke. Or seemed to have a thought. Like Charlie had cast them from plaster and animated them with the spirit of his angry, impatient God.

'Just talkin' to Susie,' Charlie said.

'Shirley,' Shirley said.

Charlie had his Bible open to Matthew 24:7. Roland sat down with the vegetable in his lap and said, '"Nation will rise against nation, and kingdom against kingdom".'

'I was explaining how Hitler was the second Antichrist.'

'Who was the first?'

Charlie either didn't know, or care. Sonia noticed how the girl was looking at her. Like she was planning violence. Jealous, perhaps, of her older neighbour's escape from this purgatory of whitegoods and memorised psalms.

'But I's explaining how there'll be others,' Charlie said.

Sonia just shook her head. 'If he was the Antichrist, how come he didn't win?'

'There are others, stronger.'

The prop boy wiped his nose on his hand, and seemed to be using his tongue to get something from between his teeth.

'Shirley!' Mary was standing under the arch on the border of their territories. 'Come on, you've got jobs.'

Shirley stood and walked away. Catholic Mary waited, her arms crossed. She couldn't stomach Charlie. She called, 'No harm meant, Griff. It's just she tends to believe what she's told.' And she glared at Charlie. 'You leave that to me, Charles.'

'We all got the same Bible,' he called back.

Mary knew that God was a bus timetable. He could be read in many different ways. But she also knew the Witnesses were evil, subverting the Word, the quiet prayer beneath the jasmine. She turned and went inside with her daughter.

'Mum's probably got the kettle on,' Sonia said, in a way that didn't imply an invitation.

Charlie closed his Bible. 'I can return, with some reading.'

'Don't bother. There are other things going on, in case you haven't noticed.' And whispered, 'Or cared.'

Roland followed Sonia in and presented his cabbage to Ena, and she said, 'It's a lettuce.'

He looked at it. 'Shit.'

Roland had made a carport from wood, but hadn't roofed it, preferring to leave the job to the wisteria. He was standing underneath it. It was nearly one in the morning, but still warm. He was smoking Capstan, looking through to the cinnamon stars, wondering. If they were a trillion miles away, what did an arbour, or painting boats, or anything really, matter? This was some consolation. Hal could've lived till ninety before the starlight had reached them. The sky was a sink with the water emptying out of it. Roland could feel himself going with it.

He heard the wheels of Hal's Austin pedal car. No matter how many times he oiled them they still turned like fingers down a blackboard, urging and receding as Hal pedalled up and down their cracked concrete river. Around the Dodge, the garden, a U-turn, back at full speed, and again, for hours, as Roland tried to paint, eventually emerging.

'Hal, could you do that later? I'm trying to work.'

He was the man who never wanted to kick the footy. Sitting on his bonnet, he inhaled and blew the smoke into the sky in a little oil spurt.

'Not too fast,' he said to a toothless, cow-licked Hal, as he pedalled past.

'I'm timing myself.'

'You'll end up arse-over-tit.'

Hal swerved and the wheels lifted. He pedalled so fast Roland could see the wheels coming away from the car (he'd only repaired them with wire), rolling down the road, as his son tumbled and his face ground into the concrete.

He heard Mary's front door opening and turned to see Sam coming out and sitting on the porch. Opening his paper, he started reading from the light that was coming from the bedroom behind him.

Roland finished his cigarette and threw it into the garden. He watched Sam studying the form guide. He'd be up at four to walk to the racecourse, to take the times for the trainer, Tim Johnson. Every weekday morning, sitting with his stopwatch in the starter's box, writing down the figures, holding his binoculars to his old eyes as he watched for signs of improvement – anything that might offer some hope (and justify his two quid).

Roland noticed how Sam stopped reading, rested the paper in his lap and looked out. He could tell his thoughts had nothing to do with horses. How he studied the ground, and seemed to sigh. Folded the paper and placed it on the table beside his smokes.

'Early start?' Roland asked.

Sam wasn't surprised by the voice. He looked over. 'Yeah.'

'You better get to bed.'

'Don't need sleep these days.'

'You need some.'

'Hardly any.' Sam scanned the street and there was a long pause as he wondered whether the conversation warranted a smoke. 'I still can't believe it,' he said.

'No,' Roland replied.

'You never think it's that bad. But it's how you see it, isn't it?'

'Yes.'

'You can only say so much.'

Roland stood. 'Well, I'm tired now.'

'Good-o.'

Roland came inside. He pulled the screen door but it wouldn't close; it had to be taken down and planed. There wasn't much point using it now anyway, there was almost no breeze. The bricks and mortar held the heat, keeping them sweating and miserable through another slightly-cooler-than-day night. Sleep came with difficulty, and it never lasted long.

He lay down in bed and lifted his legs. Woofed his jama pants to get air to his machinery.

'"Dear Mrs Griffin …"' Ena said.

'What?' Roland asked.

'Remember, that note from school? "Mrs White noticed that Hal didn't have lunch today. We managed to arrange a sandwich from the canteen." I felt so bad.'

'Once,' Roland replied. 'In how many days? Thousands?'

'Then it said something like, "If you're having problems supplying food …"'

'Nerve of them.' He wiped his forehead with the wet flannel he kept beside the bed. 'You should go to sleep.'

'No point.'

'You'll feel shithouse tomorrow.'

She didn't reply. What did it matter how you felt?

'What made you think of that?' he asked.

Ena really didn't know.

'When was it? Fifteen years ago. But you still remember what they said.'

She got out of bed and walked across the hall to the toilet. He listened as she dropped the seat, sat down and emptied her bladder. He knew how it began and how long it lasted. How long she'd wait before standing up, hitching her daks, returning to bed without washing her hands.

But tonight Ena went into the lounge room, switched on the light and sat down in the recliner. She tried the radio, searching for some piano – perhaps Lucie McCabe playing a nice nocturne. She'd grown up with a piano in the house; a sign of civilisation, her mother would explain to visitors. They had Chopin and Mozart scores, open to the trickiest-looking passages, spread out for fingers that would never play them. Lessons, lessons, her mother always nagged. Just try. But Ena wouldn't have a bar of it back then. The piano was school, sucking marrow from the bone with the promise of great things, although, from what she could tell, there was little beyond the hoover and steak-and-kidney pie.

Nothing but twangy guitars; she turned off the radio and saw Sonia standing in the doorway. 'When you gonna get an air conditioner?' she asked.

'Ask your father.'

Sonia sat down on the lounge. 'Wanna cuppa?'

'No.' Ena walked over to a glass cabinet and produced a decanter of sherry. Took two small glasses and filled them almost to the lip. She gave one to her daughter and said, 'I don't know if it's any good, it's been sittin' there for years.' Ena wasn't even sure she wanted it, but if anything warranted alcohol. 'That room's hot,' she said. 'It always got the late sun.'

Sonia shrugged. 'Back a coupla days and I'm used to it again.'

It was still her favourite room, her favourite place, in the world. Where she'd spent sixteen years with her brother – listening to his breathing, cursing, singing and, after the Change, other things. It was a small house, and there were only two bedrooms. Eventually Roland had strung a line down the middle of the room and hung a curtain for privacy. But every time Sonia looked Hal was peeping, smiling, telling her she didn't have very big tits. She'd asked for a room in the shed but that had always been her father's studio. There was nowhere to go.

When Sam suggested a sleep-out, Roland delayed, but in the end agreed. As did Ena, who saw that her children wouldn't survive a shared adolescence.

No council permit; the concrete was mixed and laid, the pine erected, the asbestos painted and hammered on, Mrs Ireland's brother brought in for the power, a set of louvred windows installed.

'What colour for the inside?' Roland had asked, and Sonia (who was at that difficult age) had just said, 'Leave it to me.'

One day, Ena and Roland had come home to find the sleep-out decorated with newspapers. Sonia had mixed the flour and glue and started work on the dozens of front pages she'd been collecting for months in anticipation of her own room: Eisenhower, Korea and Radium Hill; Elvis Presley and Doc Evatt's piercing eyes watching at night. At last, she was happy.

But now Sonia was more interested in the early days. The times they'd sleep bed-by-bed and she'd read him *Robinson Crusoe*, and he'd fall asleep as she told him about muskets and Friday. In a way, she guessed, only she knew her brother. Only she'd shared the same stale air for thousands of nights. Listened to him fart, and giggle about it. There was always something about brothers and sisters, beyond even what parents knew. Something that was given up, regretfully, when the world beckoned. He was in every corner of their room: where he'd carved his name in the mortar; drawn pornographic images (probably of her) inside the darkness of their wardrobe; spilt paint from his models on the rug; knocked in nails for his posters, leaving cracks that were never filled.

Sonia had known when she'd seen Ena and Roland on the porch. Her flatmate had watched from the hallway as her parents sat silently in the lounge. Maybe it was the same way brothers and sisters learned to communicate without words. Like she knew, and Hal knew, there was no thought or word the others could have or say they hadn't anticipated and understood. Maybe it was like mashing potatoes. You only had to be told once, and probably not that, if you'd seen it done.

Sonia had eventually asked, 'When?'

'A coupla hours ago.'

And then her flatmate had come in, and they'd all embraced, and shed a few tears, before the friend had fetched a bottle of vodka from her room. Sonia could remember lino. They'd just cleaned it, and it still smelt of laurel and lemon, and this seemed to overpower even the news of death. Now, she couldn't comprehend how cleaning and suicide could coexist in such an intimate way. But they did. It was like one was no more or less important than the other.

'How long you gonna stay?' Ena asked.

'As long as you want. As long as I feel I want to.'

'Your father would like that.'

'Until work want me back.'

'He likes having you around.'

Still listening from his bed, Roland unstuck his legs and watched the fan go round. He hoped she'd stay forever, but of course, she couldn't.

They sat in the shed, busy in their worlds: James Bailey on a fruit box, Roland on a stolen dining room chair. Bailey sketching Griffin, Griffin staring at the child in the boat.

'That boy's got Hal's nose, and mouth,' James said.

'No.'

'I'm not an art magazine, you don't have to hide it.'

Roland shook his head and made a move to attempt a few more lines. 'It's not Hal.'

'No?'

'It's rubbish, anyway.' He removed the boy and laid it on the rug, replacing it with an aborted townscape. 'Everything I do lately … looks like something else I've painted.' He opened a tin of white putty and started applying it to the canvas with a knife.

'What are you using?' James asked

'White, raw sienna, bit of black.'

'It's not that bad.'

'It's shithouse.' Roland continued removing the memory of the deserted main street that looked like a hundred others he'd attempted.

'Paul'd be mad with you.'

'Paul isn't here.'

'Paul's always here.'

Their teacher, Paul Bell, wandering the room (or shed), studying sketches and saying, 'That looks like a pig's face.'

'What do you reckon I should do, Mr Bell?'

'Cheeks, chin, something recognisable.'

'Remember what he said?' James reminded Roland.

'That was years ago.'

*'Move the lines, shape the face – no, don't throw it away! Keep at it!'*

Roland knew James was right: Paul, with his brandy breath and whistling nostrils, always behind him, watching.

1932. Roland was sitting bored in bed in hospital, his left eye bandaged. He found a piece of paper and made a few sketches of the old Greek who was sent in to clean his room at eleven every morning. Later, when the nurse saw the pictures, she said, 'They look just like Eleni, Mr Griffin.'

He'd hidden them beneath his newspaper, thrown them in the bin, but when she returned she got them out. 'You got a talent for it.'

Then the ophthalmologist came and said, 'Didn't quite go as planned.'

Roland wondered why it'd taken the doctor several days to tell him this. 'How do you mean?'

'That's the problem with a detached retina … it's tricky. But we'll see, when the bandage comes off.'

When it did, things were no better: the same blur of shape and colour. He'd tried to focus on the doctor and said, 'What's next?'

'That's it.'

'There's not another operation?'

'I could try again, if you like.'

If you like. What did that mean? I can fiddle around again, charge you hundreds of pounds, and we'll be back where we started.

The doctor was examining the crumpled sketches the nurse had left out. 'These are very good.'

'There's no other procedure?'

'I've got this friend, teaches art. Paul Bell. I can pass these on if you're interested. He learnt from Fox, and Conder. He's good.'

Roland was too angry to say no.

James had finished his sketch. He showed it to Roland, still flattening the surface of his canvas. 'Who's that?'

'No one. I've learnt from you, I don't do *real* people.' James didn't want it to go on like this, but wasn't sure what to say. Sorry for your loss? He was a good kid, wasn't he?

Instead, he put the sketch aside and took a small bottle of gold from his pocket. 'I found this at home.' He handed it to Roland, who abandoned the knife to examine it, turn it in his fingers. 'Hal threw it at me when we had a fight. I was trying to tell him something, then he's shouting at me: "And take yer fuckin' gold, too!"'

'That sounds familiar.'

'But I knew it wasn't him.'

Roland was grateful for this chunk of understanding. 'It wasn't, eh?'

'Not when I'd known him that long. I knew it wasn't him screaming at me.'

Roland had seen this version of his son a hundred times. This wasn't the way he wanted to remember him, but it was okay because it was James, and he was as close as anyone. 'He could be frightening.'

'My word. But times like that, I always remembered him when he was little.'

'That was okay for a while … till he grew muscles.'

James didn't know how to answer; this wasn't a time to make Hal accountable. 'I can remember when we found it too,' he said, examining the gold. 'Remember?'

Roland could. 'How many ounces do you reckon?'

'Dunno. It's strange he never sold it.'

'Maybe he had plans for it?'

'Maybe it was for good luck?'

Roland took a deep breath. 'Yeah, good luck.' He handed the gold to James but he said, 'No, you keep it.'

'I don't want it.'

James took it. 'Maybe I could ...' But he stopped himself.

Roland placed the canvas on the ground and picked up the boy in the boat again. 'Just keep going, eh?'

'That's what Paul would say.'

Roland worked on the child's face; a smile, or grin, full of wonder at the waterspouts and breakers, the green night and singing phosphorus. Each fine line; azures; flotsam. As Paul Bell came up behind him.

'Your name?'

'Roland Griffin.'

'Your background in art?'

'None.'

Bell had studied the drawing, but given nothing away. 'You seem to have the dimensions, and accuracy. But why couldn't you become a designer, or engineer?'

'I reckon it might be fun.'

'Fun?'

'The doctor said there might be a scholarship, if you thought there was some promise.'

'You're not meant to ask for a scholarship.'

'Sorry, sir.'

'Well, I'll tell you what. Go home, sketch some faces, bring them back in a month and we'll talk.'

'Faces?'

'Yes, faces. That seems to be what you're good at.'

Meanwhile, James was studying the several dozen photos Roland had pinned up around the benches, on the window frames, the walls. Some were studies: Shirley, turning away from the camera; Mr Ireland in his yard; a pair of Aboriginal jackaroos holding a steer's skull. There were family shots, awkwardly posed: mother and daughter standing under the arbour; a self-portrait with roses; the two artists in their shed, lighting each other's smokes. Only one showed the boy, posed with Sonia, pulling a face. 'Where are the photos of Hal?'

Roland went to the drawer of the old kitchen cabinet and took out a shoe box. Then he sat down and opened it. 'Just for now,' he said.

James pulled up alongside him on the fruit crate and took a photo from the box. It was a head shot of Hal, a study for a painting called *Figure alone in the bush*. 'I recognise this. Didn't you sell that one?'

'No.'

Roland sorted through his pile of aborted paintings leaning against the iron wall and pulled out the transfiguration of his son, standing alone in scrub. James came over and stood beside him. 'It's a good one.'

'I couldn't sell it now.'

'Yes, you could. I'll give you a bottle of gold.'

Roland placed the painting on the easel on top of the boy in the boat, and sat down to look at it.

James placed the photo on the ledge beside it. 'Every time I look at him at that age I see that movie poster, and him running around Kalgoorlie.'

Roland let out a lungful of air. 'You take it home.'

'No, but you don't want to leave it here. The heat'll get to it.'

'Take it home, please.'

Roland didn't like the undertaker's suit, or the way he looked at them like he was trying to sell them something. It wasn't like they hadn't bought his product. He didn't like the forms on the desk. Paperwork, even in death. As if they could have their son back if they filled it all in correctly. The expensive-looking fountain pen. How did that change anything? But most of all, he didn't like this Robinson man's face – shaved clean and white and pasty, like he might be trying death himself. His expression – a little head tilt, lips clicked together like Ena's purse, a sort of store-bought concern, *yes, I know how hard these things are.*

'I'd like "Abide with Me",' Ena said.

Roland still couldn't believe he was arranging these details, rehearsing the phoniness of his son's departure from a world that specialised in veneer. Hymns. A nice tie, perhaps, for the viewing, Mrs Griffin? We'll need to be in and out of the chapel in forty-five minutes. Will that be a problem? 'If your priest can't make it, we can find someone.'

Your priest? Since when did they have a priest? Do we, he wanted to ask his wife, even know one?

'Well, if there's someone handy,' Ena said to the undertaker.

Robinson picked up his fountain pen and made a note: 'No priest'. Like they'd never bothered with religion but now, of course, needed it. Hypocrites, he was really writing. In need of a wag of the tail, a few lines from Psalms, the invocation of God and the firstborn between a few awkward tributes.

They sat dutifully. Roland could see past a door to what looked like a preparation area. He imagined the car arriving with the body and men standing around smoking, looking at it and thinking, He was a young one. And the driver saying, 'Killed himself.' All of this must have gone on every day, with no one thinking much of it, like a shopkeeper arriving for work, unlocking the door, stacking the bread, waiting for the first customer.

'Just the one hymn?' Robinson asked Roland, as though he wasn't contributing enough to the conversation.

'I reckon. What do you think, Ena?'

'Yes.'

'And what about the eulogy?'

Ena had no intention of getting up. That was a man's job: to fumble scraps of paper, keep it together between memories of cricket and the first day at school, and the time the car broke down.

Robinson and Ena were waiting for Roland.

'Something short?' he asked.

'Four, five minutes,' Robinson said. 'A few moments you shared.'

A few moments. As easy as that. Entertain them, old boy. A *Reader's Digest* version of everything someone said, thought, did, wanted, hated, couldn't cope with, succumbed to, screamed about. The thought ended there, but it didn't. It just went on and on, in the same way life did, even now.

'I'll try write something, I suppose.'

'Good-o,' Robinson said.

Roland could hear them moving something in the back room. Some old girl, dead in her sleep at ninety, a nice, clean stroke, the neighbours finding her a few days later. Or maybe some wheezing wog, released from his emphysema, six months of coughing up his lungs from a two-pack-a-day habit. Or maybe it was Hal. Lying naked, plugged up at either end, someone applying makeup to the marks around his neck, doing up his old suit so the collar covered the bruise. Maybe he could look, he thought. Maybe he could ask, Can I go see him? But he didn't really want to. He wanted to visit his living son, but that wasn't possible.

'And what about flowers?' Robinson asked Ena.

She was comfortable with flowers. Carnations (and she suggested colours), mixed with roses and a spray of gypso. Flowers were cup-of-tea cheer, powder-scented, preservative-dipped. Biscuits, too. 'Do I need to supply food?'

'No, of course not, that's part of the service we provide.'

The service. The oil and lube, the wires stripped back, the mail delivered, the walls painted. Service. And here's your bill. Written up with the same rotten pen.

Still, Roland wondered what he'd really expected. There was a body to deal with; that wasn't easy. It's not like you could bury it in the backyard, or dump it in the creek. And the government needed to know, apparently. Why, he couldn't think.

'And what about the newspaper?' Robinson asked.

'I don't want all that,' Roland said.

But Ena had already decided. 'Something simple?'

'I don't see the point of broadcasting it across the city.'

Robinson was ready with what Roland guessed was a stock response. 'There are many who won't know: old friends, school chums ...'

Chums, he used the word chums.

'People he's worked with. Then, for the next few years, there'll be phone calls and knocks on the door and you'll keep being reminded, having to explain it all over again. Grieving, again.'

'It's not like we're trying to get it over and done with. He was our son.'

Robinson looked at him as if he was too stupid to get it. 'It's part of the *closure* process.'

'The closure process?'

'Allowing yourself to move on.'

I don't have to allow myself, Roland thought. Maybe I don't want to. Maybe I just want to sit in my shed and remember him, paint pictures of him. Maybe it's just your business that needs me to move on.

'Should I dictate something?' Ena asked, clutching her purse.

'If you'd like.' Robinson picked up his pen and waited.

'The details, of course,' Ena said, 'then what about, "Our loved son, the most any parents could wish for."' She turned to her husband.

'I dunno.'

'It's standard, Griff.'

'What's that mean – the most we could wish for?'

'It's just a reassurance,' Robinson said. 'When people read it ...'

Over their breakfast, or chops and eggs. 'But what does it mean?'

Ena shook her head. 'It's the sentiment, isn't it?'

Not really, Roland thought. Just more of the window dressing that made him feel so uncomfortable. The little cards (Robinson had shown them the samples) with Hal's face smiling at them, as if to say, Look what I gone done. Made myself dead. The cards people would take home and keep on the mantel for a few days, before guessing the time was up and popping them in drawers or, more likely, the bin.

Ena was trying out words: '"A great loss, but memories are our consolation."'

Roland could hear water running from the back room. They were probably washing someone down – the blood, or piss and shit that had run down their legs, the smell of acid-burnt flesh. He could still smell it. Every day he woke up and every night he tried to get to sleep. His dad moaning, his mum rubbing on the ointment, him standing in the doorway. 'See you, Dad, I'm off to school.'

'Make sure you behave yerself.'

He could remember not wanting to go in, to see the red flesh, the look on his dad's face, the table covered with medications. He felt a coward, that his dad would be hurt. But later, he realised his dad wouldn't have minded. It didn't matter that Roland didn't see him like this. Only that he got better, and life continued.

Ena still fighting with words: '"Forever remembered by father, Roland …" What do you think?'

'Fine.'

She shook her head and continued: '"… mother, Ena, and sister, Sonia." How many words is that?'

It's not a classified, Roland wanted to say. Not a birthday greeting. It's not like you die every year.

'I suppose we should include the grandparents?'

Robinson played with his pen, waiting.

Water, Roland thought. Running, filling a trough or sink, by the sounds of it. The City Baths, hundreds of dolphin-like bodies playing in the sun. Boys in thigh shorts with house keys safety-pinned to their bathers. Cross-armed girls watching them jump from the top of the tower. The smell of coconut and cooking flesh, hair oil and chlorine. The sound of lifeguards threatening ejection if you run again. Nine-year-old Hal, standing on the end of the board, looking down, mustering courage as people waited. 'Come on, we want a go!'

Roland was looking up. 'Come on, Hal. People are waiting.'

But Hal just held his arms close to his body, squeezing them (and himself), his legs shaking. He knew he couldn't go back down, but couldn't jump. The next boy in line asked, 'You goin'?'

He nodded and stepped towards the edge. Roland (in his baggy bathers) waited, hoping, but not expecting. 'Come on, son.'

Hal put his toes over the edge. It was a long way down. Surely it wasn't survivable. Here he was, holding everyone up, and he hadn't even thought about how he'd do it: head first, feet first, bomb, tumble. How had the others done it?

'Are you goin'?' the boy said.

'Yes.'

He noticed the line – nearly all the way back down to the pool. He could see his dad standing beside the lifeguard – the familiar look of expectation.

'Just jump!'

The boy saw it before Hal himself registered. 'He's pissed himself!' And then they were all laughing. 'That's disgusting!'

The lifeguard said, 'Do you reckon he can get back down?'

Roland felt helpless. Always had. Still did. As he sat listening to the running water, wanting to go in and see if his son was there, and needed help. But he knew he couldn't. Couldn't climb up and bring him down. No one could.

Hal had to wait until the other divers (dozens of them, looking at him as they walked past and threw themselves over the edge) had finished. He sat on the platform, mostly in his own piss, his arms cradling his knees and his head buried in his body, until it was safe to go down. Roland watched him descending and realised the City Baths was another bad idea. When he was down he said, 'Maybe we could just do laps. Or muck about?' But Hal turned and walked towards the change rooms.

'Fine,' Robinson said. 'It should be in tomorrow's paper.'

He led them into a side room with no windows. Roland could see where they'd bricked one in, and wondered why. Maybe neighbours, or burglars. It would be hard to explain the theft of a body.

'This one's oak,' Robinson said, running his hand across the lid of one of the eight coffins. 'Beautifully made. But it's getting buried, isn't it?'

Ena tended to agree. There was no point asking the price if you weren't going to buy it.

'Some of our Greek customers want them to last. I'm not sure why. Maybe they want to reuse them.' He half-smiled. 'Maybe something in pine?' He led them towards a pair of similar coffins. Ena studied them and was overcome. She started sobbing and Roland put his arm around her.

'This one, perhaps?' Robinson asked, refusing to be drawn.

'Yeah, that'll do,' Roland replied, leading his wife from the room, back to the desk, and the paperwork.

Robinson sat down and made a note of their choice. 'And finally, the location of the plot?' He laid a map of the cemetery in front of them.

Ena gathered her thoughts, and studied it. 'In the middle,' she said, indicating.

'Prime plots. Very expensive. Here, on the side …'

Ena looked. 'I'm not having him near a road, listening to trucks all day. In the middle, what do you say, Griff?'

Roland nodded, not thinking about plots, or coffins, or flowers. He was thinking about his son, ten yards away, waiting for him to climb the ladder and bring him down.

The night wouldn't cool. Burleigh Avenue hummed with a few air conditioners, *Blue Hills* and kids under sprinklers. Until the blackout. Silence. Tellies swallowing pictures, radio voices falling silent, books put down as lights cooled, as hands and fingers fumbled candles. Followed by a chorus of voices in the dark. 'What d'yer reckon it is this time?'

'Someone's hit a pole.'

'No, they're sharin' it around.'

It didn't really matter. There was nothing to be done. The moon cast its light on split-skin plums and the bit of water left in the birdbath Roland filled every morning. The day had roasted the sword fern and burnt the margins of leaves. Dead grass blew away in the last gasp of northerly, although it would keep trying all night. The house took a day to heat, but three to cool. Roland would even hose it, watching steam rise from the red bricks his father had laid, the walls he had never bothered insulating. It was a sun-hardened hippo, stuck in drying mud, waiting for the end. The soil played with the foundations. He'd used concrete to fill the cracks. Ena would watch him work and say, 'Shouldn't you get it the same colour as the mortar?'

He'd stand back and look. 'You can barely tell.'

After ten minutes of a hot house most people came outside. Small tendrils of life reached out and through front fences towards the footpath. Roland started watering the garden as Ena checked no one else had the light they'd been denied. A few kids got on their bikes, riding up and down in the dark. One started on his pogo stick. Sam and Mary appeared, Sam with a longneck. 'Should I get you one?' he asked Roland.

'No, thanks, Sam.'

The street had come alive, the sort of place Roland remembered from his own childhood. Singlets revealed warts and scars. Most of the women had taken off their bras; the whole day was sagging. One neighbour, a wog who kept to himself, pottered about in only his pyjama pants.

Sam went back for another beer anyway. 'I got 'em cold in the esky,' he said.

'Sam, he doesn't want one,' Mary called to her brother, needlessly.

'You comin' out?' Sam said as he passed Shirley's room.

'No.'

He went into his sleep-out, still murmuring with the Harold Park trots, the tranny he'd bought to replace the one in Griff's shed. He opened his esky, took out another beer, popped the top and spotted the drawing taped to the wall. He pulled it down and sat on the bed to study it: a horse (long, with a body twice the size of its legs), with an old man (him) riding it. He was wearing salmon and black, clutching the reins, and a speech bubble said, 'Come on, girl, you can do better than that.'

He remembered the night. Hot, like now. Hal (wearing the shirt he chewed around the collar) was standing in the doorway. 'Look what I did, Sam.'

'What's that?'

Hal sat down on the bed beside him and showed him. 'It's the one we were watching the other day. What was she called?'

'Problem Child?'

'That's her. See, same colours, and long legs, like hers.'

'She's a beauty. Pop that on the wall, eh?'

'If you like.'

'And you can come back Wensdee, and help again.'

'If Dad lets me.'

'He'll let yer. I'll have a word to him.'

Hal's arms were red, where he always scratched them, and the fleshy creases of his elbows scarred from constant picking.

'You gotta leave that alone,' Sam said.

'It's itchy.'

'Doesn't matter. You gotta leave it alone.'

Sam wasn't about to tell him the itch was all in his head (Griff and Ena had done that). That he had to stop fretting, and chewing his clothes, and scratching. He was even anxious about being told he was anxious. So what was there to do? Get him busy with the stopwatch, helping the trainers wash the horses, shovel the shit – anything, really. Horses were more useful than words.

Sam smoothed the drawing and considered taking it out. He noticed the screen door sitting open against its clicker, and remembered running inside to make the call. The same doorway Hal had stood in. He thought this was strange. How people grew, and changed, but the houses they lived in didn't; how the laundry trough had the same crack and his esky, the same leak.

He taped the drawing back on the wall, picked up the full beer and the half beer and returned to the garden.

John Carey had arrived. 'How are you, Sam?' he asked, but Sam just nodded and handed Roland the beer.

'I's just sayin' to Griff and Ena,' Carey said, 'makes you wonder, eh?'

'What's that?' Sam asked.

'Why they switch it off.'

'Prob'ly just a prang.' Sam knew that Carey wouldn't settle for such a simple explanation.

'You look at the area. I got a friend in Brighton, she never gets blacked out. That's a marginal seat. You look at Pennington. Safe Labor.'

'So you reckon someone sits there and decides who'll get blacked out based on politics?'

'Of course.'

Sam avoided shaking his head.

'Anyway, why can't they make enough electricity? We pay plenty for it.'

'Everyone's got a cooler these days,' Sam said. 'I suppose when they put in all these lines people didn't.'

Carey didn't like Sam's logic: far too understanding. Where did that get you? It just allowed the government to walk all over you. Maybe he was a Christian. Or maybe he'd been kicked in the head by a horse.

Sam wondered whether he should offer Carey a beer. Did he deserve one? Had he even extended his sympathies, asked how they were going, brought down a casserole? Unlikely. Carey was for Carey. That's why there wasn't a wife (apparently there had been, but Sam could just imagine why she'd left).

'I got a dozen chooks in the deep freeze,' Carey said. 'I bet they won't replace them.'

Roland was sprinkling his burnt-umber grass, soaking the soil, studying the cracks in each square foot. He'd tried the sprinkler.

Now Hal and Sonia were running through it, squealing, jumping, stopping and lowering their bodies over it. Hal sat down on it. He was looking at Roland, saying, 'It's going up my bum.'

'Get off,' Sonia cried.

One night like this, Roland found a tent that hadn't been used for years. He strung it up between a couple of fruit trees and filled it with water. It leaked, but took a few hours to empty. The four of them, legs and bodies intertwined, until someone moved the wrong way and the water gushed and a branch broke and the whole lot flooded across the lawn and they were left like fish out of water, flapping on the mud under the fruit trees.

'Two hours,' Carey said. 'That's what they reckon. If they get it back on before then they're not liable.'

Carey never acknowledged the kids, like the other neighbours would, if they were in the front yard when he walked past, or if they passed him on the way to the shop. 'G'day, Mr Carey.'

'Who's that? Oh, Griff's boy. How is Griff? Still paintin' his pictures?'

'Yes, Mr Carey. He's got a big exhibition coming up in London.'

'London, eh? Quite a celebrity, living in our little street.'

Sonia was sitting inside, peering out, close enough to her dad to talk to him without the others hearing. 'He's a stupid old prick,' she said.

Ena saw Roland laugh and wondered.

'You gotta feel sorry for him,' Roland said.

Ena hated it when Roland talked to himself. He could have his own thoughts, but it was different when his lips moved.

'Go on,' Sonia said. 'Tell him to stick that hose up his arse.'

Roland laughed again and they all looked at him.

'Somethin' funny?' Sam asked.

'Just remembering a joke.'

'He's such a miserable sod,' Sonia whispered, quieter this time. 'It should've been him instead of Hal.'

Roland thought this seemed fair: if all the Careys hanged themselves, instead of the Hals. But the Careys didn't realise they were Careys.

'Why don't you come out?' he asked.

'Not in the mood for chitchat.'

'Neither am I.'

'Who you talkin' to?' Ena asked.

'Myself.'

'You're goin' mad,' Carey said, but then realised.

'Go on,' Sonia said. 'I dare you. Go over and squirt him.'

Roland just smiled.

'Wish he'd drop dead. Bet he hasn't even mentioned Hal.'

'No.'

Ena realised he wasn't talking to himself. She saw Sonia's shadow. 'That'd be fair,' Sonia said. 'But it never is, is it?'

Roland watered. He felt like this was doing some good. He could feel them all watching him, but didn't care. He knew Ena couldn't help but be nice to the old bastard; that Sam just wanted to chew his ear; that Mary was happy standing back, and adding the occasional Jesus, Joseph or Mary. He looked at Sam and smiled, and he grinned, and drank, and wiped his mouth.

Father-and-son set off down the road. It was another hot night and they had to escape the house. Hal (with his newly peach-fuzzed upper lip) walked beside him. Roland guessed this was the best way – walking, talking, or at least attempting to get him to talk. That would lead to questions and answers, and Hal learning the world wasn't such a complex place.

'If you don't want to, don't. You can leave at fifteen and start an apprenticeship.'

'Like plumbing?'

'Boilermaker, whatever.'

They were reading the vacancy board on the side of the Simpson's factory.

> Boilermakers (12)
>
> Fitters (9)
>
> Carpenters (7)
>
> Refrigeration mechanics (3)

'Six years in there?' Hal said.

'Up to you. You can make some good money.'

Hal though about it as they continued walking. Good money. But that didn't seem enough. Not if you were trapped in a factory for six years, or a lifetime. 'I could paint, like you.'

'You could. But that's a hard slog.'

'So?'

They passed the school. The pool, locked up. Roland said, 'That's a waste, on a night like this.'

'Look,' Hal said. He pushed a gate and it opened. He walked into the school, and jumped a small fence onto the concourse surrounding the pool. 'Come on.'

Roland checked the street. 'Hal!'

'They forgot to lock it.'

Roland followed, watching, as Hal approached the pool and, without stopping to think about it, stripped down to his underwear and dived in. He guessed the interest had more to do with the open gate than water, or maybe it was just because no one was here to see his legs, the hair under his arms, his angry little face, and its half-a-dozen spots. He was kicking water, pushing off from the sides, gliding across.

'See, you're good in the water.' Roland slipped off his sandals and shirt and lowered himself into the water. 'Cold, cold, cold.'

Hal laughed. 'It is not.'

'It is.'

They both swam. Suddenly, Hal got out, ran around the pool and walked to the end of the diving board.

'No,' Roland said. 'The neighbours.'

But Hal launched himself into the air. He got out and did it again and again, perfectly, and ten minutes later one of the neighbours came over.

'You're not meant to be in there.'

'I'm the principal,' Roland said, quicker than he'd expected.

'Right, just checking.'

'Thanks for keeping an eye on things.'

The neighbour returned to his house and they laughed, their heads just above the water.

Roland switched the tap off and left the hose on the front lawn. He showed Sam his empty bottle. 'You got another one?'

As they walked down the drive the power came on. Sam could hear Ena's light classics. The streetlights reclaimed their few minutes of community.

Ena looked at John Carey and said, 'I hope your chooks haven't spoiled.'

She led Mary in, saying, 'It's best not to start a conversation with that man.'

Ena and Sonia stood in front of the painting, *Mother and Son*. The mother was distracted by something in an otherwise empty desert; the boy looking out accusingly, as if the viewer had placed them in this treeless wasteland. The mother's long, brown fingers trailed across the boy's white shirt.

Ena noticed that it hadn't sold. There were others that had, and they were inferior paintings. One, a collage by some up-and-coming teenager – cotton wool and torn paper, fabric, splashes of paint. *Composition VI*. Where were the other five? A tag for one hundred pounds and a red sticker. 'Who'd buy that?' she whispered to Sonia, looking around in case she was overheard, although the room was mostly deserted. A pair of old girls moved their faces to within an inch of each of the paintings they examined.

'That's all the go,' Sonia said.

'But why?'

'Someone's betting that this person's the next big thing.'

They'd been in the gallery for fifteen minutes and come across seven of Roland's paintings, none of them with a sticker. In 1950, when the mother and son were painted, he'd had a solo exhibition in the same space and nearly everything had sold by the end of the first night.

'It's about money,' Sonia explained. 'They probably don't even want to hang it. Probably don't even like it. I mean, could you like that?'

They moved to the next painting.

Annadale Galleries was white-walled and singular-fanned – an old industrial number clunking on the ceiling. The floorboards had been worn down where people shuffled from painting to painting. There were small tables in each room with vases of lisianthuses and carnations. Like a mortuary, Ena thought: a home for dead and dying pictures. There was a desk near the door where Mr Annadale sat talking to Roland. Ena could tell Roland was getting angry about something. His hands were moving, his legs crossed, in the same way Hal had crossed his legs. And she could imagine Annadale's reply: I can't help it if people are buying the new stuff.

The new stuff: planes of paint, lines that wandered over the canvas, ceramic boxes inside boxes. Roland guessed anything was valid, as long as the artist was trying to say something, to express him- or herself, to give in to the urge to *make*. But what could a single line painted across a canvas possibly mean? And if it did mean something, who could possibly work it out? And if it wasn't meant to be worked out, then what was the point of painting anything?

Roland studied his hands, and wondered; at the paint under his fingernails, the crease in the side of his finger where he held his brush.

'I really love this one,' Sonia said, as she and Ena stood in front of *The Cattle Yards*, one of her father's early experiments with light. The paint was thick, rising and falling from the canvas in painted and knifed-on patches. 'Why's it for sale?'

'Mitty gave it up.'

'Why?'

'She needs the money.'

Sonia noticed that Annadale was selling it for two hundred pounds. 'After all these years,' she said. 'It must be worth more than that.'

'You would've thought. It's one of his best.' She studied the yards at night – no shadow, just black and white (although the white had yellowed). 'It takes you there, doesn't it?' she said. 'I still remember staying in Albury, and him runnin' round at night, sketching. Do you remember?'

'No.'

'One night the coppers brought him home. Can't imagine what they thought he was up to. When we got back from Albury he just painted, for months. Had one of his … periods.' She smiled.

They both knew what this meant. Months on end when they barely saw him: up at seven and straight to the shed, in at twelve for a slice of ham in a roll, back to the shed, no responses to calls; no morning or afternoon tea. Sometimes Ena would wonder if he was okay, and pop her head in, and he'd barely look at her. 'What is it?'

'How's it going?'

'Fine, fine. Is there something you need me to do?'

She'd shake her head and close the door, cook tea, feed the kids, bath them and get them to bed. They'd want to say goodnight but she'd tell them not to disturb him. She'd sit listening to the radio. Then, at eleven or twelve, he'd come in, take his tea from the oven and eat it in five minutes. Shower. Collapse in bed, ready to get up and do it all again the next morning.

Roland was almost whispering to Annadale. 'You can't be serious?'

'I gotta do it, Griff.'

'But you haven't sold any.'

'*I* haven't? Who painted them?'

In the battle of the figs and abs, modernism was winning. Two more weeks and I re-hang everything, Annadale had explained. All this lot comes down, and we give the young ones a go. He reached down and produced a small canvas cluttered with angular shapes. 'Ask me why this is behind my desk,' he said.

Roland didn't reply.

'Because as soon as Haessler's on the wall he's gone. This little prick paints 'em as fast as I can sell them. I'm keeping this one as a favour to a good customer.'

'We were doin' that stuff in the thirties.'

'It's back in.'

Once he was Haessler, kept behind the desk, and the conversation was all about sheep skulls and barbed wire and what it meant to be Australian. 'You gotta promote the work,' Roland said.

'I do.'

'Proper catalogue, big exhibition. I can fill the place.'

'But would they *buy* anything, Griff?'

Roland felt his muscles tensing, his legs locking like overstrained wire. Annadale had started off decent but had ended up like everyone else.

Ena followed Sonia past two more abstracts. They stopped in front of a portrait of a teenage girl. Ena could tell Roland had finished this one quickly. The paint was thin, applied in confident lines. He'd sketched her dozens of times before he was happy with the result. Then it was just draw, paint, seal, sell. She could see them sitting in his shed – Shirley in a canvas-backed chair, wondering what all the fuss was about. She'd brought tea. 'Should I put yours over here, Shirley?'

'Yes, thanks, Mrs Griffin.'

'Griff, don't keep her out here all night.'

'I'm nearly finished.'

Sonia examined the rash her father had painted. 'I never understood why Mary agreed,' she said.

'She was flattered,' Ena replied, watching her husband, deep in thought, as Annadale filled out some paperwork. 'Mary's never seen her as a ...'

Now they were both thinking about Shirley, standing in the drive, hiding her face, her hands in home-knitted gloves. Straightening her fingers, attempting to stretch her arms and legs and feet. Sonia said, 'I always wanted brown eyes, like hers.'

'They're not Mary's,' Ena added.

'No, they're not.' Sonia struggled to say any more. She felt bad. She hadn't been much of a sister or neighbour or friend, or anything, really. She'd always ignored Shirley. She was a cripple. And lupus, what was that? Did it catch? Did it kill you? Far easier to bring friends home from school.

'Of course, he didn't paint the rash,' Ena said.

Sonia was confused; the red blooms were there on the canvas.

'He painted her, and showed Mary, and she loved it. But then he thought, It's not really honest. So before he sent it off he added it and Mary never knew. Or if she did, she never said anything.'

Sonia could remember a Friday afternoon in the living room with a couple of friends. They were playing records on the old stereogram, dancing, singing along, banging bums and attempting mock waltzes. She looked up and Shirley was at the window. 'What do you want?'

'Can I come in?'

'No!' And she pulled down the blind.

'Who was that?' someone asked.

'The spaz from next door.'

And they all laughed.

Shirley was still standing in the drive, outside the window, listening, when Hal rode in the gate and pulled up next to her. 'Whatcher doin', Shirley?'

'Not much. What about you?' She was holding it all in, waiting for her room. 'How was school?'

'Boring. Equations. You ever done them?'

'No.'

'You wouldn't want to.'

Roland was soon beside them. 'Where you been, Hal?'

'Riding around.'

'How are you, Shirley?'

'Good, Mr Griffin. You wanna draw me again tonight?'

'If you're not busy.'

Standing in front of the painting, Sonia guessed she felt worse than Shirley ever had. Really, really rotten. 'I was a cow to her,' she said.

'Your father really got her, didn't he?'

As Sonia thought of the thousand times and wished she could repeat them all differently. 'I was such a cow,' she repeated.

Roland had had enough. He asked for a box and Annadale said, 'Griff, they can go back up, after.'

But Roland insisted. Annadale went outside, returned with a fruit crate, and Roland began. He walked to the boy and mother, removed them from the wall and placed them in the peachy-smelling box; then the cattle yards, Shirley, James, deserts, pubs, a long-legged, small-headed man sitting on his back verandah.

'What's wrong?' Ena asked, following him.

'He's gonna take them all down.'

Ena looked at Annadale, busy with paperwork.

'For a coupla weeks,' he said.

'Griff.'

Roland took his last painting off the wall. 'He's either with me or he's not.'

The old ladies, watching from the other side of the gallery, seemed confused.

Sonia asked, 'Dad, what are you going to do with them?'

'Dig a big hole and bury them.' More to Annadale than anyone.

'Griff,' Ena consoled.

Roland stormed from the gallery and Sonia and Ena followed him. They went back to the car and he threw the lot in the boot.

'Griff, calm down, take them back in,' Ena said.

But he just shook his head. 'What's wrong with people?'

And what he meant: Why doesn't anyone understand what I've done? What I've *tried* to do?

Sonia did. She saw it in Shirley's eyes. A moment in the shed when he'd said something and she'd smiled.

Ena sat on her son's bed, lost in thoughts, but no thoughts. Roland appeared in the doorway.

'What?' she asked.

She was unsure of her husband's feelings. Although he insisted on moving on, in a way, he enjoyed remaining behind, chewing over the tough meat. There was nothing visceral, weepy, memory-littered (at least spoken out loud) about him. Like his father, he just lay in his sick bed all day, bottling up the frustrations so they might come in useful later.

'I'll cook something when I come in,' he said.

'I can do it.'

He waited.

'There's no law against sittin' for a minute, is there?' she said.

Then he turned and walked from the room.

She slid to the ground and leaned against the bed. The full-length mirror was on a frame that allowed it to tilt in the middle; it was angled up. She thought she was floating.

She pulled Hal's cricket bat out from under the bed and examined the red dents, the end ground down where he'd tapped it on the drive. Four o'clock every summer afternoon; a ball with its cork emerging; standing six feet from the side of the house: bounce, crack, bounce, crack. Listening from inside, she'd wonder if the walls were up to it.

Cricket was another casualty of art. Hal would tire of hitting the ball against the wall. He'd wander into the shed. 'Dad, can you chuck us a few?'

'In a minute. I've just gotta finish this bit.'

He'd wait in the drive for ten, fifteen minutes. 'Dad?'

'Coming!'

Roland would eventually appear, hands and arms covered with paint. 'Just a few. I gotta go in and help your mother.'

Five balls later he'd call it a day.

'Dad, a few more?'

'Tomorrow.'

Always tomorrow. Hal had played club cricket, and they'd sat watching for four hours every Saturday morning.

'Why's it drag on so long?' Roland would ask Ena, as they watched him waiting for balls that never came.

'That's cricket.'

'Can't he play something … faster?'

'If you don't wanna come …'

'He just stands there.'

And he'd wave to them.

'Not too much to ask, is it? Couple of hours on the weekend?'

Roland had thought that it was too much. He'd looked at the freshly mown oval, but only seen other landscapes. Perhaps there'd be a painting in cricket. Perhaps. As he'd thought of a couple of boys practising against a pub wall.

Ena opened the bottom drawer beside the bed. Singlets, dating back a decade, the tops chewed, bottoms stretched where he was always pulling at them. She could see his little arms hanging out of the holes: the knobbly shoulders and beginner biceps. His small naked body, jumping on the bed, dripping bath water, the pirate Griffin flicking his sister with his towel, her pinning him down, threatening to spit in his face or cut off his willy. Ena could hear the bedsprings tensing and relaxing, the mattress rising and falling. Hal! Stop it! You'll break the bed.

She searched the drawer and found the journal she'd helped him keep as a ten-year-old. It was to be a record of his child acting, his trip to Western Australia, his imaginary life as the brother of Lucie McCabe. She looked through the dozen or so pages he'd completed before losing interest. The fact that he'd kept it for twelve years must have meant something. Perhaps he'd planned on showing his own kids, or maybe he'd never got around to throwing it away.

She flicked through the blank pages and noticed red ink, and a full-page drawing. She stopped to study it: a girl tied to a stake, surrounded by what looked like fruit crates, and lengths of timber. A boy (unmistakably Hal) stood looking up at her, holding a burning stick, saying, 'It will only hurt for a minute.'

She closed the book, opened it, tried again, but couldn't understand. Searched the other pages, but it was the only drawing. She heard a voice. 'You there, Ena?'

'Christ,' she muttered, standing, returning the journal to its drawer. She walked to the front door and greeted Mrs Ireland. 'How are you, Jude?'

'Fine, thanks, Ena.' She presented a casserole dish. 'Steak and kidney. I remembered Griff liking it.'

'Yes.' She took the dish. Roland had never liked it. He'd trawled through Jude's steak and kid several times before, picking out the organ, saying, 'Who would eat offal?'

Jude Ireland waited for praise. 'I know what it's like … times like this. It's hard to convince yourself to cook.'

Ena knew Jude wasn't going anywhere, so she invited her in. As they entered the dining room Ena said, 'Where's Barry today?'

'Busy in the garden.'

'Tea?'

'Water, please.'

Ena fetched two glasses and braced herself as they sat down. The trick was to avoid questions and ignore Barry's hip, council rates, how sad it was, wasn't it, the little lass with the rash.

'Ena,' Jude said, 'I didn't want to come down too soon.'

Ena didn't respond; there was no need.

'I didn't want you thinking we weren't aware, or didn't care, but I know what it's like. Well-meaning people, those first few days.' She sipped her water slowly. Less than a mouthful. Ena divided it by the volume in the cup and realised she was in for at least an hour.

'It came as a shock to both of us,' Mrs Ireland said. 'Mr Carey popped his head over the fence and told us. We went in and made a cuppa and no one said a word for ten minutes. It was like that. Shock, I s'pose.'

Ena was curious about *their* shock. Not the shock of the hanging body, the ambulance, the doctor, the undertaker – just Jude and Barry, silent with their cups of tea.

'Just last week he walked past, going to the shops, and I said hello, and asked him what he was up to.'

Why was that so surprising? Ena thought. When he was alive he could still walk and talk. 'What did he say?'

'Told me you were off overseas again.'

'Not now.'

'No, of course.' Jude carefully timed another mouthful of water. 'I'll have some very good memories of him.'

Ena waited to hear about them.

'Up and down the road on his bike, even when he was on his trainer wheels.'

Ena guessed she'd made this bit up. She could remember Roland taking him to the tram park and letting him practise there; he didn't want him on the road too soon. This felt like scripted conversation: the requisite small talk, memories invoked, funny moments recalled (despite not having happened) before everyone got to go home and forget, content they'd done the decent thing.

Jude Ireland said, 'I had a nephew did the same thing. Of course, that was different. He was about to be married and she ran off with some other fella. Apparently, when she found out, she hardly blinked an eyelid.'

That sounds made up too, Ena thought. 'Sure you wouldn't like a cuppa?'

'No, thanks. There's a funeral?'

'Yes.'

Jude was glad Ena didn't give her any more. Funerals were a

bother, especially if you were only a neighbour (and six houses away at that). What could you do? Make up the numbers? Of course, it'd be different if he was a kiddy, but he must have been in his mid-twenties, and by that age all bets were off. 'I suppose things will never be the same,' she said.

'No, I suppose.'

'But you'll have to carry on.'

'Yes.'

'And how's Griff's painting going?'

'Good.'

She saw a little nugget glistening in the sand. 'We saw one hanging in the bank.'

'Really?'

'Barry said it wasn't Griff, but I looked and there it was: Roland Griffin. It seemed to be an old man, and his gin.'

'Yes. They made prints. I'll have to tell him.'

'It's good he's got an interest.'

'Well, it's his job.'

Mrs Ireland couldn't see how painting pictures could be a job. She'd never understood how Roland made enough money to support his family by fiddling about in his shed. She'd always assumed there was some other income: an inheritance, shares, racing horses, perhaps. 'He's sold a few, has he?'

'About four hundred.'

'That many?'

'Over thirty years.'

'That long? Well, I must get his autograph.' But how could it be anything like Barry grinding axles for forty years for the tramways?

She drank again. Ena noticed the glass was still nine-tenths full. Her back was sore. She'd had enough. Mrs Ireland was just here because she was worried about not being here. She braced herself. She planned her words (Well, Jude, we've got some visits to make this afternoon). Mrs Ireland was holding Ena's hand now, pressing it on to the table, stroking it.

'We still talk about that afternoon: goin' to the Regent to see Hal's film. We couldn't believe it, little Hal, from down the road, up there like Gregory Peck. Well, Freddie Bartholomew, perhaps. He was quite famous, wasn't he?'

But Ena felt she'd shared enough. She wanted to tell Jude to mind her own business. She wondered what Hal might say. Here, this is my autograph. Shove it up yer ... This made her feel better.

Roland and Ena walked up the hill between the chapel and gravesite. Hal was too heavy to carry, so they'd loaded him in the hearse and driven him up. The mourners, dressed in their various shades of black, had to walk, dragging their feet, towards the high part of the cemetery.

It was hot, but the worst part of the day was holding off. When Roland had finally got up to speak people had fanned themselves, wiped foreheads with ironed hankies, adjusted stiff collars and smelt themselves as they listened and thought, Terrible business, and wondered how he was managing to hold himself together. He soon had Hal wandering up and down the aisles, hitting balls against the wall, practising lines, climbing trees that reached into the rafters. Then he'd said, 'It's tough for any father, I suppose.' As if this was something most would have to do. 'No one thinks they're gonna be standing here.'

He'd said, 'Hal never had an easy time, but like any parents we tried to ...' He'd wondered why he was saying this, whose business it was, if he should continue. '... we tried to guide him in the right direction.'

It couldn't go on like this. So he'd had to lighten it again, describing Hal in his undies, at five in the morning, running around the house, jumping from lounge to pouffe, in next door, through their cupboards, back out with a bowl of porridge, Mary chasing him with her wooden spoon (as the smiles started appearing) and up a tree to eat his breakfast. 'And I'd be out, and saying, "What yer doin' up there, son?"'

'You did well,' Ena said, as they continued up the hill.

'Well, it's done. That's the best you can say.'

Sonia was walking further back, her arm in Mary's. Sam shuffled behind them, staring at the ground as he walked. Shirley followed him. She hadn't said a word all day. Hal was at her window, but she hadn't noticed him. She was still getting dressed. She saw him, covered herself, and said, 'What are you doing?'

'What's it look like?'

'I'll call Mum.'

'I'll tell her you asked me to watch. I'll tell her you showed me your thing. Come on, show it to me.'

'Get away.'

'I've seen it anyway. It's a nice little pussy.'

'*Mum.*' But she didn't say it loudly.

'Seen what you do with it, too.'

'What?'

'Don't pretend. Look, I can see round the side of yer blinds. I could tell her that too. So you might as well show me again.'

Each thought (in each head on the hill) was a version of a lost original. Charlie's was the only voice, singing consolations. *There will be food shortages.* Roland wanted to tell him to shut up. 'That man's a giant fuckin' pain. Why'd he have to come?' A chorus of footsteps, the squeak of patent leather, the tap of someone's walking stick. 'All just a big sideshow,' he said.

'You'll be glad you did it, after.'

Roland couldn't see how this could be true. How, after he'd put his suit away, and sat down with a drink, he'd think, Well, now I can get on with it. The flowers, the condolence book (where Sam had scribbled his initials like some track time), the organ that wheezed when they switched it on. How could any of this help? 'Half of them never said more than two words to him,' he said.

'Nonsense. Everyone knew him.'

'That Wyndham woman. I haven't seen her for years. Why'd she come?'

'Christ, Griff, she wanted to. People do.'

But he didn't get this. Surely, if she'd wanted to, she would've made an effort in the years between school and adolescence, adulthood and the illness. 'Hal didn't even like her.'

'He did.'

'Not after she suspended him.'

'Things improved, Griff. You don't remember.'

But he did. The letter home, the meeting, the trip to school for Saturday detention, waiting in the car as Hal emerged from the school gates.

'Anyway, she's representing the school,' she said.

'Why do they need representing? That was years ago.'

'That's how these things work.'

'That's why they're a load of shit.'

She glared at him. 'It's your son's funeral.'

'You can imagine what he'd be saying, can't yer?'

She didn't reply. But she knew. Fake. Phoney. Put-on. Ridiculous. 'You'll feel better, later,' she repeated.

He noticed the hearse on the hill. The undertaker had opened the back door and slid the trolley under the coffin. He stood waiting, his hands by his side.

'It seems like weeks ago,' Roland said.

Ena just walked.

'I try to think what he was like, those few days.' Before, he avoided saying. 'He was talking, wasn't he?' He tried to remember if he'd heard him singing, laughing at the telly, going off to visit Sam – because all of these would be good signs. 'I took him to see that film on Saturday, remember?'

She nodded. With her son sitting in a coffin at the top of the hill, it seemed irrelevant.

'It was a long one, but he seemed to enjoy it. Peter O'Toole prancin' around the desert for three hours. But I suppose it was a distraction.'

Ena wondered why he was bothering. The film, the days, what he was reading, his moods, explained nothing. She knew her son was always hidden, or hiding. She'd given up, long ago, trying to understand him. Neither Lawrence nor Arabia nor Dr Neri nor Mrs Ireland could make sense of it. Hal was Hal, and his wires were crossed, and you never knew what you were in for. It was like Christmas every day.

Roland thought maybe if he'd followed Sam's technique: watched the horses, started the stopwatch, observed, recorded times, gone down and examined the animals, got on the phone to the paper. The logical approach. Then again, it didn't always work. The wrong horse won; the right horse lost. 'I was gonna take him away on another trip. I figured, if we could go away every twelve months. But it'd been a couple of years, hadn't it?' Since their last father-son trip north.

He remembered when Hal was twelve or thirteen, when his school had organised a father-son day. They'd travelled to a forest and built a fire and swung from ropes and solved the challenge of getting the pilot (a dummy) down from a tree, into an improvised stretcher, across an abyss on a flying fox and into a tent. They'd had an hour to do it, but after this time they were still trying to get the pilot down. Then there was lunch. The boys had letters they'd written in class, telling their dads how grateful they were, what they hoped to become and the times they remembered (although most were only a few awkward lines long). They were meant to give these letters to their dad over lunch. Roland had noticed that some had, but most, including Hal, had put them back in their pockets.

This hadn't upset Roland too much. Boys were boys, and emotions were sticky, difficult things. In a few days, or weeks, perhaps, he'd be ready. One day it appeared on the telephone table. He'd thought, This is his way of doing it. Should I open it? But then thought, No, he should give it to me. So he'd waited again, and the letter had remained on the table. Then it was gone. And now he thought, What was he trying to tell me?

These were the details Sam wouldn't have missed: this boy trying to speak in the only way possible.

A few people had arrived at the top of the hill ahead of them. Roland could see the rental priest and wondered how he'd got up so quickly. He was old, and fat. Perhaps he'd gone in the hearse.

*The Lord is my shepherd …*

Pathetic, he'd thought, as he'd sat listening to this man with the buy-my-used-car grin, who Hal had never met.

'I've been told that young Hal had a habit of spending his nights out.'

I've been told. The whole time. As if he was saying, Well, the Griffins never came to church, so I can't be sure, but I'll try and reanimate him anyway because, after all, that is my job.

'And what's so different from this fella we call Jesus?'

Leave him out of it, Roland had thought. This is about my son: Hal Griffin, boy, climber, jam-maker, letter-writer, little sod, miracle. Stick to the kid in the coffin. No God, no Jesus, no one going to Heaven. Why did we even ask you?

By now the coffin had been laid on the ground beside the grave. There were cords beside it and they reminded Roland of the rope. Where was it now? Who had taken it down? The two policemen who'd come to investigate? He could see one of them fiddling with the knot, seeing how it had been tied, as if this might tell them something. Now he wondered whether they should ask for it back.

Sam too was thinking how distant this all seemed from the person

Hal was. He looked up, and the boy was there, in his sleep-out, again.

'Sam, you couldn't lend us some money?'

'Why?'

'You know, something from the shops?'

'What?'

Hal could see the jar of coins under Sam's bed. He knew how long it took to dart in, take a few, pocket them and leave without being noticed. How to walk slowly past Sam's shed so they didn't rattle in his pocket (although Sam could hear them as Hal ran back to his house).

'A Choo-Choo Bar.'

'No cigs?'

'For thrupence? You gotta be kiddin'.'

'If you save enough of them.'

'Never touch my lips, Sam. Swear to God! Just a Choo-Choo Bar.'

'And your mum said it was okay?'

'Yep.'

'Did she?'

Sam looked at the coffin and couldn't believe it had come to this. Hal was a shiny piece of granite you found on the footpath, picked up, took home and kept on a shelf because it was too good to throw away. And now they were going to bury it. Him. Hal, who'd been Sam's son as much as Roland's. He'd put so much work into ensuring this didn't happen. If he'd wanted one thing in life, it was that Hal would get better, maybe meet some nice girl (and keep her).

The priest said, 'And now it comes to us to commit Hal to the earth ...'

Hal had always been scared of the dark. More than once, Sam had laid with him, in his sleep-out, telling him there was nothing in the world to be afraid of, except fear itself. He'd invoked the trenches and the shell bursts and the nights without sleep and said even that could be conquered.

As much as Sam didn't want to see the ropes, the body (which was the least part of him, perhaps) waiting to be lowered, he knew he couldn't turn away. Because there was a chance that, somehow, Hal was saying goodbye. In a look (open-mouthed, wide-eyed), a hand run across a mare's flank, a puff of a ciggie behind the shed.

Ena knew she was out of time. She was looking at the red ink image. She was looking at Mary, and wondering. She was just waiting for the drone to finish, clinging to her daughter's arm, studying the various paths that led back down the hill.

When the shed got too hot, Roland headed inside. The hourly showers, the evening expeditions to water the hibiscus, until one day, the change. He opened the shed and was back at work.

Hal was kept alive by visits. After the funeral everyone decided it was safe to sift through the ashes. Morning and afternoon teas lasted longer. Even Mr Carey made an effort. But Roland had soon had enough. He said to Ena, 'You entertain them.'

'Thanks.'

Sonia had decided it was time to go. She was packing her few things into a case. Newspapers lined drawers Hal had inherited when she'd moved to the sleep-out. '"Miss Kathleen Whellum is wearing a long-waisted, heavy white crepe gown with a beaded collar,"' she read. '"A long veil caught with a juliet cap of pearls and beads, for her marriage to Mr Ralph Horton, RAAF." *Dashing*,' she said, showing Ena the photo.

'What year was that?'

'July 1944.'

'Yes.' Ena tried to remember the day, month, or even year she'd put it there. 'You wouldn't know there was a war on.'

'"Miss Elma Lewis will wear an off-white satin frock ..."'

'Give us a hand, will yer?'

Ena had stripped the bed and thrown the sheets into a pile. It was time to wash them, to leave his wallet (which they'd been through) and watch in the bedside drawer, to lay his washing in the spaces Sonia had left behind. Maybe, in time, all of this could be packed in a box and kept in the roof, but not yet. Maybe it could all be thrown away.

The risk was (Ena thought) that his room might become a display, a doll's house, the place where Hal Griffin, boy actor, son of the artist, had lived for twenty-two years. Somewhere people could pay to stand behind a rope and admire. Perhaps they could turn it into a sewing room, or indoor studio.

She'd fetched clean sheets and Sonia had helped her make the bed.

'It's been nice having you back,' Ena said.

'Has it helped?'

'I dunno. Has it helped you?'

Of course it had helped. And it had meant Ena could continue cooking for three. Now it would be two. 'I don't know how I'm gonna deal with him,' she said.

'Leave him alone.'

'I don't get anything out of him.'

Sonia had assumed they talked about Hal, at night, in bed, with the door closed. That they remembered the days and violent nights. She returned to packing, and the old newspaper: twelve rounds of featherweight, *A Murder Has Been Arranged*, *Tim Tyler's Adventures* and the idiot-proof crossword. 'He'll probably do a painting,' she said. 'He's thinking it but …'

Ena sat on the made bed. 'Hal never really got along with Shirley, did he?'

Sonia closed her case and sat beside her mother. 'They never had much to do with each other.'

'No, they didn't, did they?'

Sonia knew something had prompted this. 'They were poles apart.' And yet, not, she thought, both living in their diminishing worlds.

'"Bridesmaid Miss Loy Lamsheed wore green taffeta trimmed with lemon net."'

Ena laughed but then grimaced. She moved her legs apart.

'What is it?'

'My rash. It's been chaffing.' She pushed her daughter away, laughed again and lay back on the bed. 'Oh, my darlin' boy,' she said.

Sonia followed her down.

'Hal, come give yer mumma a hug.'

But Sonia was there for her instead, and they fell together, soft skin, warm breath. Sonia started improvising: 'Her tulle veil will have a coronet of roses and forget-me-nots. She will carry a sheath of white flowers.'

'Will you?'

'One day.'

'I'm not holding my breath.'

In the shed, Roland had added rocks and burnt trees on either side of the man. He sat back and wondered if it wasn't too much. There was a lot going on, and maybe this distracted from the man, front and centre, his long arms draped across a piece of granite.

No, he said to himself. That's it.

It was time. The boy was still in the boat, a sort of figurehead on the prow. The only way to get rid of him was to paint him. He was there now, sitting on the floor hammering bits of wood together.

'What y' makin'?'

'Somethin'.'

The offcuts formed a small, angular mountain. Roland realised it wasn't the product, the form or function that mattered. It was the process. Placing one bit of wood on top of another and hammering the nails. Bending them. Removing them. Trying again.

'I might paint a picture of you.'

'Should I pose?' Hal smiled his cheesiest smile.

'No, I got another idea. You just keep working.' Roland sketched as

Hal hammered, as his cheeks and eyes soon appeared on the cartridge paper.

'Paint me flying through the air.'

'Why?'

'Cos I can.'

'Can you?'

'Well, no, but you might as well, if it's a picture. No one's gonna know.'

'So you reckon some people might believe it?'

'Might.'

'I could paint you flying a plane, or doin' a heart operation.'

'Na, no one'd believe that. Kids can't do operations.'

'They can't fly.'

Hal couldn't work out why his father never made sense. 'Just make me tall.'

'You will be tall soon.'

'Why wait? If you don't have to.'

'That's good logic.'

'And muscles, give me big muscles, like a boxer.'

'Which one?'

'Bob Millick.'

'Jack Hunter's are bigger.'

'Alright, Jack Hunter.'

As they remembered their visit to Stadium Boxing, the big gorillas sweating over canvas, one in the face, flat on the back, one, two, three, knockout! And two hundred men, each with their shirtsleeves rolled up, crying out for more. Hunter versus Millick, legs like steel girders, jaws like rabbit traps.

'Maybe I could paint you as a boxer, knocking out Hunter?'

'No, I could never knock out Hunter. No man could. Not even you, Dad.'

Dad. Roland said the word aloud: 'Dad.'

Ena and Sonia walked into the shed. They came up behind Roland and the man on the easel, and Sonia said, 'That's a good one.'

'Yeah, I just keep going over it. It never makes 'em better. Just gotta sell it now.'

If anyone wants to buy it, he thought. He noticed the case in his daughter's hand. 'You off?'

'Yeah. Mum said you might drive me?'

'Of course.' He wiped his hands with a rag and looked at the spot beside the woodpile. 'It'll be quiet without you.'

'Just pop the radio on, Dad.'

He loaded her case into the back of the car. Then he got in and waited. Ena hugged her daughter, and cried, and said, 'Just look after yerself.'

'I'm not goin' to the moon. Just back to my flat.'

'Still.'

As they drove, Roland said, 'She'll be okay.'

'Keep her busy. Spoil her a bit.'

He glanced over, then back at the road. 'What do you suggest?'

'Movie, night out. Restaurant.'

'We don't go to restaurants.'

'Well, start.'

'Haven't got millions in the bank.'

'She's alone now, Dad.'

'She's not alone.' But he knew she was right. A husband was an attachment, but children were the things that made a vacuum suck.

'There's a nice place on Moorhead Road.'

'I got you.'

'What I mean is …' And what she dared not say: You can't spend all day in the shed.

'Listen, Princess Sonia, we're a tough pair of birds. Cookin' in this pot for a long time. There was a time, before you and Hal. We got by. We will again.'

Sonia wasn't so sure. 'She thinks you just want to move on.'

'She said that?'

'Not in so many words.'

'Well, she wouldn't, cos she knows it's not true.'

He stopped at a light and looked over. 'What do you think?'

'You like your busywork.'

He smiled. 'You little cow.' Then started off. 'It's all just busywork, isn't it? Or else you gotta stop and think about things.'

They passed the old drive-in, and he slowed, and said, '*Moby Dick*.' Then he pulled over next to the weeds and rough bitumen. 'All seems so long ago,' he said.

'Come on, Dad, let's get going.'

He recalled the evening in 1956. The whole family, as normal as any, the hundreds of little steel-capped cars in perfect lines. 'Pity,' he said.

She wasn't sure about what.

Roland was chasing his son through the wild oats and smashed speakers. Calling, 'Hal, what is it?'

He could remember Hal's eyes, full of a dazzling Persil whiteness. Hal ran away from him, shouting to himself, clutching his head. Then he climbed the steps to the screen, looked down at his dad and yelled, 'Go away!'

But Roland wouldn't. He waited as Hal paced, studied the sky, then grabbed a cable and jumped. But instead of touching the ground, he just swung, reaching down with his legs, unable to feel the earth. After a moment of this (and Roland trying to grab him) he let go, fell, glared at his father, then ran towards the gate.

Roland pulled out into light traffic. 'Hopefully they'll bulldoze the place soon.'

'I heard they're planning on re-opening it next year.'

Roland stopped outside Sonia's flat. She opened the back door and took out her case. 'You okay?' she said to Roland, still in the driver's seat.

'Yeah.'

He waited. 'Mum's wrong,' he said.

'How's that?'

But he just put the Dodge in gear and pulled away from the kerb.

# 1944

Sonia wasn't the most popular girl in class, but she was the only one who dared question the teacher, or tell the principal what she thought about his rusty drink fountains. This confidence, she told her friend Thea Wilson, had come from 'my time in Europe'. Six months in Paris, then a year in London, before Hitler started up, then Dad thought we better come back to *here*.

'How old were you?' Thea asked, as they walked home past Simpson's, its yard full of unpainted washer bodies sitting in the sun.

'Two.'

'And how do you remember all that?'

'Just do.' Considering the six-year-old, with her plaits and a missing front tooth, had already told Thea about the Louvre, their day picnicking in the Champ de Mars, boat rides on the Seine.

'I can't remember much before last week,' Thea said.

'Well, I do. We lived in a third floor apartment, in the thirteenth arrondissement.'

'What's that?'

'A suburb, like Pennington, but ...' Nothing like Pennington, she wanted to say, but felt she shouldn't, considering the Wilsons had no money, couldn't afford a car, and certainly knew nothing about Paris. 'There were cafes all around, and you got up in the morning and went and had coffee and croissants.'

'What are they?'

'Buns.'

'Like we get from the baker?'

'Sort of.' But Le Petit Bofinger was nothing like Mr Sneddin, plodding down their drives at 8 am, knocking, offering his stale bread and fruit buns.

'I bet you'd like to go back?' Thea said.

'One day. Maybe we could go together?'

'Yeah. When we're eighteen. Should we agree on it?'

Sonia wasn't so sure. Thea's sister had got pregnant at fifteen, and the boy had run off. A pit bull guarded their house, and the garden was just piles of junk her dad collected. 'I don't know about eighteen,' she said, as they crossed the road, headed for Burleigh Avenue. 'I might go to university.'

'You still wanna be a dentist?'

'Na, looking in people's mouths all day. Prob'ly a doctor.'

'That'd be okay.'

'But it's a lot of study. So I won't be able to go to Paris.'

'What about when you finish?'

'Perhaps. But then you gotta work in a hospital for a few years. So then I'd be, maybe, thirty.' She tried to ignore the sores around Thea's mouth.

'I could wait,' Thea said.

'What would you do?'

She indicated the giant factory, the trucks driving in and out, hundreds of artillery shells sitting inside the pressing shed. Outside, a dozen men sat in the sun eating lunch. 'Dad reckons Simpson's always need girls for the office.'

'You wanna be a secretary?'

'If I'm smart enough. You gotta be able to type quick.'

Sonia hated the popular girls. There was nothing to them, she told Thea, who (despite everything) was still a get-what-you-see sort of person. Not like the taffeta bitches, sitting in the only bit of shade sipping their cordial, laughing (at her, at Thea, she guessed) and inviting each other to parties. None of them had been to Paris, and none of them had a famous painter for a father.

Show-and-tell. Roland had given her a small portrait (of her) he'd painted. She'd taken it wrapped in paper. One of the bitches had said, 'That doesn't look like you.'

'My dad's got his own style. That's why he's famous.'

'I've never heard of him.' She'd asked the teacher, 'Have you heard of him, Mr Clarke?'

'Yes,' he'd replied. 'Roland Griffin is one of the country's best artists. He's shown all round the world.'

Of course the teacher was going to say that. It didn't make it true. 'But your arms are long, and yer skin's orange.'

'Meant to be that way.'

'And yer standing in a desert.'

'Dad likes deserts.'

The bitch clutched her bangle. She was going to tell them how she made it from seashells.

Sonia Griffin was small for her age, but she was her own pit bull. Her legs were solid and meaty, and she had nutcracker fists. They came in handy – lifting Hal, throwing him across the room when he annoyed her. She liked her hair nice, and demanded Ena spend hours brushing and plaiting it. She'd asked for a colour but was told she'd have to wait until she was eighteen.

She glanced and noticed Shirley running up behind them. 'Just ignore her,' she said to Thea.

Shirley came up to match their stride. 'Mum reckons I can walk home with you.'

Sonia didn't reply. No one, no matter how low in the food chain, talked to Shirley. She was the school retard, sitting with her gloves on, eating lunch under the pepper tree. She was awkward, and smelt, and no one could stand that *stuff* on her face. The bitches reckoned it was contagious. She'd overheard Mary talking about it: lupus – an all-over body ache, stiff joints, everything puffed up, and all the inside bits, too, if you could open her up and look.

'Wanna do homework together?' Shirley asked, as they turned into Burleigh Avenue.

Thea grinned and raised her eyebrows, but Sonia's eyes threatened to murder her.

'Sonia?'

'I'm walking with Thea.'

Shirley got it. She stopped and sat on a fence. There was no point continuing.

Thea glanced back. 'You sorta feel sorry for her.'

'You wouldn't, if you were me.'

'Why?'

'Mum and Dad always make me look after her. She goes into my room and looks through my drawers.'

'No?'

'And takes my books and …' For a moment, she did feel bad. She saw that Shirley was watching them. She almost wanted to ask her to join them, but thought, No, why should I? 'I can't get rid of her. I ask Mum to tell her to go home but she says she's not hurtin' anyone. So I say, "Shirley, Mary's calling. You better go."'

Thea was unsure about this, but still she said, 'Glad she doesn't live next to me.'

'Yer lucky.'

'I'd just put a lock on my door.'

'That wouldn't stop her. She'd just come in the window.'

They laughed. Sonia knew this was necessary. At times she felt proud, perhaps too proud, but it was a good feeling. She could see in the mirror. High cheeks, teardrop eyes. And the way some of the boys looked at her. She felt a sort of glow, like the world could just go shit itself. Until the moment passed, and she was left stranded in

Burleigh Avenue. Like always wanting to go back to Paris. Perhaps this made *her* a bitch. Although it wasn't like she was hurting anyone.

'They reckon Hitler's got these bombs that are so big they can blow up a whole city,' Thea said.

'A whole city?'

'And he's gonna start with London, then Paris, then us.'

'I hadn't heard that.'

But Thea didn't seem too worried. 'I bet them French boys are good lookin'?'

'They won't be, after the bomb.' Sonia looked back again when they reached her drive. Shirley was walking, head down, feet dragging. 'See you, Thea.'

Sonia searched the breadbox, stopped at the door to the shed and said, 'I'm home.'

'How was it?' Roland called.

'Same as yesterday.'

She walked in the back door, dropped her satchel, and found her mum in the kitchen. 'Whatcher doin'?'

Ena glared at her. 'What are you doing?'

'*What are you doing?*'

Ena was stirring a pan full of candying almonds. 'We send you to school all day, you could at least *speak* properly.'

'You don't.'

Ena raised her wooden spoon, but thought better of it. Sonia peered over the rim of the pan. 'Can I?'

Ena handed her the spoon, and she climbed onto a stool and started stirring the water, sugar and almond mixture.

'Don't let it catch.'

'What's for tea?'

'Bubble and squeak.'

'Yuck.'

'You can have a sandwich.'

'No one likes bubble and squeak.'

'Correction, everyone except you likes bubble and squeak. Even Hal.'

And on cue, the stick-legged boy ran through the kitchen with his shed-made rifle. 'Give it up, Fritz,' he said, pointing it at his sister.

She ignored him and turned to her mother. 'You'll never guess what happened today.'

'What?' She was emptying a frozen mass into another pan.

'Mrs Harper.'

'What now?'

'Hands up!' Hal insisted. He was wearing his pyjama shirt, because it resembled a uniform, even doing up the top button, because that's what the Nazis did.

Sonia kept stirring the candying almonds. 'We were all lined up in the hall, and she says, "Alright, who was it?"'

Hal gave up. He ran from the kitchen in search of missing aircrew.

'You could smell it.'

'Smell what?' Ena took the wooden spoon and stirred the almonds. 'More, keep 'em moving.' And returned it.

'Someone had shit themselves.'

'Sonia.'

'What? They did.'

Ena wasn't sure about Pennington Primary. There seemed to be lots of colouring in and collages and little lunches, but not much of what she remembered from school. Where was the cursive? The times tables? The grammar? Now the only thing Sonia seemed to come home with was bad language.

'So, she looked at us and said ...'

Or maybe it was the Wilson girl? Why on earth, with hundreds of kids to choose from, did she get around with her? It was the house everyone avoided, the mother no one spoke to at the shops (and none of them were that fussy), the drunken father people pretended not to notice.

'... she said, "If no one's getting to tell me, I'll check." So she went up and down the line looking in our pants.'

Ena turned to her. '*She what?*'

'Honest to God.'

Hal returned, emptied a magazine into them, and fled, rolling across the laundry floor, kicking open the door and disappearing.

'Let's be clear,' Ena continued. 'She pulled up your dress and looked in your underpants?'

'Yes.'

'And she did the same to the boys?'

'Yes.'

Sonia knew she was onto a good thing. She could see her mum storming in the front gate, demanding to see the principal, or at least writing a letter.

'Completely unacceptable.'

'Yep, and she didn't even find no one.'

Ena was confused. 'So, who'd done it?'

She shrugged. 'Someone musta farted.'

'Passed wind.'

'Then she said, "Well, maybe my nose is over-sensitive."'

Ena put the gas on under the tea. Sonia wasn't happy. The rage was subsiding.

'She's an old perve, isn't she, Mum?'

'She had no place doing that.'

'Exactly. She saw everyone's gear. And later, Thea said she saw Tony's dick, and he whacked her, and it was on.'

Sonia started playing with the food. Hal ran past, knocked her and she almost fell off the stool. 'Get out of it!' But he was already climbing into his Panzer lounge.

'So, what yer gonna do?' Sonia asked.

'What can you do?'

Bugger, she thought, as Harper's final comeuppance at the hands of Ena Griffin evaporated. 'You should go to the coppers.'

'You've still gotta go to school there. If they think I'm a troublemaker ...'

'But she looked down our knickers.'

Sonia had been sure this would be enough. Twelve months of hand and nail inspections, the cane and cuts, endless lectures about respect for the aged and infirm. She'd even made them join Mr Saxby's square dancing. 'I'll tell Dad. He'll drive down there now.' She switched off the almonds, trapped in their crystallising ooze.

'No, you won't. He's busy.' Ena switched the almonds back on. 'So, what did you learn today?'

'Not much.'

'You musta learnt something?'

'I before e except after c, but that's wrong.'

'How?'

'Species, science ... and what about seize, weird, their?'

'Well, there are exceptions.'

'They're all exceptions.'

Ena looked at her and thought, As you are.

Like her son, and husband, and the kitchen window that didn't let in light, and everything in this house, really.

A few hours later they sat in their spots: Hal on a cushion, shovelling the grey mass into his mouth, Sonia picking out the peas and carrots, Ena sipping tea as she watched her off-with-the-fairies husband, and Roland, eating slowly with his left hand and writing with his right.

He wrote: 'Fat on lean. Fat = oily pigment. Lean = less oily pigment.'

Ena asked Sonia, 'What happened on the way home?'

'What d'you mean?'

'You know what I mean. I spoke to Mary.'

Sonia put down her fork. 'Just cos she lives next door, doesn't mean – '

'Shirley was in tears. How do you feel about that?'

'It's not my fault.'

'She asked to walk with you.'

'I was walking with Thea.'

'So what? Griff?'

Roland looked up. 'Sorry?'

Ena returned to Sonia. 'She relies on you. Think how you'd be in her position.'

'I'm not!'

'Sonia!'

'What?'

'Don't speak to you mother that way.'

They retreated to their corners. Roland guessed it was safe and continued writing. '1st lot with turpentine – lean. 2nd paint with varnishes and turpentine (body or fatter paint).'

'Griff, your tea's getting cold,' Ena said.

'Better that way.'

'It's a bit rude, isn't it, at the table?'

But he didn't hear her. It had occurred to him that he could write a small book, or some sort of guide, to the technical aspects of painting. Nothing overblown, just a hundred pages to help the beginner, save them years of trial-and-error, poor paint, bad technique. If done well, it would sell. He didn't want a head full of knowledge to go to waste.

Ena knew there was no point. You buy your ticket. Like the Easter Wondershow tent. Ten shillings for the bearded lady (although it looked stuck-on). You couldn't ask for your money back. You had to sit and make the most of it. She looked at Sonia and said, 'She may not have as long as you.'

'Is she gonna die?' Hal asked.

'No, she's not gonna die. Not yet, anyway.'

'When?'

'Who knows?'

Hal was only four, but he could tell when things didn't add up. 'She may not have as long …?'

'To wait for a bus.'

'Does she get the bus?'

Roland shook his head. 'Just eat yer tea.'

'It'd be okay if it was just here,' Sonia said. 'But at school, every time I turn around.'

'What, you're a snob?'

'Mum.'

'Too good for her? I tell you what, that was embarrassing. Mary normally wouldn't say anything.'

'Fine, I'm sorry.'

'Good ground colour – black, white, yellow, ochre – scrub on dry leaving as much canvas as possible.' But then Roland stopped. Twenty years of work, all given away for a couple of quid?

'What you writin'?' Hal asked.

'Story about a boy who assassinates Göring.'

Hal's face lit up. 'Yeah?'

'This four-year-old from Pennington, gets recruited by the army. They parachute him into Germany and he walks to Berlin. Meets up with an agent, gets a gun, shoots him.'

'Who's the kid?'

'Let me think. Expert sniper. Speaks eight languages. Short, well-built, good-looking, like his father.'

'Who?'

'I can't say. It's secret. If I said, they'd have to kill me.'

'It's me, isn't it?'

'You? Killing Göring? Na.'

'It is.'

'Don't be stupid,' Sonia said, looking at her brother. 'He's not writing a novel.'

'How do you know?' Roland asked.

'You've never done that.'

'I have.'

'When?'

'Early days. I was either gonna be a writer or an artist. I did this novel, it got published, and won the Nobel Prize for Literature.'

Sonia shook her head and continued hunting peas. Roland concentrated on Hal. 'And they made a film of it, with Errol Flynn.'

'Griff,' Ena warned.

'Ask yer mother.'

They looked at her.

'Yeah, that's right. The Nobel Prize, Errol Flynn.'

Hal finished his tea. 'That's not true.'

'Believe what you want.'

'How come you've never showed me?'

'The book went out of print.'

'What about the film?'

'Ah, there's one copy left, and I keep it in a trunk in the roof.'

Roland studied his notes. 'Last process adding delicacies of colour.' No, he thought. That'd spoil everything. He screwed up the sheet of paper and deposited it on his bread and butter plate.

'Why'd you do that?' Hal asked.

'If the Krauts got a hold of this, they'd know.' He picked up the paper, took a bite and started chewing it.

'Yuck!' Hal said.

Ena: 'Griff, don't be ridiculous.'

'Go on, swallow it,' Sonia said.

He swallowed.

'Let's see your mouth.'

He showed them.

'Disgusting!' Hal said.

'He hasn't swallowed it,' Sonia said. 'Under your tongue?'

Roland pretended to cough, leaned over, spat it out and sat up.

'It's in your hand!' Sonia said.

'It is not.'

And she was up, around to him, working on his hand. Hal followed and soon they were both attempting to unclench his fist.

'Stop!' Ena said, but they ignored her. Roland got up, slipped from the room and they chased him. Ena could hear furniture tumbling. She thought of the Wondershow tent. Vanessa the Undresser, in a full-body, flesh-coloured stocking.

Roland had the recipe (scribbled in his journal) on the bench. This was something he'd never give away. After years of trying different combinations of turps and oil, linseed and paint, he'd eventually come up with a foolproof recipe for black oil. It only took an hour to cook a couple of jars full, but to Ena, these were the most painful hours of her life: her measuring cups given over to oil and paint, her stove marked with stains, the smell of it through the house. 'Can't you do it outside?' she'd ask.

'On what?'

'We'll get you a gas burner.'

But they had a perfectly good stove; he used his pan; he only did it at night, when he wasn't bothering anyone. Like now, stirring the molten mass, hanky wrapped around his face. Ena said, 'See, it's dangerous.'

He opened the kitchen window. 'Another ten minutes. I can't work without it.'

She just shook her head and disappeared into the lounge room.

He knew he could be obsessive. It wasn't that he wanted to be, but art was an all-or-nothing proposition. He'd learnt this many years before. If you only put a little bit of yourself into it you'd remain an amateur. You may as well breed sheep, or work in a bank.

Hal came in and stood on his stool and demanded the wooden spoon. 'Candied almonds,' he said.

'Shit.' Roland realised he was using Ena's best spoon. 'Don't tell your mother I used this.'

Hal stirred. 'Are you a good painter?'

'Average. But if I keep at it I'll get good. That's how life works.'

He often wondered if this was really true, or whether he'd mortgaged his life on some giant (soon-to-be) unfulfilled promise. But the alternative was never knowing.

It was all down to his eye. His last year at school, sitting in a history class, rubbing his eyes, staring at the board, the words becoming less distinct. Then the eye doctor, who sat him on a sort of mechanical horse, filled his eyes with drops, shined lights into them, before saying, 'Well, I'm gonna book you in for a few days in hospital.'

'Why?' his mother had asked.

'The retina doesn't look right.'

Waking up in a lemon-scented bed. The same doctor with the same worried face, the indistinct outlines. Then the sketching, the revelation that he might be an artist, all of it leading to this: black oil on Ena's stove.

'No other dads paint pictures,' Hal said.

'Some do.'

'Who?'

'Jonathon van Gogh, his dad.'

'Who?'

'Vincent. But he's dead.'

'Who else?'

'Harry Renoir. Anyway, you're lucky,' Roland said. 'It means I get to stay home with you.' He tickled Hal under the armpit. Then he reclaimed the spoon, stirred the mixture again, said, 'That's enough,' and turned off the gas.

'You nearly done?' Ena called.

'Finished.'

'Remember Sonia's asthma.'

'I remember.' He smiled at his son. *'Remember Sonia's asthma.'*

Hal laughed. 'I'm gonna be a painter too.'

'You sure?'

'Yep.'

'It's a tough way to make a living. Secret agents make more.'

'You made that up.'

Roland didn't want to talk him into it or out of it. Realistically, he wouldn't have any idea for another ten years. 'Just don't end up at Simpson's,' he said.

'Why not?'

'Anyone can get a job at Simpson's. But you, you're special.'

'Why?'

'Göring … the world's waiting, old boy.'

Roland sat on a bench in a brushwood shade house he'd built during a short-lived orchid growing phase. He smoked the remnants of a shed cigarette. He was far enough away from the house so Ena couldn't smell it. Far enough to avoid the shed, the paintings, always looking back at him; the house, shoelaces too short to be tied. But not so far that he couldn't hear Mo on the radio. 'My dear Miller, this is The Frivolity … the spiritual home of Bozo M'Haffie. It's also the Home of Clean Entertainment.' He could hear Hal's giggle, but neither his wife nor daughter were laughing.

He spread the newspaper across his lap and read by the fading light about the lifting of restrictions on the importation of carpets and linoleum. And the war. Bombers over Berlin, Great Haul by Third Army, refugee columns. The same stuff he'd been reading about for years. Knives slipped between ribs, bullets in the back, the struggle for the right to candy almonds and cook black oil. As usual, he felt bad. Eye or no eye, there must have been something he could do.

He was inside a hall, waiting. A doctor called him over. 'You've written here, slight problem in left eye.'

'It's nothing.'

'What's a slight problem?'

He knew he couldn't avoid it. 'Detached retina.'

The doctor shook his head, picked up a stamp and attacked his paperwork: 'REJECTED MEDICAL'.

'What does that mean?' he asked.

'You're no good, old man. Not with a bad eye.'

Old man?

'Next!'

'Well, I suppose, not for battle, but what about support? I can cook. Type a little.'

'We got plenty of cooks and typists. We need soldiers. Can't fight the Japs with a bad eye. You'd end up shootin' one of your own.'

He could still hear Mo, rattling on as though nothing was happening. 'Stone the crows, I'm making a hole in me manners.' An ad for Victory Loans: bonds of ten to a thousand pounds. He looked up and Ena was watching him. 'Scare a man to death.'

'We still winning?' she asked, sitting down.

He pretended to read. 'They're shelling the hell out of the Ryukyu Islands.'

She studied the sky. 'You wouldn't guess anything's happening, would yer?'

'No.'

'I'm just glad the kids are little. There's no way I'd give them Hal.'

'You'd have to.'

She thought about this: the lists of names in the paper, the sons and nephews, the kids that wouldn't be coming back to their fitter's apprenticeships at Simpson's.

Roland turned to the back page. Bob Millick and Jack Hunter were going ten rounds next Monday night. He wondered whether she'd let him take Hal. She hated boxing. 'I'll be in in a bit,' he said, handing her the paper. 'Don't bother, there's not much in it.'

Back in his shed, he started going through his latest pile of sketches. There was only one subject: Shirley. He'd first sketched her while they drank morning tea, and Mary had asked, 'What you doin', Griff?'

'Fiddlin' about. I was thinking of painting your daughter.'

'Really?'

Shirley was more confused than anyone. 'Why me?'

'A painter does what's to hand.'

'What about Sonia, or Hal?'

'Done them. Need something new. Unless you object?'

No, she'd said. No, Mary had agreed. Why not, it's just a picture?

He arranged his fresh canvas on the easel, placed his best sketch on the bottom ledge beside several photos he'd taken, picked up a pencil and began: chin, jaw, the suggestion of a mouth. He was worried he wouldn't be able to capture the thing that made Shirley Shirley.

He'd sketched her again last night. The light from the yellow globe making her face shadow. 'Should I smile?' she'd asked.

'No, just think about school.'

'I'd rather not.'

'Why?'

She didn't reply.

'Do you play with Sonia?'

'Sometimes.'

He gave up, scribbled on the sketch and started again on the other side. 'What's your favourite subject?'

'Art.'

'Sonia in your class?'

'Yeah.'

'She sit next to you?'

'No.'

'Who does she sit next to?'

'Thea.'

'You play with her?'

'No.'

'What do you do at lunch?'

She had her own spot – there wasn't anyone she felt she could talk to. But this was too big a thought to share with Roland, especially now. 'There's a coupla girls I knock about with.'

'That's good.' He seemed genuinely relieved, but wasn't sure if she was lying.

She said, 'If you paint this, will someone buy it?'

'I hope so.'

'For lots of money?'

'Not lots. Not enough to buy a new car, or bike or … no, not much. But I tell you what, whatever I get, I'll give you some.'

She didn't argue. She wondered how much: ten quid, fifty? Enough to buy a new dress, perhaps?

'It might make you famous,' Roland said.

But he didn't feel it would; not unless he could do better. There was nothing in the sketch, just features, no way of seeing behind the skin. He said, 'You might end up hanging in a gallery.'

'Really?'

She was imagining it: taking Mary and Sam, telling the whole class. That would change everything. Once you were a painting, you were permanent. Thousands of people saw you every day. Every year, for decades, long after you were dead. Roland Griffin wouldn't have bothered painting you unless you were important.

There was still the question of the rash. Roland couldn't do that to Mary, but without it, it wasn't Shirley.

'Never!'

It was Hal.

'Griff!' This time: Ena.

'Christ!' He threw his pencil across the shed, stood and went out into the night. 'Where are yers?'

'Here.'

He followed the voice around the house, down the back path to the plum tree. Hal had climbed to the highest branch. He was wearing his pyjamas. Ena was shaking a finger at him. Sonia was just standing, smiling.

'You, to bed,' Roland said to her.

'I'm not playing up.'

'Go!'

She turned and walked towards the house, but stopped behind a bush. Roland waited for his son. 'What are you up to?'

'I'm not goin' to bed.'

He checked his watch. 'It's after nine.'

'Sonia always gets longer.'

'She's older.'

'I'll sleep up here.' He pretended to sleep.

Roland turned to Ena. 'I'm puttin' a lock on that door.' Then he walked down a path beside the shed, picked up his ladder, carried it back and rested it against the tree. Hal was still feigning sleep.

'If I have to climb up …'

Then he started to snore.

'Right.' Roland ascended four steps, but Hal sat up, jumped onto the back lawn, rolled a few times and ran off around the house.

'I'm gonna kill him,' Roland said.

Sonia was laughing.

They searched around the house, went into his room, and he was in bed, feigning sleep again. Roland said, 'I should tan your bloody hide.'

But they all knew he didn't have it in him.

Hal sniffed his way to the kitchen. Scones. There were voices from the dining room: his mother, father, Mary, and a stranger. That made it difficult. He stood in the kitchen listening. This man had a deep voice, so he imagined he was tall; he was slightly husky, so he might've smoked; he laughed after nearly every line, which probably meant he didn't have kids. He heard him say, 'Mary? Jesus, she'd run a mile. Take one whiff, you know where you are.'

What did he mean? Run a mile from what? Hal knew, given this situation, it was best to stay quiet, and listen. Often, that told you everything you needed to know.

'It's hard to sleep when you're hungry,' the stranger said.

Hal's hand moved and a knife fell to the ground.

'Hal, that you?' his mother called.

'Yes,' he managed.

'Come here, there's someone you might want to meet.'

He walked to the doorway.

'Come in,' Ena said.

He took a few steps and saw him. A soldier. A khaki tunic with copper-coloured buttons; two stripes on one arm and '3 BATTALION' on the other; a hat, with a Rising Sun. The real thing. The war had come to Burleigh Avenue.

'This is Mr Grant,' Ena said. 'Mary's cousin.'

Corporal Grant stood, squeezed forward in the gap between table and wall, and shook Hal's hand. 'Nice to meet you, Hal.'

He even knew his name. His grip was firm, merciless. He wondered what it'd done. Killed Japs? Held them by the throat and squeezed the life out of them? Or was he a Bren gunner? Had his finger pulled the trigger that had cut down hundreds of fleeing Krauts?

'Trev's just back from Borneo,' Roland said.

Borneo, he thought. Where was that? That'd make it harder to imagine.

Trevor Grant sat down and smiled at him. 'I hear you been doin' yer own fightin'?'

Hal looked at Ena and she said, 'You've made your own gun, haven't you, Hal?'

'Yes, Mr Grant.'

'Call me Trev. You get many of the little bastards?'

'Trev,' Mary said.

Hal couldn't take his eyes off the corporal. Roland noticed, and saw something unfamiliar.

'I just got a pretend one,' Hal said. 'You wanna see it?'

'Too right I do.'

He ran to his room, returned with his gun, handed it to Grant.

'She's a beauty. What sort?'

Hal was surprised he couldn't tell. 'A Thompson.'

'Ah, you're a machine-gunner?'

'What you got?'

'.303.'

Hal wanted to ask how many of the little bastards Corporal Grant had killed, but it didn't seem like a polite question, and he knew his mother would growl at him.

Grant placed the wooden gun on the table and sipped his tea. Then he let the cup clatter into its saucer and picked up a half-eaten scone. Hal watched as he took a bite, wiped the crumbs from his chin.

Roland noticed his son's fascination with Grant. He certainly didn't hold it against Mary's cousin. It's just how it was.

The corporal met his eyes. 'Mary says you got turned down.'

'Yeah, the eye.'

'Can't see much, eh?'

'I can see your outline, and when you move.'

'That'd make it difficult.' He put the last of his scone in his mouth and swallowed. Hal watched the whole lot go down in a single gulp. Even his throat was big, sticking out of his bull's neck, welded onto his bumper-bar shoulders.

'So you're sticking to painting?' Grant asked.

Roland wanted to be unapologetic. 'Gotta do what you can, I suppose.' But felt traces of it in his voice.

'Course you do. If you can fight, good-o, if not …' Grant shrugged. 'What sort of things do you paint?'

'Landscapes.'

'Deserts,' Hal said. 'Everyone's standing in a desert.'

'Well, I must have a look. Mary says you're quite famous.'

'No.'

'Says you've had exhibitions in London, and Paris.'

'A few, but a lot of people have.'

'I haven't!' And Grant looked around the table. 'I can't even draw a dog.' Stopping at Hal. 'What about you, Hal? You any good with a pencil?'

'Some.' Enough about art, Hal thought. Let's talk about war.

'Follow in your dad's footsteps?'

'Perhaps.'

'A hundred years' time, that's how people'll remember us,' Grant told him. 'They'll look at the paintings your dad's doing and know what it was like.'

Ena put the kettle on again. She fetched the rest of the scones and they continued with butter when the jam ran out.

Hal was still watching Grant. 'You ever been ambushed?' he asked.

'My word.'

'When?'

'Last month. Me and a few mates got cut off from our battalion. Got dark. We had to get back, so we walked along this creek. Full moon, which is never good.'

I know, Hal wanted to say. You're meant to stay put in a full moon.

'We're spread out, guns at the ready and bang, off she goes!'

Hal waited, mouth open.

'I got behind some rocks but there were shells going off all around me. I thought, Well, this is it. Goodnight, Irene. Thought me aunt'd be gettin' a telegram.'

Roland studied his son's glowing face.

'Anyway, I thought, no use sittin' here and waitin' for it. So you know what I did, Hal?'

'No.'

'Attached me bayonet, ran into the bush, started stickin' the little yellow bastards.'

'Trev.'

'Soon there was a pile of bodies six feet high.'

Hal was imagining them.

'Got the fellas back to camp and there was Blamey, with me Victoria Cross.'

'Trev ...'

'Then the rest of the Japs surrendered. Said they'd heard about Corporal Grant, and they weren't willing to risk it.'

'Is that really true?'

'Of course. What, you reckon I'd lie to you, Hal? With yer bloody Thompson?'

Mary shook her head. 'He's makin' it all up, Hal. He's a radio operator.' Pointing to the badge on his sleeve. 'You even been in a jungle?' she asked him.

'Yeah, up Queensland, when they were training us.'

Hal wondered if he could be content with a radio operator. Was a gun worth the same if you never used it? 'So, you've never killed no one?' he asked.

'No, but ...' Grant sat forward, 'you know what they call me?'

'No.'

'Mr Magnetic.' He picked up a spoon, placed it against his chest and rubbed it a few times. He released it and it stayed in position.

'Shit,' Hal said.

'Hal!'

Grant repeated the trick with a fork and the jam spoon.

Hal couldn't believe it. 'Can I have a go?'

'Of course.'

Grant stood and Hal came around to him. He gathered all the teaspoons and, one by one, stuck them onto Mr Magnetic's uniform. When he was finished, he asked, 'How do you do that?'

'Couldn't tell you.' Grant shook himself and the spoons dropped. Hal gathered them and tried again but Ena said, 'Hal, leave him alone, he didn't come here for that.'

Hal said, 'Is it all over your body?'

Grant stuck a spoon to his cheek, his forehead, even his tongue. 'The whole lot, Hal.' He smiled. 'Well, not everything.'

After morning tea, Roland and Grant went outside, got in the car and started reversing up the drive. Hal ran out and waved them down. 'Where you going?'

'Secret government business,' Grant said.

'Can I come?'

Roland shook his head. 'It's not for kids.'

'I can help.'

Grant turned to Roland. 'He might come in useful.'

Fifteen minutes later they were driving along the highway, windows down, multiple backfires. Roland said, 'How long you home for?'

'Next Wednesday.'

'Much planned?'

'Lotta drinkin'.'

Hal liked sitting in the back of the car. You could hear all about life. The world looked good going past at thirty miles an hour.

They arrived at Strathearne Air Force Base and Grant showed his card to a man at the gate. He gave Roland directions – along a dirt road, into a hangar. They got out and Hal stood admiring a DC-3, its wheels muddy, its paint worn to the metal. He wanted to look inside, but dared not ask. Whatever the secret was, it was more important. This was the real thing, and he was part of it. It smelt of gasoline and oil, hot engines and burning dust from the arc lights.

Grant walked into a side office and talked to a man in overalls. Hal watched them laughing, checking papers on the desk. 'What's it all about?' he asked his dad.

'Can't say.'

Uniform or not, things were looking up. Hal studied the plane's wings and asked his dad, 'D'yer reckon it's got guns?'

'No.'

'D'yer reckon I could look inside?'

'Prob'ly not.'

Grant and the other man approached them. The man messed his hair. 'This is top secret,' he said. 'Has Corporal Grant administered the oath?'

'No, sir.'

'Well, he will, later. And once you've taken it, you can't say nothin' about this to no one, or else the government will come lookin' for you. Got it?'

'Yes, sir.'

Roland noticed the same look on his son's face, as Hal studied the two men. Like he'd just seen a comet for the first time. Something marvelous, new; a boy in a boat in a jungle full of panthers.

'Good. Let's get started,' the man said.

Roland was instructed to back his car up to the plane. Once he had, Grant and the man started loading wooden boxes into the boot. Then they started on the back seat. When that was full, the man covered the boxes with a tarpaulin and said, 'Now, son, your job's to sit on them.'

'Yes, sir.' Hal climbed in and the back of the car almost touched the concrete apron. Then two more men appeared at the front of the hangar. Grant said, 'Christ, who are they?'

His friend said, 'You keep them busy. You, Griffin, drive this lot out back.'

Grant went over to them. They seemed interested in what was

going on, but he had them entertained. Took their pens and invoked his magnetism. Meanwhile, they drove out of the hangar, onto the back road, and waited.

Hal knew it was his job to protect the boxes. With his life if necessary. Maybe they were full of guns, or explosives? But even this thought didn't make him uneasy. He tried to read some words through a gap in the tarpaulin.

DEWAR'S SCOTCH

Grant got into the car. 'Go!'

His dad drove off, skidding, tumbling down the road as Hal fell from side to side, hit his head on the door, the roof, fell to the floor, got back up and listened to them laughing. Grant didn't even have to show his card on the way out. All he said was, 'I'll give your lot to McVicar.'

Then they were back on the bitumen. The night blowing in the window.

Roland held *Dutton's Pub* between his fingers. James Bailey studied it – moved forward, squinted, said, 'Why's that fella squatting?'

A miner with a handlebar moustache, posed before the front door of Dutton's Market Hotel. His legs were black stilts, his shoes no more than a flick of the brush. He was holding a burnt-down smoke. 'That's what he did,' Roland said. 'Middle of the road … like he was taking a shit.'

James took another swig of whisky. He wiped the lip and handed it to Roland, who did the same. They were about halfway through the first bottle but the box, covered by an old raincoat, promised plenty more. 'You got that road nice,' he said.

Roland squinted to see: the way the red became orange became brown became black shadow.

He'd decided *Dutton's Pub* was finished and ready to sell. There were a few others: a man with his newspaper (based on Sam, James suggested), a different man feeding his dogs, a Sunday evening family portrait (a father and kids surveying the dunny they'd built too far from the house), and the medical examination. Men lined up, waiting for a doctor.

'I was in and out in five minutes,' James said.

'Half your luck.'

'They looked at my superior physique ...' He reclaimed the bottle and drank without wiping. 'Christ, that's good.'

Roland was still busy with the medical examination. 'There musta been something I coulda done.'

'Why worry about it?'

'And when it's all over, and everyone's talking about it?'

'You're not the only one. What about, whatshisname, Deary?'

'Him? He's got a hundred day cough.'

'Na ... a plate in his leg.'

Roland decided that even the whisky tasted bad. He put the bottle on the bench and corked it. What had started as an adventure had ended as an inquisition. Midnight: Ena standing in the drive with her arms crossed as they transferred the boxes from their car to one of Grant's mate's. Grant was saying, 'Keep a lookout will yer, Mrs Griffin.'

'I'm not involved with any of this.'

'There's nothing to be involved with. It's all paid for.'

'My foot.'

'It is. It's just, if we bring it in this way, we avoid customs. That's just wasted money, isn't it, Mrs G?'

Then the car was empty, apart from the one box.

'That's for you, Mrs Griffin.'

'I'm not having stolen stuff in my house.'

Roland lifted it out. 'It's fine, we'll keep it in the shed.'

'And when the police arrive?'

The magnetic man laughed. 'They got bigger problems, Mrs G.'

They laid *Dutton's Pub* on the butcher's paper. Three men stood in front of the hairdresser watching them. They all had smokes, and the one in the middle was wearing a tie. 'Did you talk to them?' James asked.

'Yeah, this one, he was the bank manager.'

As he remembered sitting at the front bar of Dutton's, and the manager taking out a roll of notes, peeling a few off, saying to the barman, 'Coupla stiffies over here, Harry.'

Roland had looked at the notes and thought, The day's deposits? The takings from the butcher shop? He guessed he'd probably put it all back in the vault, eventually. He said, 'Nice little town you got here.'

'It's a shithole.'

An hour later the front bar was sozzled. They went outside to get some air; the manager met a few mates and they stood in a line while Roland sketched them.

'Try make me look a bit younger,' one of them said, leaning on his car.

The manager turned to this man and handed him a few more pounds. 'Go on, Smithy, get us another round. And Mr Griffin, what are you drinkin', Griff?'

'I've had enough.'

'Bullshit.' And he turned back to Smithy. 'Grab a coupla jugs, we can settle in for the night.'

Back in his shed, Roland wrapped the painting and taped it. 'That was a rough place,' he said.

James could tell his friend was still there. He might've lived in the city but he was never far from the long-necked, bow-limbed men in their old suits.

Roland opened his journal and turned to a new page. Picking up a pencil, he licked the lead and wrote: 'Sent to Annadale, 2 July 1944: Duttons, Man with paper, Mwd, Sun. evening and the medical'. Then he closed it, put it on the tool bench and drank more whisky. 'I met the owner,' he said.

'What owner?'

'Fella owned Dutton's. Looked like W.C. Fields. Big red nose, the lot. Had his own side room, full of parrots and dogs. Always fell asleep when you talked to him. Asked him if I could paint him, but he wouldn't have a bar of it. Said he didn't want people coming looking for him, like he was the Elephant Man.' But Roland had sketched him anyway, dozens of times, from memory. 'He was so fat.'

'Well, that's no good. Everyone's starving to death in your paintings.'

'I can paint 'em fat.'

James laughed, sat forward and lit a half-smoked rollie. 'D'yer remember that fella Paul Bell used to get?'

'Yeah.'

'What was his name?'

He tried to remember. 'Windsor …?'

'Somethin' like that. What a repulsive-looking man.' James could see him, naked, reclining on a chair, as he and Roland and a dozen other students sketched him. 'Fat hangin' down over his old fella, remember?'

'I try not to.'

'He just sat there with his *Best Bets*. When he found a horse he'd write it down. Then his fat'd move and he'd fart and we'd all be lookin' at each other.'

They both laughed.

'I reckon that's when we met,' Roland said.

'Was it? Too long ago.' But James could remember this young man with his glasses taped. His sketch, accurate and covered with short, sharp lines. 'You still got them sketches?'

Roland stood, retrieved a box from the old kitchen bench, and sorted through it. He produced the oldest of his sketchbooks and searched for the fat man. 'Here he is,' he said.

'That's him! You got him,' James said. 'You gotta paint him.'

'Na, what about you have a go?'

James seemed interested. Roland tore the sketch from the book and handed it to him. 'Do you a deal. You do the fat ones, I'll do the skinny ones?'

James took it. He noticed a scribble in the corner. 'Form is exaggerated. Draw what you SEE, Mr Griffin.' And the initials: P.B. He said, 'He never liked nothin' no one did, did he?'

'He just didn't say. Prob'ly thought, if you got rid of every imperfection …'

James wasn't so sure.

'We talked, after,' Roland said.

'Eh?'

'After that first class, you and me. You said you were goin' to London. You hated this place and you'd never come back.'

James couldn't remember the conversation, but he knew it must've happened. 'And yet I'm still here.'

'You can only paint what you know.'

This made James think. 'Listen, if I cop a bullet …'

Roland didn't know if he was joking.

'Seriously. It doesn't bother me in the slightest. If I do, though, you wouldn't mind tidying up?'

'How's that?'

'My paintings? I've written all the dates on the back, but I'd need someone who knows what to ask for, keep a note.'

Roland picked up the whisky. 'More come home upright, you know.'

'But you would, wouldn't yer?'

Half an hour later they walked out into the night. James climbed into his car and Roland asked, 'You alright to drive?'

'See what happens. Keep left, don't yer?'

Roland went in and stood in the hallway listening to Ena singing along with Gert and Daisy: *Save a little sugar, save a little tea …*

He moved to his children's doorway, watching them sleeping peacefully. He turned to go.

'Dad,' Hal said.

Roland went in and knelt beside him. 'You still awake?'

He sat up. 'Can we look in the roof now?'

'The roof?'

'Your film. Errol Flynn.'

'At eleven o'clock at night? How about tomorrow?'

'How long is it?'

'Long.'

'Did they give you much money?'

'Lots.'

'Can I have some?'

'I spent it all.'

'On what?'

'Whisky.'

'But you got a box full.'

'I do. But you can't mention that to anyone, right?'

He smiled. 'Why not?'

'It's how the government pays you these days.'

*Save a little money if you've got more than your whack* – they listened to Ena's voice crack, and wobble around the notes. They laughed. *And save your love and kisses till the boys come marching back.* So hard that Sonia woke.

The rain followed Roland along the path. Although it was too cold for the beach there were kids in bathers, dragging towels, climbing and sliding down dunes. He could hear the sea crashing and smell it rotting behind him. The expanse: a black oil desert that had never interested him.

He got back in the car before it started teeming. Ena was sitting with a jam roll on her lap, slicing and distributing it to the kids. When they saw the ice creams they changed their minds.

'Finish your cake,' Ena said, but they weren't having any of that.

They'd just picked her up from her Women's Army Service meeting, more discussions about the spotlight they'd been promised three years before. 'Only so many times you can do them drills,' she said.

Roland had heard the complaint before: the fuel drum someone's husband had donated; the girls (in their overalls, their hair up) adjusting it to follow a flight from Alice, or birds, or nothing in particular; the evening they'd filled it with kero, and lit it, and watched it leak onto the grass and start a fire; the brigade arriving too late to save a long-drop no one fancied rebuilding.

They surveyed the beach as they ate. A father and son had given up flying a kite and were running for the cover of the jetty. Roland turned to Hal, sitting in his own bathers, ice cream down his chin, and said, 'You can't go in.'

'Why not?'

Sonia was having a few quid each way. She'd put on her bathers but covered them with a jumper and shorts.

'You can't,' Ena said. She knew what happened on days like these; she'd seen the newspaper reports. She could imagine Hal in a rip, Sonia trying to get to him, Roland running along the beach, jumping in and going out as well. There'd be a few people watching but no one would be stupid enough to try save them. 'You don't see no one else in the water.' She turned to Roland. After all, this was his fault. 'They'll get a chill, and Sonia'll be off school all week.'

Roland knew there was no point replying. By definition, everything he did was wrong. Every tap he fixed, hinge he oiled, dish he didn't dry well enough. Every bill they'd run out of money to pay. It was okay if there had been an exhibition, and he'd sold a few, but then there were the fallow periods. Then it was down to savings: Reenen money. 'It won't last forever,' Ena would tell him.

'I know.'

'Dad's been at me again.'

'I know!'

It would play out over scones: Ena's father, Nevil Reenen, sitting in his Methodist starched collar and tie, ignoring the bum artist son-in-law. 'You two doin' alright?'

As Roland thought, Mind your own business.

'Well, mostly,' Ena would reply.

He'd look at her and think, Don't tell him, but realise they probably needed to. Nevil would ask about his paintings and if, maybe, there was a more lucrative outlet for his talents (of course, it was the way he said the word – *talents*). 'What about cartoons, for a newspaper?'

'No, that's not my style.'

Roland knew, eventually, he'd put on his wire-framed glasses and get out his chequebook and pen.

'It's not like it was with just you two living it up in London.'

We never lived it up in London, Roland would think. We struggled, because I wanted to do something better than selling tap fittings. Still, there was no escaping the trinity. The old sod would hand over the cheque and Ena would fold it and put it in her apron pocket. Then he'd say, 'Hal's not very tall for a four-year-old,' and Roland would have to apologise for that, too.

The rain stopped. Hal said, 'Can we go now?'

'You can paddle,' Ena conceded. 'But not past your ankles.'

Hal opened his door, jumped out, and slammed it. Then he was across the beach and into the water. Sonia followed, but she felt no need to match his enthusiasm. He wasn't so much human as slug. She couldn't believe she had to sleep beside it: wriggling, kicking, swimming beneath the sheets in search of lost socks. And baths too, which were more disgusting than anything. The way he held his hand under his armpit to make fart noises. And how he laughed when he did – a full-on cack, rolling in the grey water, fiddling with his thing and stretching it like a piece of hot toffee.

Roland watched Hal in the shallows. He guessed there'd be a time when he ignored their advice. Sonia was still following him. Maybe she was watching him, or maybe it was because he was the brother and, like it or not, you stuck together. 'I should write back to those people,' Roland said.

Ena wrapped the roll and looked at him. 'Who?'

'The camouflage people.'

In response to the letter he'd written, explaining how, because of a minor imperfection in his left eye, he was unable to fight, but how he was convinced he could still be of some help to the war effort. 'I believe I have a good grasp of colour and form, and how these relate to the Australian landscape. It occurred to me that I might be of some use in your design department.'

And the reply: 'The present schemes were settled on some years ago, and it is unlikely things will change in the near future.'

He'd made a study of existing camouflage patterns from newspaper photos and vehicles he'd seen on flat-tops heading north. He'd sat at crossings waiting for them, picking up his coloured pencils when he heard the bells. He'd collected these sketches and thought about them: wrong shapes, wrong colours.

'All wrong. I don't think anyone had put any thought into them,' he said.

'They told you, they don't need camouflage.'

But it was more than this. 'Mr Griffin, I believe the best way you can serve your country is to continue to paint. In the past, some of our best artists have modified their subject matter …'

Which had led to a sketch of James in uniform and greatcoat, a train station instead of the shed, soldiers boarding and wives and kids saying goodbye. He'd started painting it, but felt the chasm between this and being the one boarding the train.

'All wrong,' he repeated.

'Well, I can't see you fighting Rommel.'

'He's dead.'

'Still, I don't think you've got it in you.'

'What does that mean? *In me?*' He shook his head, got out and stormed down to the beach. Even if it were true, why did she need to say it? He stood on the hard sand and had to fight to stay upright. 'Should we go back?' he asked his children.

'No, I'll blow away,' Hal said, raising his arms and running along the beach. A few moments later he returned and Roland said, 'Let's go sailing.'

'Now?'

Roland took out a notebook, removed a page and started folding. 'This thing will make it all the way to India.'

Hal was curious. He asked for his own piece and copied his father's folds. It took them a few minutes, kneeling and standing, turning against the breeze. Roland said, 'You do it right, you can put a cat in one of these.'

Hal wasn't so sure. 'Not a cat … maybe a mouse?'

'A cat, or small horse. Don't you believe me?'

Hal watched his dad as if he saw a trace of Corporal Grant in him. They launched their little boats and watched them sail away, bobbing in the waves, as Sonia came up behind them and said, 'What's the point of that?'

'If you were in it, you'd know,' Roland said.

'How?'

'You'd be hoping I got it right.'

She didn't get it, so she ran back to the car. But Roland and Hal persisted, determined to see the boats off. After a while, Hal said, 'I reckon you're right. I reckon they'll make it.'

'Course they will,' Roland said, taking him around the shoulder and leading him back to the car. On the way, Hal said, 'You know tomorrow?'

'Yes, I do. And his brother.'

'Who's that?'

'Fred.'

Hal turned to check his boat, but couldn't see it. 'Do I gotta go?'

'Nan's lookin' forward to it.'

'It's so boring.'

'Life's not a sideshow. You gotta go.'

To the home of Dr Edmund Bailey, at ten-thirty the next morning – two stories of floors to be waxed, dressers to be dusted and shirts to be washed. As Hal sat at the dining table, coloured in and listened to the big clock donging and the hoover hoovering, as Nan cleaned the old man's rugs. 'How much longer y' gonna be, Nan?'

His grandmother straightened and turned to him. 'I don't want to hear none of your complaining.' She switched off the vacuum and said, 'Just sit there. I'm gonna do the dishes.'

She was gone. He listened to the clunk of plates.

'You can put on the radio,' she called.

'No, thanks.' Hal searched the bookcase for something familiar. There were still some on the fourth shelf he'd never tried. So he fetched a pouffe and stood on it. Took out the biggest volume he could find, got down, laid it on the floor and started studying it. At least this one had pictures: someone's head, cut down the middle, and a big lamb's brain ready for the pan. There were diagrams of bodies with nothing but their plumbing, and wiring, and organs.

'What you doin'?' Nan called.

'Sleepin'.'

'How you talking if you're sleepin'?'

Pictures of eyes sliced down the middle, with labels like *vitreous humour* and *ciliary body*. He wondered if his dad could've drawn them. No pubs, no black fellas, no long-drops. Everything, it seemed, was in this book. Which meant that if you could look at all of them the whole world would be explained.

'You're awfully quiet.'

'Doin' me colourin' in.'

'You stayin' in the lines?'

'Oh yeah, I'm stayin' in the lines.'

He turned the page and found another picture. He knew it happened, most mornings when you woke, but not like this. There were whole bits missing, and it was leaning, like the tower. Nan walked in and he slammed the book closed. She approached him and picked it up. '*Advanced Physiology*.'

'What's that mean?'

'You be careful of Dr Bailey's books. I'd be working a year to pay this off if you damaged it. Come on.' She replaced it on the fourth shelf, turned and walked out of the room.

He waited, looking up at it.

'Come on.'

He followed her up the stairs and into the master bedroom. There was a big four-poster with carved supports and what he thought was a tent on the top. She picked up a nightdress, folded it and put it in a drawer.

'Is Dr Bailey married?' Hal asked.

'No.'

'Why's he wear a dress?'

'He sleeps in it.'

'Hasn't he got jarmies?'

'He doesn't wear them.'

'Why not?'

'How should I know? Likes to let his boys breathe.'

'How old are they?'

'Who?'

'His boys.'

'He doesn't have children, I told you.' She started pulling back the sheets to make the bed. 'Boys are, you know, plumbing.'

He wondered if he should ask. No, she might be shocked. She might have no idea about the tower. Instead, he moved towards a small table and examined a brush, powder, a bottle of lemon-coloured liquid.

'Don't touch that.'

He stepped back. 'What is it?'

'It's his toilet water.'

It was the right colour. But what was it doing in such a small bottle? Even he made more than that. 'What's he do with it?'

'Sprays it on. Make himself smell nice.'

He screwed up his nose.

'Impress the ladies.'

He picked it up and smelt it. It was musky. He wondered if doctors had a different smell. After all, even his own dad's pee was as rotten as his.

'Come and help.' Nan handed him pillowcases and he slipped them on. She lifted a pot from under the bed and walked out of the room.

'What's that?'

'I gotta empty his pot.'

'What pot?'

She re-entered. 'His piddle.'

'Doesn't he have a dunny?'

'*A toilet*. And no, lotta these old places only have one downstairs.'

They went back down to the kitchen and she sat him on a chair as she peeled potatoes. 'This time next year you'll be at school,' she said. 'I bet yer lookin' forward to it?' She popped a potato into a saucepan full of water. 'This place ain't much fun. Havin' to listen to me naggin' you all day.'

Hal didn't think Nan nagged. Nagging was Sonia, telling him to stop wriggling, or Mum, forever at his face and neck with soap. But Nan, she was okay. Fat, and nice smelling, and good to hug. Defending him from the threat of Dad ('Fair go, Griff, he didn't mean to') and always bringing him Choo-Choo Bars. And when he stayed in her flat (which was built onto the back of a Chinaman's home) he got to sleep in her bed and eat her fried mushrooms and wonder how she could have so little stuff after such a long life.

'Nan?' he asked, as his feet dangled.

She finished another potato. 'Yes?'

'Why's Dr Bailey got so much stuff?'

'That's life, Hal. You fix people's hearts, you get a loada money. You empty their piddle pots ...'

'You should marry him, then you'd get all this for nothing.'

She laughed. Still holding her potato and knife, she came over and kissed him on top of the head.

Waxed floors, dusters and an hour later he was waiting for her to put the last of the dishes in the cupboard. He sat at the piano and opened the lid. A Griffin hung on the wall above him. One from before his time: coloured cubes and a couple of big seedpods. He turned to the bookcase and wondered if he had enough time. He pressed a white key.

'Hal, off the piano.'

'I know a song.'

'Off!'

There were other things he needed to know. He knew, after he started school, it would be too late. He had no choice. He ran across the room, found the smallest volume and slipped it into his pocket. He felt he'd done something wrong, something he'd end up paying for, but he needed to know. They were hiding something from him.

Roland woke him just after four. 'You comin'?'

Hal moaned, but then remembered. 'Five minutes.' He jumped out of bed, turned on the light (and Sonia told him to turn it off), slipped on his clothes and ran out to the dining room. His dad and Sam were waiting, eating toast, sipping tea.

'Breakfast,' Roland said.

'I'll have it when I get home.'

'You'll have it now.'

Ten minutes later they were walking down Burleigh Avenue in the dark. Hal was between the men, and they were holding his hands. He said, 'Do you think I'll get a ride?'

'If you're useful,' Sam said.

Sam came alive in the morning. He could already see the track lights, hear hooves, smell the feed and shit and even sweat on tired flanks.

The racecourse. Red brick grandstand. NEXT MEETING AUG 3. Floats coming in and out, exhaust and horse breath clouding the still Sirius sky. They walked through the back gate and a few people said hello.

Sam was all horse. The colourised photos on Mary's walls, all of the great runners from the last forty years – stretched bodies reaching for the line, diamonds and dots and underweight jockeys with their pockets full of lead. The transistors, of course, forever calling him to prayer, scratchings and final weights, a chat with Tim Johnson before he ran his horses along the beach. And his own silks, in the back of his wardrobe, reminding him. 'If they're galloping, you keep away from them,' he said to Hal. 'Saw this mad fella once, ran onto a track, went under ten horses. When they got to him he was like a bag of bones.'

Hal imagined someone rolling him up like a rug, popping him in the post and sending him back to his family.

A jockey, with his helmet undone, riding a big horse that towered above Hal, stopped and talked to Sam. 'Tim's ready,' he said.

'Give us a tick,' Sam replied, but then remembered and said, 'You got two minutes?' He moved closer and spoke to him. The jockey smiled. 'Come on then, Hal, let's have you.'

Hal lit up. 'Really?'

'Come on.'

Roland lifted him and the jockey got him under the armpits. Soon he was sitting in the saddle, lost in the grey-grass world. The jockey moved his reins and the horse cantered. 'Should we go round?' he asked.

'Can we?'

Hal went once around the track, safe between the jockey and the lip of the saddle. He felt a hand on his side and knew he wouldn't fall. 'You gonna ride for Mr Johnson?' the jockey asked.

'Reckon I'll be too big.'

'How old are you?'

'Four.'

'Give it a few years.'

He could feel horseflesh and muscles, the jolt of his legs and knees. He looked back and Sam and his dad waved. Perhaps this could be it, he thought. Horses. It was the best thing he'd ever done. There was nothing better than horses. He studied its mane, its big head and brown eyes, its nostrils, sucking in air, and a trail of spit coming from its mouth.

'What d'yer reckon?' Sam asked, once Hal allowed his father to lift him down.

'I might be a jockey,' Hal replied.

'Dunno. You're a solid piece of work.'

Hal knew that Sam had plenty of time for him, but less when horses were involved. He knew the glaze in his eyes when they were talking and a race came on. 'Ssh, just a minute, boyo.' He knew you had to be quiet when he phoned the racing editor. Lots of money was involved. If, for instance, he didn't tell the editor how Geronimo's Dream hated a wet track, then someone might do a hundred quid. Although Sam was an old man, living in a sleep-out in his sister's house, cutting his nails in bed, drinking brandy from a jar, he was still an important man.

They climbed the metal steps to the starter's box. Hal clung to the handrail. He realised they were as high as the top of the grandstand, above it, and he could see the city, Pennington itself, their own roof, Sonia and Ena still sleeping inside. They went into the small box with its all-round windows and little desk for the starter to keep his notes.

Sam lifted the binoculars and checked the stables. 'Come on,' he said. 'Stop muckin' around.' He held his stopwatch, waiting.

'How many horses does Mr Johnson train?' Hal asked.

'Plenty. But they're all sleeping by the looks of it.'

A horse came onto the track and the jockey cantered the hundred yards towards them. As he approached he got faster, then galloped. Sam started his watch. They all observed the gelding's progress. He slowed, but the jockey encouraged him, and a minute later he passed them again. Sam stopped his watch and wrote the time on his pad.

Then he looked back, waiting.

Hal thought he understood Sam. How horse poo didn't worry him; how he carried it on his boots into his sleep-out; how it crumbled onto his rug. His little room smelt of leather from a saddle he kept under his bed. Hal guessed Sam liked this smell, as, if he'd wanted, there was plenty of room in the shed. And he thought it was great how one thing could keep you happy. He often wondered what his one thing would be. It probably wouldn't be horses or paintings because you had to find your own thing.

Sam continued timing. He and Roland talked about horses, and the sort of money people were betting. 'They certainly aren't spending it on bonds,' Sam said.

'You think they'd crack down on it,' Roland replied.

'The war's a long way away, if you know what I mean.'

Hal thought that seemed obvious: Germany, New Guinea. 'Can I have a go at timing one?' he asked.

Sam handed him the stopwatch, gave him his binoculars and told him not to drop them. Then he turned to Roland and said, 'When you off?'

'Wednesday.'

'Big job, is it?'

'A hundred miles, right along the Murray. Hal's comin' with me.'

Hal was too busy to respond.

'So, what, they want you to draw the river?'

'Drought scenes.'

'Dead animals?'

'Empty dams, paddocks, anything. So people can get some idea of how bad it is.'

Hal took the binoculars from around his neck. The sun was coming up, and he decided it would be more fun exploring. 'Can I go sit in the grandstand?' he asked.

'Thought you were helping?' Roland said.

'He's alright,' Sam said. 'Just watch when you're crossin' the track. And stay outa people's way.'

Hal jumped down the steps, three at a time, and ran towards the grandstand. He passed the betting ring, climbed the stairs to the top of the stand and sat down. His dad and Sam were still at it.

Maybe horses wouldn't be his thing.

He reached into his pocket and produced the book he'd taken from Dr Bailey's house. He opened it. Ant trails across musty-smelling pages. There were pictures: a tall man with a beard, rough clothes and a musket; a younger man, nearly naked, kneeling in front of him. Further on, the first man was building what looked like a fort. Then he was firing his musket at what might've been Aborigines, although they were funny-looking black fellas. Later, both men were sitting around a campfire eating fish. Now the second man was wearing clothes. Perhaps the first man had given him some. He tried to read the words: '… the devil was God's enemy in the hearts of men.'

God. He recognised this. Maybe the first man was God? He looked a bit like the God, or was it Jesus, hanging on the wall in Mary's lounge room.

'Come on,' Roland called from the bottom of the stand.

Hal closed the book and ran down the steps. They crossed the road and headed home.

'Can we go back later?' Hal asked.

'Another day.'

The book dropped out of his pocket. He stopped to pick it up and Roland said, 'Where'd you get that?'

'I found it.'

'You found it?' He took it from him and opened the front cover.

*Ex libris*: Dr E. Bailey

'What's this?'

Hal could feel his fingers trembling, then his hands. 'I borrowed it.'

'What, you asked him?'

They were out in the open, and there was nowhere Hal could go. 'No.'

'Well, how did you borrow it?'

'I was gonna return it, next time. He wouldn't notice it. He's got hundreds.'

'But what if he did? Nan could lose her job.'

That was a good point. Dr Bailey might even call the police – Nan, in prison, or if they found out it was him …

'We didn't bring you up to … Christ, Hal, why'd you do it?'

Hal couldn't think of any reason except he liked books. 'I don't know … I'm sorry.' He started crying. Roland grabbed him by the hand and dragged him along.

Hal could feel it warm down his leg.

Roland noticed and stopped. 'Jesus Christ! Not again!'

'I didn't mean to.'

'What d'yer mean? How could you not *mean* to steal something?'

'I didn't mean to …'

Roland saw how the pee had soaked Hal's socks and got into his shoes; how he was shaking; how his own son was terrified of him. He felt this wash over him.

There was a bus stop, and a bench, and he walked over and sat down. Hal followed him, seeing that something had changed. 'Dad?'

'I'll give it to Nan. Maybe he hasn't noticed.'

Hal had stopped shaking. He noticed the sun above the horizon. 'It's about a man trapped on an island,' he said.

Roland said, '*Robinson Crusoe?*'

But Hal didn't know. 'And his friend …'

'He saved him from the cannibals.'

'What are they?'

Roland stood, took his son's hand again, and they walked home. 'They eat their enemies.'

'So, they were gonna eat him?'

'Yep. Feed a family for a week.'

They turned into Burleigh Avenue.

'Mum's gonna let me have it.'

'Don't worry, she'll be asleep. We can rinse 'em. She'll never know.'

Ena hated it when Charlie came around, standing at the back door, calling, peppering his conversation with 'shit from the Bible', as she always let slip. But there was the cancer, and he wasn't harming anyone, as such. So she'd send Hal out to sit with him, listen to his sermon for the day.

Charlie had settled in beside the geraniums with Hal and Sam. Together, this Trinity (although Charlie wasn't the slightest bit Catholic) sat talking as spent wisteria settled on their shoulders. Charlie was wearing the usual beige suit, carnation, bow tie, ivory cufflinks. Sam couldn't understand him. Fair enough, he'd been a tailor (and a good one, apparently), but a man didn't need to bring his work home (unless, of course, a saddle needed sewing).

Charlie said, 'I had Bradman in one time.'

They'd heard it before, but Charlie was a sick man. Sam said, 'For a suit?'

'Double-breasted, pinstripe.'

'What sort of man was he?'

'Never said much. This was just after he started stockbroking. Said he wanted to look the part. Hodgetts was with him.'

'Harry Hodgetts?'

'Yes. Rolls of cash, and he'd just peel it off. Best you got, he'd say. Imported fabric, Charles.'

Sam noticed Charlie's blue veins, his meatless fingers, his sucked-in neck and hollow skull that rattled on his shoulders. 'Did he talk cricket?' he asked.

'Nothin' like that. Just what they were buying and selling. Almost ignored me.'

'You shoulda got his autograph,' Hal said.

'I'm no fan. The most boring game on God's earth.'

God. They worried he might start. Hal said, 'Not when he slogs them.'

'You play?' Charlie asked.

'You gotta be seven to start.'

Charlie sat back and got his breath. Sam studied his face, his chest rising and falling, and suspected they might not have to put up with him much longer.

'If God wills it,' Charlie said.

Shit, Sam thought. He tried to ignore him and refocus on rations. He'd taken leftover pages out of his meat ration book and was sewing them into the Griffin's. It was the neighbourly thing to do. He said, 'Life's tough enough without going on about bloody pestilence.'

Charlie just took a deep breath. 'I'm not going on.'

Sam knew that life itself was rationed, and had to be prized, like a long-odds mare coming up on the outside. 'Just make the most of every day, Hal,' he said. 'Don't go worrying about all that business.'

'"He that does the will of God remains forever,"' Charlie said.

Sam tried to ignore him. Invoked Mary's patience, and forgiveness. The old fool had blood cancer. Sam wanted to use this as proof against his theories, but you couldn't kick a dog when it was down.

'1 John 2:17.'

Sam looked at the ration book. 'You'd never tell.'

Charlie was determined. 'There's no great sadness, Sam,' he said. 'Long as you're ready. "God shall wipe out every tear and death shall be no more …"'

Sam ran the white cotton through a cup of cold tea. It emerged brown, aged. Then he threaded it through a needle and continued sewing the pages into the ration book. All this time, Hal just watched the two men. Charlie said, 'Good of you to do that for Ena.'

Sam guessed it was a peace pipe. 'Well, Mary doesn't eat much, and Shirley, she just picks at her food. But Hal, he's a real carnivore.'

'What's that?' Hal asked.

'Meat-eater. Like a lion. Show Charlie how you can roar.'

Hal tried.

'Frightening,' Charlie managed.

Sam knew it would give them an extra sixty vouchers. But the butcher wouldn't suffer any tampering, so he had to do a good job. He followed the holes in the card, blew on the wet thread.

'Still got your pigeons?' Charlie asked.

'Let 'em go. Not worth the cost of the feed.'

Hal could remember standing beside the hutch, opening the doors, the dozen pigeons flying off, but returning that night, clinging to the chook wire, before Mary ran out with a broom and shooed them.

'Never minded a pigeon pie,' Charlie said.

'Dirty bloody beasts. But they did have their uses, especially when you got difficult neighbours.' He looked at Hal.

'Me?'

'No, but when people give you trouble.' He was happy with the book. He held Hal's knee. 'This is confidential. What you do's, you wrap up some cotton, soaked in metho, light it and tie it to their legs, and they fly off and land on your neighbour's roof, and poof!'

'You never did that,' Hal said.

'Wanna bet. Talk about the end of the world. "Nation will rise against nation, neighbour against neighbour." Fire and brimstone, Hal. You don't wanna worry about God, not when your neighbour's got pigeons. They reckon Hitler's got millions of them, and he's training them to land on London.'

'He has not.'

'He has, hasn't he, Charlie?'

'My oath. Millions of them. And Tojo, too, and they reckon he's teaching them to fly to Australia.'

Hal shook his head. 'They can't fly from Japan.'

'These ones can. They got special feed.'

'But they'd catch fire.'

'And suits. Little pigeon suits. Asbestos. So they don't get cooked.'

Hal liked it when the old men worked together. But he also liked it when they argued. It was a pity Charlie was so sick. But that was okay. These were his Last Days, and this seemed to make him happy.

Roland continued north. After four hours of driving he felt tired, the wheels slipping from the edge of the road, the engine running in the red. The vegetation had turned mallee and he could see hundreds of rabbits moving from hole to hole like small hoovers removing everything from the landscape. Some farmers had planted crops but most, faced with their fifth year of drought, had decided to cut their losses. Dry paddocks had succumbed to weeds, and cracks that could fit a fair-sized child. The remaining stock wandered in the heat searching for something to eat. They licked stones and fence posts and tore at stubble. The sheep were all rib, small heads and big eyes, sniffing the remains of their weekly bale.

He slowed for a stock grate. The car bounced and settled.

'How would he make clothes?' Hal asked, holding up his book and showing him a picture of Crusoe.

'Kill animals.'

'What sort of animals?'

Where was the island? Somewhere near South America? 'A bear, perhaps.'

This seemed to satisfy Hal. He continued looking at the words, trying to make sense of the images. 'What's *roaming*?'

'Walking about.'

Hal tried to imagine Crusoe walking between paddocks; he could see Friday following him, holding down fence wires so his master could slip through. 'Musta been a lot of people got lost out here,' he said.

'Lots.'

'And if no one came along?'

'There was one boy, and his parents owned a petrol station. And one day someone stopped with a horse float.'

Hal guessed horses didn't float, but now wasn't the time.

'They let the horse out to stretch its legs and it took off into the desert. And you know what this boy did?'

'No.'

'He thought, How proud will Mum and Dad be if I get it back. So he took off into the bush, and walked for hours, then realised he didn't know the way home. Then it was night, then day, then he was scared.'

'Like Crusoe?'

'Crusoe was an adult, so he figured out what to do, but this boy, he had no idea. They had a hundred people out looking for him, but he'd gone too far.' He wondered whether Hal needed to know how it ended. Crusoe was rescued, but Crusoe was a made-up story.

'So?'

'They found him a week later, and he was peaceful, like he'd fallen asleep.'

'Was he dead?'

'Yes. And his parents cried and cried.'

'Did they find the horse?'

'No.'

'That's bad.'

'Very bad. But that's what people have gotta put up with out here. There's no deli. Not even a tap if you're thirsty.'

'Pennington's better.'

Hal returned to his book, and Roland returned to the road. The wheels were stuck in orbit, pushing time forward.

When Hal gave Nan the book, Roland looking on, she'd growled at him too, telling him trust was the only thing that really mattered. It had made its way back with a note, now used as a bookmark.

> Dear Master Hal – Your dad's probably reading you this letter, but soon, I hope, you can read it yourself. I noticed you borrowed ROBINSON CRUSOE from my library. You chose well. Mr Crusoe is every man, and boy. Enjoy! The due date for this book is your 100th birthday. If I'm not around, you may consider it yours. Regards, E. Bailey, Doctor of Bums and Broken Bits

Driving, staring at the bitumen, Roland guessed it was partly his own fault. He'd never bought books. There was a Pollyanna and Heidi, and Alice with a broken spine, but Sonia was more interested in Tim Holt and Liz Taylor. 'When we get home I'll take you to Preece's,' he said.

'Who's he?'

'He's a bookshop.'

Roland saw his kids were standing at the shed door, waiting, but he only ever closed it. Hal, for instance, coming in with six lumps of wood, a hammer and nails. 'Dad, can we make a box?'

'Now?'

'I know how the nails go in.'

'Later.'

Later, he'd found Hal hammering, hitting his thumb, the wood full of bent nails. 'How's it lookin'?'

'Can you help now?'

'I've gotta finish a painting for Tuesday.'

The following day he'd found the box on the table under the arbour: wood held together with crooked nails. He'd realised this angular lump was the very best and worst of Hal. It was the hours, and days, and years, perhaps. It was everything, and it was nothing. Overcome with private grief, he'd taken it all apart, straightened the nails and reconstructed it as a perfect box. He'd though: A gift! But then: No, what did the box have to do with anything? So he'd taken it all apart, left it on the table, and waited till Hal got home. 'Come on, boyo, we've got a job to do.'

So, in the end, Roland realised, as he searched the desert for something worth sketching, the box was always waiting.

He leaned over in the car to touch his son's shoulder, and squeeze it, and couldn't believe his love for him, creeping up over the years, overgrowing the back shed like wisteria no one could remember planting. 'You're not gonna be bored?' he asked.

Hal looked up. 'No.'

'I'm gonna be busy.'

'I can draw things too, and the paper man can say which he likes best.' He closed his book and squinted at a flat-topped hill in the distance. 'Someone chopped the top off.'

'That was God.'

'You don't believe in God.'

'He did that before I stopped believing in him.'

'When was that?'

'Last Tuesday.'

Hal smiled. 'How much longer is it?'

'Six foot.'

'Why'd you gotta draw dead sheep?'

'Most people who read newspapers live in the city. They don't know what's going on out here. So the journalist will write his bit and they'll publish my drawings, then they'll know.'

'And how will that help?'

Roland wasn't sure. 'People just need to know. And I've gotta do my bit.'

'Cos you can't fight the Japs?'

'Yep. That's why.' He wondered whether this might suffice. Droughts affected food production, people had to eat, to make guns and bullets, to keep the soldiers fighting. 'Like James, he's doing his bit.'

'But he's fighting the Japs.'

'And he needs food to do it, and this is where it comes from.'

Hal could still see James in his uniform, carrying his duffle bag, his rifle across his shoulder, waiting for the train at the station. They'd got up early and driven in. There were hundreds of soldiers and it had taken half an hour to find him. They'd gone for tea and biscuits in the Cheer-up Shack, and managed to talk above the noise. Hal had run his hand over the wood of the .303. 'Where's yer bayonet?'

James had said, 'We haven't got it yet.'

Roland had been watching this, and watching the hundreds of soldiers – some much older than him, limping, fingers missing, and thought, All cos of an eye … He'd given his friend a few notebooks and pencils and said, 'When you get back, you'll be painting this stuff for years.'

Roland turned off the road and they drove down a dirt track. Ten minutes later they pulled up in front of a house, beside several sheds, stockyards with collapsed panels and gates lying on the ground.

They got out.

'Hello?' Roland called, but there was no response. He didn't think there would be. The house had been left open and sand had blown in. They approached the door, called again and entered. The rooms were mostly empty. There was a sofa in the living room. Someone had rolled up a rug and leaned it against a wall. 'Where have they gone?' Hal asked.

'Moved out.'

'Why?'

'That's why we're here, boyo.'

There was a radio in the kitchen. Hal plugged it in and switched it on but nothing happened. '*Howdy-do, Daisy,*' he said. '*Good morning, Gert ...*'

Roland opened the drawers and found mouse shit and chewed newspaper. He pulled a sheet out and noticed the date: 1941. The days of flour and icing sugar, dripping and arrowroot biscuits. A calendar on the wall: June 1943. Someone had written 'vacsinations' on the third.

'Do you think they're comin' back?' Hal asked.

'No.'

They went out to the sheds and found fencing wire and posts, but no machinery. Roland said, 'Wait,' and went back to the car to get his camera. Soon he was busy photographing the house and surrounds, the old pepper tree where the family had once sat, broken chairs and a vase on a table. Then he fetched his pad from the boot and started sketching. It was what the world expected of him, he supposed: red sand and ruins, a windmill that still turned on its axle, but clunked, a short-drop with no door but plenty of paper.

Hal was hot and hungry. He carried the basket from the boot and laid out sandwiches and cups with cordial from the thermos. They ate in the shade of the pepper tree, Roland clutching his food and pencil in his sketching hand. 'It's a pity,' he said.

'How's that?'

'This was someone's home, and they had to leave it.'

'Maybe they wanted to.'

'Would you want to leave our place?'

'Perhaps.' Hal knew this wasn't true. A house was most of your life. 'I wonder if they had a boy.'

'Probably,' Roland replied, pointing to a bike lying in long grass. Hal jumped up, ran across and pulled it out. Both tyres were flat and the frame and spokes were rusty. This didn't stop him. He walked it into the compound and, still holding his sandwich, tried to ride.

'Careful,' Roland called, still caught up in charcoal.

He couldn't ride without trainer wheels so he fell, got up, and tried again. This time he rolled down an incline, into a fence. 'Dad!'

Roland ran across and pulled him out of a mess of wire. 'This is exactly what I warned you about,' he said.

'Sorry.'

Even before he was out, Roland could see the gash. Two inches, across the soft, meaty part of his arm. 'Christ,' he said. 'You had tetanus?'

'What's that?'

'Come on.'

The front bar of the Commercial Hotel was deserted. The publican, Percy Bliss (or Smith, Roland hadn't quite caught it), explained that it was too late. 'When there was money around they'd stay all hours, but no more.'

Roland and Hal sat at the front bar. Percy's wife, Sue, had placed the roast of the day in front of them: a small mountain of lamb, a scoop of mashed potato, pumpkin and something green-grey floating in a sea of gravy.

Hal hadn't begun. The publican's wife was bathing his gash, padding it with cotton and bandaging it. Meanwhile, Roland was halfway through. 'Nice bita meat, Mrs Bliss.'

If the name was wrong, she didn't say. 'It's getting dear.'

'I'd imagine. At least you got a few animals to hand.' And he thought about the sheep he'd seen earlier. 'Course, at some point, it'd cost more to feed them. You reckon it'll break soon?'

'Soon.'

Without asking, Percy poured him another beer and placed it on the towel. You didn't go to church to read the newspaper.

'Thanks,' Roland said.

'If you study the meteorological data, Mr Griffin, you see a pattern.'

'How's that?'

'Every twenty or so years it dries out, but it never lasts more than five years. Then it's wet for five years.'

'So you're due?'

'Another twelve months you won't be able to get a seat in here.'

Roland hoped he was right. He cut another piece of lamb, put it in his mouth and chewed. It was so tough he had to make himself swallow. Percy was watching him; there was only so much chewing you could do before it became rude.

'Killed this morning,' Bliss said.

'That's fresh, eh? The stuff we get in town, you wonder how long it's been sitting in someone's back room.'

He eyed the dog sitting beside the pool table. That was an option, but how much worse would it look if they caught him feeding it?

Mrs Bliss pinned the bandage in place. 'All done.'

'Thanks,' Hal said.

'You gotta be careful with cuts,' Percy said, but didn't explain why.

'She'll be apples,' Roland said, and he felt he was laying it on a bit thick. He drank half of his beer. 'Called my wife, Ena. She said he's had his jabs.'

'Good-o.'

The phone call when they'd come in: the local operator. 'I'm putting you through now.' The wrong number. The second attempt. Sonia answering. 'Hi, Dad, how's it all going?'

'Good. Is your mother there?'

'She's talking to Mary.'

'Well, she can stop for a minute.'

'Shirley had an accident.'

He made himself ask. 'Nothing bad?'

'No, she tripped on the gutter.'

'Fine, your mother?'

Ena had come on. She'd told him about the accident, Shirley's front tooth knocked out, the trip to the dentist (on the bus, the bleeding and crying). Then he'd said, 'We've had a bit of drama too.' And he'd explained.

'I knew this'd happen. Were you watching him?'

'Of course. I can't be … he was twelve foot away. It coulda happened anywhere. He's fine. The publican's wife's gonna fix him up. Reason I rang, couldn't remember if he's had his tetanus.'

'Yes,' she said. A can't-trust-you-for-a-minute yes. 'It might get infected.'

'It'll be fine. She's got all the gear. She used to be a nursing sister.'

'Put him on.'

Roland knew he had to.

Whose bike was it? Why were you riding it – you don't know how to ride? (I do so!) We told you, if you go, you sit and wait for Dad. No muckin' around. (I didn't!)

Hal started eating his meat. He chewed, and swallowed, unconcerned.

'So, you're a proper artist?' Percy said.

'Yes.'

Percy didn't seem to believe this. Artists came from London and

Paris, and they looked different, spoke different, they were poofters (he guessed) and had no idea what life was really about. But Mr Griffin, he was alright.

'I worked for a year on a farm when I was younger,' Roland said.

'Where was that?'

'South. Citrus. I was an overseer.'

'Why'd you give it up?'

'Just did it for a while. Keep my old man happy. They weren't paying nothin' for oranges, either, so we were bulldozing trees. Hundreds. Cheaper than watering them.'

'What year?'

'Let me think ... 1932 and 1933.'

Percy did the maths and frowned. It didn't fit his scheme. 'Dry years?'

'Wet. Too many oranges, prices dropped.'

'Ah, that'd explain it.'

'Lotta empty places round here,' Roland said.

'A few. Most'll hang on. They got money in the bank.'

But this didn't agree with the FOR SALE signs along the highway; the closed schools; the empty bays at Privett's Farm Machinery.

'Droughts are part of the grand opera, Mr Griffin. You paint us now, come back in twelve months when everything's green, paint us again.'

Roland admired this habit of seeing everything with a hundred-year perspective. It made any given day, month or year bearable.

'You got yer newspaper payin', you wanna drink up,' Percy said, as he placed another beer in front of him.

Roland wondered whether Percy wanted him to finish the keg, to justify opening a new one. 'So full of beer I can't eat,' he said.

'Killed that this morning,' Percy said again.

'So where do you recommend I go?'

Percy stopped to think. 'We got a nice rose garden, down by the Freemasons.'

'No, they want drought scenes. They thrive on bad news.'

'Maybe you could paint me?'

Roland sent Hal to their room to fetch his pad and pencil. He got Percy and Sue to stand under the front verandah and sat sketching them while Hal, inside, worked his way through a mousse. 'Nice and natural. Like I wasn't here.'

After ten minutes, Sue Bliss asked, 'How's it goin'?'

'Nearly there.'

And after twenty minutes she said, 'I gotta get back to the dishes.'

'Wait on,' Percy said. 'We might end up in the paper.'

'Or hanging in a gallery,' Roland added.

'I wouldn't want that,' she said. 'People laughin' at yer.'

'Why would they be laughin'?' Percy asked her.

'Look at what we're wearin'. Could you imagine? My fat arms?'

Roland had got those. And her tired shoulders, heavy eyes, hard-working hands and broom-bristle hair. 'Don't be upset when you see it,' he said. 'I like to be honest.'

'Your tea'll be getting cold, Mr Griffin.'

'I'm full up, Mrs Bliss.'

'It's Smith, Mr Griffin. *Smith*.'

When he showed them the sketch they took a few moments. 'Jesus,' Percy said. 'We're eight foot tall.'

'That's my style,' he explained. 'Big landscape, like it was stretching people.'

Sue couldn't understand. 'My kids looked at this, they wouldn't even know it's me.'

'Yes, they would. Look at your nose, your chin. I tell you what, I reckon this'd make a decent painting.'

Sue Smith wasn't so sure. 'What would you do with it?'

'Sell it.'

'And we'd be hangin' in someone's house?'

'Possibly.'

She shook her head. 'Right. I can warm up yer tea, Mr Griffin.'

He just smiled and held up the sketch. 'What do you reckon, Perce?'

Mr Smith was saved by a ute pulling up, and two men coming in for a drink. 'Reckon we can crack that other keg,' he said.

They walked towards the river. Past Boston's Motor Repairs – a long, sky-lit shed with part of its roof caved in. 'Look!' Hal said, and ran inside.

'Hal!'

But he was already past the empty workbenches, over the service pits, picking up a tractor tyre and rolling it. Roland came in and shouted, 'Hello?' He watched pigeons fly into an opening of blue sky. Hal kept rolling the tyre in orbits, until it fell, jumped across the concrete floor and settled.

There were even fewer people on Ayr Street: Norrie Carmichael working in his shop, still buzzing, flies on tiles and angled mirrors; two men in overalls talking out front of Goldsborough, Mort and Co.

They looked in Alan Bowey's window. All three walls were lined with shelves, each chocker with labelled jars. Laskaris had come to cook fish and chips, but left. Gibbs and his mower repairs had gone, but the Savings Bank and Walker's Men's Store had survived. They crossed into the middle of the road. The grass was mowed, neat, dead in the evening sun.

'It's too tight,' Hal said, picking at his bandage.

They sat down opposite the war memorial and Roland unclipped the safety pin, removed the bandage and started reapplying it.

The plinth was carved with the names of Great War soldiers. A granite Anzac stood at ease in the shade of a fig tree. Hal said, 'He's got the same gun as James.' He hooked a finger under the bandage and loosened it. 'Sam said he had the same one when he was in France.'

'He told you about that?'

'Yep.'

On a cold, July night, as they sat in his sleep-out. Hal noticed a photo in a book beside Sam's bed. Took it out and studied it: a soldier, hands behind his back, in front of a studio rendering of the Great Pyramids. 'Hey, Sam, who's this?'

'Who do you reckon?'

'Were you in Egypt?'

'Yes.'

'What were you doin' there?'

'Selling hair oil.'

Hal didn't react.

'Killing Germans.'

'D'yer get many?'

'A few.' He shook his head. 'You know, it wasn't a night out. And them over doin' it now, they got it worse.'

Hal just waited, studying the image. 'How many d'yer reckon?'

'Ten.'

'D'yer get 'em with yer knife?'

'Aren't you meant to be somewhere?'

As if he'd heard, Roland called from next door. 'Hal, bedtime.'

Hal asked if he could have the picture and Sam said, 'No, you can't.' He grabbed it back as Hal ducked out the door.

As Roland fixed the bandage, Hal studied the Anzac and said, 'He looks like Trevor.'

'Does not,' Roland replied.

'We shoulda brought him along.'

Roland almost laughed. 'That would've ended well.'

'What?'

Because Trevor, back staying with Mary, had asked if he could come, saying he knew a few blokes up that way and they could stay with them, and one of them sold tractor parts, and they could get them for a decent price and re-sell them. But Roland said no. Not just for Ena's sake anymore, but his own. For the sake of the law. Of a good night's sleep.

They continued along a rough path beside the river. The water sat still in a deep channel. Dead fish on the margins. They found a log, sat down, and Roland started sketching. He made the river look sicker than it really was. Although it was documentary, he added a man fishing, waiting in expectation of the little bit of life the waterway could still muster.

'Where we goin' tomorrow?' Hal asked.

'Follow the river. Back to where I used to work.'

'Where was that?'

'Cobdogla.'

Hal started throwing stones into the water.

'Don't do that.'

He wandered off into the nearby scrub, and started poking an anthill with a stick.

'Don't *do* that.'

'They'll make a new one.'

'How'd you like someone to do that to your house?'

Hal didn't get his dad. Maybe he never would. He kept on at the ants.

'What did I just tell you?'

'I'm bored.'

'I warned you. Now you'll just have to put up with it.'

Hal started crushing ants. He couldn't see where he fit in to all this.

A week passed and Roland was sitting in his shed, studying the dozens of sketches from his journey. Lots of desert, and dead trees, the gougings of land that used to water people's livelihoods. But mostly, the people. Simple, no-fuss, boiled-mutton people, with all their scars and accidental arse cracks. The memories of Perce and Sue Smith.

He admired the sketch, and the photos he'd taken (Percy peeling potatoes, telling him the best way to kill rabbits) and started on a canvas – a few hesitant charcoal lines, until the instinct took over. The images coming in a simple alchemy he had no control over, no desire to control. Then the picture of the elongated publicans standing on their verandah as two boys rode a goat-cart down the road.

They'd driven through Cobdogla, but most of that was boarded up, too. Later, on the highway, they saw farmland that was more desert. Dead cattle, legs splayed, as though they'd just given up.

He'd submitted his sketches, and a few had already been published. Even written a bit about Percy, and others, but the paper had gone for the journalist's copy. Everything could be reduced to numbers. As Percy had explained, there was an average of twenty-three years between droughts. Just long enough to get the house swept out; the bodies buried, and almost forgotten.

Roland noticed Shirley at the shed door. She was wearing a smaller version of her mother's apron. Her hands were twisted, clenched, but there was no sign of pain on her face. She held a small basket full of eggs. 'Mum wants to know if you need any?'

'Yes, thanks.'

'I'll give 'em to Ena.'

'No, don't worry, I'll take them in.'

He moved his sitter's chair to the middle of the shed. She knew the drill: sat down, the eggs still in her lap.

'I'll take those,' he said. He put them on the ground.

'Mum says they're not laying so many.'

'We've got plenty.'

'She reckons they're too old. Reckons Uncle Sam should knock 'em on the head.'

He sat and replaced the Smith canvas with *Shirley*. He'd already started painting – filling in the blocks of colour that would become sky (she was sitting under the arbour), skin (and the rash was still unresolved) and apron. 'I wasn't sure about your eyes,' he said. 'I reckon I got them too big.'

'I don't mind,' she said.

He started working on the canvas, changing the roughed-in eyes with his charcoal stick. 'You've got small irises,' he said.

'What are they?'

'The bits you see through. They reckon you can tell a person by their eyes.'

She smiled. This seemed silly. If you had eyes without a person, you'd never be able to tell who they belonged to.

'Look at me, I'm eyeless.'

'You got one good one.'

She always avoided his bad eye. She was never sure what he was seeing: shadow, shape, movement? Maybe he thought she was pretty. Maybe that's why he was painting her. Or maybe it was because of her disease. All of Griff's paintings showed people who weren't quite right. There were no beauties: Happy Jack the simpleton (who looked like he'd been dropped on his head), the half-caste woman with her big lubra nose.

She studied the photos around the walls and window frames. 'Sonia's real pretty.'

'You reckon?'

'Plenty of people say so.'

'Who?'

But she couldn't think of anyone.

'You play with her?' Roland asked.

'Not much.'

'Why's that?' He sat back and examined his changes.

'Dunno.'

'You're mates. That goes for home, and school.'

Well, I don't reckon she sees it that way, Shirley thought. 'She's off with these other girls.'

'Well, she should include you.'

No reply.

'She do something to you?'

'No.'

'Say something?'

'Nothing.'

Just the sound of the charcoal stick, rubbing, crumbling, Roland smoothing and changing lines with his fingers.

Shirley still wasn't sure what was expected of her. Was she a sort of vase, arranged on a table, or did her words, her ideas, matter somehow? 'How did you like it up the river?'

'Good.'

'Mum's got all yer pictures, from the paper.'

'Really?'

'She cut 'em out, stuck 'em on the fridge. She reckons yer famous.'

'I'm not famous.'

'More than us. We've never done anything anyone's noticed.'

'What about all those blue ribbons?'

She shrugged. 'They don't put photos of yer scones on the front page.'

He put down the charcoal and wiped his hands on his pants. 'I reckon that's just about ready for paint.'

She stood, came around and looked. She wasn't sure. Her face seemed featureless, her hands like stumps. And the rash? 'That's how it's gonna look?' she said.

'Mostly.'

She picked up the eggs. 'I'll give them to Ena.'

He waited until she disappeared, realising he'd made her uncomfortable. Called out, 'Tell Sam, if he needs a hand with the chooks.'

'Griff.' Corporal Trevor Grant stood in the doorway. He'd traded his uniform for civvies. Hadn't shaved for days, and his unoiled hair hung in his eyes. He dropped a jammed-full duffle bag. 'You busy?'

'No.'

Trevor came in, took a carton of cigarettes from under his jumper and handed them to Roland. 'Another thank you, for the other day.'

Roland smelt them. 'We didn't do anything wrong, did we?'

'No, it was all paid for, eh?' Trevor smiled.

Roland noticed how he kept adjusting his shirt, scratching his face, flicking the tip of his nose. 'You alright?' he asked.

'Fine.' Trevor looked at the painting. 'That's a good likeness. She's a good kid.'

'Yes.'

'That rotten disease, though. It'll kill her.'

Roland found it strange that he'd say this; that he was leaning in so close to him; that his breath smelt so strong. 'Why d'you say that?' he asked.

'Mary tell you much about Davo?'

'No.'

'His mum was dead at thirty-nine. Cruel fuckin' disease. Why they ever had kids, I don't know. Still, Shirley seems happy enough. Although I reckon she gets a hard time.'

'From who?'

'At school. She's always comin' home and cryin', and Mary just says, "Stop it, listen to yerself, girl."'

'Who are these kids?'

But Trevor was preoccupied. 'I'm about to head off.'

'I thought you were staying for another two weeks?'

'I was, but I'm in a bit of trouble.'

'How's that?'

Trevor smiled. 'Various things. Mostly, these fellas I've been gettin' around with. Turns out some of them are … anyway, I've heard I'm a wanted man.'

'Anything to do with our excursion?'

Again, Trevor just smiled. 'Mary doesn't know a thing, and I wanna keep it that way. She's got enough to worry about. But I thought I'd have a word to you. So *you* can talk to her, after I go.'

'None of my business, Trev.'

'I know, but as a favour. I've packed a few things. One of me mates is pickin' me up.'

'You're deserting?'

'Yes.'

'You'll be in a shitload of trouble.'

'Less than I mighta been in.'

'Where you gonna …?' Roland realised it was better he didn't ask. 'You got somewhere lined up?'

'A place on the river. Bita fruit pickin'. We might head north, coupla stations looking for people.'

'Shouldn't you talk to someone?'

'No, I'll slip out, and you can tell Mary. And when they come looking for me you tell them I didn't want no part of it, but they made me go along with it.'

'With what?'

'Tell 'em I was suicidal. Tell 'em I'm willing to testify.'

'Testify?'

'If they can cut me a deal.' He took out a notepad and scribbled a phone number. 'This is the place I'm stayin'. Don't give it to no one, promise?'

'Yes.'

'But, if they reckon they'll listen.'

Roland wasn't sure if this was real. It felt like a radio play. 'So, no one knows about the airport?'

'I don't think.'

'You don't think?'

A car pulled up out front and sounded its horn.

Trevor extended his hand. 'That's me.'

'They can shoot you for this.'

'They gotta find me first. They reckon Hitler'll be finished in twelve months. Then we'll see how it goes.' He picked up his duffle bag.

'Trevor, you should stay. Think about Mary.'

'Nice to meet you, Griff. Say goodbye to Hal for me.' He reached in his pocket and produced a Rising Sun Badge. 'I thought you could give him this.'

Roland took it, studied it. When he looked up, Trevor had gone.

Returning to Shirley, Roland only saw patches of white canvas – the bits he had to fill in. He mixed a slightly paler version of his usual skin colour and began.

An hour later Mary came in. 'You haven't seen Trev, have yer?'

He avoided looking at her, thought, What's it got to do with me? Tried to work, but couldn't.

Mary noticed the painting, smiled and said, 'That's her, is it?'

'Yes.'

'I can see her eyes.' She wanted to ask why he'd painted her this way. Was it because he wanted to make her, Mary, feel better? She wanted to say, I don't need to feel better. My girl is as perfect as your kids.

'Listen, Mary. You gotta wait till it's done.'

'Good-o.' Then she remembered. 'So, you haven't seen him? I reckon he's gone. He's taken his gear. Maybe he's stayin' with a mate?'

Roland couldn't see a way around it. 'Mary, he asked me to have a word.' He stood, and offered her the seat. 'I don't know if any of this will come as a surprise.'


The Griffins walked through the State Art Gallery. Ena's arm was bandaged from where the spotlight had burned her. From where Mrs Sneddin had turned it without warning, collecting several bodies, arms, melting Ena's dress and removing layers of skin. Years of drills, manuals and 44-gallon drums had done little to get them ready for the real thing: the grey lamp on its pedestal in the yard behind the cold stores. Ena had tried the handle that turned it, but the bending had finished her back.

They moved into the main gallery. The walls were ochre, but Roland knew there was nothing outback about the place. Nothing of Perce and Sue, and the Commercial, cattle caught in fences and living rooms full of sand. And the people looking at the paintings: striped ties and hankies in pockets, wives in taffeta dresses, cardigans, gloves, even. Why did you need gloves to look at art? What were you going to touch?

Roland examined a Lucas sketch of an approaching storm and admired the lines, the tinted paper, every pebble on the beach. He heard a man's voice. 'Too much of the Biblical.'

And his wife said, 'No, they're Greek. Look at the columns.'

Roland returned to Ena, studying the deaf-mute son of King Croesus attempting to stop the Persians from killing his father. Hal said, 'They're gonna run him through.'

Ena looked more closely. 'Who's the son?'

'That one.'

'He doesn't look too worried.'

Roland thought it was the worst sort of art: photographic people playing out history. They should've been wearing their own cardigans and gloves. 'This place makes me sick,' he said.

'Why?'

'You wouldn't know you're in Australia. They don't give a shit about – '

'Ssh,' she said, aware of the other couples.

'So? A few Heysens, Tom Roberts, Conder, if yer lucky. But what's happened since then?'

She knew he was angry that they had at least four Griffins in storage. 'Where's this one you wanted to see?'

They collected Sonia from the European modern section and made for the back of the gallery. A special area had been set aside to show the winner of the 1943 Archibald Prize. They went in, waited, and eventually came face-to-face with Joshua Smith. Ena said, 'He looks like one of yours.'

'He does,' Sonia agreed, stepping closer, examining the paint, the lines, but then just turning and shrugging. 'Hard to see what all the fuss is about.'

'He's nothing like mine,' Roland said.

Hal didn't seem to care either way. He just sat on a leather lounge and kicked loose parquetry with his polished shoes.

Ena waved her hand, like it was a disappointing home renovation. 'He is, look: long head, big ears, body all out of proportion. No, I don't like it at all.'

Roland had entered a painting of a man standing next to a bowser in a small-town petrol station. It hadn't even been shortlisted.

'That's nothin' on yours,' Ena said. 'You had that real country spirit, but him, he looks like a ... what d'yer reckon, Sonia?'

'He looks creepy. And why's he sittin' on the edge of his chair?'

'Didn't you meet him once?' Ena asked.

'Yes. Nice chap.'

'Who?' Sonia said.

Roland admired the image. 'Dobell.' At least, he supposed, there were people looking at Australian art. And it wasn't all bushscape and lost children. But this didn't make it easier. He wanted to turn to the small crowd and say, I did one of these, but it's in the basement.

They walked to the cafeteria for tea and sultana cake. Roland thought the tea too strong, the cake stale. He gave his to Hal and watched him eat – feeding the slab into his mouth. 'Slow down.' He noticed the Rising Sun Badge pinned to Hal's shirt. He'd been wearing it for days, transferring it from one piece of clothing to another, even pyjamas, except for the time Roland had needed it to show the detective and policeman who stood in his living room. 'I'll be quite honest with you, Detective.'

'Good-o, Mr Griffin.'

'I guessed he was up to something, but I didn't want to ask. I thought, If he tells me, one day you fellas will arrive and I'll feel compelled to tell you.'

The detective, a tall, lanky man not unlike Joshua Smith, had said, 'I understand all that, but you were the last person he spoke to. He must've given you some idea of where he was going?'

Hal had been listening from the hallway. Roland had seen his shadow against the wall. 'Hal, get to bed!'

The detective had said, 'It's not inconsiderable, what they've stolen.'

'No?' He thanked God he'd packed the whisky and cigarettes into his car, and driven them (at midnight) to the big bin behind the metal works.

'You know much about that?'

He wondered how much he could afford to play with the truth. 'I guessed it was whisky. I saw a few bottles, but I didn't want to say nothin'. I mean, it wasn't none of my business. He might've used his money to buy them.'

'So, he never actually gave you anything?'

'No.'

'But you suspected?'

'Well, you would, wouldn't yer?'

The detective sat down and started rolling a cigarette. 'He didn't say he was headed interstate?'

'No, but he said if you wanted to go after these other fellas, and you got 'em – he'd help you out.'

'Help us out?'

'Testify.'

'Right.' He licked the paper. 'So, if I told you now, that's a goer, how would you contact him?'

'I'd have to wait, and eventually, I'd hear something.'

The detective wasn't happy with this. 'That's what he told you? *Eventually*?'

'Yes.'

Back in the cafeteria, Roland wondered if he'd done the right thing. Maybe it would've been better to say nothing. That'd been Ena's opinion, when he'd told her the story the night of Trevor's flight.

'I told you no good'd come of it.'

'How was I to know?'

'I told you! Christ, listen to your wife sometimes.'

There'd been the usual dumb husband lecture, finishing with, 'Stay right out of it. The coppers come, you tell 'em we said hello, had a cuppa, and that was it. Otherwise, you could get in a loada trouble.'

'How was I to know? He asked for a lift. That's what you do, isn't it? Help people out?'

They left their crumbs, and sweet dregs, and headed back to the main door. There were still discoveries to be made and, although the kids ran ahead, Roland lingered around a few portraits. 'Bugger me,' he said, completely taken back.

Ena smiled. 'See!'

A Griffin! An early painting, saturated with cubism: a man and his son standing in front of a shed that was a confusion of line and colour. The trees were angular, leafless skeletons with dead fruit hanging from the tips of cast-iron branches. He read the label: 'Roland Griffin, Australia. 1936. *The Storm and the House*'.

The kids came back to look. 'Who's that one?' Hal asked.

'Your father,' Ena replied.

'In here?' he said.

# 1948

They'd worked out it was the manager's bedroom. He'd left a four-poster, and it was mainly intact; a mattress, its springs emerging; a wardrobe with 'Commonwealth Bank of Australia' stencilled on the back. A certificate pinned to the wall: 'Terrance Graves Best Employee Western Region 1919'. Roland wondered why this man (and he could see him, done up in a double-breasted suit) had come here. Maybe he'd been transferred; maybe he had no choice. Osmond Hill, the streets paved with gold (although the streams and hills had stopped yielding). A new start for his family (and there were clues, a rusted-out spinning top in the kitchen), a shot at management. The room, like the dozen others in the abandoned bank, was a mess of crumbling mortar, honeycombed floorboards (Roland reckoned he could hear the white ants), piles of old ledgers and burnt walls where someone had started a fire.

He shifted to the edge of the bed as Ena moved further onto his side. As was her habit. It didn't really bother him. He never fell. It was as though his body knew the few inches he was allowed. Ena had made the bed up with clean sheets but it still smelt like the old mattress.

If he closed his eyes he was in London. It was 1938, and they were in their two-up two-down. It smelt the same; the walls were just as damp, the floorboards just as soft, although at least here there was no one next door shouting at Faye to shove her head in the oven and do everyone a favour.

Ten years ago, he thought. To the month, the day? The 185 to

Lewisham at their front door – the first bus at 5.15 am, the last at 12.48 pm. The White Swan on Vauxhall Bridge Road – sly grog on the pavement at one in the morning, Ena opening the window and calling, 'Get home, or we'll call the police!' Laughter. 'You call 'em, love!' The upstairs bedroom, Sonia (getting them up three or four times a night) in a bassinet at the end of their bed. The downstairs kitchen-lounge. A gas ring to cook mutton (if they could afford it). A small laundry cum studio. It serviced all eight flats, so he could really only work at night. Still, these had been some of his best paintings of outback grocery stores, fingerless ringers, old fellas and their gins living in galvanised-iron shacks. Perhaps it was the longing that did it.

He looked out of the window. The sun had risen a full fist above the horizon. He could hear James and the kids downstairs making toast.

'Ena, we better get up,' he said.

'What?' She turned to him, opened her eyes, and closed them again. 'Rotten bloody night's sleep.'

'I's just thinkin', reminds me of Pimlico.'

She couldn't see it. 'It's a long way from Pimlico.'

Half a world; dreams of artistic greatness evaporating as Hitler rattled his sabre, as, one day, he said to Ena, 'If it starts, I don't fancy being stuck here.'

'So, what are you saying?'

'There's nothin' I can't do here that … we'll be cut off.'

But he'd been talking about London for years – how it was the only place, really, you could become a proper artist.

'Nine months, and you wanna go home?'

'I don't wanna go home, I'm just saying. There goes Austria, Czechoslovakia. He won't stop.'

'Rubbish. The place is full of fellas like that. What's his name, Mussolini?'

But Roland wasn't so sure. 'We could be stuck here for years.'

'You wanted to be!'

'It's just … Sonia.'

But she knew it wasn't really Sonia. He'd tired of putting pennies in a gas meter, lining up for shanks, the grime, everywhere, on everything.

'Stay there, have a sleep-in,' he said, but she didn't reply. He slipped on his dressing gown and went into the hallway. The kids' room was almost empty. They'd found two more mattresses, and Ena had tried to make them up, but Hal wasn't interested in sheets. He'd slept in his singlet, beside a set of stamps he'd found downstairs. He'd stolen some of his dad's Indian ink and started a collage of words – FINAL PAYMENT DUE, IN ARREARS, ACCOUNT CLOSED – and left it beside a bookcase containing a single small book. Roland picked it up, leafed through, blew the dust. Rimbaud. He'd heard of him; wrote a few poems, gave up before he was twenty-one. Maybe that's what I should've done, Roland thought. The paper was yellow, acid-eaten, and smelt good. He read a few lines. 'I have come to know skies splitting with lightning, and waterspouts …' He put it in his pocket, for later.

Several treads on the stairs were missing. James had told the kids to be careful, but Sonia had already fallen: a tumble, a grab for the banister (which came away in her hands), as Hal, standing at the top, laughed.

'You're such a shit.'

'I didn't say a thing.'

'I wish you weren't my brother!'

When Roland arrived in the kitchen, James was sitting sketching, Hal eating and Sonia making a cup of tea. 'I'll have one,' he said.

'I didn't boil enough water.'

'Boil some more.'

She glared at him, but took the kettle from the Primus stove and filled it from the tap that still worked.

He sat down. 'Busy already?' he said to his friend.

'Havin' a go at this villain.' James motioned to Hal.

Hal smiled. 'I'm not a villain.' Then he looked sideways at the pencil image. 'You gonna paint me?'

There was little of the bony boy left. Hal'd filled out. Tissue more than fat, but his cheeks were still hollow, and his eyes still low-tide blue. His long bones had stretched and he was nearly up to his sister (who was Ena in miniature). He had a long neck (as Roland had) and a strong jaw. His fingers were fleshed-over paperclips, and his nails had a lunar glow.

'Should I?' asked James.

'I'd be better,' Sonia said, waiting for the kettle to boil.

James turned to Roland. 'Ena sleepin' in?'

'She was up half the night chasin' mozzies. Then she came down for water. Then she started talkin' …'

'We can stay the day, go home tomorrow afternoon,' she'd said.

'No, I said a few days.'

'But it's so primitive.'

'That's the whole point. No distractions. We can get a heap of work done.'

'What about the kids?'

'They'll love it. All the old buildings to discover. They won't wanna go home.'

Ghost towns were all well and good, but a person needed a shower, a shop, communication. 'Day after tomorrow,' she'd conceded.

'We agreed, a week.'

'I didn't know it was gonna be so basic.'

Sonia placed the cup of tea in front of her father. It was milky and weak. They'd forgotten to bring sugar. He tried it. 'Perfect.'

'When can we go exploring?' Hal asked.

'After breakfast,' James said.

'What about now?'

'After breakfast,' Roland agreed. 'I don't need you falling down a mineshaft.'

James said, 'This place was worked for forty-eight years. They sunk hundreds of mines. Some are covered with iron, and that's covered with dirt. So you wouldn't know till yer halfway down.'

'I'll be careful.'

Sonia stood behind James as he worked. 'Why'd you buy it?'

He looked back and smiled. 'How else can you get your own bank? Your own town?'

'But it's not really a bank.'

'It was.'

'A long time ago.'

Sonia was a sensible ten-year-old. She'd discovered the usefulness of facts. People couldn't argue with facts, although they tried to ignore them, even parents. If a ten-year-old was meant to get ten hours sleep, and she got up at eight, then there was no reason for her to go to bed at nine. This was the sort of thing she felt she needed to remind them – and Hal, especially. He had no idea of facts, of anything, really.

'I just wanted somewhere to come, somewhere quiet, away from noise and annoying people, so I could paint,' James said, and Roland nodded. That's why they'd come.

'But I suppose you should fix the stairs?' Sonia suggested.

'I suppose.'

They'd arrived at sunset. Down the main street of Osmond Hill, Population One. James had been waiting. He'd shown them around the bank he'd bought for fifty quid. The main chamber with its leather seats around the walls, the hardwood counters, the cast-iron grilles. They'd looked through the offices and the vault with its door removed, just in case. There was a staff kitchen, and a lounge room that had become a studio. This was the only room he'd swept out, mopped, taken any time over. Although his bed was upstairs, he generally slept on a couch beside his easel. Roland had said, 'Fifty quid?'

'They would've taken less.'

Roland had turned to Ena. She'd shaken her head. 'No bloody way.'

James had said, 'The old pub's in good nick. Bigger than this place. You'd get it for a hundred.'

Ena had said, 'You can't even fix a tap at home, why'd you want a pub?'

The kids had been on his side. 'Come on, Mum, it'd be fantastic.'

'No.'

This was the problem with wives, Roland guessed. They had no intention of letting a man return to his childhood, which, it seemed to him, was the only place worth returning to. They wanted them working, earning, saying sensible things, not painting, dreaming away the days, making unfunny jokes and buying ruined buildings in ghost towns. Men had to be made sensible.

Finishing his breakfast, Hal stood up. 'Can we go now?'

Sonia shook her head. 'In yer undies?'

'I'll get changed.' He was off, up the stairs (he knew which treads he could trust).

James showed Roland the incomplete sketch. 'I don't think he'll stay still long enough.'

They left Ena in bed, awake. She didn't think there was much to get up for. Why hadn't someone just demolished the place?

The four of them started on top of the hill – the Church of England, minus its stained-glass windows. The gaping holes had let in dust, which had settled on the carpet, the pneumatic organ and altar. There was a single pew, and they sat on it. Hal stood and said, *'Jesus cast them aside! He saw Sonia and thought, What have I done?'*

She shook her head. 'Is this meant to be funny?'

Roland studied the numbers on the hymn board: 16, 75, 108. 'Are You Washed in the Blood?' He didn't think so. Although perhaps it helped. He thought of Charlie Bass, beaming, standing at his front gate saying, 'How are yer, Griff?'

'Good, Charlie. Haven't seen you for months, thought maybe …' But stopped short. Thought maybe you'd finally died, laid down the Bible.

'Fit as a fiddle,' Charlie had said.

'Don't say?'

'Three hours of prayer every day. What did I tell you?'

'Prayer, eh? And a bita treatment, too, eh?'

'Perhaps. But they'd all written me off, Griff. Said it was time to stop treatment. And yet …'

'Cosa God?'

'Got a minute? I promised Him, I said, "If you save me I'll devote myself to spreading your word." '

'Sorta busy, Charlie, but I'm glad you're feeling better.'

They left the church, walked down the hill past rows of old pressed-tin cottages. They picked through one and found a pram, a meat safe with its door off, and a few knives and forks. Hal wanted to take them but Roland said they'd have to stay. It would all have to stay. The place, he said, wasn't there for their amusement.

Back on the main street, they trawled through old shops. Casey's seemed to have sold everything. There was a catalogue on the floor. You could buy sailor suits and girls' dresses and lanterns and spirit levels. Hal searched the cupboards. 'What a load of junk,' he said.

Then out to a big house set off the main street: Spanish Mission, bay windows, and a bull-nosed verandah that ran between them. A brass plaque: 'Councillor Hayman'. They went through Hayman's empty rooms, and out into his stables. There was a saddle, but the leather had cracked, and there were no horses anyway. 'Spend your life painting this place,' Roland said.

'Perhaps I will.'

'We can come live here,' Hal said. 'I can be Councillor Hayman.'

'What you gonna eat?' Sonia asked.

'Vegetables. Didn't you see the plots?'

'You hate vegetables.'

As they continued down the main street, Roland said, 'Problem is, who do you talk to all day?'

James was thinking of the barracks, the three hundred men, the smell of boot and floor and every other sort of polish. Standing in the showers with twenty others. No privacy, as they did what needed doing, as they discussed rifles.

They passed a shed with James's car's snout sticking out. 'My garage,' he said.

'Wasn't for that you'd be in Hobart,' Roland said.

James had wanted to head south, to buy a small house on the banks of the Derwent, paint in the mornings and sail in the afternoons. But then, one day, he had appeared in their drive, revving his new Austin. 'Comin'? I gotta run it in.'

Roland had dropped his brushes and got in, without even telling Ena. They'd driven north, into wheat country, taken a few side roads and, hours later, spotted the small town in the distance. 'What's that?' James had asked.

Roland had checked. 'Not on the map.'

Once they'd driven into it, James had stopped his car and got out to look. He'd called, 'Hello? Anyone?' But there'd been no reply. He'd said, 'Christ, this might do.'

'Go on, I dare you!' Roland and James heard Sonia call.

Around a corner, a house with its side missing where Hal had pulled a mattress out of the bedroom. He was standing on the roof, his arms spread.

'Go on,' Sonia said again, laughing.

'Get down,' Roland said. It wasn't much of a mattress – flat, lifeless. 'That's not gonna stop you.'

'*Ralph Rivers, Private Investigator, alias the Crimson Comet, is just*

*leaving his office in the metropolis when a panic-stricken girl crashes head-*
*long into him ...'*

'Hal!' Roland glared at Sonia. She stopped laughing. 'And when he breaks his leg?'

Ralph Rivers knew these people, holding out in their ghost town, were smuggling whisky. He'd seen it. There was a war on, but these master criminals didn't care. 'I can see what you're doing!'

'Hal!'

He jumped, landed roughly, rolled a few times and ran down the street. Sonia cracked up. 'Go the Crimson Comet!'

Roland turned to his mate. 'I'm not sure exactly how much painting we're gonna get done.'

That afternoon, James and Roland went sketching: paper and charcoal, sandwiches and a thermos of black tea. They headed west, away from town, towards the old diggings. Past poppet heads, tailings that had leached calcium brown, and open shafts.

A track led down to a valley. There was a stream at the bottom, and they could see where miners had dammed it to make smaller watercourses. Time and rain had deepened these channels and now the earth was honeycombed. 'You gonna become a hermit?' Roland asked his friend.

'Why not? You would, if you didn't have a wife and kids.' James said the last word slowly, as if he was taunting him.

They climbed a hill, found a few granite rocks, sat down and started.

'I just wanted some quiet,' James said.

He'd never told his friend the whole story: six weeks in the jungle, the majority of time on his tummy, clutching his rifle, waiting. Birds that never stopped squawking. Insects, all day and night. Listening for a broken twig or footstep. 'Gave you plenty of time to think,' he said, drawing Hayman's House on the distant hill. He could see Hal on the porch, running in and out, moving on to the next building.

'About what?' Roland asked.

'For one, why anyone'd bother doing this.' Indicating his sketch.

Roland could see it. A one in a million shot at greatness. Boiler-making made more sense, but a man couldn't always choose what he did with his life.

'I used to think, if I got back, I'd do something useful,' James said.

'Like what?'

'I was gonna buy a car dealership. They make a shitload of money.'

They worked in silence for ten minutes.

'Sometimes you could feel it.' James tapped his forehead.

'What?'

He continued drawing. 'A bullet, right through yer head. Someone taking aim, watching you. That's what it was like. So I'd move a few inches, so he'd have to aim again.'

In three years all Roland had heard were made-up war stories that Hal had asked for. Did you kill many Japs? Did you stick it through them? James had told him how he'd machine-gunned a vipers' nest full of the slippery bastards, how they'd pleaded for their lives, but how he'd just laughed.

James stopped to pour two cups of tea. 'And plenty of fellas got the shits. Then you were in trouble.'

Roland saw Hal climbing another roof. He stood and called across the half mile, but couldn't be heard. Hal jumped, and Ena came down the street after him. She was shouting, but there was no sound.

Back in town, Hal was looking at James's car. He ran a hand over the hubcaps, the wheel arches, the door trims. He got in. Opening the glove box, he found a tin of travel sweets and put one in his mouth. He moved the gear stick: 1, 2, 3, 4, R. He knew what that meant. You had to start slow and get quicker. There was a brake to stop and an accelerator to go.

The key was in the ignition and the garage door was open. He could feel his fingers tingling. Turned the key but nothing happened. Checked the buttons on the dashboard, switched a few, but there was no response. He tried the key again, and this time the dash lights glowed. Nearly there. And further, and the engine humphed, shuddered and died.

Of course, the clutch, he thought. He reached down, pressed it and tried again. The car roared to life. 'Jesus!' he whispered.

He kept the clutch down. It was difficult; he could only just see above the dash. He didn't want to release it – he guessed it would cut out again.

Sonia ran into the shed at the sound. 'What are you doing?'

'Goin' for a drive.'

'Dad's gonna kill yer.'

'Come on, get in. It's easy. They'll never know.' He moved the gear stick to 1. As he released the clutch his body lifted and he could see where he was going. The car seemed reluctant, and he remembered. The handbrake! Then it was happier. It moved out of the garage into the street. Too slow, he thought. He pressed the clutch again and tried 2. It worked. He turned the wheel and he was moving. Sonia walked beside his window. 'Press the brake!'

'Hop in.'

'It's not our car.'

'James won't mind.'

Meanwhile, half a mile away, Roland said, 'That's funny.'

James was unwrapping the sandwiches. 'What?'

'Where's Ena going? She can't even ... Christ!' He ran down the hill, James close behind. By the time they arrived on Argent Street it was too late. The car was sitting, chugging, its right fender against the wall of the RAOB temple. The impact had cracked the mortar and loosened a few bricks. Hal was attempting to push the car back onto the road.

'Christ!' James stood with his face an inch from Hal's. 'What were you thinking?'

'I's just givin' it a test.'

Sonia was standing nearby, her arms crossed. She dared not smile. Now was not the time.

Hal said, 'I did it all right – clutch, gears. Dunno what happened. It sorta jumped, then went real quick, and I couldn't get to the brake in time.'

'It's new!' James shouted.

'Sorry.'

James reached into the car and turned off the ignition. Then he returned to Hal. 'Nine hundred quid! You gonna pay me?'

Roland was happy to watch; he knew this was the only way his son would learn.

'What made you think …?' James examined the fender more closely. 'Look, the side panel, it'll all have to be fixed.'

Hal held his ground. He didn't seem especially terrified. 'I thought you wouldn't mind. Not many kids can drive a car.'

James looked at Roland, who said, 'Silly thing to do.'

'Jesus!' James grabbed Hal's forearms. 'That's it?'

'Said I's sorry. What else can I do?'

'Silly boy.' James's face was red now, his arms and hands tight.

'That hurts.'

James started shaking him. Hal resisted, but the hands were too strong.

'Stop it!'

Roland stepped forward.

The boy's head shook on his shoulders, and he was unable to speak.

Roland moved over and steadied his friend's hands. 'Come on,' he said to James.

'You seen what he's done?'

Hal broke loose, and ran off.

James was left standing. His arms were still raised, his hands clutched. 'You mighta hurt him,' Roland said.

Roland walked up the hill before tea, escaping the heat and awkwardness of the kitchen. They could head home, but that was admitting defeat – abandoning James, perhaps. This ghost, rattling his chains, living in place of the thousands who'd given up on Osmond Hill. As each of the treads gave way, the walls collapsed, there was less of the place, and him, and all of them, Roland suspected.

He went into the church, sat down on the pew and started sketching. Two figures: a boy, watching his sister, who was grinning at the artist. The boy had a long neck, and small teeth, and he might've been singing. The girl might've been telling a joke. They weren't particularly handsome. Neither glowed with intelligence. They were much the same as a million other kids scattered in a thousand other schools across the country.

He drew the arches where the windows had been. Then filled in a leadlight of uniformed Christs with whisky bottles, an Austin with a dented bumper, old bikes and Bibles. He wrote the words: 'There are many rooms.'

He stood, approached the organ, and pressed several keys. There was a mechanical clunk, and he could remember this, too: Ena, in a dress they hadn't taken up in time, him, in his dad's old suit, and three hundred people sweating in the January sun.

Clunk – *Bring me my bow of burning gold!*

He smiled at Ena, but her eyes were cast down. She'd chosen the hymn but she had no intention of singing it.

*Bring me my arrow of desire!*

It had been a long wait, but now they were nearly there: the small hotel, the top-floor room. As he stood, waiting for the hymn to finish, he had to stop himself from thinking about it. The thought could consume everything.

*Bring me my spear! O clouds, unfold!*

It was a hearty crowd. They knew every word, and were determined to prove it. It was the least they could do for a free feed of fish.

James was behind him. 'Thought I'd find you here.' He sat down where Roland had been sketching. 'You are a very spiritual man, are you not, Griff?'

'I am not.'

'You believe in Him?' James inspected Roland's sketch, as if he might find proof.

'I do not.'

'Why, for instance, have you chosen an ecclesiastical setting?'

'It might save the boy's soul. Maybe God can sort him out.'

James tried to think how to say it. 'I wasn't that concerned about the car.'

'No?'

'I told him I was sorry … then he says, "Okay then, tomorrow, I'll have another go, with you next to me."'

'Little shit.' Roland played a dissonant triad on the organ.

'So, I agreed.'

They sat silently.

'How about tomorrow, we try something different?'

The next morning the expedition set out after breakfast. It had rained most of the night and James promised they'd now have a creek. They found one, managing to pass its trickle from hill to valley, but it was more a tap-left-on sort of flow. 'Still,' Roland said, 'it'll do. If there's gold we'll find it.'

So, James, with his skillet, with its handle removed, knelt down and showed them how to pan. Hal watched excitedly; he'd heard stories of monster nuggets on top of Osmond Hill, thousands of men lining the creeks, digging the pits, shouting 'Eureka!' as they ran for Hayman's house.

The previous evening, around the table, Sonia had said, 'A couple might've got lucky over the years, but what about the thousands who found nothing?'

'They didn't stick at it long enough,' James had explained. 'There's gold down there. It doesn't come looking for you.'

James kept working the fine gravel in the bottom of the skillet. 'Every pass, get rid of the big stuff,' he said to Hal.

'Have you found much?'

'Have I what. Little sugar grains, but when you put them all together …'

Sonia resorted to crossed arms. 'How much were they worth?'

'That car, remember, the one you pranged? I call it the gold car.'

'You got that before you moved here.'

Hal thought it all sounded reasonable. If you were smart and stuck at it you'd eventually make money. Sam had explained: there were mug punters who rocked up every Saturday, flashed some cash, put it on the favourites, went home broke. Then there were those who studied the form, track, weather.

James handed Hal the skillet and he began. A handful of gravel, water, agitation, keen eyes. He got to the bottom and there was nothing but sand.

'Try again.'

So he did. You couldn't expect it first go.

Or second, third, fourth. Roland produced a frypan and gave it to Sonia. She moved to a different part of the creek. After a few minutes she said, 'James, what's this?'

He looked. 'That's it! First go! Nice-sized specks.' He picked them out and laid them across the back of her hand. She opened a hanky and gathered them, then turned to Hal. 'How you going?'

He refused to move until, after another few minutes, Sonia found more. He crept closer to look. 'What if you did this all day, and found nothing?' he asked. 'What would you eat?'

'Bread and water,' James said.

Roland sat back on the bank and rolled a cigarette. 'It's like art, Hal. You gotta be a bit wrong in the head.'

Sonia wiped hair from her face. 'How much d'yer reckon I'll get?'

'Thousands,' Roland replied. 'You can buy a house.'

'Why do you gotta be wrong in the head?' Hal asked his father.

'If you know there are better ways to make money ...'

Sam: only a mug'd race horses. Sometimes you won, but mostly it was like shovelling ten-pound notes into a fire that never went out. Hal supposed horses were a little bit like creek gold. 'I'm bored.' He dropped the pan in the creek, stood and walked up the bank.

Cigarette in mouth, Roland jumped down the few feet and started panning. 'I got a good feeling.'

Hal walked through ankle-high grass. He wanted to go home. He'd explored every building and basement, every storeroom and workshop. Junk. That's all this place was. His mum was right. Someone needed to demolish it.

Then something caught his eye. It was half-buried. He leaned over and uncovered a small bottle. He picked it up and held it to the light. 'James,' he said.

James saw the glint. 'Whatcher got there?'

'Gold.'

James, Roland and Sonia ran over to Hal. They looked at the chunks of gold.

'Jesus!' Roland said. 'What is it, James?'

'Where did you find it, Hal?'

Hal showed him.

'Can I?'

Hal let James hold it, but said, 'I found it.'

James shook it, examined it more closely. 'It's gold,' he said, smiling at Hal.

'I'm rich?'

'Well, it's a good amount. Coupla hundred quid.'

Hal jumped about. 'Eureka!'

Sonia took it, studied each of the lumps, the specks that had settled in the bottom. She handed it to her father and he loosened the lid, looked inside, replaced it, studied it from every angle and said to James, 'Someone might've spent years getting this.'

'And he mighta spent a long time trying to remember where he'd buried it.'

'I can keep it?' Hal said.

'That's the law.'

Hal turned to his sister. 'Beats working for it, eh?'

'You were lucky.'

'And James, I'm not gonna sell it.'

'No?'

'Keep it till I'm twenty, then I'll buy a car.'

'You could buy me a new one?'

Hal wasn't so happy about this. 'I suppose I could sell a few bits, so you can get it fixed?'

James just ruffled his hair. 'Don't worry, it's insured. Perhaps you could give it to your dad?'

He wasn't happy about this either. 'I could …'

'No,' Roland said. 'You found it, it's yours.'

Hal smiled at his sister. 'I bet you're spewin'?'

'Righto, enough of that,' James said. 'I reckon the lake might be full.'

They walked a few minutes to a murky-looking pond. 'Is it clean?' Roland asked.

'Bita dirt,' James said. 'This is my bath, when it's full.'

Hal didn't need any convincing; swimming in dirt looked like a lot of fun. He took off his clothes, hid his gold in his shirt, and stood in his underwear. 'Come on,' he said, before running down the hill.

'Don't jump in,' James said. 'It's only four feet …'

But he already had. There was a splash, a gurgle, silence, and Roland wondered whether he'd done it, at last.

But then there was a head. 'Come in, it's warm.'

James was next: down to his underwear, in, one step at a time, until he floated like a stale egg. 'Beautiful. Who's next? Come on, Sonia!'

'I'm going back.' Turning, she walked up the hill.

'Come on, y' chicken?' Hal called.

'Get stuffed!' And she was gone.

They waited for Roland. 'Doesn't seem much point,' he said.

'Why not?' James asked.

'Just get dirtier.'

'You don't get in to get clean. It's called fun. Remember that?'

'Come on, Dad!'

'No.' He sat down in some grass.

James smiled. 'You worried we might see what you got to offer?'

'Don't be stupid.'

'All men here, aren't we, Hal?'

'Yep.' Hal flexed his biceps to prove it.

'The shy painter,' James said. He turned to Hal and splashed him. This was a sign they were both men, and able to do men things. 'Your dad,' he said. 'In one of Bell's first live model classes we had this tall, gorgeous-looking creature. She was lying down on a couch. We had to sketch her. In he comes ...' James looked up the hill. 'Remember?'

'No.'

'And he sees her and says, "Ah, What happened to the bowl of fruit?"' James laughed. 'Like that: "What happened to the bowl of fruit?"'

Hal was giggling. He didn't care if it was true or not.

'Then yer dad says to me, "Oh, I can't do this."'

'Did yer?' Hal asked his dad.

'No.'

'But he starts drawing her head, shoulders, then, you know what comes next, Hal?'

'What?'

'Womany bits. You know, boobies.'

'None of this is true,' Roland said.

'He starts to draw them but his hand's shaking and they look wobbly, and Bell walks past and says, "Ah, Mr Griffin, you're having a little trouble?"'

Hal was enjoying every moment. His toes and feet had sunk into the mud.

'So, he starts again, and his hand's shaking, and this time they look like a couple of old prunes, and this bird's looking at him … shall I finish?'

'No, you shan't. He's eight years old.'

James said, 'I gotta stop there. That's all he wants you to know.'

'Dad!'

'Do you a deal, Griff. You come in, my lips are sealed.'

Roland turned the idea over, stood, took off his clothes and walked down the bank.

'No,' Hal said. 'Don't come in. I wanna know.'

'You never will,' Roland said. He tried a toe, a foot, and soon he was up to his chin.

'Damn,' Hal said. He swam over to James. 'Tell me anyway.'

'No. I promised.'

'Hey!' Sonia was standing beside Hal's clothes. 'I found some gold.' She held up Hal's bottle.

'Put it back,' Hal said.

'Finders keepers. It was just sitting here.'

Hal swam to the bank, ready for action. She ran. He was out, up the hill, and down the other side.

After tea the men sat in the lounge room cum studio. James was painting the main street – as he had a dozen times before – at dusk, dawn, after rain, summer sun. Roland was sketching the room: the clock that hadn't worked for decades, his own son, sitting in a corner, sketching him.

Hal felt his pocket. It was safe. She wouldn't do it again in a hurry. He'd launched himself at her, she'd fallen against a tree and hit her head, he'd prised her fingers open and reclaimed his gold. There'd been blood on her face, but it hadn't bothered him.

'What's wrong with you?' she'd called, as he'd returned to the pond.

No reply.

'I wasn't going to keep it.'

He'd turned back. 'You spoil everything!'

Hal sat drawing his father's face, his cloudy eye, his bottom lip with the indent where he always bit into it. It was funny how you could know a person so closely but not at all, really. You might know there's a mole under their arm, but you couldn't tell when they'd strike out, hitting you for something you hadn't done.

'Gis a look,' Roland said.

'It's not ready.'

'Don't draw me sideways. I'm not an Egyptian.'

'*I won't!*'

'The arms are in *front* of the body.' Roland stood, and came over. Hal tore the sketch from the pad and ripped it into small pieces. 'That's what I think about drawing.' He threw the pad across the room and walked out.

Roland sat down. 'Righto then …'

James knew that when Hal was in one of his moods you couldn't reason with him. It would last a few days, then he'd be Hal again. He was a good son, but an absent one. All artists' kids were, he supposed.

'We might head back in the morning,' Roland said.

'You're welcome to stay longer.'

'Yeah.' Roland knew it was too late. 'Thanks for havin' us.'

Hal sat in Sam's shed. It was nothing like theirs: no canvases, paints, machine-gun wood; no photos of front bars and Aborigines; no almonds to be cracked or knives to be ground on the wheel that made sparks when you jabbed it with a file. Just a big table, covered in reins and bridles, and Mary's mixing bowls, full of warm water and saddle-soap.

'Go on,' he said to Sam.

'Shit.'

'Another one!'

Sam reached into his pocket, produced a penny and dropped it in the swear jar.

'Once more,' Hal said.

'No.'

'What did they call Jesus?'

'Christ!' Sam reached in again, found another penny and put it in the jar. 'Don't let Mary hear that,' he said.

'Why not?'

'She still thinks He's runnin' things.'

Sam saw her, kneeling beside her bed, praying for the infirm; *Jerusalem, lift up your hearts and sing*, the holy card of St Sebastian and his lions on the fridge, the every-Sunday-morning-guilt: 'Come on, it'll do you good.' As he turned up his tranny: 'Me?'

Hal said, 'Dad reckons that's all shit.'

Sam held out his hand. 'Right, your turn. Gis a penny.'

'Haven't got one.'

'You owe me one.'

'He reckons that's for the *feeble-minded*.'

'Well, Mary ain't feeble.'

'That's what he said.'

Sam wasn't willing to argue. Jesus or no Jesus, the horses kept running; God didn't affect the odds, and he certainly couldn't pick a winner. That was down to horsemeat. 'Keep workin',' he said. 'Can't pay you for talkin'.'

Hal ran the bridles through his fingers, rubbed the soap along their length, worked it up, rinsed, and rinsed again. A line of them hung ready for oiling. 'Why can't the strappers do it?' he asked.

'Cos they do a rotten job.'

'So why we doin' it?'

'We'll show 'em how it *should* be done.'

Hal guessed this was fair. And anyway, there were a lot of pennies in cleaning bridles. He looked at the swear jar. 'Bloody strappers. Useless, aren't they, Sam?'

Sam just ignored him. He'd slipped in a dozen bugger, bum, shits, but that was enough. He turned to Shirley. 'How you goin'?'

'They've all come undone.' She showed him the stitching on the saddle rugs she was repairing.

'I might be a strapper,' Hal said.

'Y' reckon?'

'Must be good, leadin' 'em out on race day?'

'It is.' Sam could remember this – twenty years of it. His 4 am walk to the track: the smell of morning grass, the baker's van, the main gates with their million smoked-down Capstans, the gassy horses waiting in the dark. 'Early mornings.'

'That doesn't bother me.'

The cold water on his red hands, the twitching flanks, the kicked knees. 'I can't see you shovelling shit,' he said.

Hal smiled.

'I'm not payin' for that one. Shit's shit.'

'Three pennies,' Hal said.

Shirley smiled and met Hal's eyes, but it was like he was blocking her out of the conversation, the space, the words and intimations that made up her own life. Like he was trying to overpower her, grind her into the shed floor. He was saying, What's so funny about that? She returned to the needle and thread, her raw fingers, refusing to move.

'Righto, like I told yer,' Sam said to Hal.

Hal removed the bridles from his improvised rack. He placed them in a separate bowl and covered them in olive oil, working it in.

Sam said, 'Thing about strappers, get all the hard work, none of the glory. But he's the one the horse knows.'

'It's a big job,' Hal said.

'Too right. And when they're sick, you're the one sittin' next to them all night.'

Shirley noticed that Hal was still staring at her. The expression of an asbestos tile. He never blinked, never moved his focus from the centre of her face. She never knew what he wanted.

He even spoke as he looked at her. 'Sometimes they break their legs, don't they, Sam?'

'Sometimes.'

'And they have to put them down?'

'Yes, and they spook. This one time a mare slipped from my hands, straight across the course, out onto Torrens Road.'

'No?'

'And she's galloping towards the city. I couldn't stop her.' He could remember: the asphalt beneath his feet, a moving van veering onto the footpath. 'I's calling for the coppers, but in the end we didn't need them.'

'No?' Hal asked.

'She went straight through a red light.' He wondered why Hal wasn't concerned. He looked at him, then his niece. 'Shirley?'

'Gettin' sore,' she said.

'Try again tomorrow?'

'No.' She glared at Hal. '*What*?'

He didn't reply. Instead, 'You could get me a job, couldn't you, Sam?'

'If you're a hard worker.'

'I am, aren't I?'

Sam took the oiled straps and started piecing them together. 'I reckon you could do better, Hal.'

'How's that?'

'What about a vet?'

'That's a lot of study.'

'You're a smart boy. What d'yer get for maths?'

He shrugged. It was an A, but that didn't matter.

'I was gonna be a vet,' Sam said.

'Why didn't you?'

'I got into university, and I did a year, but then my dad died.'

Shirley noticed Hal again. He was looking at her body. He was studying her chest, her arms, her hands. 'Wanna turn sewin'?' she said to him.

He didn't answer.

'So, that was the end of that,' Sam said. 'I walked over the road, in the gates, and asked Mr Johnson's dad for a job, and he put a shovel in me hand.'

'Sam!' Mary's voice came from the house.

He wiped his hands. 'What's she want now?' He stood. 'Back in a minute.'

'I'll go,' Shirley said.

'Wait there, it's probably a lid.' He hobbled out of the shed.

Shirley worked on the rug. It was in good condition, but it was hard getting a needle through leather. She looked up and Hal was staring at her again. 'What's wrong with you?'

'I found a bottle of gold.'

She ignored him.

'Gonna buy Sonia a horse.'

'Are not.'

'Dad a car, Mum a new house.'

Sam, she wanted to call. He's at it again.

'You havin' trouble doin' that?'

'I'm alright.'

'What's that thing you got? Lupus, wasn't it? Isn't that what you put in soup?' He smiled.

It's not funny. But she wouldn't say that.

'Does it get itchy?' he said.

'No.'

'Maybe you could paint over it?'

She saw him smile. Every time, he seemed to be going further.

'Remember that time you lost your hair and Mary made you wear that beanie?'

She was sitting alone in the schoolyard, adjusting it over her ears, looking down at the ground.

'And that Christmas morning,' he said.

On the lounge, waiting for her presents. That's all she could remember. But she'd slipped to the ground, jumped about like an eel (Mary's words), before falling into a deep sleep. Sam had wanted to take her to the hospital, but Mary had known better.

'Can they cure it?' he asked.

'No.' She knew he knew.

'So, what's gonna happen?'

She sat up. 'I hate you, Hal.' She threw away the saddle blanket and stormed from the shed. He heard her open the back gate and run down the road, crying.

He looked up at the swear jar, and listened for the back door. Nothing. He stood, climbed onto the table, and took a handful of pennies from the jar.

No, he thought, he'll hear them rattling in my pocket. So he ripped a corner from his rag, wrapped them, tied them up and put them in his pocket.

Sam walked back in and saw the finished bridles. 'Nice job,' he said. 'Might even pay you.'

Hal sat in an antiseptic foyer watching a man with a buffer. He moved it in circles, stopping to look what he'd done, using his foot to shift stains. There was a table with magazines about beautiful homes and how to grow roses. His mum and dad stood waiting at an enquiries desk. They seemed upset, but he was sure it was nothing. Shirley was often in hospital. It was all part of her disease.

A soldier sat down next to him, stretched back, seemed to chew over a few thoughts, then picked up a magazine and leafed through. Hal wanted to ask if he knew Trevor Grant, although he'd worked Trevor out over the last few years: overheard conversations, snippets around the roast lamb and teapot, the hushes and stares. And now he was back with Mary and Sam, and had a job at Wyndham's, the timber people.

'Hal!' Roland called.

They walked down a long hallway that had just been buffed. An old woman was cleaning windows. It could've been Nan Griffin; she was always doing Dr Bailey's. This made him think of Robinson Crusoe, and Don Quixote, and Pip, wandering the moors, and the note that was always tucked in the covers: 'Dear Hal, try this one. Jo. Conrad was a sea captain, and you'll love the way he describes storms'.

The gathering of books, together with the teaching of words, had allowed him to enter the doctor's world of geishas, tree houses and rainbows. Most of it was nonsense, but some writers made sense. Some described the trenches. This tallied with Sam's descriptions of life in Flanders. Some described the way early motor cars killed children who ran out in front of them. Hal guessed a lot of them would've been brought here.

'Come on, keep up,' his dad said, and he followed them into a lift.

It moved slowly. Hal could hear the groaning of cables. 'What is it this time?' he asked.

'What do you mean *this time*?' his mother said. 'You could be a little more empathetic.'

He had no idea what that meant. Just watched the lights: One.

How could it move that slowly? What if it was an emergency? What if you'd been hit by a truck? You'd be dead by the time you got there. Perhaps there was a faster one, for the patients.

His dad said, 'The heart, that's worrying.'

His mother didn't reply. This generally meant she agreed.

Two. They stopped and waited for two nurses. They pushed the down button and Hal said, 'We're going up.'

One replied, 'We'll come with you.'

He looked at her legs. They were nice. And the other one's, but they were all scaly and horrible. He realised it had taken forever for the doors to close and the lift to start. 'We shoulda taken the stairs,' he said.

No one replied.

The nurses smelt good: musky, like the lollies Nan gave him when he got bored. But was it any wonder? Eight years of cleaning the doctor's house. Luckily, school had saved him from the worst of it. But there were still weekends and holidays. The doctor would always need his toilet scrubbed (because he was too lazy to do it for himself).

Three. The nurses go out. 'Weren't they going down?' Hal said.

'Changed their minds,' his mother replied, without looking at him.

The doors opened and they walked into a ward, through doors marked, 'Silence!' and, 'Visiting Hours Strictly 4 pm till 6 pm'. His parents asked at another desk and they went into a room with four bays. Sam and Mary were waiting. There was a curtain around a bed and he guessed Shirley was in there. He could hear someone talking to her. 'No, don't try to get up.'

As he entered he noticed Mary watching him. She didn't say a word. Usually she'd ruffle his hair, and pinch a cheek, but today, nothing.

'Hi, Hal,' Sam said.

'Hi, Sam.'

Mary was whispering to his parents. 'We found her wandering. We brought her home.'

'You shoulda called us,' Roland said.

'Trev was handy,' Mary explained.

Then there was quiet.

'Down, Shirley,' the doctor, or nurse, said, from behind the curtain.

'What's wrong?' Roland asked.

'It's her heart again. They reckon it's inflamed. But it should settle, given time.'

Heart. That sounded serious. Although she wouldn't actually *die* … would she? Anyway, if she'd overreacted, and run off, and wandered the streets for hours, that was her choice. She did the same thing at school. A teacher would say something and she'd run out of class, all the way home, and the front office would have to check to make sure she was okay. All he'd done was mention lupus. He was just trying to show concern, like his mother had said he should.

'She's had it before,' Sam said. 'She'll come good.'

Hal saw something strange in Sam's face – like he'd changed his mind about something important.

'What brought it on?' Ena asked.

'We're not sure,' Mary managed.

Hal was unsure too. 'She was sewing the saddle blankets.'

'And what happened?' Ena asked.

'I dunno. She started crying and ran off.'

'For no reason?' Roland asked.

'I think her hands were hurting. I told her she should stop but she wanted to go on, didn't she, Sam?'

He waited. 'Yes.'

'You told her, didn't you, Sam?'

'It wasn't that, Hal.'

Two of the other beds were empty, but one held an old woman with no teeth. She opened and closed her mouth, like she was trying to eat a piece of rubber. Her gown was loose at the front, and Hal could see her wrinkled skin.

The nurse opened the curtain. 'All done.'

Shirley was sitting up, supported by two pillows.

'Good as new,' Mary said. 'Aren't you, Shirley?' She turned to the nurse. 'How is she?'

'Blood pressure's coming down.' She placed a set of notes in a sleeve attached to the bed.

Mary went around and kissed her daughter. 'You are a worry,' she said.

'Sorry.' Shirley saw Hal and her smile disappeared.

'She'd fainted,' Mary said. 'We got in Trev's car and drove round, right down to Torrens Road.' She shook her daughter's arm. 'How long had you been walking?'

'Not long.'

'And that park, on the corner, she's on the bench. We thought she'd fallen asleep.'

Hal slid down into a chair. Ena took a box of chocolates from her purse and laid them on the bedside table. 'For later,' she said. 'Soft centres.'

'Thanks, Ena.'

Sam was looking at Hal, who noticed and sat up and said, 'I hope you get better soon, Shirley.'

'Thanks, Hal.'

Hal turned back to watch the old lady. She'd picked up her false teeth and was trying to put them in. He glanced at his mother and met her eyes.

As they drove home, Ena said, 'You don't know nothin' about all that, Hal?'

'We were working, then she says, "I'm goin' for a walk."' He could feel the tension through the road, the absorbers, the seats. 'You reckon I did it?'

'No one said that,' Roland replied.

'You do. I'm her friend.'

'We know.'

'What about Sonia? Her and her friends, they're always laughin' at her, to her face. Why don't you ask her?' He'd almost convinced himself. Yes, it was Sonia. *He* was the one who'd sit with Shirley, helping her peel potatoes, as the third from Randwick echoed in their ears. 'Last time I do nothin' with her.'

Now he owned the anger. When they got home, Ena handed him a pound note and asked him to walk to the shops to buy custard powder. He went into his room, retrieved the hanky full of pennies from behind the wardrobe and set off. When he got there he paid for the custard powder, then said, 'Pack of Craven A mild.'

The man said, 'For your dad?'

'Yes.'

He paid separately. He said his dad needed a box of matches, too.

He walked around the block. There was a bus shelter and he sat and opened the smokes, took one out, and lit it. He'd worked out that if you inhaled slowly you wouldn't cough. The smoke would just drift into your lungs, and you'd feel relaxed. You could get them from Trev's pack, of course. He never noticed a few missing. But it was safer this way. There was a gap behind the wardrobe, and an inch of dust. He knew his mum never cleaned there. The future seemed limitless. Sam would always swear and the jar would always be full.

An old woman walked past and saw the smoke in his hand. He tried to hide it but she could tell.

'You're a bit young,' she said.

Hal hid his cigarette again as Trevor drove past. There were chickens in the back of the Vauxhall. Trevor stopped, reversed, and wound down a window. 'What you doin'?'

'Nothin'.'

'What you got there?' He noticed the smoke rising.

'Just tryin' one.'

Hal found Trevor back at home with his dad who was unrolling a length of wire, nailing it to posts he'd buried in the ground. Trev was burying the fringes of the mesh in the garden. Two posts supported an old door that would become the entrance to the new chookyard.

Ena stood with her hands in her apron pockets. 'There's no room,' she said.

'Plenty of room,' Roland said.

'You just wait,' Trevor said to her. 'Once they get laying ...'

She watched them, growling when they stepped on flowers or dug another post hole.

'You just wait,' Trevor said again. 'They'll be poppin' 'em out.' He turned to Hal. 'What d'yer reckon?'

Hal examined the box of hens. A dozen Rhode Islands, pecking at sawdust, peering out of the air holes. 'I'll collect the eggs.'

'Good on yer.' Trevor returned to Ena. 'See, there's yer worker. You'll have a yard full of busy cloacas. Speakin' of which ...' He paused, waited, and sang, *Listen to this, too good to miss* ... Farted.

Hal laughed. Roland smiled. Ena sighed. That was the problem with having Trevor around: he was a door to everything crass, mindless, and (although he'd promised he was on the up and up) illegal.

*Here comes another one just like the other one* ... And again, this time a little squeaky thing.

Hal broke up. Ena shook her head.

'Sorry, Ena.'

She knew she couldn't ban him. Mary and Sam had taken pity on him, setting up a temporary canvas stretcher that had become permanent. Now he was always around, sharing tea, telling them about some girl he'd met in a wine bar, or recalling stories about his mate Jimmy, the hangman at the gaol. 'Once they get old I can knock 'em on the head and we can have a roast.'

'How d'you do that?' Hal asked.

'Blunt end of an axe. Or you can dislocate their neck.'

'How?'

'One hand on the body, the other on the head … pull hard.'

'Trevor,' Ena said.

'Snap, breaks the spine. Bit like the hanging tower.'

'Trev, I don't know if it's appropriate for an eight-year-old.'

'Go on,' Hal said.

Trevor knew Ena had claws, and fangs, and that it was better to keep the peace. Still: 'It's a quick death.'

Hal's face lit up with mock horror.

'Down they go, bit of a quiver, it's all over.' He spoke to the chooks. 'What do you think, ladies?'

Ena shook her head again, but she knew she couldn't win. 'You'll give him nightmares.'

'Mum! It's okay.'

Trevor knew he couldn't give up a good story. You never took a bone from a hungry dog. 'They pre-stretch the rope, Hal, so it doesn't snap. Some of them crims are fat bastards – sorry, Ena, fat people. I used to go watch Jimmy prepare. Help him hang the weights off the ropes the night before.'

'Hal, come with me,' Ena said, attempting to cut her losses.

'He could hold this,' Roland said, indicating a post.

Hal jumped up, ran over and smiled at his mother.

She walked off in disgust.

Then Trevor said, 'He let me see 'em afterwards.'

'No?' Hal said.

'And the neck, long, and covered in burst blood vessels … horrible sight.'

Roland said, 'That was your job?'

'Yep. Some worked in the laundry, some cooked, some in the workshops, but not me.'

Trevor always talked about prison as if it were some job he'd had during the war: floors to be mopped, potatoes to be peeled. The nature of the crime had never been stated, but they knew. From the time he'd contacted them from some shack on the Murray, from the meeting in the shed Roland had organised. Trevor handing himself in. From his emergence in handcuffs, the three-day trial (he'd admitted the lot), his testimony (from behind a screen) against his mates.

But as to what or how much had been stolen, no one was sure. If asked he'd say, 'Just a few bits and pieces sittin' around, no one was using them. We didn't think for a moment …'

But that was how he always talked. Hal thought it was exciting to have a proper criminal living next door. Roland didn't see the problem. Ena did. But Roland'd say to her, 'The man's done his time.'

'Once bad …'

'Then we had to bury them,' Trevor said.

'No?' Hal said, adjusting the pole so it was straight.

'Me and Jimmy. Had to be done the same day. Between the walls. I dug, in they'd go, then we'd cover them with lime. That'd eat 'em away quick smart.' He farted again. 'They reckon there's nothin' left a week later.'

'Did you ever get to pull the lever?'

'No. That was Jimmy's job. But I stood in the room beside him. They'd bring 'em in. Some had accepted it. They were quiet. They just wanted it over with. But others, they fought to the end, screamin', kickin' the guards.' He put on his stern face. 'I tell you what, Hal. Once you see that you don't do nothin' wrong again, ever.'

'Hear that?' Roland said.

'Nothin'!' Trevor said, glaring at him.

Hal was unsettled, but content. This was Trev's warning, and it would end there: Pick up another smoke, and I'll turn on you too. I'll stand behind a screen, and I'll tattle. Trev nailed the last of the wire. Checked to make sure there were no gaps.

The yard was ready. Trevor turned to the box of hens. 'Time, ladies.'

The three of them headed over and Trevor lifted the lid. They watched the twelve hens scratching the plywood floor. 'Another week and they'll be laying,' Trevor said.

'What do I owe you?' Roland asked.

'Nothin'.'

Nothing was a dangerous price.

'Honest to God, Griff. He'd had a gutful of the farm, he'd given away his sheep, and cows, and he was gonna kill this lot.'

Roland smiled. It was impossible to know. But maybe it was true. No one would bother stealing chickens, surely?

Trevor handed Hal a hen. He showed him how to hold her, and they had them in the yard in less than five minutes. Then Trevor said, 'Beautiful. Let 'em have a peck. Then we can build some laying boxes, eh, Hal?'

'Too right.'

'Your job, watch 'em for ten minutes, make sure they don't find a way out. They'll try.'

'Righto.'

'Any problems, come and find me.'

Yes, sir, Hal wanted to say, remembering the uniform, the badges, the rifle. But that wasn't Trev. He was a soldier of misfortune, lurching around a jungle of roses and burnt camellias.

His mother's bell rang. He knew it was time for a cup of tea, but he couldn't go. If he did the hens would get out and they'd be chasing them down Burleigh Avenue and cars would collide and chooks would get squashed and the whole thing would end disastrously. So he sat on the bench and watched.

There was interest in worms. When this was exhausted they started scratching around the fenceline. They seemed like stupid animals.

Hal looked up, and Sam was standing beside him. 'What you up to?'

'I'm watchin' the chooks, in case any escape.'

Sam sat down. He held his tranny; the patter of names and weights. 'Nice pen you made.'

'You wouldn't wanna be a chook,' Hal said.

'Why's that?'

'Not much to look forward to.'

'True. But there's not much to worry about.'

True, Hal thought. Maths, history, cursive. Didn't matter if you were a chook. He suddenly felt bad. Sam was only ever good to him; taking him to the races, talking about problems (girls, especially), giving him chocolate bars he'd bought from the cafeteria at the track. Only ever decent. Sam had been there since he could remember; since he'd started smelling wisteria, listening to magpies on the front lawn every morning.

'You know what happened to Shirley?' Sam said, as if he'd heard Hal's guilt.

Hal didn't know what to say.

'Her dad left. He didn't want a bar of her. Not when he knew …'

Hal noticed a hen sticking her snout under the wire.

'The thing was, his mum had had it, and she'd died at thirty-nine. So he didn't want to go through all that again, I suppose.'

'That's pretty miserable,' Hal said.

'Yes.'

Sam turned down the radio. 'It's pretty rotten when a kid loses her dad.'

Hal wanted to get up, walk off, but couldn't.

'Could you imagine if your dad … you wake up, and that's it. Gone. No note, nothin'. What would you think?'

Hal shrugged.

'Well, Shirley thought it was because of her, and no matter what me or Mary said …'

'Dad'd never go.'

'Probably not.'

'Dave could've stayed?'

'Perhaps.' Suddenly Sam said, 'I can smell them on you.'

Hal looked at him. 'What?' But then remembered. 'A kid from school said ...' He stopped, realising he couldn't do what Trevor could. 'You gonna tell Mum?'

'What if you grow up smoking and it makes you sick and I'm left thinking, I could've stopped him?'

'Never havin' another one.'

'No?'

'Did Trev tell yer?'

'I can smell it.'

Hal held his hand to his face and exhaled. He couldn't smell it. 'He told you.'

Sam smiled. 'I put a mark on the back of the jar. If you're gonna steal you wanna make sure you can get away with it. Look at Trev. If you'd only taken one penny each day I mightn't have noticed.'

'Sorry.'

'I had to do a lot of swearing for your smokes.'

'I'll pay you back.'

'Will you?'

'Yep.'

'Okay, but not with pennies.'

Hal didn't get it. That's what he'd stolen, so that's what he'd have to return. 'What with?'

Sam turned up his radio. 'You decide,' he said. He stood, and shuffled off.

Hal didn't feel so good. But he knew what Sam wanted. He thought how he might do it. Then he had an idea.

Going into his dad's shed, he searched through his old canvases to find one painted white. He took a charcoal stick, and returned to his seat in the garden. He started: the gum trees, the fences, the pen. Small, fluffy hens with beaks twice the size of their heads. Then (having decided the chooks weren't about to escape) he returned to the shed. He found a palette and some paints and squeezed them out, and started painting.

When his father returned to his shed from tea he sat on the toolbox reading the paper, occasionally checking the chooks that were growing bigger than the gum trees, but not saying anything to Hal.

When Hal took it next door, Sam held it and nodded. He showed Mary. 'Hal wants to give it to her, don't you, son?'

And Hal said, 'Yes.'

That night he asked his parents if he could go to the hospital with Mary and Sam. They went in on the bus, and walked along the Terrace. His painting (still tacky) was in a pillowcase Mary had given him. As they got into the lift he took it out and discovered it was smudged. He said, 'Shit.'

Sam said, 'It doesn't matter.'

They went onto the ward, and into the room, and Shirley was sitting up, reading. She told them she was feeling better.

Hal gave her the picture and said, 'It's pretty rubbish, but I thought you could put it up somewhere.'

She smiled. 'Thanks, Hal.'

He couldn't believe it was that simple. So, he sat down and told her about the chooks. He turned it into a story, and in this story all of the chooks did escape and run down the road. And she laughed. And he felt better.

Sam was watching him. When Hal looked up he saw that he'd repaid the pennies.

Roland and Ena braced themselves as they walked into the foyer of Pennington Primary. Roland took a deep breath and said, 'Still use the same stuff on the floors.' There was an honour board, but their kids weren't on it: 1947, 1946, 1945 – all Thomas. The wretched Welsh woman and her buffed-up kids: school captains, best and fairest of everything. Sheena *Tom's-arse*, Sonia called the daughter.

They found the notice that told them Mr Saxby was upstairs in room seventeen. One step at a time, dreading what they were going to hear, ascending treads with bits of gum and old lunch ground in, posters warning them of the horrors of unwashed hands, the penalties for lateness and laziness and an explanation of what Katy did next.

'Just don't argue,' Ena said.

The previous year, a just-out-of-college teacher telling them that Hal was too argumentative. Roland had said, 'Really? He does what he's told at home.'

'Well, not in class.'

Roland'd just thought, You have to *make* him behave.

They arrived at the top of the stairs and started along the hallway. A swarm of cardboard bees threatened them with their pipe-cleaner stingers. 'Which one's Hal's?' Ena asked.

Roland remembered sticking it together, coating it with black oil, making egg-carton eyes. And Hal arriving home a week later: 'She only gave me a C.'

Roland had been livid. 'What, others did better?'

He couldn't find the Griffin bee. 'The bloody teacher never bothered hanging it up.'

'It's probably a different class.'

'Yeah, of course, everyone makes a bee. How about they teach them to write, or add up? That'd be useful.'

They arrived outside the room and sat down to wait on chairs that had been set out especially. Kids' chairs. Roland's knees were up past his ribs. He could feel the legs splaying under his weight. He wondered whether he should let them slide, break off. Yes, it would make a point, but he'd end up on the floor, and there were other parents, Mrs Tom's-arse, coping quite nicely on her undersized chair.

He managed to hold on to the lockers and pull himself up. Ena soon did the same.

Roland moved closer to his wife and nodded to indicate a woman standing beside the door, waiting.

'Don't say a word,' Ena told him.

Ruth Philips approached them, almost kissed Ena, half-smiled at Roland. She told them about a stomach bug she'd had for three weeks; how she was worried it was something more ominous. Then she said, 'You still painting, Roland?'

He nodded, wondered what sort of pictures Ruth Philips had hanging in her house: a faded seascape in the toilet? Vincent's *Irises* above her bed of little joy or pleasure?

Ena could see it in Roland's eyes. He'd say something he'd regret. Ruth would tell the other parents. They'd avoid them.

'You do landscapes, don't you?' she asked.

'Yes.'

'But they're *modern*, aren't they?'

'Contemporary. I wouldn't do Renoir, cos I'm not him, or anyone else. I'm me.'

Ena took a deep breath. 'How's Gary?' she asked.

'Good.'

'Still with the Highways Department?'

'Yes. He's writing tenders now, which is what he's always wanted to do. He's too old to be out digging up roads.'

Of course, Roland thought. Tenders.

Ruth was still looking at him. 'If you want, he might be able to put in a word for you.'

'Sorry?'

'If you want a job?'

Roland studied the network of capillaries across her nose. 'I've got a job.'

Ena was determined. 'And how's Gary's arthritis?'

Roland wandered off. There were collages, too: strips of gold and silver paper cut into irregular shapes and stuck together. He couldn't see how this was art, or anything, really. He searched for his son's name again, and this time he found it. The shapes hadn't been cut, just torn; most of them were only half-stuck, and bits of white showed.

Ena managed to escape the woman and join him. 'She's just so ignorant.'

Roland preferred just to hate her.

An old man stuck his head out and called, 'Griffin?' Then went back in.

They went in and sat in front of Mr Saxby's desk. There was nothing on it except an ashtray (full), a newspaper, a bulging wallet and a *Best Bets*. He said, 'Hal said something about racing?'

'Racing?' Ena asked.

'He goes to the races?'

'Sometimes,' Roland explained. 'But it's mainly track work. Our neighbour used to be a strapper, and now he's a clocker.'

Saxby lit up. 'Well, horses, that might be just the thing for young Hal.'

'How do you mean?' Ena asked.

'He can't sit still. Whatever we start, he gets up, wanders.'

Roland wondered whether Mr Saxby mightn't have started on something more positive. 'He does what he's told?'

Saxby indicated a chair in the corner, facing a wall. Someone had written 'Hals chair' on it. 'That's where he generally ends up.'

'Cos he won't stay still?'

'But maybe he'll make a good jockey.'

'How long's he spend sitting there?'

'Hour a day.'

'An hour?'

'He's gotta learn.' And then, 'I've got an interest in racing. Part-own two mares. Kitchen Hand, you heard of her?'

Roland searched for signs of education. There were papers on the ledge behind Saxby; a textbook, a box of readers. The blackboard was clean, and looked like it had been for some time. 'I think ten minutes, perhaps, and he'll get the idea. I don't want him missing out on … whatever it is you do?'

'I like to get my message across,' Saxby said.

Ena noticed a cane in the corner. 'We were wondering about his maths, and spelling?'

Saxby opened a desk drawer, produced a roll book and used a yellow-tipped finger to look. 'Tests,' he said. 'Speed and accuracy … all out of ten.' He seemed surprised. 'Ten, each time.'

Ena was relieved. 'He's always done well with maths.'

'If he'd just sit still long enough …'

'And spelling?'

'Nine, ten, nine, nine. He's got a brain in his head.'

Ena noticed that most of Mr Saxby's hair had gone, and what remained had been oiled and cut in the shape of a soup bowl.

'I've been doing this forty years,' Saxby continued. 'There are very particular *types* of children. Some are like blocks, and they just drop into their holes, and some need a bit of sanding down, but Hal … kids like Hal are in their own world.'

'How?' Ena asked.

He leaned forward. 'Let me give you an example. Last week, a girl comes running in here and says, "Sir, Hal's in the girls' toilet."'

Roland turned to his wife.

'"Sir, he pulled down his pants and took out his thing." So I went out, and Hal's standing in the hallway, and I say, "Well?" And he says, "I was just getting a drink."'

Ena was confused. 'But we didn't hear anything about this.'

'Because I wasn't sure.'

'So, the girl might've been making it up?'

'Perhaps, but she's reliable. Anyway, he ended up arguing with me,

I told him to go to the office, he ran off, we spent an hour searching for him and the groundsman found him in the shed.'

'Seems very out of character,' Roland said.

'If he's a square he needs to go in the square hole,' Saxby said. 'Otherwise, by the time he's fifteen or sixteen …'

No one spoke for a bit. They could hear Mrs Philips and Mrs Thomas talking about their pop-in-the-hole children.

'Hard to see him … exposing himself,' Ena said. 'I couldn't see why he'd …' Although, she could.

They walked home at dusk. Roland said, 'If he can survive that old bastard …'

Ena wasn't sure. 'He hasn't said much.'

'Maybe he likes staring at the wall?'

And they both thought, Maybe Saxby knows best? Maybe, after forty years, he's good at hammering pegs?

They turned the corner and Hal was waiting, sitting on a fence, his hands in his pocket. 'What did he say?' he asked.

They continued walking and he followed them. Roland said, 'Maths, excellent, English, excellent. Saw some of your artwork.'

'That all?'

'Why? You expecting something?'

Hal didn't reply.

'We saw your chair.'

'Not just me.'

'No?'

'Anyone who gets up, he shouts at them and they gotta sit there.' He came up beside them.

Roland tripped, but kept on. He picked a sprig of jasmine from a fence. 'He told us what happened in the girls' toilet.'

Hal stopped in front of them. 'What?'

'You tell us.'

'I went in there cos it was quicker. The boys' toilet is at the other end of the hall. Didn't think no one was around. But *she* came in.'

'Who's she?'

'Gillian. And she screams and runs off and tells Saxby.'

'Mr Saxby reckons you pulled down your pants.'

'No.'

'Showed her your thing.'

Hal shook his head. 'That never happened.'

'You sure?'

'Don't you believe me?'

'Why would Mr Saxby have said it?'

'Because *she* made it up. She hates me. She always has.'

'Why?'

Hal tried to think. 'She just does.' He tensed, clutched his fists, waiting.

'Hal, don't be silly,' Ena said.

'I never showed no one nothin'. But he believed her cos she's a girl. He likes girls. He makes them stand with him and he ...' He turned and ran off.

'Hal!' Roland called. They couldn't chase him two more blocks. When they came up the drive, Hal was standing with one of Roland's recent paintings, his farm children. He waited until his father was closer then lifted it and started smashing it on the concrete. Roland made no attempt to stop him. Ena did, but he pushed her away, and she stood back, waiting for her husband. Hal kept going until the frame shattered and the canvas collapsed. Then he laid it on the ground and stepped on it.

He raised a shaking hand to Roland. 'I never did it.'

Roland didn't care about the painting. He just wanted to know what to believe.

Hal locked the door, pulled down his pants and began. He could hear Nan Griffin telling someone how she had no choice. How her son and daughter-in-law had a big do at the gallery and how, despite the boy's age, they weren't happy leaving him at home. How there'd been a history of experimentation.

Hal examined a few drops of pee on the seat and wondered whether he should wipe them. It wasn't his job, but the next old girl might assume it was him. There was more on the ground, and the smell wasn't pleasant: old-lady smell; my-husband-was-killed-in-Flanders smell; Legacy-smell; fifty-women-and-a-dance-band smell.

'What you doing in there?' Nan asked.

'Peeing.'

'Hurry up.'

He stood, zipped up and looked at the concrete wall. Was it? Yes, it was. A stripe, where someone had wiped it off their finger. He studied it more closely. It was dry, and parts had crumbled off.

'Hal?'

He exited, and she was waiting. 'Come on.'

She took him by the hand and dragged him back into the hall. He said, 'Dad lets me go alone.'

'I don't take no chances.'

And to prove this (she knew he needed a firm hand) she sat him down at their table, placed his Coke in his hand and said, 'Don't move.'

'Can't I dance?'

'I'll be back.'

He watched her walk across the hall. She found another table, with a different group of women in loud, showy dresses, and her expression changed. She smiled, pawed at them, laughed. He knew he wasn't welcome. He'd overheard her saying it: 'Yes, a fifth limb, but what do you do? Leave him home alone and the house'd be burnt down.'

He watched the four men in the band: a pianist with a big moustache who kept looking up and smiling, a drummer, a double bass player and an accordionist with a dangerous-looking forward lean. They finished an instrumental and the pianist adjusted his microphone. 'Any of youse ladies from Ireland?'

A few hands shot up.

'This one's dedicated to you.' And he began playing, and singing, telling them about smiling eyes, which Hal thought stupid. Like ears that could taste or a nose that could speak. Or a Legacy widow who hadn't actually lost her husband in either of the big wars.

Hal could remember Pop Griffin. He'd been there for a few years, before dying of his wounds. *Of his wounds*. His father's words. But these were the burns he'd received at the chemical works. So they weren't war wounds, and Nan wasn't really a Legacy widow (unless Australia was at war with a drum of potash). In fact, Pop Griffin hadn't fought at all. He'd been rejected because of his eyes. This, Hal's father had explained, was the curse of the Griffins.

Hal had often been subjected to the old girls, and they'd always tell him about their husbands, and how many Germans they'd killed, and how hard it had been bringing up seven kids by themselves, but God bless Legacy for helping out. Then there'd be a photo of the uniformed subject and stories of how they'd met and lived in a two-bedroom cottage and suffered years of drought and lost their farm and blah blah, on it would go, as he sat sipping warm Coke, allowing his cheek to be pinched, which was fair, seeing how their husbands had got a bullet through the head.

The band finished with Irish eyes and played another instrumental. Hal suspected the pianist didn't like singing, and he really wasn't very good. He spoke like Mr Saxby calling a square dance: *do-si-do and round she goes*. Nan had sat down. He wondered if he should go over, but knew how it would end.

He took the fireworks from his pocket: seven brightly coloured Roman candles with rat-tail fuses. He examined them, ran his fingers over their glittering cases, made sure the tops were secure.

'You're Hal?'

He shoved them back in his pocket and looked up. Nan Griffin was standing beside an old man wearing an even older suit. She said, 'This is Mr Dalrymple. He used to work with Pop.'

Mr Dalrymple extended his hand and Hal shook it. He sat down and Nan gave Hal a warning look before returning to the other table.

Mr Dalrymple was quick to get started: he told Hal about the acid vats, and the accident, but how your grandfather was lucky, cos several men died after falling in, and the management refused to put up rails, so there was a walk-out, then there were rails, but believe me, it was a bitch of a place to work (Pardon the French, how old are yer, nine? You woulda heard all that before.)

Hal checked his pockets for the matches. He'd been painting with his dad when Trev came in and showed them: hundreds of Catherine wheels, cakes, mines and candles.

His dad had kept working. 'Where'd you get them?'

'I bought them.'

'You did, eh?'

'Honest to God. From the factory door.'

Hal had examined the fireworks, and said to his dad, 'Come on, just a few?'

'No, thanks. I've had the law before, I don't want them again.'

'I'll convince you,' Trevor had said. He'd taken the box, walked out to the drive, lit a few and thrown them down. They'd hissed and sizzled and danced about before popping with red and blue flashes.

His dad had leaned on the doorway, half-smiling, as though encouraging a child. Ena and Sonia had come out too, and Mary had called from her window, 'Trev, what are you doing out there?'

But when it was all over, and Hal had let off a few and danced about with joy, and pleaded with his dad to buy a box, Roland had said, 'No, thanks.' He'd returned to his shed, and the canvases that wouldn't get him in trouble.

Trev had packed up and said to him, 'Bad luck, Hal.'

Hal wasn't about to let the opportunity slip. 'Can I buy a few?'

'Na, your dad wouldn't like that.'

'He wouldn't know. I wouldn't tell him. I'd let 'em off down the paddock.'

'If yer silly with fireworks you could lose a finger.'

'I know.'

Trevor had reached in, taken a handful, and given them to him. 'Go hide them. Don't say a word. Griff'll kill me.'

'Of course.' Hal had shoved them in his pocket, shaken Trev's hand (because that's what men did when they made a deal) and ran to his room, and his hiding spot behind the wardrobe.

Mr Dalrymple said, 'Your Pop, he was a good man.'

Hal wasn't sure what to say.

'Most of the time he made fertiliser.'

Hal wondered why none of the Legacy girls were interested in Mr Dalrymple. Why they mostly danced together, like they were part of some secret community, nymphs, or Amazonians. 'Why didn't you get killed in the war?' he asked.

'I didn't fight.'

'Why not?'

'I had a disease when I was a child, and it left me lame.'

'What disease? Lupus?'

'Polio.'

Hal had heard of it. It was lucky, really. If Mr Dalrymple hadn't had polio he'd probably be dead, like all the other husbands.

Mr Dalrymple said, 'You're lucky, gettin' brought along by your Nanna.'

'Mum and Dad made her bring me.'

'Well, it looks like you're having fun.'

'Not really. They make her take me everywhere. She cleans Dr Bailey's house, and I gotta go and sit and wait. That's boring too.'

'We all gotta work.'

'And the Legacy shop.'

'Where's that?'

'It's a shop full of old stuff. They got people's pants and shirts. They sell 'em to make money. And I gotta sit behind the counter and read while she sorts clothes and puts a price on them and hangs them out.'

'So, you're a shopkeeper?'

He really didn't like how this man couldn't see the problem with anything.

'People don't want to pay.'

'Sorry?'

'Say a shirt costs threepence. They'll come up to the counter and say, "If I buy this one can you throw in these?" But it's all old crap that someone's donated.'

'I'm sure it's not crap.'

'It is. It's all musty.' Like this place, he wanted to say. Old dresses that should've been thrown in the bin.

The pianist was promising to take Kathleen home.

Hal looked at Mr Dalrymple and said, 'I killed a chicken.'

'Really?'

'Don't tell Dad.'

'No.'

'He reckons I'm too young. But Trevor let me. One swipe, bang, and off it comes. Then y' gotta hold it down until it stops kickin'. It took about a minute. Even then it kept twitchin', but Mary just started pluckin' it – said she couldn't wait all day. You ever killed a chicken?'

'When I was a young man. We had a farm.'

'It doesn't matter. They're dumb animals. They don't mind.'

'No?'

'They probably like it.'

'How?'

But he wasn't sure. He finished his Coke and put the glass on the table. 'This is better than the shop,' he said. 'There are toys for sale, and a train set, and I set it out on the ground and this lady tripped on it and fell over and Nan was screamin' at me.'

Hal watched her and a few friends walk onto the dance floor. They embraced (awkwardly) and started dancing. He said, 'That's a bit strange.'

Mr Dalrymple tended to agree. 'Too much for one man. I get handed about like a pipe.'

'At least chickens don't have to dance with each other.'

'No.'

'I reckon they'd rather get their heads chopped off.'

'Quite possibly.'

'You dance with someone if you wanna fall in love with them. Get married, have babies. Mr Saxby makes me dance with Kenny Sutcliffe. Don't wanna have babies with him.'

'No.'

'It's poofy.'

This was grey territory, even for Mr Dalrymple.

'You know, when two men do it.'

Mr Dalrymple looked horrified. 'Did you get to eat your chicken?'

'I can't work out what'd happen. Do you know?'

'Your Nan thought I could tell you a bit about your Pop. He was captain of the bowls team for seventeen years. Did you know he played bowls?'

'Yes. There's a couple in the shed.'

'You should take it up.'

'It's for old people.'

'Not at all.' Mr Dalrymple was happy. The boy had accepted bowls. It wasn't his job to explain homosexuality. He stood, took Hal by the hand, led him onto the dance floor and delivered him to one of the ladies.

Hal felt betrayed. Mr Dalrymple made for the bar.

The woman spoke over the music. 'You know how to waltz?'

'No.'

But she made him anyway. Nan Griffin watched, smiling, content.

The band was ramping up. The drummer had come to life. He jumped about, hammering the cymbals. The man with the accordion stood and swayed with the music.

The woman sang, *Someday my prince will come …*

Hal doubted it. He watched how she seemed in raptures, how she lifted her head and surrendered to the music. He decided: it was time. He waited until no one was looking, then ran behind the stage.

One, two, three … He took out his matches and lit the first, slid it across the polished floor, and waited.

It seemed louder in the hall. There was some screaming, of course, and the old girls scattered, but that gave him enough time to light the rest, throw them out, and hide behind the stage again.

It made a good show. The only lights were on the band, so the copper-blue and barium-green lit up the hall. He was sure they'd all be grateful. Blueberry scones were one thing, but this was Guy Fawkes and New Year's Eve and every party that had ever been.

Then he felt the pain in his ear. The accordionist pinched his lobe and dragged him into the middle of the dance floor. 'Who owns this?'

The lights came on.

Nan was trying to calm the women. Several had collapsed into chairs. But she stopped to claim him. 'Are you happy?' she asked.

He wasn't sure if she was truly grateful. This would be a Legacy dance they talked about for years to come.

He noticed the burnt scraps on the floor. 'I got a couple more,' he said.

But she had him out the door, into the cold night, and they were running after the Pennington tram.

# 1950

Sam asked Hal to wait outside the couplings. 'Not a place for a boy,' he said.

'Why?'

'Language's bit rich.'

Hal was left standing, waiting. The small pub promised 'Portahouse how you like it!' and, by the smell of it, plenty of beer. Men emerged wiping their mouths, hitching their pants, checking their stubs for a win or place. One of them said to him, 'What, you lost, son?'

'No.'

'What's yer name?'

'Hal.'

He smiled. 'You watch out for Hotspur, eh?'

Hal had no idea what he meant. It was probably a horse. Perhaps he was giving him a tip. Perhaps he should tell Sam.

He was left watching the concourse: the bookies with their big bags; the thousands of punters and their sweat-soaked hats; the cloud of smoke that never lifted; the calls ('Come on, fellas, two minutes to close!'); and, distantly, the thump of hooves on the track.

The little pub had saloon doors, but one was hanging loose. He leaned against a wall and waited. Men emptied their beer dregs and threw their butts onto a pair of rubber plants in pots before heading for the bookies.

It all reminded Hal of his dad's new painting. *Mad Ernie's Shop* showed a fat storekeeper standing in front of a store in an outback town. A greyhound stood in the middle of the road sniffing a piece of newspaper that had probably had fish or lamb's brains wrapped in it. He'd said to his dad, 'Why's he mad?'

'That's what you gotta work out.'

'Did he kill someone?'

'Perhaps.'

Hal waited, but there was no sign of Sam. He thought of heading home. It was a warm Saturday afternoon, and jackets had come off, revealing braces struggling against gravity. Bellies emerged from shirts – inners and outers, too – and the bits of pants that should've been under bums were closer to knees. Some of the men had binoculars. Some ate sandwiches from wax paper. He hated wax paper. It made sandwiches sweat.

Sam came out and gave him a bottle of Coke. 'Come on, I got a bita business.' He led, and Hal (who was tall for ten, nearly shoulder-height to most of the sagging men) followed him through the crowd, catching glimpses of sky through the chaos of race day, Cheltenham.

'I just found out Dave Butler's riding,' Sam said.

'You gonna bet on Hotspur?' Hal asked.

Sam checked his form. 'Which race?'

'Dunno.'

'How'd you get the name?'

'A man told me. Said I better look out for him.'

Sam could remember something about Hotspur, and one of the King Henrys, Prince Hal, a battle. 'That's who yer dad name you after?' he asked.

'Who?'

'Prince Hal.'

'Who was he?'

'Look it up.'

Sam led him to the saddling enclosure. There were a dozen horses. Some were saddled, and the jockeys were up, but others were jumping about, spooked. Sam said, 'You gotta judge their mood.'

'Who?' Hal asked.

'The horses. Like you – some mornings you just don't feel like going to school. Horses are no different.'

Hal finished his Coke and put the bottle in the bin. The men had a smell. He knew it well. Hair oil, and cheap perfume (or whatever it was called). Leather from the binocular cases. Beer breath. Shit they'd stepped in. This all added up to one smell: the racecourse. It was the best smell in the world. It meant Saturday afternoon and early mornings, before anyone was up; sitting in the empty stands watching trackwork; hot tea in the strappers' rooms (they put rum in it). He returned to Sam and said, 'Who you bettin' on?'

'Haven't worked it out.' He indicated one of the jockeys and said, 'Him and that horse aren't matched. Tim shoulda got someone else.'

'Why?'

'He doesn't sit right. Maybe the horse doesn't like him.'

'How can you tell?'

'Just can.'

Sam could tell a lot of things about how man and animal, and man and man, got along. Trevor, for instance. He'd always understood him, and said things to Hal like, 'He'll end up with a knife between his ribs.'

'Why's that?'

'Some blokes just don't know where to stop.'

Sam saw his boss, Tim Johnson, and called him over. 'I thought Harry was riding Gifter?'

Johnson shook his head. 'If you can tell me where he is.'

'Hasn't shown up?'

'No. And that's it. You tell him when you see him.' He walked off.

On the way back to the stand Sam said, 'You still in the bad books?'

'I guess.'

'You don't talk to yer dad like that.'

'His fault.' Although Hal knew Sam wouldn't accept this. 'He pushed me.'

'Why did he push you?'

They found a spot in the stand, sat and waited for the next race. Sam was watching the gates, noting the horses that resisted.

'Cos I called him an arsehole.'

'Your own father? You called him that?'

Sam knew the sequence of events: Hal sitting on the lounge reading comics, refusing to help out around the house, telling his sister she was fat – until Roland came in and told him to stop being so goddamn rude. Then, the to-and-fro that had developed over the last twelve months: the ferocious boy who'd stand up to anyone. Followed by him running from the house, climbing onto the roof of the new chook shed, sitting for hours, throwing plums from the overhanging tree at anyone who came near. Until Roland got the ladder, climbed up, grabbed him around the neck, dragged him down, stood in the drive having another shouting match, eventually losing his temper and pushing him.

Sam said, 'No problem's ever solved through screamin'.'

'He started it.'

'*He, he.* It's always someone else.'

'He lets Sonia get away with everything.'

'Rubbish. I see her out hangin' clothes on the line.'

'Sometimes.'

Sam turned to him. 'Thing is, you can whip a horse, and he might do what you want, but he'll hate you for it.'

Hal knew where it was going.

'Or you can train him up, slow, try get some *understanding*.'

'He didn't have to push me.'

There were still two horses refusing to enter.

'Your dad, he's a good man. You're a lucky boy, Prince Hal. Look at Shirley, growin' up without no one.'

That's not my fault, thought Hal.

'I can tell yer, he's damn proud of you. He's always showin' us your art, or yer school work. If you decide you don't need a father …'

'I never said that.'

The bell rang. They were off. Hal noticed how Sam wasn't that interested.

'I don't get you, Hal.'

'What?'

'Most dads'll be down the pub – and kids, they're just there, in the way. But Griff, I reckon there's only one thing he really cares about.'

Four-thirty. The best part of the day, Sam thought. After the last race. The last drink. The horses fed and watered. The sun low in the wintry sky, a light breeze, barely noticeable through the louvres. Viburnum, and jasmine, and Mr Hessian's chicken shit, and the hundred smells of his neighbourhood that became one smell. Kids calling each other, and these voices becoming those of everyone who'd ever played or hung out washing or had a ding-dong, or lived, in Pennington. The sort of moment it would be good to die. Mary would find him lying across his bed, his tranny still going, wearing his socks and sandals and singlet. She'd just turn off the radio and call for Shirley. 'Heart just stopped, I reckon.'

They played an ad for Lawlor's the White Ant People, and he stopped to think. Something was meant to happen at five. Five? Of course! He fiddled with the knob on his radio. The signal was getting weaker. He couldn't find the station. So he turned it off and ran next door. Arriving in the lounge room he said to Roland, 'Can I use your radio?'

A moment later they were all gathered around, listening to the ABC. Ena was wearing slippers that showed her toes, and Hal was holding cotton over a bleeding scab he'd picked. Sonia was sitting on the lounge, arms crossed.

A voice described the essay competition that had been held: entries accepted from schools across the state, a winner selected. And now, ladies and gentlemen, we hear the winner reading her essay. Shirley was introduced, and Hal said, 'She sounds funny.'

'The radio does that,' Roland explained. 'You can't expect it – '

'Ssh!' Ena said.

They all listened.

'My essay is entitled "Five Years to the Day: How the war changed our lives forever."'

Ena gave Sonia her could've-been-you expression. Sonia didn't care. Who'd wanna read school stuff on the radio? Radio was Frank Sinatra, Count Basie, Judy Garland, perhaps. Not boring essays. And who'd be listening on a Saturday afternoon?

'"It's five years, almost to the day, since Russian troops overran Berlin. I can remember reading the news in the paper. The Germans were fleeing; Paris was free; Hitler had retreated to his bunker."'

Sonia wasn't jealous. It was only school. And what did you get? A book voucher for five pounds. So what? There were plenty of books at school, in libraries, and no one read them. Unless you were a hermit (and that explained it); unless you didn't have friends (again); unless you were twelve going on fifty.

'"Although we were a long way from the war, it affected all of us. Not just rationing but the constant fear that we could be invaded. Our dads and brothers and uncles were all involved. My uncle for instance …"'

Sonia knew Mary had helped, giving her ideas, writing sections, editing them. Or at least this is what she suspected. Otherwise, how could she have won? Against all the kids from the rich schools?

Ena said, 'It was a good topic she picked, wasn't it, Sonia?'

'Yes.'

Compared to Sonia's tribute to her father: 'My dad is quite well-known as a painter. He paints pictures of old pubs and houses and old cars and stuff. The pictures don't look like real people, or towns, but that's his style, he says. He told me his theme is alienation. This means people who don't get along with other people. He painted a picture of me and my brother Hal but it doesn't look much like us, and no one's bought it yet, although he reckons someone will one day.'

'She reads well, doesn't she?' Ena said to Sam.

'She's been practising for weeks.'

Sonia just listened. She couldn't understand why it meant so much to Shirley. Ena was watching her.

'What?'

'You listening? Maybe you could do one like this next year?'

'Maybe.'

'"My uncle fought in New Guinea. He was on the Kokoda Trail …"'

'Was Trevor at Kokoda?' Ena asked Sam.

'She's gilding,' he explained.

'Ah. Are they allowed to do that?'

Sonia thought, Of course. She's made it all up. I coulda done that. I coulda said my dad was the greatest painter in Australia. It's all a lie. Shouldn't she be disqualified?

'"He won an award for attacking a Japanese machine-gun post. He killed seven soldiers and allowed his mates to advance. These are the sorts of stories he tells me, as do a lot of dads and brothers with their families. We really have so much to be grateful for. Without their sacrifice we mightn't be sitting here today."'

Christ, Roland thought. Sacrifice? Trev?

'"We all grew close during the war years. Our street was, and is, a great place to live. We look out for each other. My friend Sonia is more like a sister. And I think this is because of the tough times we all shared back then."'

Ena waited for her daughter's response. Hal, Roland and Sam turned to Sonia too. Ena said, 'Nice of her to say that?'

'Yes.'

Sonia and Sheena, who was in her art class, were riding their bikes up and down the road, and Shirley was waiting for a go (Ena had made her promise). But they just rode off, around the block, and when Shirley called after them they rode off again. 'Come back! Mum said I could have a shot.' But they just laughed.

Sonia didn't feel so good. Perhaps it was something about being twelve. Her eyes started to water, she ran to her room, closed the door and crawled under the bed so her brother wouldn't find her.

Roland stood but Ena said, 'No, stay here.'

'"Of course, if the Japanese had come south we would've fought them. Each of us, in our own streets, because that's what you've got to protect. Your house, your family. That's all we've got, really."'

Hal had noticed the signs on the racecourse fence weeks before: 'The Coming Storm of the Lord'. He'd seen the truck arrive the previous Wednesday, and a dozen or so men (he'd watched from the starter's box) raise the enormous tent, its red and yellow striped roof, its stage for praising the Lord, its lighting and sound systems. He'd told Roland, who'd laughed it off, and Ena, who'd told him to stay away. Then they'd had a visit from Charlie Bass, and he'd given them the literature: 'The Lord will arrive like thunder, and lay the fields of man flat with his fury'.

Hal had said, 'How do they know it's going to rain?'

Charlie had smiled. 'You think God doesn't know?'

Charlie seemed a powerful man. God had cured his cancer. He'd given him three wives, and he'd outlived them all.

Shirley had been listening to this conversation, and Mary had come and dragged her away.

Saturday morning arrived and Hal stood in the lounge room of number seventeen, listening at the window, the sounds of amplified hymns and brass bands blurring across Torrens Road, along Burleigh Avenue, down the driveway. 'Carn, Sonia, let's go see.'

'Mum and Dad said we shouldn't.'

'So what? They won't be back from the shops till two. They won't know.'

She thought about it, bit her lip and said, 'You'd just get yourself into trouble. You can't help it. You were born bad.'

'That's why I need to be healed.' He grabbed her arm, dragged her out the door, down the drive, and Mary, out trying to pull a few weeds that Sam had missed (since Cheltenham was closed for the day, he'd gone to Morphetville), said, 'Where are you two off to?'

'Shops, for Mum,' Hal said.

'She's gone to town.'

'She left a list.'

They were gone, across the road, into the racecourse, mostly deserted, except for a few people drifting in and out of the tent. They stood and listened a few feet from the entrance, and someone asked them where their parents were. Hal said they were in the tent praising the Lord. This seemed to do the job. Then Hal said to Sonia, 'You wanna go in and sing?'

'No, I don't. I only came to make sure you didn't kill yourself. Let's go home.'

'No chance.' He ran into the tent and looked around – the crowd of two hundred or so people in their Sunday best, a small band playing a dissonant dirge with words. At the front, up on the stage, Charlie Bass was playing the organ, surveying the assembled as some sort of preacher, with whiskers that followed his chin line, waved his hands about in the air.

'Let's go,' Sonia said.

'In a minute.' Hal pretended to sing along, dance, even turning circles and praising a Lord he'd been warned off, mostly.

The preacher introduced himself as Pastor Nicolas, and promised, before the arrival of the storm, to change lives. Only one way. Jesus Lord our Saviour. He invited his son on stage and explained how the ten-year-old had nearly died in an accident a few months before. How his boy could now describe the very clothes Jesus wore, the whiskers on His face, the sandals on His feet. Saved by the Lord's intervention. This man who'd pushed the boy from the path of an oncoming bus.

Hal said to his sister, 'He doesn't mean that Jesus actually saved him?'

'Of course not. It's all made up. They're religious fruitcakes, soft in the head.'

Some old woman turned around and Sonia just smiled a smile every bit as phoney as the bossa nova pre-set on Charlie's Hammond. Then she said, 'We gotta go. Mum and Dad'll be home soon.'

But Nicolas took his son's hand, held it up and said, 'For my son and wife and family, and every man and woman in this tent, Lord you're with us, your love informs every thought and feeling and action and seig abordoma furto neftum ghetish orandy ...'

Hal loved it. Glowed. He moved closer to Sonia and said, 'What's that?'

She didn't know.

'God, you put us here for a purpose – to live for you, through you, to make your will known, and manifest. "I shall not die but live and declare the words of the Lord." Psalms 1:18, 17. God's gonna need miracles today and I pray the power of the Lord, the Lord Jesus our Saviour ab demo thateris fitin sumbola defret ...'

'What's that all about?' Hal asked his sister, but she shrugged, and Nicolas kept babbling, morphing between sermon, psalm and gibberish, and Hal seemed to warm to it, and whispered to his sister, 'Gud juser tima suds goij suma Sam and Mary sud fer Sonia and her big fat arse.'

She kicked him, as the prophet of Cheltenham racecourse sang his sermon of the hundred-yard line, a truncated race call as good as anything Sam could manage. Then Charlie Bass started the band playing, and the music and sweat and non-words and crying and calling and shouting and praying reached a crescendo, at which point the rain began. Soft at first. Then heavy. The promised downpour, as this fugue of everything rattled in Hal's ear like a Nazi machine gun, and Nicolas's son fainted and fell into his father's arms, and a group of people, including Charlie Bass, approached the boy and put their hands all over him and said more words. And then Sonia said, 'I'm going.'

Hal wasn't happy with this. She obviously didn't feel the spirit. 'You can't, you gotta look after me.'

She turned and walked out into the rain.

'Sonia.' Hal followed and said, 'You're meant to make sure I don't get into trouble.'

She kept going.

Hal turned, noticed a few of the ropes that held up the tent, approached one and worked it loose, then called, 'Hey, Sonia.'

Still nothing – she was almost to the road. So he released it, and part of the tent fell in, and he heard voices from inside – a different sort of chaos and strange singing.

'Sonia?'

This time she stopped, looked back, and he said, 'Dare me?' He didn't need encouragement. Finding another rope, loosening it, watching more of the tent fall in, more voices, louder, men calling from within the canvas temple, chairs and scaffold and framework collapsing.

Roland wasn't in the mood for crowds, but he guessed he better make an effort for today. He wore his dad's suit – that would do; polished shoes; his fedora with the yellow paint fingerprint rim.

Ena had Hal in his longest shorts, and socks, which meant there was only an inch of exposed knee; his cotton jacket with its pockets full of dried gum and loose tobacco. His woven tie, pulled loose.

They walked along Commercial Street. It was busy for a Tuesday. Roland chose the gutter but Mary and Ena, and Hal in their wake, headed straight down the middle of the footpath. Stevenson's clock, hanging on a frame above the jeweller's door, tolled noon. Ena checked, just to make sure. 'We better hurry,' she said to Mary. 'I thought we'd be finished by one.'

Hal had been given the day off school. This was the rarest of events, but it was called for. There was only three days before they left. Firstly, for Western Australia, where he was to become John McCabe, brother of Lucie, running around the Kalgoorlie goldfields in search of a piano. Secondly, for London, where Roland's new exhibition was opening.

Mary encouraged Hal to catch up. 'They'll put you in those magazines.'

'Which ones?' he asked.

'You know, Hollywood, with all the stars. You'll become famous and you won't want anything to do with us.'

'I don't think so. It's a Pommy film.'

'Doesn't matter. Million people might see you up there. What did you say it was called?'

'*The Blue Lily.*'

'And who was the woman?'

Ena said, 'Lucie McCabe. You've heard of her?'

'Yes, she was a pilot?'

'No. A pianist.'

Mary licked her thumb and cleaned jam from Hal's face. 'Are you excited?'

'Na.' But his smile gave it away.

'You know all yer lines?'

'Yep.'

'You do not,' Ena said. She'd sat on the lounge the previous evening, reading the underlined dialogue, testing him.

'Right, this is the scene where Lucie walks in, and the new piano's there. She says, "I never woulda thought". She looks at you and you say?'

'Something about the fellas at the pub?'

'No.'

'I ask her how she reckons it got there?'

'No. You either know it or you don't.'

'I did. I forgot!'

'Well, you better hurry up and remember, otherwise they'll forget why they've chosen you.'

Hal still couldn't understand why they had chosen him. It wasn't like he could act, or had acted, or even been that interested. But his Greataunt Gwen had come to their house to visit, to sip tea in their dining room, and she'd said to him, 'You've got the most intriguing little face.'

Later, Hal had said to his mum, 'Why's she going on about my face?'

'She does it for a living.'

'How's that?'

'She works for a casting company.'

A few weeks later she'd returned. Another cup of tea and Gwen had sat Hal down and said, 'After I left last time, I was looking at some photos of this John McCabe kid, the one we want for the film, and Hal, you know what?'

'What?'

'You. You're him. John. Your face, the way you talk. Ten years old. You'd have to do a screen test, and the director, Michael, who's coming out from England, would have to think you're suitable. But he goes on my advice.'

Ena had said, 'He's never acted.'

'That's just the point. We don't want one of these little darlings. We want the real thing.'

Hal turned to his father as they walked into Myer. Roland wasn't listening, of course. Wasn't impressed by films. He thought they were phoney, but Hal didn't get how they were any more phoney than his paintings.

They stopped in Women's Dresses. Mary picked one out and said, 'It's pretty, eh?'

'Yes. Why don't you try it on?' Ena said.

'Na, I got plenty of dresses.'

'Go on.' She steered Mary towards the change rooms.

'No, we're here to get some clothes for Hal.'

The Griffins stood waiting. Ena said to her son, 'Excited?'

'Yeah.'

'Not long and you'll be standing in front of the cameras. What d'yer reckon, Griff?'

'Eh?'

'It's exciting, isn't it?'

'Bloody oath it is.' He squeezed his son's shoulder.

'People all over the world will be watching. But ...' Ena smiled. 'I shouldn't go on. I'll make you nervous, eh, Hal?'

'I'm not nervous. Just say me lines. That's all they reckon.'

'Of course.'

They. Michael Grady, sitting behind a desk, Aunty Gwen, Mrs Woodward, the producer, and two other men in suits, poring over documents on the table, looking up, writing notes, rearranging their papers before losing interest.

Michael had said, 'So, what sort of hobbies have you got, Hal?'

'Just muckin' about, I s'pose.'

Gwen had handed him the script. 'Let's get going. I've underlined your bits, Hal. Just read 'em out. Natural. Don't try to act.'

This had seemed reasonable. How did you act, anyway? Talk funny? Gwen had read: '"I don't reckon Dad can afford it, John."'

'"Me neither,"' he'd said. '"But them nuns, I reckon they got a piano, Lucie."'

'"Do they? Maybe they give lessons. D'yer reckon?"'

'"You can only ask. This girl in my class, she takes lesson, but she's a horror. And she's no good at it. But you can do it without trying, Lucie."'

'That'll do,' Michael had said.

Hal had looked up. 'I can do it differently.'

'No, that's fine. You'll do.'

This had taken a while to sink in. Ena, who'd been sitting at the back of the room, had clutched her purse.

Hal had said, 'I reckon this John boy, he might be a bit like me.'

'I reckon, too, Hal.'

Mary emerged a new woman: low-cut (and she kept covering her chest), arms revealed almost to the shoulders. 'It's not me,' she said.

'Nonsense,' Ena replied. 'For going out.'

'It's nice. I like green.'

'That's it. Get it off, we're buying it. Hand it out.'

A routine of sick child, candied almonds, cups of tea and all-day-scratchings had taken a toll. Ena could see it in Mary's face, hear it in her voice. She took the dress to the till and opened her purse. Roland followed. '*We're* buying it?'

'It's the least we can do, for what she does for us.'

Ena handed over the seven pounds and six and the till rung.

'I agree, she does a lot, but can we afford it?'

'Yes.'

'If you wanna buy clothes for Hal?'

She glared at him. 'We can afford it.'

Mary emerged in her old dress, saw what was happening, and came over to them. 'No, you're not paying.'

'Already done,' Ena said, handing her the bag with the dress. 'Think of it as payment. Ten years' worth. What do you reckon, Griff?'

'We got the money, Mary.'

The bag was heavy in Mary's hands. She wished she'd never come.

They headed upstairs to boyswear: new pants, shirts, socks, undies, the lot.

Hal trudged back and forth from the change room and, in the end, didn't bother – just slipped off his pants where he stood, tried on one, then another, as Ena and Mary pulled at them, felt around the legs, checked for hems (they'd still have to last a few years).

Roland sat watching, but soon he was off, on the main street of a small town, noticing the characters, their features, the clothes that just asked to be painted.

Sometimes Ena would ask his opinion. 'Griff?'

'Eh?'

'What do you reckon?'

He'd look at his son's latest shirt. 'Yes, nice. New man, aren't you, Hal?'

'I hate doing this,' Hal said.

'It's part of the movie actor's life,' his mother explained. 'What do you think of this one, Mary?'

'Yes, nice collar, bit of formality.'

'Aren't you meant to ask me?' Hal said.

But they ignored him.

They descended the stairs with bags of clothes. Placed them on the floor between their legs in the tram on the way home. Carried them the two blocks, and down Burleigh Avenue. All of this time, Hal was aware of his father, dragging his feet, not saying a word. He wondered if there was any point making the film.


It was Thursday and Roland had to wait for the paint to dry. He always fiddled with the sky. There was one cloud, but he'd never seen a sky with one cloud. Perhaps the intellectuals could read something into it: the drought had sent Ernie mad; life was always about the promise, but never the delivery.

He could hear the phone ringing. 'Ena,' he called. Waited. 'Christ!' He stood, went inside and said, 'Where are you?'

No reply. He picked up the phone. 'Hello?'

'This is Mr Griffin?'

'Yes.' Short; sharp. These sort of people always rang when he was trying to work. Some fella from the gas board; one of Ena's friends, determined to discuss the price of bread.

'This is Bernard Harris, from Pennington Primary. We've had a few problems this morning with Hal.'

Roland allowed himself the luxury of a seat. 'What sort of problems?'

'Well, firstly, he might be home soon.'

'Why?'

'I was gonna call you to come get him, but he just ran off.'

'Right.' Like an unpleasant diagnosis you suspected, but kept avoiding.

'There was an incident in the classroom.'

'An incident?'

'Hal got upset and there was an argument with Mr Coates. He threw a chair and myself and Mr Coates and another teacher had to restrain him.'

Ena was in the doorway, holding clothes she'd ironed for the trip.

Roland whispered: 'Hal … in trouble again.'

The air emptied from her lungs and she sat across from him.

'Go on,' he said, back into the receiver.

'We got him back to the office, he seemed okay, but then he just stood up and walked off.'

Hal was standing in front of them. He threw his satchel on the table.

'Righto, he's here now. Perhaps if we have him back in the morning?

You could talk to him then? And then you know we're away for a few months?'

'Righto.' Not a hopeful righto, more a return-him-if-you-must righto. A go-away-for-as-long-as-you-like righto.

Roland hung up.

'He told you I ran off?'

'Yes.'

'But he didn't tell you why?' Hal walked into the kitchen, opened the fridge and took the cordial. He brought it in and sat down, drinking from the jug. Ena wanted to say it, but dared not.

'Lisbeth,' he said.

'Who's she?'

'Coates has a seating plan, and her name's Green, so I get to sit next to her.'

Lisbeth Green, turning to her friends and giggling, pulling faces (his), moving comments from desk-to-desk like checkers when Coates's back was turned. 'She said I'm schizo.'

'She wouldn't even know what it means,' Roland said.

'Said her parents told her. It's when you don't think right, or you act funny.'

'None of us think right. All of us act funny.'

But Lisbeth was grinning at him, explaining. 'Dad's a psychologist. He told me. "Be careful of him. If he's turned, there's no telling what he'll do."'

'She sounds like a nasty piece of work,' Ena said, looking at Roland 'Maybe we could ask to have him moved.'

But Roland knew that wouldn't solve the problem. 'We'll talk to Mr Harris in the morning, explain. Maybe he can deal with her.'

She was writing now. Her head was low to the desk and her eyes were following her words. 'You know what they do with your type?'

He didn't respond.

'Glenside. And when it gets bad enough they lock you in a padded cell. And you stay there forever, cos they can't trust you to be around people.'

'Quiet!' He stood.

Coates turned. 'Hal, sit down.'

'She said – '

'Sit down!'

He stood back, lifted his chair and launched it across the room.

'Maybe there's something wrong with me?' he said to his dad.

'Na.' Roland sat next to him and held his knee. 'It's a boy thing. I was the same, wasn't I, Ena?'

'Still are.'

'Things don't work out, y' get shitty, and it feels like the world's falling in. But that happens to everyone. This little *bitch* …'

Hal sat up. 'I'm not goin' back.'

'Cos of her?'

'No, I'm just not. I hate the place – the teachers, the shit about Hastings and Nefrititi.'

'Hal, it's just cos they're all jealous. Going away, the film.' Roland studied his boy's face: the skin, like candle wax, the few freckles, the clear eyes. 'Another day, then we're off.'

'See how you feel in the morning,' Ena said.

But the next morning things were no better. Hal stayed in bed. Ena called, Roland called, his uniform was laid out, his lunch was put in his box and packed in his bag, but he wouldn't move. At five to eight Roland was standing above him. 'Come on.'

'No.'

'I'm coming with you. I'll tell him about that girl, and say I want something done.'

Hal couldn't see how this would help. Harris would just call her to his office, growl at her, send her back; she'd be there, an hour later, doing the same thing.

The other boys had given up on him. They couldn't understand why he got so angry; why he couldn't take a joke. If they ran off with his marbles he'd chase them, and hold them down, and shout in their face. They couldn't understand why he wouldn't talk to them for days, until he seemed to improve, and returned to the group. But mostly, he couldn't understand himself. How people made him mad; how he didn't want to be around them; how all the voices and calling out and shouting and skipping and running and everything just made him feel sad.

'You can't fix things by lying there.' There was no point waiting. Roland pulled back the rugs and Hal grabbed them. He curled into a ball. Roland took hold of his legs and pulled him to the edge of the bed and he kicked. 'Listen, you can't stay home.'

'Why not?'

'It won't fix things.'

'The film starts in a couple of days.'

Sonia stood smiling in the doorway. Hal noticed and shouted, 'Get stuffed!' He threw his pillow at her and she retreated into the hallway.

Roland tried again: legs, body, up. Then they fought over socks, pyjama pants. 'This is ridiculous. How old are you?'

Hal waited, then decided. He leaned forward, picked up his shoes and put them on.

As Roland drove him to school he said, 'One word from her …'

Hal didn't feel like answering. Maybe she was right?

They went in and sat with Mr Harris and Hal managed to apologise, but explain why it had happened. Harris said, 'Well, if you hada told me that in the first place …'

'So what can we do about her?' Roland asked.

'Don't you worry, she'll get a good talking-to. I know our Lisbeth, she's got an opinion on everything.'

By nine-thirty Roland was back in his shed. He sat looking at Mad Ernie: his store, the pub, the dog, even. Something was wrong. He squeezed purple, and dappled it on the shop. Better, he thought. But Ernie was the real problem. He didn't look mad.

How could you really tell the story? How Ernie's dad had struck him (aged seven) with the blunt end of an axe? How, after that, he'd never been quite right. How his dad had said to his mum, 'Righto, he's all yours' – before disappearing forever. How Ernie had been teased at school, and how his mum had removed him, aged ten. How he'd got a job sweeping the floor at the butcher, chopping meat, making sausages, before there was an incident, and the butcher told his mum it'd be better if he wasn't around knives. How he'd had jobs at the sawmill, down the mines, cooking at the Commercial, but how they'd all ended the same way ('For everybody's safety, Mrs S'). But how, when Mr Graetz, the provision store owner, had died, the will was read and there in black and white: 'My store, all the stock, land, yards and c., to Ernie Smith (on his 18th birthday)'.

Some said Ernie was Graetz's son (although his mum laughed). Graetz, the life-long bachelor, had heard and listened. A store would be good for the boy. He could use the till to add up and Lena, the shopgirl, knew what to order when.

Roland almost wished he could write all this down. But he'd chosen canvas, so people would have to work it out for themselves. He turned on the bar radiator and left it in front of the painting while he went in for a cup of tea – to tell Ena about the interview with Mr Harris.

When he returned he said goodbye to Ernie, laid him on brown paper and wrapped him, thrice, before securing him with string. Then he found a pencil and wrote: 'P. McKeever, Leicester Galleries, Bloomsbury Square, London, WC1A'. He stood him beside the other nine paintings he'd send this afternoon. There was a tenth, James in front of the church at Osmond Hill, but he didn't want to sell it. He'd managed a good likeness – something that words couldn't match. He supposed this was the other side of the coin. Paintings said nothing, but they said everything.

Then, it all started again. He placed a canvas on the easel. Taped a sketch (four boys in front of a ruined house) onto the top corner.

Picked up a charcoal stick, studied the shape of the house, and attempted to transfer it. A few tentative lines. No good. Rubbed them out and tried again. Sat back. He just didn't feel like art. If art was concentration, then his life was all obligation and interruption. He could hear Mary's vacuum, Sam in his shed, Ena's mixer.

He noticed the old book from Osmond Hill on the bench. It was covered in dust and webs. He picked it up, cleaned it off and opened to a page he'd marked. And read what he thought he remembered, and knew, now more than ever: '… a child squatting full of sadness launches a boat as fragile as a butterfly in May.' The picture started forming in his head: the boy in the drunken boat, marvelling at the jungle. Like everything after this day would be some sort of anticlimax, the worst sort of disappointment.

Roland heard footsteps in the drive and knew right away. He went to the door, shielding his eyes from the brightness. 'What yer doin'?'

He followed Hal into the house. Ena heard them and came into the entry porch. 'What you doin' home?' she asked.

Hal turned on them. 'Right across the yard: "Schizo!" I told yer.' He walked down the hall, into his room, and slammed the door.

'Bugger it,' Roland said, walking back into his shed. 'We'll deal with it when we get back.'

Hal avoided the ten-thirty cuppa. He went into the backyard, sat on the grass and watched the hens searching for feed. One was lame. At first she hopped, and he thought it was funny, but then she just stood looking at him. He picked up a piece of bark and threw it at her. She didn't move. And again. So he went into the yard, and the drum where they kept the pellets, and scooped a cup full and emptied it in front of her. The other chooks ran over but he shooed them. He stood and waited, watching her peck at the plum-stone, chicken-bone dirt.

He went looking for Sam, and found him in his sleep-out. 'What you doin'?'

Sam was sitting on his bed, hunched over a table, clutching a paintbrush. 'Tinting.'

Sam had cut the photo finishes from the paper. He'd piled them up, and now he was hand-tinting them, mainly the jockeys' colours. He knew each combination, every dot, every stripe, every colour. But it wasn't just this. The jockeys themselves were tinted peach, the saddles bark-brown, the grass a wash of lime. He'd written legends and stuck them on the bottom: 'Apache Cloud (2nd), Miss-a-sis (3rd) ...' Eventually they'd join the others hanging around the house.

'This here, this is Bedwellty Viking.'

Hal sat down on the bed beside him. 'Is that the one I rode?'

'No, no.' Sam smiled at him. 'God, we couldn't get you on a horse now. You should stop growing.'

'Well, I'm not gonna be a jockey.'

'No?' He adjusted the glasses on his nose. Then he rinsed his brush, mixed the water with paint, and started again, this time on the boots.

'Why d'you paint them?' Hal asked.

'Why not?'

'Doesn't look real.'

'Your dad's paintings, do they look real?'

'That's different.'

'How?'

'Just is. He's an artist.'

'So am I.'

'No, you're not. You're a ...' He didn't know exactly what Sam was: an old man who hung around the track, a strapper, a clocker, advice-giver, growler, shouter – anything that needed to be done or said in Cheltenham.

Sam said, 'It's so I can remember the races. One day I'll grow senile, and I won't remember, and I'll be able to look and remind myself.' He finished the boots, rinsed, and started on the horses.

'What's *senile*?'

'That's them old fellas that just sit there staring at the ceiling, and you think they've gone back to their childhood. Like babies.'

Hal had never seen anyone like this. 'Do they cry?'

'Sometimes.'

'And wet their pants?'

'Yes, they do that, too. My theory is, they're remembering, all day. Like when they were kids, runnin' about teasing chooks.'

'I don't tease chooks.'

'Didn't say you do. They're with their mums and dads, who are long dead, and they're eating tea, ploughing fields, all kind of things.'

Hal didn't think this sounded bad.

'But the problem is, Prince Hal,' and he squeezed his knee, 'that's *all* they do. There's no comin' out of it. So they don't even know who's around.'

'That'd be the worst.'

'What?'

'You know, bein' there, but not knowing.' He thought of Sonia – even she had her uses. 'And Mum and Dad ...'

'That's why you make the most of it while you can.'

'And when do you go senile, Sam?'

'Not everyone does. But it wouldn't start till you're at least seventy.'

Seventy? That gave him a good sixty years. So, there was no point worrying yet. But his dad, he might be senile in twenty-five years. 'Better pull my socks up.'

'Eh?'

'If Dad was senile and he didn't know I was there, and the last time he'd seen me I'd ...'

Sam messed his hair. 'Don't worry, your dad won't go senile.'

'How do you know?'

'Just do.' He placed a cutting in front of him and handed him a brush. 'Get busy. If I'm senile, you can show them to me.'

Hal painted the grass and purple hills, the horses, the saddles.

Sam said, 'Heard you had a bad day?'

'She's such a bitch.'

'She called you a name?'

But he didn't want to repeat it. He didn't want Sam thinking he was schizo, senile, stupid, or even bad. He wanted him to think he was still Hal, and always would be. 'They won't do nothin' about her,' he said.

'No one's gonna fix yer problems for you. You gotta fix 'em yerself.'

Hal rinsed his brush. 'How's that?'

'This girl, she's a bit trashy?'

'Yes.'

'So, you do the same. You say, "Good morning, Trash." She's probably quite common. Making up for something she's not happy about. So you say, "You can call me (whatever it is) cos I understand what's going on at home." Then she'll say, "What?" Then you say, "Having to live in a shed with your fifteen brothers and sisters."'

Hal smiled, thought about it, and then said, 'I'm not going back to school.'

'No? Gonna be a movie star?'

'It's just a small role.'

'That's how it starts. Errol Flynn, his first movie he was a barman.'

'Was he?'

Well, he might've been, Sam thought. He checked his apprentice's work. 'And you'll never come and visit me. You'll be in Hollywood, with all those stars, and you'll forget.'

Hal looked up. 'No, I won't Sam. You don't forget people cos you make a film. That's stupid.'

'Yes, it is. Stupid, eh?'

Hal noticed a bullet casing on the ledge above Sam's bed. He reached up, retrieved it and studied it. 'Where'd you get this?'

'A souvenir.'

That was it. The bullet wasn't to be discussed.

'Of what?'

'France.'

'When you fought there?'

Sam wished he'd never got it out, never kept it. 'Yes.'

'It's never been fired.'

'No.' He guessed there was no avoiding it. 'Look on the rim. See, it's been struck.'

'But it never went off?'

'No, that's why I'm sitting here talking to you.'

Hal didn't get it.

'I went into this blown-up café, and I'm searching about, and this Fritz comes around the corner with his rifle pointed at my head, pulls his trigger, nothing. So I take out me knife, jump on him and …'

'What?' Hal asked.

'You don't need to know.' He reclaimed the bullet and put it in a bedside drawer. 'Just keep it, to remind me.'

'Like the horses?'

'Sort of.'

'But what happened?'

'It's not a movie. I'm not Errol Flynn.'

'What did he look like, when he looked at you?'

'What's it matter?' Sam returned to the horses, but then felt bad, and put down his brush. 'He probably had a sister, too, and a niece, and a kid like you, living next door.' He could hear his voice going, like when he had a cold. 'And every day you wonder about that, Hal. And you feel really rotten … rotten.' He took a moment then picked up his brush and continued. 'After the war I tried to find out who he was, so I could write, and explain, or maybe say sorry. But I never had any luck.'

The sound of brushes being rinsed.

It made sense. Why Sam never talked about the war. Perhaps he just sat wishing the bullet hadn't misfired. That way he wouldn't have had to feel bad every day.

Later, Hal went to his room, lay on the bed and stretched out with his hands behind his head.

'Pretty blue eyes,' he heard Sonia say.

He sat up, moved to the front window and saw Sonia and Thea sitting together, studying a copy of *Photoplay*.

You better give that back, he wanted to say to his sister. But didn't. It was too good an opportunity. If he listened long enough he'd hear something she didn't want him to know.

It was obvious she'd stolen it. The magazine was Shirley's one treat. Trev had bought them for her. They came all the way from America, and now she had them sent by air mail. Mary moaned about the expense, but Sam said it was alright, everyone needs something to take their mind off Pennington.

Thea said, 'And her lips.'

'They're not natural,' Sonia said.

'Why?'

'They're too red. Someone's painted over them.'

Thea looked carefully. Sonia was probably right, but she was still Elizabeth Taylor, and she could do no wrong. She was marrying Nick Hilton and they were honeymooning on the Riviera. 'Imagine that,' she said.

'It's close to London.'

Thea wouldn't have been surprised if Sonia had made up everything about having lived in London. She was prone to fantasy.

Hal kept silent. All very boring, but he knew, if he waited. Soon it would turn to boys, and Thea wouldn't be able to help herself. It would all come out.

Mr Carey walked past and said hello to them. 'You must be very excited,' he said to Sonia.

'Oh, I don't know,' she replied. 'I'm growing tired of London.' She wasn't Sonia Griffin; she was Liz Taylor in a wedding dress, a lace veil over her head, white gardenias in her hand.

'And I hear Hal's actin' in a film. Who'd a guessed?'

'It's only a small part.'

Not that small, Hal wanted to say. Jealous. But like a good infantryman, you couldn't give your position away.

'I'll keep an eye on the house,' Carey said, and passed, mumbling. None of them were quite right. The husband, stuck in the shed till all hours; the boy, on the roof; the snooty girl. Ena was okay, but she had a lot to deal with.

'Hal might be in here soon,' Thea said, flicking back through *Photoplay*.

'Unlikely.'

'Why?'

'It's not a *Hollywood* film. Just some people from England.' She studied the New Hollywood Diet, with full plans for safe reducing exercises.

'Has he gone nuts lately?'

'What do you mean?'

'You know, like he did at school.'

Sonia didn't want to talk about it. 'He just gets the shits on.'

Thea wasn't so sure. 'That Dylan kid, Hal really let him have it, didn't he?'

Hal had guessed it was common knowledge. He could tell from the way people watched him as he got around, followed him until he was out of sight, and mumbled things to each other as he went.

Sonia didn't answer. Dylan Brook, and his little gang of inbreds. 'He's an arsehole, isn't he?'

'Who?'

'Dylan.'

'But he got away with it, eh?' Thea said.

Sonia remembered: Dylan (with a black eye, front tooth broken) standing in front of three hundred kids at morning assembly. Mr Saxby hitching his pants and saying, 'Righto, who was it?'

Everyone standing silent in a sign of anti-Dylan solidarity. Saxby had gone up and down the rows, stopped in front of Hal (he knew, it was always Griffin), and even a few of Dylan's henchmen, but they weren't talking. Chances are things would change, and you didn't want to be left in the wrong camp.

But Hal had got away with it. Dylan wouldn't say the S word again. And there was the warning, to anyone who was thinking of spreading it around.

'Sonia!' It was Ena, from the kitchen. When she shouted, Burleigh Avenue knew what she wanted.

'Hold on,' Sonia said. She stood and went inside.

Hal watched as Thea studied the magazine, thought about it, then took out a pen and drew. She started on Betty Hutton: horns, a moustache, wrinkles; Jeanne Crain's little boy: a fountain of spew from his mouth, landing in his mother's face.

'You better not do that,' Hal said.

Thea looked at the flywire. She could see his outline.

'It's Shirley's.'

'So what?' And she continued. Janet Leigh: fangs, and snot dribbling from her nose.

'She loves her magazines. She keeps them in covers.'

But Thea didn't stop. 'It's just a laugh. She won't mind.'

'She will.' He came out of his room, the house, approached her and took the magazine. 'She gets them from America.'

'So what. She's a monster.'

Sonia was behind him. He showed her the magazine. She noticed the pen in Thea's hand. 'Why'd you do that?'

'Cos it's Shirley's. You're the one saying …' But she realised something had changed.

Sonia took her friend by the arm and led her down the drive, under the arch that had become an artery between families, next door. 'Shirley!' Inside, past a confused Mary, busy stirring apricots on the stove, and into Shirley's room. She was on her bed, horrified to see all of them, even Hal, in her doorway.

Sonia threw the magazine on her bed. 'Look what she did.'

Shirley didn't understand. 'How did you get it?' she asked Thea.

'You left it in my room,' Sonia said.

Shirley leafed through the pages, noticed the drawings, and looked up. 'Why?'

Thea tried to smile. 'It was just a joke.'

'It wasn't a joke,' Sonia said to her.

Mary was behind them in the hallway, her arms crossed. She wanted to slap this girl, but was overcome with something stronger: Sonia, at last, growing up.

Thea took coins from her pocket and threw them on the bed. 'There, happy?'

'No, she's not,' Sonia said. 'You can't get old issues.'

Shirley didn't care about the magazine. She was trying to work out why Sonia had brought Thea into her room. Why she hadn't drawn in it, too, and left it somewhere for her to find.

Thea turned on her friend. 'You're such a bitch!' She stormed from the house, slamming the door. Sonia sat on the bed. She picked up the magazine and flicked through, seeing how much damage had been done. 'You didn't leave it in my room.'

Mary waited; Hal backed into the hallway.

'I took it when you were out.'

She apologised to Mary, who just said, 'The fruit's burning,' and left. Hal followed her.

Sonia could feel her heart racing. 'She's a bitch,' she said.

Shirley smiled. Sam had told her it would happen, but she'd just have to wait. People had to work these things out for themselves. 'Pity,' she said. 'It was Liz Taylor's wedding.'

'I don't reckon she's all that good looking,' Sonia said.

'No?'

'Look, Esther Williams, she's got the perfect proportions.'

James was in the driveway at 4 am. Roland brought out the cases and tried to squeeze them all in the boot, but they wouldn't fit. So they left it open, tied down with string. Mary came out in her dressing gown. She'd pre-cut a slab of sultana cake and wrapped it in foil. Ena thanked her and smelt it. 'The flight's a good five hours,' she told her, and showed her a thermos of soup, and one of tea.

'Can you move about?' Mary asked.

'Not unless you have to.'

Sam and Shirley had come out, too. They stood together, watching, like the world was about to end and there was nothing they could do about it. Sam said the tea wouldn't taste the same every morning, and Ena told him it was only six weeks. He said that was still a fair whack.

Hal, saying his goodbye to the hens, realised it was all because of him. The four layers of clothes, the jam-roll underpants and shampoo wrapped in plastic; the yawns and bleary eyes – all for him to be John McCabe. The cold morning and black sky and Pennington-as-a-hole-in-space, sucking up any noise in the pre-rooster dawn. The water turned off, the note for the milkie: 'None for 6 weeks pls.'

They said goodbye, and Mary cried, and Shirley gave Sonia a *Photoplay*. Sam told them not to worry, the place would be safe. He had the key and he'd check every day and call if anything was wrong.

They drove north to the airport, on the edge of the city. The streets were almost deserted. 'Never seen it like this,' Hal said, squeezed up against the window.

'Best time,' James replied.

'Any word from London, call me,' Roland said. 'It's the Commercial, Second Street, Kalgoorlie.'

'Don't worry, I got it.'

Hal agreed with James. He liked the world like this: the stoplights that stopped no one, and made you wait, regardless. The closed shops, some with a light left on, mannequins still pretending to play tennis. Someone else's milkie, the baker, even a police car. When it was gone, James drove through a red light.

'I must admit,' James said. 'I am jealous.'

'What, you wanna be an actor?' Roland said.

'No, yer exhibition.'

'Nothin' stoppin' you.'

On the outskirts of the city, where houses stopped and market gardens began, an old man was already out on his tractor, working up a paddock.

'Least Bell's proud of yer,' James said.

Roland didn't reply. He watched how the tractor's lights cut through the last of the darkness.

'It was good we went, eh?'

'Yes,' Roland said. 'He didn't look well.' Their old teacher, Paul Bell, sitting up in bed; his gaunt face and hollow eyes. They'd sat beside him and James had told him Roland was headed to London.

Roland had felt guilty. Surely they should talk about something else. 'I got a show at Leicester Gallery.'

'Ah, they're very good,' Paul managed, before slipping back into his pillow. 'Don't let them take too much. They'll try for fifteen per cent, but five'll do 'em.'

Both men knew they were limited in what they could say. It wasn't like you could talk about treatments or cures. It was past that.

'This is where I wanted to be,' Paul said. 'See, look how the light falls on the ground, from that elm.' And he showed them the view from the window. 'If I could paint it I would. I always envied the impressionists. That's the only way you can paint light.' And he kept studying the elm.

'I dunno, I reckon you've done a decent job,' James said. 'I wouldn't be no good without what you …' He stopped, realising it sounded too much like a eulogy.

Roland was more pragmatic. 'Problem is, the world moved on.'

'Yes, it did,' Paul agreed. 'You had to find your own way, didn't you, Griff?'

'Yes.'

'You couldn't borrow … I don't think I borrowed.'

'No. That's why you're hanging in, how many galleries?'

Paul had smiled and said, 'They'll soon take you down once yer dead. Still, it doesn't bother me. Whether it lasts. Nothing really lasts, does it, Griff?'

'Not forever.'

'Cos you only do it for yerself, no one else. In a way, it's just being selfish.'

'That's what Ena reckons,' Roland said. 'Says I should spend more time with the kids.'

Paul had nodded his head, but even this seemed to tire him. 'Yes, that's right. You should. Unless you know why you're really doing it.'

Roland wondered what Paul had meant by that: *why you're really doing it*. He had no idea. Except that a man had to do something to stop himself going mad. He could still feel Paul's hand on his – guiding him. That made him just as much a father as his own. Which meant it was all happening again – dad in his bed, bubbling skin, calling for tea. It seemed cruel. That men (no matter how well, or smartly, or bravely they'd conquered the world) could be reduced to piles of flesh and bone. And that they wouldn't rage or roar anymore, or correct you, even. That they wouldn't get angry or short-tempered or impatient about anything. That, after rushing to get everything done, now they just sat waiting.

They arrived at the airport as the sun nudged above the horizon. As they got out, Hal could smell the kerosene. He walked to the wire fence and saw a TAA DC-3. Sonia joined him. 'Do they let you go to the toilet?'

'No,' James said, behind them. 'You gotta cross your legs for six hours.'

She looked at her mum.

'Course you can go to the toilet.'

They went into the terminal and James helped Roland with the cases. It wasn't busy: just a few families, men in suits, a younger man with a surfboard. The pilots emerged from a side room. Hal sat back, admiring their uniforms. *A pilot.* What better job! He watched how they walked, opened the door to the tarmac, arrived at the plane and climbed the stairs. To think, those two men would lift that lump of steel into the air, guide it across the desert and land it in Perth. 'I might be a pilot,' he said to his dad.

Roland smiled. 'You're not gonna be an actor?'

'No.'

'So, why we doin' all this?'

He shrugged. 'Cos Aunty Gwen asked.'

The engines started. Hal stood, walked to the window, and pressed his face against it. He turned back to them. 'I reckon it's time.'

Roland swapped seats and found his sketch book in his bag, and started. A line for the railway, and the road, and some sort of lake that had bled into the desert. There was an artery leading away from it, and capillaries, and each of these formed a sort of floret. Despite all this, no one else bothered looking out. Sonia said, 'It just goes on and on.'

'It's a desert,' Ena replied, glad she'd persuaded Roland to fly.

Hal watched his dad. Even now, he thought. Even in a plane, with free biscuits, with take-offs and landings, with the propellers humming a few feet away – even now.

Roland was excited. The land was changing. It had blue-tongue shingles with interlocking plates which were white on the outside and brown in the middle. He could see clouds of dust lifting where animals, cattle perhaps, were moving. 'See, look at that,' he said to his son.

Hal was now busy with his script. 'What?'

'Cows.'

Hal didn't bother looking. 'Can you test me?' he asked.

'Just a minute.'

Red dirt, and spinifex in half-moon crescents. This was real country, minus its gins and mad storekeepers. It had nothing to do with people.

'Dad!' Hal said.

'Okay.'

Hal put the script between them. 'So, we follow our mum into this tent we gotta live in. She's looking around. She's not impressed.'

Ena was listening. Women always followed, she thought, and tried to make the unworkable work.

'Right, you be my mum.'

Roland squinted to see. '"Right, you kids, over there."'

'"Whatawe sleep on, the stretcher?"'

'"Yes."'

'"We thought there was gonna be a house."'

'"Stop whining and get yer stuff. You can put it in the dresser."'

Sonia gave Ena her *Photoplay* and looked back. *'Aw, John, what do we gotta live here for?'*

'Don't interrupt!' Hal said. He saw through the curtain: the captain coughed, sat up and coughed again. Was he choking? Had he eaten anything?

'Come on,' Roland said.

*'Carn, John!'* Sonia added.

What if he blacked out? What if they both did? The plane plummeting, heading for the red dirt. You couldn't survive. What if you wanted to change your mind and get out?

'Hal?'

Hal closed the script. 'That's enough.'

The desert lost its features. Roland sat with his pad in his lap and noticed his son, busy watching the pilot. Paul was saying, 'You only do it for yourself.'

Hal turned to him. 'You gonna paint the Nullarbor?'

'Na ... there's nothin' down there.' He put the pad away.

Mary had never believed in dreams, crystal balls or cards, just God. But this dream, about six weeks old, was different. She'd been walking along the road with Sam, and they'd looked up and seen someone's featherless cockatoo sitting on a powerline. There were shrikes all around it – diving, flapping their wings midair as they tried to scare it away. It had just sat motionless, refusing (or unable) to move, and (seemingly) consuming itself, working away at its skin with its beak.

Mary had seen it for what it was: Shirley, out in the world, after her and Sam had gone. And she'd said, 'That's what worries me the most.'

'What?' Sam had asked.

'Where she'll go.'

He'd just shaken his head. 'It'll work out.'

'No, why should it?' she'd asked.

Mary and Shirley worked on the apricots: out of the pot into jars, an hour to cool, the wax paper and airtight lids. Syrup had burned on the stove and dried on the floor. They walked through it. There was no point cleaning anything until it was done.

Shirley said, 'It would've been good.'

Mary was stirring the pot. 'You'll get your go. They were all paid for.'

Shirley knew this was the case, but that didn't make it any easier. She was most jealous of the plane trip. Or perhaps the drive to Kalgoorlie (all dry country, she'd looked it up in her atlas), the wildflowers, the small towns. 'She's lucky. Gettin' to stay in London.'

Mary didn't reply. Who cared about London? All you needed was a house, a bit of land, the giving and receiving of love, the races (all day), people happy to potter about. 'The more you get,' she said.

Shirley hated this. 'It's alright for you.'

'You're not even thirteen. You'll get there.'

Shirley felt faint and missed her step. She dropped a jar and it smashed on the lino; the apricots floated in their syrup; she moved, stepped on one, and slipped. She held the side of the table.

'Shirley?' Mary said.

She felt hot, her heart racing, and then everything went dark. When she woke she was lying on the lounge. 'Mum?'

But then it was dark again.

Sam stood watching his sister taking her pulse. 'I can go next door, call an ambulance.'

'Wait.'

They both knew: the inflammation moving from joint to tissue; her enlarged heart, working to get blood around her body.

'We shouldn't wait,' Sam said. He took the key from its spot, jogged out the back door, through the arch, and stopped in the driveway. He looked at Roland's car. Yes, yes, yes. Went to the Griffins' back door and opened it. Into the kitchen and found the keys on the bench. Back out, opening the car, neutral, the key in the hole, turn. It started first time, chugged, and waited for him. 'Right.' He went back into his house. 'Ready to go.' There was no time to explain.

'You called?'

'I'll have her there in five minutes.'

Mary wasn't so sure. 'Call the ambulance.'

'Come on, five minutes.'

He picked up his niece. Could feel the muscles in his back pulling, one causing pain, but it would heal. He carried her out the back door, across the yard, stood beside the car. 'Get the door.'

Mary was still at the back door. 'I dunno, Griff won't be happy.' But she came over and opened it.

'He won't care.' He placed Shirley on the back seat.

'I gotta turn off the apricots.' She ran back inside. Sam waited. Forever, it seemed. 'Mary!' he called. 'What yer doin'?'

She reappeared carrying her handbag, still wearing her apron and slippers. She sat on the back seat, laid Shirley across her lap and said, 'Don't speed.' She pushed the hair from her daughter's face. This is why you had to stay home: so you could deal with the little disasters. What good was the Royal Albert Hall, or Turner's clouds, if your heart didn't tick?

A minute later they were driving down Torrens Road.

'How is she?' Sam asked.

Shirley was looking up at her mum. 'I felt …'

'Ssh.'

'Let me sit up.'

Sam swerved around a truck, and re-entered his lane.

'Slow,' Mary said. 'She's alright.'

He didn't hear this. He was stuck behind another car. Changing lanes didn't help; a Vauxhall drove beside the first vehicle, forming a barrier. He tooted his horn but neither moved. 'What's wrong with these people?'

'Sam.'

It's the heart, he wanted to say. You can't muck around. Shirley was the sum of his small world. They should've done something before now. Medication? What did that hopeless doctor say?

She was only ten. She came into his sleep-out and sat on his bed. 'Can I tell you something?'

'What's that?' (He'd been cutting his nails, but stopped.)

'It's about Hal.'

'Go on.'

'And his friends. They went past, and Hal started singing …'

> *Don't you laugh as the hearse goes by,*
> *For you might be the next to die …*

'What did he sing?' he'd asked.

'There was ten of them. I don't understand why he'd ...'

*They wrap you up in a big white sheet,*
*From your head down to your feet ...*

Sam'd said, 'Boys that age don't think about anything. They're idiots. Even Hal, he's an idiot.'

To Shirley, this seemed at odds with all the attention Sam showed him. If he was an idiot, why did Sam take him to the track, or help with his homework?

'You gotta understand. That's not really him talking. It's some monster. A boy monster.'

'Can you tell him to stop?'

He'd started clipping his nails again. 'I could, but you gotta learn to ignore it.'

Hal had come into the sleep-out the next day and asked, 'Can I go with you in the morning, Sam?'

'No, I don't think so, Hal.'

'Why not?'

'Going to the track is a treat. You gotta earn it. What were you singing?'

'When?'

'At school? With your mates? To Shirley?'

'I dunno ... just some song someone had made up. Ben, he was singing it, and I joined in.'

'You gotta think how Shirley feels.'

'I know.'

'And you, there's the home Hal and the school Hal. But it doesn't work like that, does it?'

'No.'

And he'd left it there (agreeing to take him to the track the next day, and Shirley saw them leaving, and couldn't work it out).

Sam slipped between the cars, sped up, and continued along Torrens Road.

'Uncle Sam, I'm okay,' Shirley said.

'I'm still under the limit.' He changed up, the gears crunched, and he tried again.

'Don't ruin his car,' Mary said.

'You wanna drive?' Sometimes she made him angry. It was like he'd been put on earth to solve her problems. Everyone's. He noticed a red light on the dash. Fuel. 'Shit.'

Aunty Gwen met them at Perth airport. She led them through the terminal, the city, along the Great Eastern Highway, through towns full of mad Ernies and nuns in too-hot habits. Roland asked her to stop at a weighbridge that was really a shed. He photographed the children in front of it. Then, to the roadhouse, where they ate shepherd's pie and drank rust-coloured tea. There were dozens of flies, sauce stains on the tablecloth, and two old men talking about tillers.

An afternoon of wheatbelt that stretched to the horizon, fences that had no purpose but to separate things in people's minds. The farmers had left a few trees, but only because it was high or low ground, too rocky, too close to the road. Apart from that it was just blue sky.

'You could paint it,' Gwen said, clutching the wheel, shooing flies.

Ena said, 'This'd be no good. It's too pretty for Griff.'

Hal had half a script on his and his sister's leg. '"Ladies and gentlemen, this is my sister, Lucie McCabe. She wants to play a song to thank yers."'

'"Not here,"' Sonia said.

'"Come on, they paid fer yer pianer."' Looking up again, he asked Gwen, 'Do you think he'll be happy with that?'

'I reckon that'll be close enough.'

During the late afternoon the wheat receded. It left roasted soil, deep brown, losing its colour. There was head-high mallee, then spinifex, then the dug-up landscape around the town. Skeletons and poppets of the gold age, steam and smoke of working machinery, men, real, with their overalls three sizes too big. The smell of redgum stumps and lanolin for sunburn, and the vapours of hope that kept the town alive.

They checked into the Exchange Hotel. There was an all-round balcony where people had hung shirts and shorts, a proud little tower with a turret with a flag. Hal found the door, climbed up and looked out over Kalgoorlie. There was a wedding-cake post office and hotels with names like Metropole, Piccadilly and Inland City. A train crawled around the edge of town, spreading coal and dust over pegged petticoats. The little tin cottages and their Mr and Mrs McCabes surviving in hot rooms with yards full of gold-less quartz.

'Hal!' he heard his mother cry.

'Up here.'

She came out, and stood at the bottom of the steps he'd climbed. 'Get down this instant.'

'You can see everything.'

'Now!'

As they walked down the stairs she said, 'You can't just run off.'

He lifted his leg over the banister, ready to slide.

'Off!' She held his arm and pulled him, a tread at a time, towards the dining room. 'Now, Mr Wallace has arrived.'

'Who's he?'

'A very famous comedian. He's playing the stage manager, remember?'

He couldn't. 'Do I have any lines with him?'

'No.' She straightened his jacket. 'Try and make a good impression. The whole country used to listen to him on the radio. *The Boy from Bullamakanka*.' She leaned down and pulled up his socks.

They went into the dining room. Aunt Gwen, Roland, Sonia and George Wallace were sitting around a table. The great man was bent over, a rug around his chest and neck, protecting his sandpapered face, his grey whiskers, his bloodshot eyes.

'Here he is,' Gwen said, standing, fetching Hal and presenting him to Wallace.

'This one plays the piano?' he asked.

'No,' she replied. 'That's his sister, Lucie. Hal is playing her brother, John.'

Wallace didn't seem to get it. 'Lucie, that's the one I met earlier?'

'Yes, Teresa.'

He messed Hal's hair and said, 'I had a dog looked like you.'

Hal wasn't sure. 'What sort was he?'

Wallace didn't reply. He returned to his soup. 'Loada fuckin' salt in this,' he said.

Gwen sat Hal in front of his own soup. They all ate and watched Wallace, waiting for a line, a lyric, a raised eyebrow, anything. Most of the other tables were empty. A husband-and-wife set sat silently eating. The bread rolls seemed a fair substitute for conversation.

Wallace looked at Hal. 'What other films yer done?' he asked.

'This is my first.'

Wallace smiled. 'Make it yer last.'

'Why?'

'You'll see. I did one called *The Rats of Tobruk*. Stuck out in the desert for a month. Conjunctivitis the whole time. And you know what they paid me?'

Hal waited. They all waited.

'Two hundred quid. And yet Charles Chauvel was one of the richest men in Australia.' He gave up on the soup and pushed it away. 'That's what I'm sayin' ... John, was it?'

'Hal.'

'When yer a performer, everyone wants a bite of the cherry.'

There was a long silence as the roasts were brought out and laid in front of them: two slices of wafer-thin meat, a pile of boiled cabbage and carrots, a single potato, floating. 'Disgrace,' Wallace said.

The waitress asked for an autograph but he told her to come back later, after he'd gone.

The meat wasn't as bad as it looked, but all flavour had been boiled from the vegetables. 'To think this is where she came,' Aunt Gwen said.

'Who?' Wallace asked.

'Lucie McCabe. When she was a kid. To play the piano.'

Wallace noticed the Bösendorfer sitting in the corner. 'Bet it doesn't get used much. Fuckin' miracle, isn't it? A concert pianist, from this.'

Hal wondered about the George Wallace his mother had mentioned. Maybe he was a hen, waiting on his perch for sunrise. Maybe it took the smell of makeup, or lights on his face, to tempt him out.

'That's the beauty of the story,' Gwen said. 'She overcame everything.'

Wallace couldn't see how anyone could overcome the boiled carrots. He turned to Roland. 'You the boy's dad?'

'Yes. Roland Griffin.' He stood, leaned over the table, and offered his hand. 'I'm a big fan of your radio show.'

'Griffin ... not the painter?'

'Yes.'

'I seen some of your stuff. Outback, isn't it?'

'Yes.'

'Dogs rootin' fence posts?'

'Well, there's one with a dog, but he's not actually – '

'Saw that in the gallery. Liked that one.' And at last, he smiled. 'You in the war?'

'No. Detached retina.'

'Ah. Me neither. But they made me sing.'

'Of course,' Ena said. '"A Brown Slouch Hat"?' And she began. *It's a brown slouch hat with the side turned up, and it means the world to me …*

Wallace was intrigued by Hal. 'Listen, son, we should have a few lines.'

'It's a pity you don't,' Gwen said.

'We can come up with something. You could steal me shoes, Hal, and we could have a bit of business?'

Gwen wanted to be clear. 'Just the scene at the concert, George.'

'Come on, that's not enough. Me and Hal. What do you reckon, boyo?'

'I reckon.'

'I go outa me room, you come in, take me pants, then me shirt, then me singlet? I'm too shickered to know.'

Gwen drew breath. He smiled at her, and sang, '*Don't you thrill as young Bill passes by?* That's what they want, in't, Gwennie?'

She kept working on her potato.

Then he said something else to Hal. Hal couldn't understand him. 'Pardon?'

Wallace cleared his throat. 'It's not the grog, John.'

'Hal.'

'I was born in a tent in the middle of winter. Fuckin' freezin'. Me mum and dad had left me with a nurse – an old sour-faced number. A Scot. She gets it in her head to feed me hot porridge. *Hot.*'

Ena winced. 'It's lucky you lived.'

'Perhaps.' He laid his fork on his plate. 'Maybe not. I wouldn'ta hadta eat this.' And pushed it away.

Roland bit his lip. 'George, I remember seeing your first film. Bloody funny.' He turned to Hal. 'Mr Wallace was a stagehand and he fancied this girl. What was her name, George?'

Wallace stuck with Hal. 'But if she hadn'ta fed me porridge, things mighta been different.' He turned to Sonia now. 'You're not Lucie, are yer?'

'No. I'm Hal's sister.'

Wallace tried Hal again. 'I don't blame her.'

'Who, Mr Wallace?'

'The nurse. She didn't know no better. We were poor. That country out past Aberdeen, it was like a desert back then.'

The waitress appeared beside the table. 'Is one of youse Roland Griffin?'

'Yes,' Roland said.

'Phone call.'

He turned to Ena, but she couldn't think who it was. He followed the waitress out, leaving the rest of them to push around the remains of the roast until he returned and sat down.

'Who was it?' Ena asked.

'Sam.'

'Nothing's wrong?'

'They borrowed the car.'

Wallace, unconcerned, asked Gwen about dessert.

Roland shook his head. 'Cleaned up the gutter. Took out the front wheel. Had to get it towed.'

To Hal it was all too distant. He was interested in Wallace.

'*His Royal Highness*,' Wallace said to him.

'Sorry?'

'My first film. The Poms loved it, but those idiots'd laugh at anything. They'll love this one, won't they, Gwennie?'

'They will, George.'


The next morning the director, Michael Grady, stood inside a tent with his co-writer, Barbara, and Hal. She studied a script on a card table, crossed out lines, asked Michael for his opinion, and finally turned to Hal. 'Would that be okay?'

He studied the changes. 'I suppose.'

Michael Grady was a big man. It was early, not particularly hot, but he was sweating, wiping his forehead and face with a rag, clearing his throat, and spitting into it. 'I think we should get started,' he said to Hal.

'Okay.' Hal was nervous. Up to now it had just been an idea, an adventure, something to tell people, but now he had to act. He could feel his hands shaking, and he hoped this tremor wouldn't affect his voice.

'Excited?' Michael asked.

'Yep.'

'Just say the lines. Your voice, yer face, that'll do the job.'

Hal wondered what job he meant. To be funny, boyish, brotherish, or just a prop for his soon-to-be-famous sister? *She* was the star – there was no doubt. The way they'd welcomed her the previous evening, given her the biggest room – tea, scones and jam for breakfast. She, Teresa Martin, the eleven-year-old prodigy-in-the-making. She'd stepped out of her car, looked him over and asked, 'Oh, so you're my brother?' She hadn't even waited for an answer before going in.

They walked to the setup: a camera on a dolly; the director of photography, changing lenses; a sound mixer; George, sitting under a piece of rigged canvas, calling out, 'Remember, Hal, yer not meant to look at the camera.'

'I know.'

His parents and Sonia stood at a distance, smiling, his mum indicating he should pull up his pants.

Sonia said, 'Maybe it'll do him some good.'

'What's that mean?' Roland asked.

But she just grinned.

'You're not jealous?'

'Why? I couldn't think of anything worse.'

Roland and Ena smiled.

'I couldn't. I just mean, it might make him, you know, responsible.'

Hal stood next to Teresa. They'd already practised the lines;

walked up the hill, across the road and into the pub where she was to hear her first piano. A young woman was fixing her plaits.

'Can't I have it in a bun?' she asked.

'No. The script says you're rough and ready.'

'But I woulda had a bun.'

'It's what Michael wants.'

Teresa couldn't argue with Michael. But she still thought an eleven-year-old living on the goldfields would've had a bun. She turned to Hal and said, 'What else have you done?'

'Not much.'

'I was in a crowd, for the Manly Players. They did *Oliver Twist*. But I'm gonna do more films.' A film with British Empire could take you far. 'What about you?'

'Perhaps. I was gonna be a strapper.'

She didn't like this lack of ambition. Films were the domain of the serious-minded, the professional. 'You might get famous,' she said, but what she meant was, *she* might. 'What's a strapper?'

'Puts the saddle on a horse, and looks after it.'

'So why you makin' a film?'

'Aunt Gwen reckoned I'd be good.'

Michael Grady told them where to stand. 'Up the hill slowly, like you're looking for a bita gold, or something fun to do.'

There was a creek, and three men panning; a few horses tied up; someone's mother shelling peas on a verandah.

'Remember, when you hear the piano, Teresa, it's like, a revelation. Got it?'

They both nodded. The crew was ready. The camera rolled and Michael called, 'Action.'

They walked up the hill. Teresa stopped, bent over, and showed him a fleck of planted gold. '"D'yer reckon it's worth much?"'

'"Na. Come on, let's find Dad."'

They ran down to the creek. The camera descended beside them.

Hal remembered what he'd been told: stay close; smooth movements. After a few moments he forgot what he was doing. It was like running down Burleigh Avenue, finding a decent tree, climbing it. All you had to remember was the made-up bit: the lines, the fake sister. They arrived at the creek. He said, '"Hey, Jo, you seen Dad?"'

'"No, sorry, John,"' a miner with big whiskers said. '"You two behavin' yerselves?"'

'"Yes, sir. Mum wants him home. Reckons she's feeling crook."'

'"Nothin' serious?"'

'"No, sir. I don't think so, sir. She didn't really say, sir."'

'Cut!' Michael came forward. 'Why do you keep calling him sir?'

'It's in the script, isn't it?'

'No, it's not,' Teresa said. 'It's just, "No, I don't think, she didn't say."'

Hal couldn't see how it was any of her business.

They started again. Back up the hill, down, the same lines, minus the sir. Ena was whispering to Roland. 'Did he get it wrong?'

'It's nerves. That's what happens. They gotta do it over and over. Sometimes a dozen takes.'

Hal muffed another line, and Teresa stopped and said, 'We coulda had this done.'

Hal didn't think a word here or there mattered. Teresa told him what he should've said, and asked, 'There, you got it now? We can't afford to stop again.'

Michael held her shoulder. 'Teresa, you just do your bit, right?'

But she just glared at Hal.


Roland wandered the streets of Kalgoorlie. They'd laid a strip of bitumen in the middle, but it wasn't wide enough for a car. He lined up a shot, framed it in the finder and photographed the street. The corrugated-iron bakery, a blackboard out front: 'Whats not sold by 4 is half price'. A young girl in a dress with puffy shoulders in front of a pram. He could tell it wasn't a baby. Toys, mostly, and a piece of painted cardboard: 'Penny for everything'. Another girl on a bike stopped. She looked into the pram and said, 'They're Ned's,' but the first girl said, 'He'll never know.'

He continued around the corner. A woman with a basket heavy with food. 'Mind if I take your picture?' he asked.

She smiled. 'Why you doin' that?'

'I'm here with the film.'

'Ah.' Her eyes lit up. 'Lucie?'

'Yes.'

'My mum used to play with her.'

'Really?'

'But she reckons, you know,' and she checked the street, just in case, 'she was a real little bitch.'

He took the photo and moved closer. 'That's what the pictures don't tell yer, eh?'

'Spot on. Now everyone will be thinking …' She couldn't bring herself to say it. 'Anyway, I got butter in here, so good afternoon.'

Bits of galvanised iron (different bits, with different sorts of paint) nailed together to make a fence. Another pub, with another wide verandah, although there wasn't a soul to be seen. Two cars were parked out front, so someone must have been drinking. One was parked under a tree but the shade was going the other way.

He looked across the road. A young boy ran along the footpath. He seemed to be crying. The child passed a side road and a car (the only one he'd seen for an hour) had to brake hard to avoid him. He saw his clothes, his face. 'Hal?'

Hal kept running. To the end of the block, around the corner.

Roland followed as fast as he could. 'Hal?'

Hal slowed, stopped, turned and faced his father. 'I'm not going back.'

'What's wrong?'

'She said I was hopeless.' Then he was crying.

A few minutes later they were sitting in the dust, hard up against another iron wall.

'I'm not going back.'

Roland had seen it coming, but hadn't thought it would be so quick. 'You gotta finish your scenes. You got a lotta people depending on you.'

'What do you care anyway?'

'What do you mean?'

Hal wouldn't explain. Some things were so obvious they couldn't be said. 'We were doing this scene,' and he tried to get his breath, 'and she said, "I refuse to work with him. He's hopeless. Hopeless."'

The girl with the pram walked past. It was still full, but she didn't seem bothered.

'You gotta learn to ignore people like that.' Roland noticed the shadows getting longer, warping, like his characters. This was the best time to take photos, but he supposed it could wait until tomorrow. 'You've got to go back.'

'I don't.'

'George won't be happy.'

Nothing.

'You know, he really hates her too. He told me. He said, "The only way to deal with people like that is to be better than them."'

Hal guessed it was a trick, but he didn't mind.

'To upstage them. That's what he said. So that when the film comes out, and they're writing reviews, everyone mentions *you*. *Oh, Hal Griffin, what a talent!*'

Hal almost smiled.

'*The next star to emerge from Australia.*'

'You're just saying that.'

'Without a word of a lie. George reckons you can show her up.

Make her look bad. You know what they say? Revenge is a dish best served cold.'

'You're sayin' it to make me go back.'

'Fine, don't go back.'

Hal studied his father's face. 'That's what George said?'

'Yep.'

'He didn't.'

'Okay, he didn't, but he did. You can't stop her being a cow.' They stood, and started walking back to the set. 'And apparently I don't care about John McCabe?'

Hal felt bad for having said it, but that didn't change the fact. 'You just like your paintings. You don't care what I do.'

'Bullshit.'

'It's true.'

'I care. All those years wiping your bum … I care.'

'You had to do that.'

'And when you broke your arm on Commercial Street, who picked you up and ran all the way to the Emergency Department?'

'You had to do that too.'

Roland put his arm around Hal's shoulder, and Hal allowed it, but he wasn't sure. Not even about Teresa, or George, or Michael, or anyone. People were just magnets, and if you hung spoons from them, they stuck.

# 1956

Although the drive-in had been open for six weeks, there was still a line. Every night. Customlines and Austins snaking a mile down the highway. Ena had suggested they leave early, and Sonia and Hal had said no, because she was always planning for disasters that never happened. But they'd struck a compromise: left home at six for a seven-thirty film. Still, there were plenty of cars, and they had to wait, Hal complaining that Sonia's fat arse was taking up too much room.

'Seems strange,' Roland said.

'What?' Ena asked, opening a thermos of tea.

'Cars are for getting places, not ...'

Shirley came too, because Ena had offered to take her, as no one took her anywhere, which was a pity (Ena said) because Shirley was just about the biggest Gregory Peck fan in the world.

It was a big thrill for everyone. An area that Roland remembered as a knackery, levelled (except for the little hill that made your car stick up), poles with speakers planted every ten feet, and a big, white screen reflecting the lights from the candy bar, although they'd never heard a deli called a candy bar before. A thrill. Driving in, finding a spot beside another car, so that you could look in, see them talking and eating and laughing. Like a little bit of privacy had been given up for a night of entertainment. Little living rooms with wheels, containing the same arguments, hosting the same battles. But that was alright because after a while you felt like no one was there, or were, but had disappeared into the ether of 'Please Dim your Lights' and 'Dagwoods 3 for £1'.

Sonia wasn't convinced that Peck made a good Ahab. 'As if a sea captain would speak like that.'

'They've left half of it out,' Hal said. He was sitting in Dr Bailey's lounge room, Melville on his knee, reading. He was caught up in the great swells, and the search for the whale. Dr Bailey came home early. 'What you reading, Hal?'

Hal showed him.

'You know, Melville's wife thought he was an idiot.'

'How?'

'Told him to get out, earn some money. Then he dies, and years later they find his books in a packing case. Publish them … next thing everyone's reading *Moby Dick*.'

Hal said he didn't think he'd make it far, because Melville used ten words when four would do and a lot of adjectives that sounded impressive, and that made it hard for a kid to understand. Bailey said, 'You've gotta persevere. All of the great writers use big words.'

'Why?'

'Cos they can.'

'Cos they want to sound smart.'

'No. They want to write well. Keep at it, young Arthur. If you don't know a word, look it up.'

So he'd taken the book home, sat, for hours, looking up words like perdition and leviathan, and eventually made it to the end. Told his dad, who ruffled his hair and said, 'You're gonna be a clever boy, Hal.' Like that; in a ruffled hair sort of way. Like his dad didn't really mean it, or care, or take the time to think about what he meant.

Back in the car, Hal said, 'This is just *Moby Dick* for idiots.'

'Pardon us,' Ena said.

'It's not meant to be about the whale, it's about Ahab.'

'What about him?' Roland asked.

'How he goes loopy, because he can't see things for what they are.' The conversation died, the sound of the projector, only a few cars away, and people talking, someone who'd put on a car radio.

Roland thought about Ahab in his drunken boat. He could see his son in his oilskins, holding a harpoon, calling for the whale. The waves tossing him, but him standing tall, determined, eyes scanning the ocean. He thought this might make a good painting; realised it already was – all these colours splashing around on this gigantic canvas someone had erected only a hundred yards from the abattoir. Cattle, finally realising, groans to match the whale, as Gregory Peck with immaculate sideburns launched his harpoon (although it barely scratched the skin).

Ena said, 'What do you think about it, Shirley?'

'Big.' All she offered, although no one was sure if she meant the whale, or the film, lighting up the tube-steel playground beneath the screen, dozens of bored children going up and down the slippery dip, falling from the monkey bars into an ocean of wild oats.

'You read the book?' Hal asked her.

'No.'

'Not surprised.' He sneered. 'I shouldn't have come.'

'Why did you?' Sonia asked.

He just glared at her.

'I mean, apparently you're the expert.'

'What?'

'All those people that saw *your* film. How many? Nineteen? Twenty? Although that's not counting us.'

Hal said, 'At least I made one.'

Sonia just grinned.

'Move yer arse, you got most of the seat.'

'Hal!' Roland said, feeling the night starting to come apart.

'What? I'm squeezed in.'

'You are not!' Sonia said.

'Move.' He pushed his arse against her, and she pushed back. He shoved her, she shoved him. Roland shouted at them, Hal shouted back, got out, said he was going to the candy bar, and walked through the jungle of cars, the eyes of a hundred hot Hillmans flicking on and off every time Peck threw his harpoon. Roland watched him go and said, 'I'll go after him,' but Ena held his hand and said, 'Let him walk it off,' and insisted he watch the film. Which he did, sort of, nudging the beats, as he trembled at fifty leagues' distance and remembered the book from Osmond Hill: the groans of the Behemoth's rutting, the dense Maelstroms. 'He'll do something stupid.'

'Again,' Sonia said.

'Let him go,' Ena insisted. 'You know what will happen.'

Roland had to agree. Hal took a good half-hour to calm down these days, and sometimes more than that. A night spent sleeping on the lawn, under the arbour, and once on the oval at school (Roland had found him, asleep, at three in the morning).

So he waited. Watched all the business in the cabin, the arguments, the dramas, and pretended they were just as bad, or worse, than his own.

Hal didn't care. He knew this place suited people, because people were lazy, and didn't like to think, and needed comfort, and distraction from lives full of two-part epoxy and gas bills. He looked around the candy bar: the drinks, the chocolates (slipped one in his pocket), popcorn (and he took a tub, and walked out, saying, 'I paid the other girl'). Then he stood in the shadow of the building. The light that seemed hot and pink and charged with electricity; the sound of the sea from a speaker that ensured you didn't miss the movie; the posters with their autumn leaves and forbidden planets.

He turned and noticed the girls' toilets, and the way the door was so far ajar you could see in, with the girls' knickers around their ankles, and hear what they said to each other, before standing, flushing, coming out into the night.

Shirley approached, and Hal slipped into a shadow, kept still, as she went into the toilet. He moved around. Looked in. Her little legs, spiky at the ankles, and her panties, all pink and frilly the way Mary made them. He took a few steps forward. 'Hey, Shirley.'

He could hear that she'd stopped pissing. 'Hal?'

'I got a big white whale.'

Voices, from in front of the candy bar. He moved back, pretended to watch the movie, as two women entered the toilet. Soon Shirley came out, and half-ran back to the car.

He smiled. He knew he'd be okay. Poor old Shirley.

The stands at Cheltenham weren't as full as they used to be, when he was a kid, when they came for the gallops. People were losing interest. The number of meetings had been cut – this made him mad. People had to be brought back; careers on the track encouraged. He said to Hal, 'It's easy. You just let it flow.'

Hal wasn't so sure. If he was going to be involved with racing he wanted it to be with horses. The jockey idea had gone out the window when he'd hit six foot, when his arms and legs had stretched beyond anything useful, his head had become a lump that dangled from its scaffold, his feet even, beefsteaks for which his parents had ordered special shoes.

'Keep your eye on the favourite,' Sam said. 'Here, race three, Gypsy.' He showed Hal the form. 'The only horse that might threaten is Jasper. Remember the colours: salmon and black, blue and green. Got it?' Sam studied the horses as they were led to the gates. Hal did the same with the binoculars Sam had given him the previous week, explaining, 'A race caller.'

'Sorry?'

'A race caller. Perfect for you. Ted's retiring next month, and there's no one else. If you can master it, it's a job for life.'

'Don't they need strappers?'

'They need race callers more.'

'It's worth a try,' Roland had said. He couldn't see that Hal (who was struggling at school) would become any sort of intellectual. Management, perhaps. Certainly nothing creative.

Sam had said, 'Listen, come to a few meetings, we'll work on it. If you hate it, nothing lost.'

'So, who's who?' Sam asked.

Hal studied the horses. 'Cavalier, going in now, Gypsy, she's settled, Jasper, Mr Darcy, and what was it, Tinkerbell?'

'Good. Forget the rest. They're all nags. Just get the colours in yer head.'

Hal studied the polka dots and stripes; he thought he had them.

'I'll do the first half,' Sam said, 'then you can take over.'

Hal had a swig of Coke. The mornings were harder now. Sprawled out in bed, he'd often wake to a knock on the window. 'You coming?'

He'd turn over, cover his head. 'I got school.'

'Just for an hour?'

'Maybe tomorrow.' Then he'd hear footsteps down the drive, and feel guilty. He'd run to the front door, open it and call, 'Hold on, I gotta get dressed.'

On the way to the track he'd think of saying, Listen, Sam, I'm not a kid anymore. It's not like it was.

But he couldn't bring himself to say it. Sam was still determined to help him; there were still horses to be timed, washed, exercised. Racing was the world (as it extended across Torrens Road, into Pennington, down Burleigh Avenue). There were other bits (eating, keeping the peace) but mostly it was just horse flesh.

They waited for the last of the horses. Hal asked, 'It's decent money, is it?'

'Yes, yes. I mean, it's not every day, but you pick up other work. For example, I was thinking …' and he took his time, 'if you *did* take it up, I'm gettin' on … you could have my job, timing, in the mornings.'

Hal didn't like the sound of this. 'You been doin' that for fifty years.'

'That's the point. I can't go on forever. I'd still come over, of course. But it'd be your job, and your money. And together with the calling, you could make a decent living.'

It seemed as though Sam was saying, I'll cut off an arm, and you can have it. A leg. Every limb. 'That's a pretty decent offer, Sam.'

'Well, it's just practical. That's the way the world works.'

But Hal knew it was more than this; that Sam would've happily died in the job, if not for him, and his issues.

Sam squeezed his knee. 'I guessed you wouldn't become a painter.'

'Why?'

'Just did. Yer not like yer dad.'

'Why?'

'Just aren't. But that's okay. You gotta be your own man.'

Your own man. That was the problem. Hal felt like there wasn't a lot he'd take from his father. Job, disposition, world view.

'One thing leads to another,' Sam said, as the last of the horses were loaded. 'You could write for the paper, interview jockeys, owners. Work your way up.'

This seemed reasonable. Hal didn't (he believed) have a problem with hard work. He'd mucked out a thousand stables for pocket money, washed horses, even ridden trackwork before the Change. What he didn't get was sitting in a hot classroom trying to solve simultaneous equations, or coming up with nine hundred words about the causes of the Bolshevik Revolution. That didn't seem to lead anywhere.

'You don't have to decide any time soon. You'd probably want to finish school next year. Yer mum and dad'd want that.'

If he could survive that long.

'How are your grades?'

He didn't reply.

'That good?'

'I got a B for English.'

'Right.' Sam was studying the jockeys, the way they sat, how they gripped their whips.

'But I wanna get out.' It wasn't just the grades. 'Bevan Richards. If it wasn't for him …' He knew Sam had heard all of this before.

'You steer clear of him.'

'I try.' But it was hard. The kid who'd goaded him into a fight the previous year. Three-thirty on the mound outside school. A crowd of nearly a hundred cheering them on. Solid hits, too. Fists to the face, ribs, neck. But he'd won. He'd stood up (his face bleeding, a tooth hanging from his mouth) and looked at Richards, lying on the ground. He'd kicked him in the side. This is what had done the damage. Ten minutes later, when everyone had gone, he was still lying there, his face red, bleeding from deep cuts. Hal had leaned over to check him. He'd heard the gurgling. 'Christ.'

A man from a house across the road had come over, shouting at him, and examined the body on the ground. 'You're a bloody idiot,' he'd said, running back to his house, calling an ambulance. He'd returned with his wife and other neighbours and they'd tried to sit the boy up, but someone had said, 'No, it'll kill him.' So they'd laid him back down and waited.

Hal had said, 'I didn't mean to hit him that hard.'

'You're a bully,' one of the women had said.

'I didn't mean to …'

Still, he'd waited. Curled up in a tight ball. For the ambulance, the policeman, the trip home, the talk with his parents, the four days in his room, the filthy looks as food was deposited on his dresser.

Binoculars to their eyes, they waited.

Bells, lights. Sam sat forward. 'Away they go at Cheltenham. Cavalier was quickly out of the gates. Gypsy shows some good pace and so does Jasper. They settle out in order. Gypsy's a length and a half on Mr Darcy.'

A four-horse race. Hal took over. 'Cavalier sits off the fence and stalks her way up. On her back is …'

'Tinkerbell.'

'The pace is even as the little filly Grow Girl pilots away. Three quarters of a length away is the monstrous mare Gypsy. Coming up, Gypsy is going to head for home, her stable-mates right with her – she lowers and the crowd go with her …'

Sam could recognise his own phrases (which he'd stolen, years before, anyway). The dozen or so people around them were listening, intrigued by these improvisations. Someone said, 'Bit louder, son.'

'Gypsy goes straight past Jasper, she's singing her lungs out, and she's got it!' Hal's voice was swinging, fists in every direction, like he was back on the mound. 'Gypsy smokes away past three lengths on Jasper and down to the post. We've never seen a horse like this before. Gypsy wins by four lengths. Jasper, Cavalier and Mr Darcy were across the track for the minors and Tinkerbell brings up the rear.'

He pulled up, cantered and stopped. 'What do you reckon, Sam?'

Someone called out, 'Give him the job, Sam.'

Sam bought him a beer and gave him the usual mints to hide his breath. Then they walked to the stables, and helped wash Gypsy.

Don Cole squeezed Sonia's arm. 'Come on.' He dragged her along Burleigh Avenue. 'What number is it?'

John Carey followed. 'Seventeen.'

And behind Carey, Shirley, her arms folded, her face involved but cold.

Sonia pushed away from the newsagent, tried to reclaim her arm, but he just tightened his grip. 'You know what this sort of thing costs me?' he asked, waving a *Photoplay* in her face.

'Let go,' she said. 'This is assault.'

'No, shoplifting.'

'I wouldn'ta never thought,' John Carey said. He'd seen it all. Left the newsagent with his Capstan and papers and there she was, hiding the magazine up her jumper. Now he was waddling. He wanted to tell Don Cole to slow down but realised justice had to be swift.

Sonia pulled her arm free. 'I don't need to be led.'

They walked down the drive, in the back door, and found Ena in the kitchen, confused. Mr Carey, in her house, without being asked?

'Bita trouble down the shop,' Cole said. He threw the *Photoplay* on the bench.

'Griff?' Ena called.

Roland came in and Cole explained, while Roland picked up the magazine and flicked through, as if it might help him understand. 'You stole this?'

'Yes,' she replied, looking at Shirley, who turned and walked from the house.

'Why?' Ena asked. 'You've got money, haven't you?'

'Kids do dumb things,' Carey explained.

'I'm not a kid,' she said. 'I'm nearly eighteen.'

'You've never done anything like this,' Roland said. He used a rag to wipe paint from his hands, unconsciously, a habit of twenty years' work. 'Why?'

Ena sighed. If it kept on at the same rate she'd have one in gaol and the other locked in her room for life. 'Well?' she asked her daughter.

Sonia turned to Cole and said, 'I'm sorry. I shouldn't have done it. I wasn't thinking.'

But even this didn't convince Roland.

Carey said, 'Mr Cole could call the police, if he liked, couldn't you, Don?'

'I'm not gonna call the police, John.' He looked at his best customer. He stocked canvases for Roland, paints, brushes, tobacco, papers, and an art magazine he had to get in from London. He knew he'd made enough from the Griffins to pay for a hundred *Photoplays*. 'Don't apologise to me, Sonia. Make it up to yer parents. There's no law against stupidity. It's just a bit of a slap in the face for yer mum and dad.'

John Carey wasn't about to let it go. He indicated the magazine and said, 'That's handled now, Don. You can't ask full price for it.'

Cole just said, 'Don't worry about that.' He noticed the red marks on Sonia's arm and guessed he'd overreacted. 'How yer studies going, Sonia?'

'Good, thanks.'

'You decided what you gonna do next year?'

She almost smiled. 'Might try be a journalist.'

'Well, I suppose you'll make a good job of it. Good head on yer shoulders, girly.' And he smiled, took his magazine, and walked out. John Carey followed, left with his flagging fury. 'I saw her stuffin' it up her jumper. I didn't know what to think.'

None of them replied.

'Right, must be off. Good-o.' And he almost jumped through the back door.

They went into the dining room and Roland and Ena sat opposite her. 'I don't understand,' Roland said.

'You can only be dull for so long.'

'What's that mean?' Ena asked.

'If you always follow rules. At some point, you're not thinking for yourself.'

Roland thought this seemed reasonable. He didn't want to raise a sheep. 'So, you thought you'd have your own little protest?'

She shrugged.

'He coulda called the police. Then it would've been on your record. Mighta stopped you getting a decent job. Did you think about that?'

'It was dumb. I've apologised.'

'Shirley will tell Mary,' Ena said. 'What will she think? She won't want you going out with her again.'

'That won't happen,' Sonia said.

'You wouldn't see Shirley … What sort of influence are you?'

Sonia couldn't comprehend how Ena understood so little.

Hal came into the kitchen, opened the fridge and drank milk from the bottle.

'Get a glass!' Ena called.

Sonia watched her face: the lines of distress. 'Anyway,' she said, 'it's sort of strange. I remember something about some stolen alcohol?' She turned to her father. 'And after that, what was it, smokes? And underwear? Didn't he give you underwear?'

Roland hesitated. 'I always felt guilty. I never slept well with that grog in the shed. That's why I got rid of it.'

'I never liked that man,' Ena said.

'Who?' Hal asked from the doorway.

'Trevor.'

'He was great! You could hang a hammer from his face.'

'Well ...' She crossed her arms. 'I wouldn't think that's much of an achievement.'

'Can you do it?'

She refused to be sidetracked. She returned to her daughter. 'Two wrongs don't make a right.'

'Mother! Don't be so predictable.'

'Don't tell me what to do. You're the one shoplifted.'

Hal's face lit up. 'Did yer?'

Sonia wouldn't answer, arms crossed.

'It's nothing to be proud of,' Ena said.

'Go, Sonia!' Hal said. 'Signs of life. I bet it was old King Cole? What did you get?'

'Hal!' Roland growled.

'Next time,' he said, 'ask me. If yer gonna do it, you wanna make it worth while.'

Hal tore into a piece of bread and left the room, smiling. 'I knew you had it in yer. Just takes a while, eh, Mum?'

Sometimes, Ena thought, life would be easier without kids. They were meant to be past the hard part. 'Well, we're disappointed,' she said. 'But people test the boundaries. Let's hope you've got it out of your system.'

Sonia hated how her mother spoke in aphorisms, scraps of Bible, homilies, anything handy on the kitchen bench. Just say what you mean, she'd tell her. If I'm a bitch, call me one. 'Can I go now?' she asked.

'Yes. I'll explain to Mary.'

That night they lay awake, Roland with his hands behind his head, Ena with the sheet up under her chin. 'Not for the life of me ...'

'Don't read too much into it.'

There were long slabs of silence as thoughts were chewed, swallowed and regurgitated.

'Can only think what Mary's said.'

'What's it matter?'

'It matters.' She pulled the sheet to get her fair share.

Hal could hear everything: the echo chamber of his parents' room. He could hear them move, and fart, but other things (he remembered) had stopped. There was no longer any need to close his door, to block his ears, to sing to himself.

Ena turned to Roland. 'Put your arms down, I can smell you.'

He did as he was told.

'If it hada been Hal.' It had been; finding food and books and records under his bed. Asking where he'd got them from.

'I used my own money.'

But they knew better. Also knew, he could get away with it. So they'd retreated. Now it was generally best. He wouldn't back down on anything. He'd stand and dig his toes into the floorboards and shout and maybe run off, or just go to his room, and slam his door, or, once, go out to the shed, return with a can of royal blue and start painting Sonia's newspaper walls.

Roland said, 'How's Shirley faring?'

'I don't think there'll be any lasting problem, physically.'

Hal almost stopped breathing to listen.

'They got it all out of her system. Hadn't taken enough, apparently. Mary reckons she was better the next morning.'

Hal stood, crawled to the door, opened it, and listened.

'The real issue is … if she'll try again.'

'She'll come good,' Ena said. 'Few weeks. And they'll find another school. Mary says some of them girls have been giving her hell.'

Hal had worked it out. The ambulance in the driveway last Friday, his mum and dad telling him to stay in his room. And this time, when he'd offered to visit her in hospital, they'd all told him Shirley was too tired, and she'd be home soon anyway. A few days, and she'd just stayed in her room, and he'd been kept away. All of this down to her lupus, apparently.

'Sleep!' Ena demanded, securing even more sheet.

And the light went out.

Hal crawled back to bed. There was no doubt: she'd had a rough trot. But Mary, and Sam, especially, they'd look after her.

Ena wasn't feeling well, so it was down to Roland. He'd left plenty of time, but they were late anyway. Father and son walked down Commercial Street, through the little spaces in the crowd. Hal didn't so much dodge as stop, wait for people to pass, and carry on. Roland kept looking back. 'Hurry up, it'll be started.'

Hal couldn't avoid the muscular arms, soft suits and satin dresses. They continued parallel to the road. Some people changed course and went into shops. It was a swarm. There was no one person. Hal didn't feel part of it. Perhaps no one did. Perhaps he was overanalysing again. He listened. Only a few voices, but footfalls, bells on doors, a truck reversing into traffic and a bus stopping suddenly to avoid it.

Roland stopped, came back and took his arm. 'I thought you wanted to meet her?'

'I do.'

'Well, come on!' He pulled him along, using his hand to clear a path.

It's not my fault, Hal wanted to say. You're the one stayed too long at the gallery, searching for a Griffin, complaining they'd taken the only one down, and what a lack of respect, of gratitude, typical!, if we lived in another state, or country, they might appreciate me.

They approached the Regent. The billboard read: AUSTRALIAN CLASSIC THE BLUE LILY.

'How's it a classic?' Hal asked, as they went into the cinema.

'It did well.'

'Seventeen screens. And the reviews ...'

'That's just someone's opinion.'

'"As crumbly as an old sultana cake."'

'That's what they're paid to write.'

But thinking back, Hal couldn't believe the real Lucie would've been anything like Teresa Martin, the stage manager like the late George Wallace, him, even, like the brother. The words sounded less like real words with every passing year. The phoney sets (built once they'd left Kalgoorlie so they could re-film several scenes); Emmie Drury, who was more like a nun than a goldfield mum. He'd lost interest. (Although it wasn't the full story. A yard full of kids calling him Gary Cooper and Jimmy Stewart, pouting stage-kisses, rehashing lines through crustless lunch hours.) No more films. Until they'd received a phone call from Aunt Gwen: 'You'll never believe it, Griff! Lucie McCabe is playing at the town hall. We've decided to screen the film.'

'They've kept a copy?'

'Don't be smart. We've hired the Regent for Saturday week. Lucie's the guest of honour. Unfortunately, none of the other actors can make it, but what about Hal?'

Hal, walking into a foyer of summer frocks and elbow-length gloves. 'Who are all these people?' he asked.

'I don't think they're here for us,' Roland said.

One old girl saw him and said, 'You're John?'

'Yes.'

'Oh, look how you've grown! Six years, and you're a different person.'

It happens, he wanted to say, but she was already pinching his cheek, which had gotten whiskery, sprouted a few pimples.

'I loved your performance when I first saw it. To be honest,' she leaned forward and looked around, 'I thought you stole the show.'

Gwen came over and saved them. 'You're late.'

'Bus was slow,' Roland said.

She turned to Hal. 'Well, come on, it's time.'

'For what?'

'To meet her!'

She dragged him through the swamp, the big laughs, rattling bangles, spilt champagne. They arrived in front of the great woman. 'Hal?'

He extended his hand but she leaned forward and kissed him on the cheek. 'After all these years. I'm so glad to meet you.'

She was tall, gangly, with golliwog arms and wiry hands. He noticed her dress: cheap-looking, pleated. He said, 'Teresa couldn't make it.'

'I know. She's living in America.'

'Hollywood.' Searching for stardom. Her mum and dad had taken her (sold the house, bought near Venice Beach, close to where the canals smogged up every afternoon, vowed never to return until she was famous). They'd found a few roles – girls in the background, a line or two, but no Liz Taylor.

Roland introduced himself and explained, 'We tried to encourage him after the film. He was offered another role but didn't want to do it.'

'Which?' Lucie asked Hal.

'With Chips Rafferty.'

'Why did you pass it up?'

He shrugged. 'Lost interest.'

The bell rang and they went in. Hal sat next to Lucie. She smelt like moth balls. He thought the film had the same aroma. And Teresa. The phoniness seemed to be there, even in her acting. The way she turned up her mouth, and stared into the distance; the way she delivered lines, short-and-sharp, but took her time if it was Emmie or her father. He remembered how much he'd really hated her. He turned to Lucie and whispered, 'She was a pain in the arse.'

She smiled.

'She told me I'd never make it because I didn't have the face. It was too round. You're not meant to have a round face.'

Hal studied the boy on the screen but couldn't recognise him. It wasn't just the round face. John McCabe seemed to be able to flit about, jump the big hummocks, fall, roll, get up and carry on. Now Hal felt he dragged himself through life. This boy seemed to run at everything, bark like a dog, demand attention. He didn't know who he was. This made him feel bad. He dropped his head, and felt himself descending. He was looking in his lap, but he was hearing himself. He was trying to forget, but couldn't. There was another seventy minutes. He didn't want to sit through it.

He could hear Lucie playing in the pub. The coins they were throwing at her, so she could become famous. Christmas carols, and the gift they'd given her: a piano, sitting in the corner of their living room. It was all so unreal. If he could go back to being ten, he might (he thought), but failing that, he didn't want to be reminded. He whispered to his dad, 'I'm goin' the dunny.' Then stood and walked out.

Fifteen minutes later, Roland found him sitting in the foyer. He sat next to him and said, 'What's wrong?'

Hal took a moment. 'Stupid film.'

'We better go back in.'

'I don't wanna see anymore.'

'But everyone's expecting you.'

'So what?'

They watched a young man using a long brush to sweep rubbish into a dustpan. Hal thought this seemed much more interesting than the film. 'She's okay,' he said.

'Who?'

'Lucie. But she's nothing like that little bitch.'

'Is that why – '

'No.' But he couldn't tell him the real reason. Maybe no one liked being themselves. Maybe that's why people made movies.

They decided to give up on the film, and walked back to the bus. Past Maugham Church, with its own Charlie Bass set up out front, a few banners proclaiming the End. They stopped to listen. Roland thought it funny. The way this man was so convinced of his own correctness. 'No Unlawful Sex' and 'Come Try Jesus', like He was some new sort of jam. And again, the thought occurred. What if he himself was a preacher of his own faith? Hollering to the uninterested, the unconvertable. What did that make him? Hal was intrigued by what this man had to say. Not so long ago, he'd tasted Mr Jesus. Found the Griffin family Bible in the bookcase, read Genesis to Deuteronomy before giving up. But returned to Psalms, underlining selected phrases, reciting them as he lay in bed each night. He'd torn out pages and stuck them on Sonia's wall, and told her, 'It's the truth.'

'What?'

'Can't you see? Christ?'

'What are you talking about?'

Roland and Ena had become worried. Jesus was welcome in their house, but only as far as a two-bob crucifix above the door. No one took God that seriously. So when Hal had begun preaching across the dinner table, they'd started worrying.

'Maybe if we surrender to Christ?'

'If who does?' Roland had asked.

'All of us.'

Roland had tried to work out what he really believed. 'You've become a Christian?'

Hal had started going to church. Asked them to come, but they wouldn't. Not that they would've minded, but they couldn't afford to encourage him. It hadn't come from them. Someone, somewhere, must have had a word to him, given him some literature. Perhaps Charlie, although he'd been in hospital with a hip replacement. Maybe all the business with the tent revival, but that had been years ago.

But the phase had passed. Thankfully. By the time Hal was fifteen he was lost again, Godless, wondering and wandering.

They arrived home and Roland went into his shed, back to the canvas he'd been pecking away at for years. The boy in the boat, the Redskins, watching him from the banks, naked men nailed to stakes. Lush vegetation; convolvulus, bougainvillea, philodendron a mile high. The sort of plants he'd never tried painting. He examined this canvas and wondered how he'd ever get the colours right. Deserts were so much easier. A Turner sky of approaching storm, and he didn't think he had that right, either. And finally, the face of this boy, still blank, like he couldn't work out, or dare to imagine, his expression.

'Griff!'

He ran out, followed the voice to the side of the house. Ena was looking up at Hal, sitting in the jasmine, breathing deeply, smiling. Sour apples, and a bird pond of green water.

Roland sighed. Three brush strokes before the interruption. Typical. 'Would you just get down here, please!'

Nothing.

'Right!' He walked to the chookyard, returned with the ladder, rested it against the house and started up.

'What if your father falls?' Ena called to Hal.

Roland got onto the roof. 'Come on, people are watching.' (Mrs Ulit, from number five, although she was pretending to pull weeds). He slid over and touched Hal. Hal reacted like he hadn't noticed he was there. Then he stood and walked across the roof.

'Careful!' Ena called.

Hal waited a moment on the gutter before jumping down onto the lawn. He rolled a few times and stood up. Then he went into his room, and they let him go.

When Roland checked the room at twelve, Hal was asleep. He closed the door. He'd attached a bolt to the outside, and he slid it closed. He'd done the same to the windows, so he went out, onto the verandah, and closed them too.

Now they could sleep, knowing he'd be there in the morning.

A week later Hal was in the box, waiting for his big moment. The usual caller, Ted Feltus, had agreed. Sam had been nagging him for weeks: 'One race, something next Tuesday? We never get many on a Tuesday.'

Feltus could see the need for new blood. Still, there were only four callers in the city, and the market wouldn't accommodate another. But Sam wouldn't relent. 'Of course, he doesn't want to start for a few years yet. How old are you, Ted? Sixty? And yer voice, after fifty years of fags, it won't hold out forever.'

The box had evolved into a small lounge. Roland and Ena sat on a couch behind Hal. Ena wasn't sure about race calling. It wasn't a job, as such. But she felt she had to encourage her son. 'You've got all the colours?' she said.

'Yes, Mum.'

'Their numbers?'

'Mum.'

'Have you got water?'

'He won't have time for that,' Feltus explained.

Sam tended to agree. 'Fifty seconds and it's over, Ena.'

'You gotta have yer wits about you,' she said to Hal.

'*Ena*,' Roland said.

Hal knew the stakes would increase. On Saturdays, it was broadcast: a whole city of singleted men listening. That scared him.

Roland sat back. Maybe Hal would settle into calling, and fiddling about at the track all day. Life had a way of taking care of itself: he'd never set out to be a painter. Mothers, though, were born (or made) anxious. Everything was of the utmost importance. Nothing could be left to chance, although everything was.

'What else might you do?' Feltus asked.

'Simpson's?'

'You good with yer hands?'

'Sort of.' Mainly, Hal was just glad to get a day off school. It was a long, drawn-out death. It didn't promise anything except fifty years welding washer bodies. At least this was solid, reliable, clean. The only problem was the microphone sitting in the middle of the table, waiting, saying, Come on, Hal, give it yer best, son. Don't fluff it up.

'You gotta find what you're good at,' Feltus said. 'Million men can make dryers, but not many can call races, or paint pictures, like your dad.'

Hal ignored this comment. For once, he wasn't going to allow art into the room.

Feltus turned to the microphone. 'They're lining up for race three, the Modbury Stakes.' He motioned for Hal to sit forward. 'Today, ladies and gents, we have a treat. An apprentice caller: Hal Griffin. Not yet eighteen, but an enormous talent.'

Hal saw the hundreds of faces turn and look towards them. He waved, and felt like an idiot. He could feel his hands shaking so he put them between his knees.

'Moving up,' Feltus said. Then he placed the microphone in front of Hal.

Ena said, 'You'll be fine.'

Sam shooshed her.

Hal could feel his body shaking, but there was nothing he could do. 'All in,' he said. He could hear his voice spreading, amplifying, settling in every crack of the grandstand floorboards, on every blade of grass. But they weren't all in. 'Waiting on Jeebers …'

He noticed his dad; he gave Hal the thumbs up. His mum; she smiled, but it was her mother smile, saying, Go on, don't make a mess of it. He stared at the microphone, its fabric cord, its iron stand. It was a no-nonsense object.

'Settle,' Feltus said, pushing a kill switch on the base. 'You okay?'

Sam said, 'Focus on the horses, Hal. You know who's who. Just tell us what they do.'

Feltus released the button.

'Lights, away they go,' Hal said. 'They bounce pretty well … Force Command might've been a touch slow to go and Stanley's been eased to the back in the early stages … Jeebers is storming forward with Last Lap and also heading forward is Sheer Talent.'

Good, he thought. It's coming. But then realised he was thinking; that another voice was trying to interrupt.

'They settle themselves out in order and Jeebers has the lead from Sheer Talent … a length and a quarter back on the inside is Last Lap … he occupies third with Practicality.'

He could hear himself speaking, and thinking, and the thoughts were winning.

'Jeebers has it in front and leads as they head towards the corner … Sheer Talent is on the scene immediately to challenge him.'

The voice wouldn't stop. It drew his eyes from the horses to the hands, his mother's, clasped tightly together.

'Force Command eases up into the race and then comes Bass Strait …'

Every finger, her ring, even. And when he looked back at the track, he had no idea what was happening. The voice said, That's better, forget it. There are too many.

Silence. The horses kept running, but nothing came out of his mouth. Feltus quickly reclaimed the microphone and started with a semi-shout. 'Grand Emperor looks for inside runs ... Jeebers leaves the fence and Last Lap starts to get through ... down the outside is Sheer Talent and You're So Good. Last Lap gets a little margin on Sheer Talent ... Last Lap is going to win!'

Feltus switched off the microphone and turned to his apprentice. 'You okay?' He held his shoulder.

Hal broke free. From his hand, his words, Sam's anxious face, his father, sitting forward, his mother, upright, her hands still locked in her lap. 'You happy?' he asked her.

'What?'

'You made me fuck it up!'

'Hal!' Roland said.

Sam was standing in the middle. 'That was near perfect. Just gotta keep going, till the end.'

'Of course you've gotta keep going,' he said. 'I fucked it up. It was awful.'

Feltus shook his head. 'Na, they wouldn'ta even noticed. You did well. My first call, I only remembered three names, and I got them mixed up.'

But Hal couldn't see this. He stormed from the room, the grandstand, across the betting ring towards the gates. Ena and Roland followed, and behind them, Sam. He tried to keep up, but couldn't. 'Tell him I'll see him later,' he said, clinging to a post.

Hal ran across Torrens Road and walked through the empty block that was a shortcut to Burleigh Avenue. His parents followed through the weeds. 'Hal, wait,' Roland called.

Hal turned the corner and sprinted for home. Roland gave up, and waited for Ena. As they walked he said, 'What did you say to him?'

'Nothing.'

'Why's he think – '

'I just said it's a funny way to make a living.'

'Funny?'

'Unreliable.'

'So? If he likes it.'

'Wouldn't you prefer to see him with something more … solid?'

'No. Look at me. Hardly solid.'

'That's different.'

'How?'

They crossed the road. Ena said, 'I'm the villain, aren't I?'

Roland didn't reply.

'Considering, he's gonna need some stability.'

They arrived home, and Sonia was standing at the door. 'Bet he was good.'

'Very,' Roland replied, going in.

'Why's he got the shits on?'

Ena came in after her husband. She spoke quietly, so only Sonia could hear. 'He muffed it up. Ted Feltus had to take over.'

They found Hal lying on his bed. 'Get out!'

'You did a fine job,' Roland said.

'It's your fault!' he said again to Ena.

'How?'

He stood, approached her, used his body to push her away. 'Why did you come?'

Roland tried to move between them.

'Why?'

Hal lifted his hand and pushed her. She fell into the mirror, on its little frame. There was a cracking of glass.

Sonia saw what was going on, came in, and pushed Hal onto the bed. 'You little shit.'

Roland helped Ena up. She brushed herself off. 'I'm fine.' And looked at her son.

'Enough!' Roland said. 'Enough.'

They left him alone and he fell asleep. Roland bolted him in, regardless. Then he went out to their new car (a Dodge station wagon), wound down the back window and opened the door. He fetched their sleeping bags from the shed and loaded them. When he turned to go back in Ena was there. She said, 'Can't it wait till the holidays?'

'No, it can't.'

He found the tent under a pile of timber, dragged it out and asked her to help him load it. 'We've got one chance,' he said.

She guessed he was right. Hal was nearly a man, beyond reasoning with, or physically controlling. At some point the bolts wouldn't be enough. The dozens of times he'd escaped through his window. Stayed out all night, coming in as they were having breakfast. They'd ask where he'd been, but he'd just smile. That was all part of the game.

Roland was jamming the gear into the back of the car. Sam was watching from his window; Shirley, hers.

'Sonia's not coming,' Ena said.

'She doesn't have to. She can look after herself.'

'I'm getting too old for camping.'

'It's not what you want …' He knew that Hal could only be made better under the stars. Time had proven this. Six months with the Pennington Boy Scouts. A camping trip to the Flinders. The fire; the marshmallow sticks; toes warming by the flames.

'Coupla nights?' Ena suggested.

'No, a coupla weeks. Months, perhaps. We'll see how it goes.'

'But we haven't prepared. We can't just drive off.'

'Why not?' He slammed the back door. 'Pack the basics,' he said.

'We can wash clothes. Two pairs of shoes. Togs. We might head north. There are a coupla nice waterholes at Kakadu.'

She shook her head. 'Kakadu?'

'Or Melville Island.'

'You wanna …?'

'I wanna get him away from everything.'

She noticed the cut in her dress from the mirror glass. 'What about food?'

'We'll get it on the way out of town.'

'What about we leave on the weekend?'

'Six am tomorrow. If you wanna keep him, Ena.'

She sensed there must be an easier way. 'What we talked about then?'

He stopped, studied her, to see if she was serious, or just trying to block him. 'Once you start …'

'Rubbish. Don't you reckon a doctor'd know best? Start him on a small dose.'

Roland continued packing: poles, ropes, cast-iron cooking pot. 'If we agree … for now, we try the simplest solution. Get him out under the stars, talk, keep busy.'

'How's that fix anything, if it's biological?' Standing on the cracked drive, wondering what might come of it, Ena said, 'Anyway, he won't go.'

'Yes, he will.'

'Alright, you can tell him.'


When the landscape was real, things were different. Hypnosis of tyres, the unreliable growl of the engine. The temperature needle kept creeping into the red. Roland had already stopped, waited for the radiator to cool, topped it up. As he said to himself, I bet it's the thermostat.

Ena wasn't so worried. Although it was dry country, it had its own beauty. The more you looked the less you saw, until it became the strange mix of colours Roland always had on his hands. Maybe that's it, she thought. No given tree or rock or shrub, just the sum of these things as they rushed past the window.

Hal had found the book his dad had brought. Poetry, of all things. Who read poetry? Shit. Maybe it was his father, every day, drifting further into the clouds. Roland had bookmarked one poem, underlined certain passages, written notes on the side: 'catch this in oil, the gaze, hand with boat, anticipation'. A child launching a boat as fragile as a butterfly. '"Lighter than a cork, I danced on the waves,"' Hal read aloud. 'Sorta like that painting you're doing, Dad.'

'He's been working on that one for years,' Ena said, hands crossed in her lap.

'It's me,' Hal suggested.

'Could be anyone,' Roland said.

'But it's me.' Reading: '"... skies splitting with lightnings, and waterspouts ..."'

'Shit!' Roland slammed his fist on the steering wheel.

'What?' Ena said, but she could see the steam escaping from the engine.

Roland pulled over, popped the bonnet, felt the hot radiator. Ena told him he should have checked it, but he told her he had, a pressure test, the lot – now this. 'Twenty minutes to cool down.'

Ena said, 'How long was that? Three hours?'

'Four,' Roland said.

'What a disaster.'

'The first little thing to go wrong and you ...' He had faith. It was a perfect day: the breeze, which was warm, but not too warm; the sky, so light the blue had leached out. He got his things, sat down and started sketching. Charcoal on cartridge paper.

But Ena wasn't finished. 'And you wanna go to Kakadu?'

'I'm not going to Kakadu,' Hal said.

Roland refused to argue. They'd come around in a day or two. His sketch (which showed an unhappy Hal resting on a shredded tractor tyre beside the road) would become a record of the journey that had saved them: 'Day 1, sketch 1 – Worried faces'.

Hal stood, picked up a handful of stones and threw them at a crow. They didn't reach. It didn't move. 'What's the purpose of this?'

'To have a holiday,' Roland said, blending charcoal lines with a finger.

'In the middle of term?'

'Why not?'

'Cos I fucked up?'

'No.'

'Cos of what I did?'

Ena approached the car and examined the radiator. 'I reckon it's ready to go.'

'Ena, you're not gonna make the time go any faster. The more you fret …'

'I don't have to come,' Hal said, wandering into the middle of the road.

'You don't.'

'I can get a bus home.'

'You can.'

'I'm nearly eighteen.'

'You are.'

Then he walked over and stood in front of his father. 'If you think this is gonna help …' He sat down and took a deep breath. 'I coulda tried again on Saturday. Ted woulda let me.'

Roland scratched his nose. 'There's plenty of time for that. I wanna go to a bush race meeting. Sounds like a lotta fun. Maybe you could ask to call it?'

'I think I'll walk home,' Hal said. He turned back, towards the city, the three hundred miles he'd need to go.

'Off you go,' Roland said.

He started walking – a hundred yards or so, but then slowed, looked back and rested on dead branches.

Ena opened the passenger door and sat in the car. 'Stupid bloody idea. Sometimes, Roland Griffin, I don't believe I even married you.'

'Well, that was a long time ago. People change.' He checked his son, a small crow in the distance.

'The problem is, Griff, you don't think things through. How's this gonna help? We need to get a proper doctor.'

'Rubbish. A waterhole. A hill to climb.'

'You could make things worse.'

'Perhaps.' He wiped charcoal from his hand. Then he turned to his son and called loudly, 'It's a bit hard doing this from memory.'

Hal noticed a small bird on the road. It was grey, with a few blue feathers in its tail. He threw a stone but it didn't move. He stood and approached it, but stopped as a car hurtled towards the bird. Thankfully, it missed. Hal walked out again, knelt beside it and said, 'Come on, old boy.'

Roland watched Hal pick up the bird and start back. When he arrived he said, 'It can't fly.'

Ena wasn't interested, but Roland said, 'Maybe it's busted its wing.'

'Maybe.'

'You wanna hold on to it?'

'I reckon … maybe I should.'

Half an hour later they were moving at speed. Hal had wrapped the bird in his jumper and kept checking it. 'What do you feed birds?' he asked.

'We could find some good soil, and dig for worms,' Roland said.

'Maybe I could get a cage, and take it home?'

'You could get some others. When we go north, you wait and see. Millions of 'em. Bita birdwatching. Did we bring the binoculars?'

Hal was aware of what his father was up to. He thought, perhaps, he should throw the bird out of the window. That would get them back to where they started. But he felt its soft head, and knew he couldn't.

'You'll see wedge-tailed eagles,' Roland said. 'Keep yer eyes open. They're up high, circling, having a look for lunch.'

Hal scanned the sky, but he couldn't see any.

'Beautiful creatures,' Roland said. And thought, Beautiful day. He turned to his wife. 'Now we're livin', eh?'

'Yeah.'

'What d'yer reckon, Prince Hal?'

'Sorry?'

'Now we're livin'?'

Hal wasn't sure about this. Another one of his dad's ideas. Like Scouts – hiking for six hours through scrub; scratched legs and dry lips, sores on the bottom of his feet, and the leader calling, 'Come on, Hal, we'll never get there at this rate.'

All designed, apparently, to improve his character.

'Yeah, livin',' Roland said.

Roland spent the afternoon watching his temperature gauge. It drifted into the red, back down, up (dangerously) – so they stopped and waited. Once it had cooled again, he said, 'Hal, you wanna go at driving?'

Not that he had a licence. He'd tried. Two lessons with his father – shouting, slammed fists on the glove box: 'Stop! Drive home! That's enough!'

Hal drove for an hour. Long, straight roads, but it was all good practice. They were only stopped again by the needle, in the red, and the steam, still percolating under the bonnet.

It was getting dusky, so they set up camp in a patch of scrub beside the road. The tent went up without too much trouble. The fire lit, the pot put on to warm. They ate bully beef with cold beans, and drank warm cordial. Hal mashed a bean with water and offered it to the bird, but it didn't seem interested. Ena, washing the few dishes in a bowl, said it was a bad sign. 'They just decide.'

'What?' Roland asked, propped up on his swag, one shoe off, sketching gum trees destined to become coat hangers.

'To die.'

'Bullshit,' Hal said, picking it up and stroking its head. His mother had no idea. Everything was prescribed. Life was a self-administered medicine. You took it, got well, carried on. But it wasn't like that. 'You've got to get into the spirit of it,' he said to her.

'Pardon?'

'We're here now, you may as well.'

They fed the fire as it got darker. Read by the light of the kerosene lamp. And then, bed. Watching the stars, Ena waited for sleep for an hour. 'I'll be awake all night.'

Then Hal said, 'Roland's Girl came out slow but she moves up the field … length and a half away My Husband's gaining … moves to the inside and passes …'

'Hal!'

'But here comes Never Been Happier … long odds and short legs, but he's gaining on Roland's Girl … she's slowing … she's full of bully beef and beans …'

Roland was laughing. Ena hit him.

'My God, she's fallen! She's sitting on her back, kicking her legs in the air … keep away, she's one angry mare … here comes the vet, he's gonna put her out of her misery … but she's back up, and running … she passes My Husband, Never Been Happier, and she wins! Roland's Girl takes out the Outback Stakes!'

Several types of birds called out. Roland took it as a good sign. Day one, and everything except the radiator was working.

Hal woke first, and found the bird frozen like one of the specimens he remembered from the museum, posed on bark and leaves inside a glass cabinet, cowering from a stuffed eagle. The godwit, or finch, or whatever it was, was cold. There was nothing in his or her small brown eyes. Dead. Like some of the horses Sam had showed him. Shot for a broken leg, or eye cancer. And then, as the cold and damp settled on his skin, he felt like going home.

His mum and dad started packing, walking between camp and car. Ena tried to drag the heavy tent to the boot, stopped, and said, 'Hal, you can't just sit there.'

He refused to look at her.

'See, this is the problem. This is why your father did it.'

'Ena,' Roland said, squeezing the tent in the back of the car.

'What?'

'It's not helping.'

She shook her head, walked over to the camp and picked up the pots and plates.

Hal studied the bird. Of course, they'd been right. He should've left it. It would've ended up under someone's tyre. Or made it to the bush where a snake would've eaten it. There was a scheme. Everything had been worked out. The god of sticks and granite watched over every creature, no matter how small.

Roland and Ena kept packing. Soon, they were ready. Roland said, 'You coming, son?'

Hal picked up the bird and threw it in the scrub. Then he stood, walked to the car and got in.

There was no one else on the road. Just bitumen, growling under new tyres, the needle, hovering on red, his mother eating almonds from a jar. Hal could smell them: the mix of grease, nutshell, black oil, fresh from the stove. He could hear them crushing, mixing with her saliva, the clunking jaw. He felt hungry.

A thousand galahs passed in front of them. 'Look at that,' Roland said. Light flashed off their wings. He drifted into the middle of the road and Ena straightened the wheel. 'Careful.'

'Wanna drive?' Roland called back.

'No, thanks.'

'This is the most dangerous sort of driving. Straight, monotonous – sends you to sleep. Then you're on the front of a truck. Or rolling.'

That was an idea, Hal thought. He could see the camping gear tumbling in the cabin, his mother slamming against the roof, screaming (until they were unconscious).

Roland said, 'In my day you just paid yer two quid, but now they want to see that you know what you're doing.'

Hal refused to fall for his father's most obvious trick.

'Hal?'

'For Christ sake, say something!' his mother said, turning.

'I haven't got anything to say.'

'Grow up!' She returned to the road. 'We'll all sit silent … how would that be?' She looked back. 'How? *How?*'

'Do what you want.'

Dirt turned orange and small trees gave way to native grass. Powerlines sagged from pole to pole, veered away from the road, out into the desert, and disappeared.

'You've always been hard-headed, haven't you, boyo?' Roland asked, peering into the rear-vision mirror.

'This is where I talk about myself?'

'I mean, once you decide … but that can be a useful. Like with yer race calling.'

'I don't wanna be a race caller.'

'But you're good.'

'So what?'

'The main thing is, don't take it out on us. We've only ever tried to help.'

They stopped at a town called Lifton. The main street was dominated by a railway station that hadn't seen smoke for years. They read posters promising Western Australian holidays, the offices, still full of cabinets and broken desks, the rotten sleepers, carrying lines that only ran to the edge of town. The main street was a two-minute walk: a proud town hall, a bakery, a pub. They went into the dining room and sat down and a girl came out. Roland noticed her cold sore, and the way she kept licking it. She said, 'Can't give you any bread, sorry.'

They ordered, and hoped for the best.

As they sat waiting, Roland said, 'Good old country pub.' He studied the salt and paper shakers, mostly empty, then asked, 'Hal, what would you be doing now?'

'I dunno, maths.'

'You're actually quite good at maths,' Ena said. 'Jude Ireland's son had a good mind for all that. He became an engineer. Chemical. Works for Shell.'

Hal wondered what she was saying. 'That's what you reckon I should do?'

'It's an idea.'

'So, that's the point of this trip? Get me sorted?'

'No.'

'It's to have a bita fun,' Roland said.

'Are you having fun?'

Roland waited, unsure.

Hal stood and went to the toilet. Nearly all the tiles had lifted, and the urinal had turned brown. He went into the cubicle, shut the door and sat down. He needed to go, but couldn't. When he returned to the table his mixed grill was waiting. He lifted the lamb chops and sausages with his fork and examined them.

'Eat up,' Ena said.

He tasted the meat. 'I can't eat this.'

'Go on,' Roland said. 'You'll get worse where we're going.'

The girl brought his parents' meals: steak, fish and chips.

Hal said, 'Can I have the fish instead?' And handed her his meal.

'Is there something wrong with it?'

'Dry, and …' He picked up the sausage and tapped it on the plate. It made a hollow, ringing sound.

Ena leaned forward. 'Here, have mine.'

'No. It's yours.' He returned to the girl. 'Please?'

'We don't swap stuff just cos you change your mind.'

'I didn't change my mind. I just can't eat it.'

'Looks okay to me.' She took the plate, examined it, and put it back down.

'Hal,' Roland said.

'It's shit.'

Ena said, 'If you could just replace it?'

'*Mum*, I can handle it.'

There was a moment's silence. Then Ena stood, and walked from the room.

Hal glared at the girl. 'And you might wanna clean yer fuckin' toilets.' He picked up his plate, dropped it on the ground, and waited for the waitress's reaction.

Roland took his arm and led him from the room.

They gathered Ena from the lounge and went out through the front bar. Hal turned, and walked down the road.

'Hal,' Roland called.

As he went, Ena said, 'I told you this would happen.'

'And I told you it'd take time.'

'It won't. He'll just get worse.'

They waited for a few minutes. When he hadn't returned, they walked down the street to the bakery, and had lunch there. They bought him a pasty.

By the time they found him, sitting, waiting for a train, the day was getting cold.

Emily Creek was dry. They'd set up on the banks, high enough to avoid a flood but low enough to avoid the noise from the road. There were gidgee trees, and empty flagons, and native grasses that grew down to the waterline in search of a drink.

'I can't take it,' Ena said, sitting on a fruit box inside the tent, looking out.

'There's plenty of water,' Roland replied.

'It's not the water … why anyone'd live here.'

Alice Springs, a few days later, in the middle of a run of a century-plus days. Hal was standing in the sun, watching his own shadow, staring into the desert beyond town.

'Come in the shade,' his mother called, but he didn't respond.

Roland looked up from the watercolour resting in his lap. 'You listening?' he said.

No reply.

Ena wiped her forehead and pulled the sweat-soaked dress from her body. 'You never mentioned anything about this.'

'I said we'd head north.'

'I say we find a room for the night.'

He took a while to respond. 'Why?'

'*Why?* Cos it's hot!'

'You wait. About seven, there'll be a nice breeze. Beautiful sleeping weather.'

'You can stay, I'm gettin' a room.'

He washed his brush in a jar of water, and mixed more paint. 'We're meant to be camping.'

'When someone says camping you think green hills, creeks, or maybe the beach. You don't think this.'

Roland coloured great swathes of cartridge paper. 'We'll get to the beach, you'll have your hills.'

'I don't think so. Hal! Get outa the sun.'

'Come on, Hal.'

Roland knew he could've got Hal to sit down, but he didn't want to. He wanted the image on paper. Perhaps this was a selfish thing to do.

'You reckon it's about him, but all you do's paint,' Ena said.

'That's part of why we came.'

'Well, why did I come?'

Roland was starting to settle in. The car, even, had decided to stay below the red. The tent, the sanitary arrangements, the dehydrated meals, everything was going fine. The first few nights of sleeplessness had given way to adenoidal slumber; he'd relearnt the technique of shitting in a hole.

Unlike Ena, calling him from the bush the previous night. 'I'm outa paper.'

He'd fetched another roll. A few minutes later she'd said, 'This is the low point.'

Even Hal had smiled.

'What's wrong, dear?'

'It's all over my dress.'

Sitting around the fire, the boys had cracked up.

'It's not funny!'

She'd returned in her petticoat, carrying her dress, and thrown it in his lap. 'You get the water and soap and wash it!'

Roland knew. Once she'd decided somewhere was a funny sort of place, or not much of a place, that was it. Driving into town that morning. 'Strange sorta settlement.'

'How's that?' he'd asked.

'There are no factories. What do people do?'

'There are shops.'

'Not many. There's hardly anyone about.'

'Maybe they're inside, keeping cool.'

First impressions counted more than anything to Ena. So the little groups of Aborigines, sitting in the shade, obviously meant it was a dangerous place; the men with sandals and socks, it was backward;

the ladies with their gloves and stockings on in century heat, the natives were slow. 'No one's got no grass.'

'Well, you wouldn't, would yer?'

'And they've got their dogs chained up in the sun.'

Roland continued painting. 'You can see, he's coming out of his shell.'

'Nonsense.'

'You can't see it.'

'Why wouldn't I see it? I'm his mother, aren't I?'

He turned and smiled at her. 'How about we cook something exotic tonight? Chow mein?'

'If you like.'

'Hal, what d'yer reckon, chow mein?'

'Okay.' He sat beneath a tree, crossed his legs, and continued his meditation.

'What you'll find,' Roland said to Ena, 'is the longer you go the more it'll feel like home.'

'This place?'

'Camping. You just gotta get on, like you do at home. You don't wanna starve yerself. You don't wanna live on chops. Chow mein.'

'I'll have to buy some curry powder.'

'Just think how good that breeze'll be tonight.' He sat back and admired his watercolour. 'That's about it.' Lifting it and showing her.

'Another one of Hal,' she said, and asked.

'He was standing there.'

'How come you never paint me?'

'I've painted you.'

'Once. You mustn't think I make a very good subject.'

'Come on.' He stood. 'We better get that curry powder before the shops close.'

Ena wasn't impressed with Alice Springs. The sun had stripped the paint from the stone buildings (which were the only ones with any character), fences had come apart, and people were shut up inside, down dark hallways, in basements. Most corners had a pub, and most of these bled distant races onto footpaths dotted with red-faced men waving fingers in each other's faces.

Then, out of the monotony of the late afternoon, there was a carnival. Packed up, scissored, compressed, slid onto the back of trucks: a ferris wheel and carousel, bumper cars and sideshows. If the purpose was to drum up a crowd, it wasn't working. The men didn't even look. A few kids, perhaps, but mums were having none of that, grabbing arms and pulling them into haberdashers.

They approached an old woman sitting against a wall. She was wearing a cotton dress with long sleeves. Clutching a sign with mission-schooled copperplate: 'Lord Jesus loves you'. She was singing: *By the rivers of Babylon* …

Roland took his camera out of his backpack.

'Leave her alone,' Ena said.

He asked, 'Do you mind if I take your picture?'

She smiled. … *where we sat down, hey-hey we wept* …

He took a few pictures as Ena stood smiling back. 'That's such a pretty song.'

She didn't reply.

'My parents made me sing it on Sundays.' Ena opened her purse and searched for a cup or hat to throw a few coins, but couldn't see one. 'You after a few pennies?'

'No.'

'Right. Come on, Griff.'

They entered a grocer and found mince and curry powder, but the cabbages were no good. 'Not at all crisp,' Ena said, feeling one.

'It'll have to do.'

As they passed the PMG depot on the way out of town, Ena said, 'I can feel my gout.'

'You need to keep up your fluids.'

'I have been.'

Roland waited, then, 'It's funny how you get it now.'

'What does that mean?'

'Five days into a trip you didn't want to make.'

'You think I'm making it up?'

'I didn't say that.' But his look said, You ate tomatoes. You drank red wine at the Sea Breeze. They walked in silence. Then she was limping.

'You weren't limping on the way in,' he said.

'It's getting worse.' She stopped, looking at their campsite up ahead. 'Christ!' She was off, limping towards the creek. Roland followed her. They arrived, and stood, trying to take it all in.

'Hal!' she said.

'Hi, Mum.'

Hal seemed genuinely happy. The seven or eight Aboriginal men who sat with him did too. They were all drinking beer from the Griffin esky, but these men (sweaty, pants hanging from their bony hips) had brought more of their own. Women (seven or eight, their wives perhaps) stood in the tent rummaging through their bags. Some were holding clothes up to their bodies, posing, laughing.

Hal didn't seem concerned. 'They're just looking. They won't take anything.'

Ena ran into the tent, pulled the clothes from the women's hands, and shooed them away. They complied, laughing, like it was a game. Then she turned to Roland and said, 'There, are you happy now?'

He didn't know what to say. The women were walking away, still laughing. The men didn't seem to care either way.

'How's it my fault?' he asked.

Hal stood up. 'Everyone calm down.'

'It's you,' Ena said to Hal. 'You've got it all worked out, haven't you?'

'How?'

'You want to kill me. You want me to die.'

Hal didn't get this at all. 'Why would I want that?' He sat down, picked up a bottle, and drank. 'And I'm the one who's not right?'

'You don't say that to me.' Throwing the clothes at him.

'We were having a drink.'

Then she turned to her husband. 'I'll pack my things. You can drive me to the airport. I'll wait for the next plane home – I don't care if it's not till tomorrow.'

Roland wondered if it was a promise he should've made: an Alice Springs to Ayers Rock driving lesson. They were nearly there (he could see the little knob on the horizon) but it had been a long slog. 'What's the limit?'

'Sixty.'

'What are you doing?'

'Sixty.'

'Closer to seventy. Slow down.'

'You speed.'

'Yes, cos I'm experienced.'

Hal said, 'If Mum hada been there last night, you woulda sent them packing.'

Returning from the airport at 9 pm, the men still drinking. Roland had joined them. They'd brought more grog than they'd taken. Ten, eleven, all around the campfire. An old man (who wasn't drinking) had looked at him and said, 'Your old lady not happy?'

'No.'

'Fella and a woman, not the same up here.' He'd tapped his head.

The speed kept creeping up. 'What sign did we just pass?'

Hal shrugged.

'You gotta watch.' Roland thought back to Hal's comment. 'Anyway, it's more complex than that.'

'How?'

'If we all went through life doing exactly what we wanted ...'

Hal couldn't see the problem with this; life would be a lot simpler.

'You wait.'

'For what?'

'Till it gets complex.'

'My life's never gonna get complex. I'm gonna get a shack, grow some carrots, coupla sheep.' He indicated and turned.

Roland had known it would get to this point – when he'd start talking, out of boredom if nothing else. 'I could go through the options alphabetically. Architect, baker, boiler-maker – '

'Or I could just grow carrots?'

'You could.' He read the next sign: AYERS ROCK, LEFT TURN, 200 YARDS.

'I see it,' Hal said, slowing, turning, heading towards the orange lump on the horizon.

'Let me think: dentist – '

'You missed C.'

'Can't think of any C jobs.'

'Cardiologist.'

'Exactly, you could do that. You've got the brain.'

The road widened and the bitumen began. The big rock loomed.

'You do that you could make a million pounds. Invest it, retire at forty. I once knew this fella – '

'I'm not gonna be a cardiologist.'

'What, yer gonna grow carrots?'

'I don't know what I'm gonna do. Won't know till I know. Perhaps not even till I start doing it.'

Roland was happy with this. 'What about a race car driver? You seem to have the knack?'

'They all end up dead.'

'We all end up dead.'

'Not smeared across a road.'

'I dunno, the way you're going.' He checked the speedo. 'Seventy.'

'Just under sixty.' But slowed anyway.

They could see the wrinkles in the rock, its various shades of colour, its shadows, its light.

'People don't exist in isolation.'

'What's that mean?'

'Sometimes it feels like you're not part of the family.'

It's just how I feel, Hal wanted to say.

'The other night, at Saxby Downs … you coulda come outa yer room.'

'I did.'

'Eventually. They were decent people.' He had to interrupt this thought to tell him to slow for an approaching T-junction. 'A person withdraws so much, it's not healthy.'

'That's rubbish.' Hal stopped, looked both ways, and turned left towards the rock.

'They end up doing stupid things.'

'Cos I wanted to rest, I'm gonna kill myself?'

'I didn't say that.'

Hal sped up.

Roland checked the speedo. 'Sixty,' he reminded, but Hal just kept going faster and faster, heading towards the rock. He saw the truck too late, tried to correct, and fought with the steering wheel as they ran off the road into a gully, the car coming to a stop, the engine still running.

They got out.

Hal said, 'That was your fault.'

'You were doing eighty.'

'Your fault.' And he stormed off, into the desert.

'Hal?' Roland walked around and turned off the engine. Too much too soon, he thought. 'Hal? Come give us a hand.'

A few minutes later Hal returned and said, 'I do everything you ask, and where's it get me?'

'You were doing eighty.'

'Everything you ask!'

They stood silently in their spot beside the road.

Roland said, 'I'll push.' He stood behind the car while his son drove out. Then they inspected it. There were scratches, and a small dent in the front wheel guard, but apart from that, nothing.

They drove in silence, watching the rock slowly consuming the sky. Soon they were standing in the car park, looking up.

They climbed for twenty minutes before Roland decided the view from the top couldn't be much better. 'That'll do.' As they surveyed the desert.

Hal wasn't so sure. 'Someone's gonna ask if we climbed Ayers Rock, and we're gonna have to tell them.'

'Come on then.'

Half an hour later they'd made it. They turned circles, stumbled, and clung to the chain. They were the only ones looking out. The sun was setting, so they sat down to watch it.

Roland said, 'Definitely worth it.'

Hal agreed, without saying.

'It's like, when you were born, I said, Let's get started, let's feed him and send him to school and drive west and climb Ayers Rock.'

'What comes next?'

Roland thought it was probably like a painting, how you were always tempted to add another stroke.

'I suppose we gotta climb down.'

Four days later they were sitting on the banks of the Adelaide River. Hal had taken off his shirt, and allowed the sweat to bathe his body. Occasionally it would drop onto the canvas he was working on: his father bent over his own painting, caught up in his own world. He'd mix the sweat with the paint and it would dilute and run. They'd had to carry their gear from the rough road they'd come in on – through thick scrub, swampy ground, down steep granite rock faces. But now Roland said, 'We might just stay here forever.'

'Even you'd get bored,' Hal said.

'Not bored. Hungry, perhaps. But it's only an hour to town. We could learn to hunt.'

'What?'

'Crocs.'

The trip north had provided humidity, wet heat that clung to every panel of the Dodge, and empty hours they had to fill with conversation. The more Hal had accepted it, the more Roland had determined to keep going: Darwin, Broome, down the coast to Perth, back to Kalgoorlie (looking for traces of John McCabe), across the Nullarbor. He knew that when they returned things would be different. The house, and its demands, would alter the landscape they travelled every day. The need to pay bills, the ten-thirty cuppa – all little chains they'd need to re-attach.

Two days prior, they'd gathered around the phone at Richard Fong's pub. 'Yes, it's me, Mary, how are you?'

'No dramas. It's been so long. How are you coping?'

'We could just keep driving. So much to see.'

'Really?'

'Listen, I've called home a few times, but no one's answering. Is Ena about?'

'Yes, yes.'

'Why doesn't she pick up?'

'Her gout. She's in bed. Can't even put a sheet over it.'

'What about Sonia?'

'She went to the Mount for a few days with a girlfriend.'

'How's she coping?'

'Sonia?'

'No, Ena.'

'She's coping. We take her meals in. Check her every hour. Help her to the toilet. I told her she should come and stay with us for a while, but she wouldn't have a bar of it. We left her window open, and gave her the bell, so she rings if it's anything urgent.'

Roland had pressed his ear close to the phone to hear her; the dozen or so drinkers were making enough noise for a hundred. 'If I called at nine in the morning, could you have her by the phone?'

'Yes, I suppose.'

'We're leaving for Adelaide River, so I'd like a word before then. We won't be reachable for a few days.'

'Nine. That's no problem, Griff. We'll have her up and fed.'

And when he'd called the next morning: 'How bad is it?'

'Bad as it's ever been. Worse.'

'You got your tablets?'

'Tablets? I'm out.'

'Go get more.'

'Haven't got anyone to drive me.'

'Can't Mary or Sam go?'

'It's not *their* job to fetch me pills. Don't worry, it'll go in a day or two.'

'You want me to head home?'

'By the time you got here it'd be gone, wouldn't it?'

Then the operator had asked for more coins.

'I better go.'

'How much longer?'

'Few weeks. Things are going well. We might head west.'

'*West?*'

Back beside the tent, Roland said, 'You better write Mum a letter.'

Hal looked up from the river he was painting. 'Why?'

'If you don't …' The sentence didn't need finishing. 'That is, assuming you want to continue?'

'Of course.'

'Cos that's not how it sounded at the beginning.'

'I'm getting used to it.'

'That's what I was trying to tell your mother.'

Hal had added colour to every part of his picture. He showed it to his father and said, 'What do you think?'

'Not bad.'

'But not good?'

'Hal, it's what you think about your own work.' He sat with his brush hanging from his hand. 'Like I said, you don't want to make it too literal. If you're gonna do that you may as well take a photo.'

'You think it's too literal?'

'Well, look at the figure. Is it meant to be me, or a version of me?'

Hal shrugged. He should have known better than to sniff about for a bit of encouragement – whatever he did wouldn't be right, because it would never be Roland Griffin. 'I don't reckon it's bad.'

'It's a decent rendering. *Adelaide Creek, 1956.* You can show that to yer kids.'

A decent rendering? That was all he could hope for. And not just in art. He stood up, threw the painting into the scrub and walked off. Then he stopped, came back, took the rifle, and headed down to the river. 'Gonna shoot a croc,' he said.

'Careful.'

He walked through scrub, feeling his shoulders and chest burning. He lifted the rifle, checked the breech, loaded a bullet and continued. .22 calibre. A rabbit, perhaps, but a croc? The sign on the way in had said so.

He arrived at the water's edge. The river was green-grey, the mud cold and plastic between his toes. Gum trees cast branches across the river, dipped, and drank. A fallen trunk seemed like a good spot to take a shot. So he walked over, and out.

There were two eyes above the water. Or were they? He lifted the rifle, pointed it, and waited.

Roland had set his painting aside. He felt like he was pushing against a wall. In the meantime his son was wandering the world with a gun, looking for a target. Suddenly, the thought terrified him. The six gold bullets he'd loaded into the magazine. Why had he brought it?

He sat up, almost expecting the shot before he heard it. Standing, he ran towards the water. Through the sedges, his feet sucked into the wet ground, slipping on sand. 'Hal!' Down the hill, along the river, until he saw him standing on the log.

Hal turned. 'I saw one!'

Roland was part relieved, and part terrified that his son was standing fifteen feet from land. 'Come in!'

'I shot it!' With that Hal slipped and fell back into the grey water, kicking, raising his head, half-calling. The rifle gurgled its bit of air before sinking.

Roland ran into the water. A few moments later he was beside Hal. He took him around the chest and started kicking towards the bank. Up, up, onto the mud, saying, 'Quickly, help yerself, son.'

Hal lay on his back and Roland sat beside him. The amphitheatre they'd fallen into amplified bird sounds, insects, even the scraping of leaves on water. It was a full minute before Hal said, 'Did you hear me calling?'

'I heard the shot.'

And Hal thought, You couldn't paint a corpse.


They walked along the road (although it wasn't much of one) talking to Dot, who seemed to have more authority than any of the men on Melville Island. She said, 'This forest here – everything we need.'

'Can we have a look?' Roland asked.

She motioned, and they turned off along a track that got darker as they descended. She showed them several types of berries and Hal (who'd decided this might be a decent lifestyle) tried them all. 'And what sort of meat?' he asked.

She used her hand to indicate fish. 'You wanna go?'

'Fishing?' he asked.

She nodded.

'That'd be great.'

'Boys can take you. What about you, Mr Griffin?'

'Griff, please. I'd love to.'

It was decided. She'd ask her husband and the boys (they'd seen them sitting outside the store) to take them later that afternoon. 'Plenty of gear,' she said, rubbing her stomach. 'We get a fire going.'

Dot led them further into the forest. She pointed out several species of birds, highlighting the ones they could eat. Roland thought they might be worth painting. 'Beautiful colours,' he said.

'Good tucker.'

Their tour had begun outside the Milikapiti Store. They'd been told it was Dot you've gotta see (after they'd paid for a pair of five-pound chops). She'd promised to show them around – a three-hour walk along beaches, past swamps, through forests – for a ten-pound fee, each. Roland had thought about it. After all, they knew how to walk, and he just wanted to see the scenery, make a few sketches, take a few photos. But it seemed this was what was expected. Dot had seven or eight children hanging around, and they needed to be fed. So he'd handed over his twenty quid. She'd given it to some bloke in the store, and he'd started spending it straight away.

As they walked, she said, 'You like Darwin?'

'Yes,' Roland replied. 'But you never get used to this humidity, do yer?'

'Plentya grog in Darwin,' she said.

'That's what people seem to like doing.'

'You live here long enough, you like it too.'

'We went to the outdoor cinema last night,' he explained, and showed his mosquito bites to prove it. '*South Pacific*. You seen it?' But then wondered why she would've. She had her own Bali Hai, of sorts, although there weren't many grass skirts or enchanted evenings.

She led them out of the forest, along a high cliff, towards a bay in the distance. 'You going any further?' she asked them.

'Heading right around. Back to Darwin, then Broome.'

She said to Hal, 'Good you go with your dad.'

'Good,' he managed.

Roland noticed several people following them. He asked Dot, 'Did they want to join us?'

She waved to the women who kept hiding, darting into the scrub when anyone turned. 'Don't worry, I told them to keep out of the way.'

'They're doing the tour too?'

She almost laughed. 'Na, they're protecting you.'

He checked again. They were no longer hiding, content to follow at a distance.

'We got spirits watchin' the place,' she said. 'And they don't like strangers. So they gotta look after you.'

Roland felt, somehow, more comfortable. The contingent explained the fee.

Hal imagined generations of Griffins might've been watching – gathered around with a cup of tea and a biscuit, shaking their heads, cursing him.

They walked down the hill to a waterhole. Two men and several children were swimming, naked. Dot asked her visitors if they felt like cooling off.

Roland shrugged. 'Good water?'

'Cool off.'

He turned to his son. 'We may as well.' He ran down the hill, stood on the bank and stripped down to his underwear. As he did, the swimmers made comments, laughed, encouraged him. One said, 'Father Christmas.' The children hid their thoughts behind their arms and hands. Hal was beside him, down to his undies, running and slipping in the mud and jumping in. Soon they were both splashing.

When they emerged twenty minutes later, Dot had gone. They dressed and headed back along the path. As they went Roland said, 'Maybe we should head home?'

Hal said, 'Why now?'

He thought, Maybe we've done what we came for? But said, 'That's a few weeks of school, and by the time we get back …'

'That didn't bother you before.'

'Still doesn't.'

'I'm not worried about school. Gonna be a race caller, aren't I?'

'I dunno. Still reckon you might be a painter. What I meant was, you seem to have settled. Which is funny, isn't it? Being on the road?'

Hal thought about this. His dad was right. Maybe he could travel for a year or two, pick up work overseas. See life beyond Burleigh Avenue.

Eventually they decided to keep going. Everyone had been telling them about Broome.

They turned back onto the main road. They were close enough to see Dot sitting in front of the store. Roland said, 'Maybe I haven't been a lot of help.'

'How's that?'

'Sittin' in me shed. Caught up with … I mean, it's just canvas, isn't it? And paint?'

'Never thought I'd hear it.'

'It is.'

'But if that's the case, why's Sam bother with his horses?'

Silence, broken by a loud bird.

'Or anyone with anything?' Hal thought of the letter he'd written to his dad, their father-son day, all those years ago. He could still remember what he'd said, and felt like reciting it (as a sort of charm, against the millions of ghosts listening). But he couldn't. Instead, he ran towards town. 'Two quid for the first back.'

Roland watched him go – his long legs, his awkward head, sitting on its drainpipe neck. He wanted, more than ever, to do whatever it took to make him happy. He knew this was almost impossible. He wished he could make the journey for him, and meet him on the other side. Perhaps love was enough to get him there, but he feared it wasn't. Advice, favours, money – all of these things might help, but nothing would guarantee success. He wanted to hug him, but knew his son wouldn't let him. To tell him he loved him, but realised he was beyond this. He felt, maybe for the first time, what it was to be a father. To *not* be able to fix things. He could remember sitting beside his father's bed, looking at his red skin, smelling it. Asking, 'You gonna be alright, Dad?'

'Of course.'

'They said they got you out in time.'

And then he'd cried – all at once, without having chosen to, or being able to control it. He'd managed, 'Nothin' bad's gonna happen, is it, Dad?'

'Of course not.'

'I'm sorry I broke that winder.'

'You're alright, son.'

He'd pulled himself together, because he figured that's what a man had to do: to be there for others.

When he arrived his son was sitting on the verandah of the store, drinking a Coke. 'What took you?'

Dot was waiting. She said, 'I let you be.'

'Why's that?' he asked.

'All them dead fellas, they reckon you're okay.'

# 1962

Hal felt it pressing around his head. Although it was unpleasant, the effect wasn't. For a while he could relax, close his eyes, descend into the sort of landscapes his father painted. Just wandering, or staggering through dry creek beds, past the partly rotted corpses of drought-dead cattle, out onto some vast gibber where the corrugated earth made walking difficult.

Or something lusher. The previous Friday, after he'd bought a few joints, he'd walked the mile or so to the swollen river (it hadn't rained for weeks, but they were releasing water from the dam). Sat on the edge watching the torrent rushing over rocks, hammering the bank. Then he'd seen a big log, and had an idea. Walked over, got on, and pushed off. At first he bobbed and picked up momentum, watched the approaching rapids (although it was just a swell under the William Street Bridge), marvelled at his world of familiar things. That's what the stuff did. Made the ordinary magnificent, the mundane bearable. But then the log had rotated, and he'd come off, but tried to hold on. Unsuccessfully. Struggled, thought he was drowning, before someone pulled him out, saying, 'How stupid can a person be?'

But today was different. He'd avoided any stuff since the previous afternoon. Still, there was enough in his system to keep him going.

He was back at Dr Bailey's. Hadn't returned for years. The days of being looked after, keeping Nan company, sitting, reading, as she cleaned around him. Dickens became Conrad, Henry James, Nabakov. Dozens of them. All with *part* of the picture. The encyclopaedias: *sabre, saffron, Samoa, saw-cut* … Somehow, he sensed, the whole world beyond Burleigh Avenue lived between the covers.

*Tiger, titration, Trinidad* … It was all there, if you had enough time. But in the end, this wasn't enough. Whatever lay beyond Pennington needed finding, digging out of the ground, examining.

'Two shakes,' his Nan called, from the laundry.

Dr Bailey's: same carpet and rugs, worn to the floorboards where the doctor moved from room to room. Same paintings and prints, furniture, silverware that Nan kept polished every fortnight, month, year, despite the fact all of this stuff (he guessed) was never used. Dr Bailey's house was a museum of Dr Bailey. But he was a good employer, paid well, didn't complain if she missed something.

There were millions of things to do in life, but all you needed was one thing you were good at, and could bear repeating every day. And this, Hal thought, standing in front of Dr Bailey's overfull bookcase, was the one thing he'd failed to do. Since he was a kid, fucking up his movie career, studies, relationships. Since he was a teenager, screwing up his race calling, various apprenticeships.

One of the first was a panel beater. Three months of hammering bodies, welding, grinding, puttying the gaps and sanding until his fingers were raw. Three months. Every time he learned something new it was gratifying. But then he was repeating himself, and his mind wandered, and he cut an acetylene line and people were running about shouting, although nothing had happened. And another boss screamed at him, and he just stood, walked out, went home to tell his parents the bad news.

The longest had been as a printer. This, he'd said at the interview, was a job with his name on it. He could sit and read books all day. He loved how the old ones smelt, and the mystery of how they were bound and, a hundred years later, still hadn't fallen apart. The love of typeface. He had a book, he explained, with hundreds laid out in alphabetical order, and he could admire them for hours, sans serif, the minor imperfections in woodcuts, all of it, for some reason (and you'll think me mad!) fascinating.

He'd started, done well, mastered typesetting and letterpress, offset, come home with inky hands and the lunch he'd been too busy to eat. He'd learned how to quote jobs so there was a decent profit, but not too much to lose the work to a competitor. Roland and Ena had never been happier. Roland would say things like, 'See, I told you, Ena. Patience.' And she'd say, 'So what was the point of all those trips around Australia?'

Hal had got the key to the office, and taken his new girlfriend, Alice, to show her around: some of the pamphlets and books he'd set, printed, bound.

But it hadn't lasted. For some reason (and even now he couldn't say why) he'd lost interest, started arriving late, failed generous deadlines. And when he was eventually called into the boss's office, he said, 'I think I know what you're going to say.'

He took a book down from the shelf, opening the front and reading: 'Ex libris, Dr E Bailey', and Hal's addition ('also read by Hal Griffin, 9 and a halve'). Hundreds, he guessed, had been marked. Dr Bailey had never complained.

Which made him think of other books. Not just dirty books. Filthy books. He reached into his pocket, pulled out a clipping. Six or seven people caught in a confusion of limbs, reaching, grasping, holding and feasting like they'd never been fed.

Nan came in with a bucket and said, 'If you want the job, you can't sit reading all day.'

'Sorry.' He helped her, carried the bucket of hot water to the entry porch, dunked the mop and squeezed it out. Then started working.

'So this is the list,' Nan said. She produced a folded sheet of paper from her apron pocket, opened it and started reading. '"Ten am until ten-thirty: mop all floors – entry, kitchen, bathrooms, toilets" (as well as outside).' She watched him work. 'Got that? Half an hour for the mopping and no, no.' She took the mop and showed him how. 'Squeeze out all the water, every drop, then long strokes, overlapping, or else you'll have a sore back before lunch.'

He reclaimed the mop and did it the right way, but she kept correcting him, then returned to her list. '"Ten-thirty until eleven: make up bed with clean sheets and take the old ones down to the laundry".'

'There's no point, Nan,' he said, stopping. 'I won't remember it all. Maybe you could give me the list?' He held out his hand, hoping she'd just go away. It was a job you could do without much thought.

'Righto,' she said, 'but you gotta stick to these times.'

Hal took the list, put it in his pocket and said, 'I'll get this done first, eh?'

Nan went out to put the kettle on.

Nan's gift: her job. She'd had a word to Dr Bailey, said how poor Hal was having trouble finding work, or at least keeping it, but how he was a good boy (Dr Bailey didn't need persuading) and a good worker and just needed some space where he could be left alone, not prodded and pushed and bullied, like all the other places. Dr Bailey had agreed. 'It's fine by me, but I always thought it was something *you* liked?'

It will be simple, Nan explained to Hal. You arrive ten minutes early, find the key in the gas box, open the door and start filling your buckets. Never touch his personal items, but you know that, don't you, Hal? Never eat his food (not that he'd mind, but it's not your place). Stick to the schedule. Don't get distracted with books. The money. He'll leave it here, see, inside this vase.

Hal closed his eyes, rocked to and fro to the rhythm: the Redskins drumming from a distance, some sort of song. He'd seen the bodies tied to trees, parts of their heads missing, blood everywhere. Pleasing, because the sexual attraction of corpses remained. He could feel this now, and wished Alice was still with him. Then he heard Nan going upstairs. He couldn't help himself. Quietly opened the front door, slipped out, took the smoke from his pocket and fumbled in his daks for the matches.

'Hal, where are you?'

Shit. He pocketed the stuff, went in and said, 'I's looking for a broom.'

'Why do you need a broom?'

He returned to the mop, and the pulse in his ear.

Nan made the tea, and called him. They sat on the lounge and he said, 'Mum said to say thanks for the job.'

She smiled. Despite all the bullshit, she loved him more than anything. Giving up her job was nothing, if it might fix things. She knew she'd give up a lot more if it would do any good. She'd give him money, if it would help, her flat, anything.

'*Mum* said to say thanks?'

'Me too. Thanks.'

'That's fine. You just gotta set your mind to it. It's not much work, for now, but it could lead to other things.'

He wondered how many times he'd heard this. Could remember Sam explaining his future in racing, Mary, as a cook (another phase: her teaching him dozens of recipes, encouraging him to apply to the army, because soldiers didn't always fight wars, but they always needed to eat). He studied the carpet he'd nearly memorised, then looked up. 'I don't know what I'm gonna do, Nan.'

'What do you mean?'

'Everyone just gets on with things, and I ...' He waited, noticed how she smiled. 'Cleaning'd be okay, wouldn't it?'

'Bloody oath.'

'I mean, it's not glamorous, but ...'

She watched how his head dropped when he ran out of words. She stood, took some cash from the vase above the fire, handed it to him and said, 'Your first pay.'

'Not all of it. You take half.' Although he wanted all of it. He knew what it could buy.

'Keep it. Don't spend it on smokes. You don't, do you?'

'No.' He wondered if she could see it: his red eyes, the way the stuff made his face gaunt, pale, no matter how hard he sucked mints and drank water and stood in the sun. 'I know I tried a few, when I was a kid.'

'Your mother was horrified when she found out.'

'Kids do stupid things, don't they, Nan?'

'They grow out of it.' Although she didn't seem sure. 'Now, you won't need to clean next fortnight because he's going overseas for three weeks. But I asked him if you could pull some weeds, and he said okay. I'll show you on the way out.'

'Fine.' He folded the pound notes and put them in his pocket.

After tea he returned to the foyer with a buffer. Nan had showed him how to add wax to the pads and let it move in circles to get the best shine. He could feel himself returning – the ease of speaking, the way everything made sense. He didn't like it at all.

He waited until he heard Nan upstairs, and escaped back to the front yard. Quickly found the rollie and the matches and lit up. Started taking it all in. Felt himself lifting, up into the pine trees that had consumed the powerlines, and sky. Lungs so powerful he could consume a quarter of the cigarette at a time. As he heard Nan upstairs doing the job he should've been learning. But everything got done, one way or another. And so what if it didn't? What did it matter? He stumbled, squatted in the pine needles. A neighbour or someone walked past, looked at him, smelt him perhaps, but Hal just said, 'What the fuck do you want?'

Hal sat in the car and watched a small tornado gathering dust, scraps of plastic and paper, moving them across the little car hills of the drive-in, before another gust of wind knocked the first one, and it ceased to exist. No dramas, no crying, no eulogy. This seemed strange. Insects born and dying. Birds. All without comment. It was only people who made a fuss. Why, he couldn't think.

Roland had parked in the middle of what was left of the drive-in. The screen had yellowed and the steel ribs were showing, like someone had tried to starve it to death. The blue metal was full of weeds, the speaker stands rusted, the speakers broken, lying about. As Hal remembered the first time they'd come. Five, six years before? And the movie? Gregory Peck? Yes, *Moby Dick*. He tried to imagine the white whale on the screen, but only saw where someone had painted their name, and a few willies. He wasn't sure why it had closed, but it had. They'd gone to pick up Sonia for tea, and on the way home had driven past, seen it padlocked, the CLOSED sign, the cafeteria boarded up. Roland'd said, 'It only just opened.'

'It's been shut for years,' Sonia had said.

'But why? It was popular, plenty of people went.' He'd slowed, pulled over, driven up to the ticket booth. 'Everyone I know says they've been.'

'Mum's expecting us.' Sonia becoming bored.

But Roland wasn't happy with that. He'd checked the gates, discovered they just pushed open, drove in and parked in the same spot they had on the night of the whale. Then he'd got out, stood staring at the screen and said, 'What a shame … nothing like a night at the drive-in.'

'Why did we only go once?' Sonia asked.

'I meant to get back but …'

Hal remembered Shirley in the toilet. The way she half-ran and half-walked back to the car. He felt bad. A stupid thing to do, really. People were generally decent. Like the previous day, waiting to buy smokes at the deli, and some old fella was served ahead of him, and he thought to say something, but didn't, and then some girl said it was funny, wasn't it, how people saw what they wanted. Next thing they were talking about how people were so selfish these days. All with a stranger. Better than the volumes of philosophy he'd read, the novels, the explanations of human behaviour.

He remembered standing outside the toilet. The colour of Shirley's panties. He felt bad for the thousand times he'd given her grief. And although he didn't anymore, it seemed there was no way to fix the damage. She had to choose to forgive, or not. All the times he'd stood outside her window.

As they'd driven into the deserted drive-in, Roland had said, 'What about it, Hal?'

'What?'

'This place. You and me. We can buy it, do it up, get it going again.'

Hal wasn't sure if his dad was joking.

'No, serious. Bita work – you can be the projectionist if you like.'

'You wouldn't buy a drive-in.'

'I might.'

'Yer too busy painting all day.' Hal found it hard to believe his father cared about drive-ins, or Hal Griffin's prospects. Roland was always for Roland. Or Sonia – like now, the two of them talking, laughing, walking around what was left of the playground under the screen. Sonia pushing him, him replying with a shove, a few words, a flurry of wind and dirt whipping up, dying away. He wondered what they were saying. Sonia, no doubt, asking if he'd been acting normal, and his dad muttering a few comments. This could explain why they kept looking at him. In a way, he was no longer a member of the family, just an attachment, a steel tube for getting to difficult places. Roland was standing at the base of the screen, looking up, like it was some enormous canvas he had to paint.

Reaching into his pocket, Hal found half a cigarette. He got out of the car, lit it, hid beside the toilet door, and ascended again. But there wasn't much of it. So he felt in his pocket and found the half-inch square of paper. Bond. Sixty years old, perhaps, smelling of ethyl hexanol. With a few words where it'd been torn: 'unhappy in its own particular way'. It had cost him considerably more, and he hadn't been brave enough to take it, yet.

Why, he thought, do things change so quickly? Flicker and disappear. A sign telling you to wait while the film is fixed, or asking if Dr Randall was in the audience, as he's wanted at the hospital right away. All unreliable memories, made indistinct by the last minutes of sun.

'Come over here,' Roland called to Hal, motioning. But turned away just as quickly, and continued talking to Sonia. Or Ena. Mary. Sam. James, especially. When James was around no one else mattered. 'Hal!' his father called again.

Hal placed the piece of paper into his mouth. Nothing, for a moment, then he felt lightheaded, fell against the wall, slipped to the ground. The feeling overcame him and he could see lights, hear the jungle, the roar of a panther, toucans. Taste it all, even. The old meat that hadn't quite rotted from the droughty carcasses.

'Hal?'

His father and sister were standing over him. Roland said, 'Are you feeling sick?'

Hal didn't want them to know. He noticed the paper beside his open fingers, but then the breeze picked up, and it was gone, and he thought, Maybe they'll think I died of disappointment.

'Hal.' His dad was shaking him.

Despite the sensation, Hal felt he had a mission. So he stood, got his balance, and said to his dad, 'I'm fine. Something in the guts, I guess.' And remembered John McCabe, and his celluloid sister, the set, the bed, telling her he had bad guts, although then his mum had come in and made him drink castor oil.

He walked a few steps towards the old cafeteria. Went in, Sonia and Roland following. He heard Roland say to her, 'He's taken something.' Felt his dad in his pockets, searching, and pushed him away. Roland fell, Sonia screamed, and Hal called her the universal slut, get away from me or I'll claw yer fuckin' eyes out. And then Roland was back beside him, holding him, trying to push him down, but he kept going. Picked up a chip stand and started smashing a register, the remains of a candy display, a swing at his father, Sonia, as they backed off, towards the door, and Sonia said, 'What should we do, Dad?' and Roland said, 'Keep back.' Then, 'What did you take, son?'

*Son.* As if, Hal thought. His eyes wide, terrified, glowing with the reflection of the fires along the river, in the Todd, cooking black oil on the stove. 'Put it out!' Hal called, smashing a mirror, a fridge, a deep fryer full of asbestos and concrete from the walls and ceilings.

Roland could see the boy tossing in the waves, terrified. At first, he'd mistaken this look for awe. Like any child faced with Blackbeard, a mare three times his size, the crocodile that had probably never existed. But now he saw the heart of it. A child who was destined to be here, throwing spears, from the moment he was born.

'Hal, you gotta tell me, what was it?'

'You should know,' he said, throwing away the metal stand, staggering around, using a hand to block the light and sound.

Sonia stepped forward and said her brother's name. But he just looked through her, like he didn't recognise her as a person, let alone a sister.

Then he ran. From the cafeteria. Towards the main road. Roland followed for a distance but couldn't keep up. He watched him run across the main road, down a side street, away from home. Then he was gone. So Roland just held Sonia and said, 'You okay?'

She didn't reply, and it was getting dark. Roland wondered where the hell they'd start looking for him.


'Dr Bernard Neri': gold letters on a wooden plaque that sat on the front of his desk. Hal guessed that made it official. He wondered what nationality he was: dark skin, flecked with liver spots, and lines around his eyes. He could ask, of course, but Neri might get shitty. The doctor said, 'I'm just interested.'

'My neighbour, Mary, first suggested it. She thought it might help, since everyone had decided I needed help.'

'So?'

'Every day I read an entry. For example, yesterday, Our Lady of Mount Carmel.'

'And?'

'I say my prayer. It can't hurt, can it?'

'But do you think the saints hear you?'

'Of course not. But it's like those pills you prescribed. You gotta try everything.'

Hal turned to his parents, sitting at the back of the room. His father, in his blood-spotted shirt with its missing buttons, Ena, still in her apron. He knew they were standing outside his door, peering through the crack. His dad was thinking, Christ, not all this again. Another straw to clutch: St Guy of Cortona in the early hours, *God of power and mercy* …

Neri said, 'Do you have a patron saint?'

'No.'

'Do you speak to these saints?'

'That'd be crazy, wouldn't it? I'd have to be mad. I mean, actually mad. Or am I already?'

'Of course not. Young people are often *confused*.'

'That's a euphemism, isn't it?'

'No, it's a description.'

Hal was feeling his way, unsure of the doctor. 'Mad? Like Joan of Arc. She kept hearing St Michael. Can you imagine what her friends were thinking?'

'But you haven't heard voices. You don't believe in God.'

'You'd have to be simple. That some fella made everything. That *is* mad.'

Neri wrote more notes.

'What are you writing?'

He read: '"Plain, clinical view of the world, and its creation."'

298

Hal seemed happy with this.

'How have you been feeling, in yourself?'

Lysergic acid, marijuana, he wanted to say. It all helps. But he guessed the blood they'd taken would soon tell them that. So all he said was, 'No different.'

Ena told the doctor he'd been in bed for the last week.

Hal turned to glare at her, clutching her purse. 'He didn't ask you!'

No one challenged him. They all knew what that would mean. Roland, especially, had learnt to read the signs. His son, lying on the lounge room floor, watching television; his wife, coming in and asking a simple question. 'Hal, you couldn't bring in the washing?'

'In a minute.'

'*In a minute*. It's always in a minute.'

He'd say, 'Ena, leave it.'

'He can help.'

'He will, won't you, Hal?'

'I'll do it. Can't you wait?'

Sometimes he'd stand and lead his wife from the room, or if it was too late, try to calm his son. This wasn't as easy as it used to be. He could no longer manhandle him into his room. Now he was taller, bulkier, fatter (from the endless hours spent sitting in front of the telly). If he lost his temper there was nothing they could do. They would retreat to their rooms, and wait. Listen to him hammering walls, or smashing windows. And if it went on too long, call for help. The police in their drive again, handcuffs, their son face down on the drive with a knee in his back.

'So, tell me what happened,' Neri said.

'I can't remember.'

'You were at the drive-in yesterday evening. You got angry, stormed off, and returned home. Got the spade …'

Hal knew there was no avoiding the facts, the blood, the fluttering wings and the way the birds stopped working when you hit them.

'The chooks were loud. Maybe there was a snake in there with them. They just kept making this noise ...'

He wasn't sure if he should say more. How he carefully opened the gate his dad and Trevor had put up, and started swinging; how some chickens went flying, but others, if they were positioned correctly, had their heads removed; how he then used the sharp end of the blade to attack them, to cut them in sections, to remove limbs.

'And then your dad arrived home, and tried to stop you?'

'Yes.'

Pulling the spade from his son's hands as Ena stood crying, calling for help. Sam arriving, going into the yard of red feathers. Both men managing to contain him. 'Ena, call the police.'

And again, two constables holding him down in the chook shit, tightening the handcuffs.

Ena saying, 'They're too tight. He won't have no circulation.'

Neri said, 'The police aren't happy with you. You hit one on the jaw. He had to go to the doctor.'

'He had his knee on my neck.'

'Maybe he had no choice?'

Hal sat up. 'You know, you're quite a nice fella, but this habit of questioning. *Why do you think that is?* Then I'm meant to answer, because blah blah, then I see the error of my ways and everything's fixed. But it doesn't work like that, does it?'

'I don't mean it that way. It's just my manner.'

'No, it's not. It's what they teach you at university. But in this case it doesn't work. I mean, considering all the pills you've tried, and how long it's been, I think we're past all that. Considering I just killed, how many was it, Dad?' He turned.

'Nine.'

'Nine chooks. I mean, how could you talk me around? I think it's horrible I did it. I've been looking after those chooks for years.' He stopped and lowered his head. 'Trevor wouldn't be happy.'

'Who's that?' Neri asked.

'Mary's cousin. He used to steal everything that wasn't nailed down.' He turned to his father again. 'Whatever happened to him?'

'He died in prison. You knew that.'

'Did he? How did he die?'

'He had bowel cancer. Remember, me and Mary went and saw him in the hospital.'

Neri asked, 'Trevor got your chooks, did he?'

Hal wasn't sure this was any of his business. It was a long time ago, when he was a boy. When he was confused, but not fucked up; heard things, but didn't respond. He said to his father, 'I can't remember him dying.'

'You went to his funeral.'

'Did I?'

'Yes. Remember, Mary all upset. Me and Sam were pallbearers.'

Hal couldn't recall. He wished he could. He'd liked Trevor. What you saw was what you got. He had no pretence (unlike this doctor). He didn't use rhetorical questions, or hide behind a desk, or write notes on legal paper with an expensive fountain pen. He just was. 'What year?' he asked his father.

'Fifty-eight. After our second trip, remember?'

They were in Cloncurry when they'd got the phone call. Ena saying, 'Mary reckons any time now.'

'Should we come back?'

'No, he wasn't family. You keep going.'

Under canvas, Hal settled. Beneath the stars, became whole. Perpetual motion was a perfect pill. But you couldn't spend your whole life travelling.

'That was a good trip,' Roland said. 'Remember? Brizzie, Maryborough, Bundy, then up north, then inland.'

Hal felt good. He was sitting beside his father. The old Dodge (and it had done a million miles by now) was purring along the highway.

The needle seldom moved. He was watching colonies of bats in fig trees: how they clung, despite the wind bumping them about.

Neri said, 'We've decided to keep you in for a few days.'

Hal didn't argue. It wouldn't do any good. They liked to observe him after an episode. It made everyone feel better. Charts were filled in, notes made, measured portions of beef served.

As Hal's way of atoning, he turned to Roland and said, 'Maybe Sam could come in tomorrow?'

'I'll tell him.'

'If he can't, tell him I'm sorry.'

'He'll understand.'

'I think I mighta hit him, too.'

'It was just a cut lip.'

A cut lip. Twenty years of helping him, and that's what it had come to. Hal looked down at his pants – the blood, the few small dried feathers, bare feet. He wished he hadn't done it. But it just kept happening, again and again.

Neri asked, 'How's Alice?'

'I dunno.'

'They broke up,' Ena said.

'That's a pity. How long had you been together?'

'Nearly two years,' Ena said. 'And she was such a nice girl.'

'Mum.'

'She was good for you, Hal.'

Hal turned all the way around. 'Good for me?'

'You know what I mean. That other week, you were in your room for days, you wouldn't come out. She arrives and ten minutes later there you are, bright as a button, "What's for lunch, Mum? Me and Alice are a bit peckish." And then a day later you call her up and say, "That's it." All off, no reason.'

Hal faced forward, and shrugged. 'It'd run its course.'

'Every relationship runs its course, but you stay with it,' Ena said.

He turned again. 'Why?'

'Because it's stable. That's what we all need, stability.'

'Bullshit.'

'It was a shame, wasn't it, Griff?'

'His life, Ena. He's old enough to make his own decisions.'

Ena wasn't happy with this. 'You could call her back?'

'I'm not.'

Neri had been happy to let them talk; that was always the best way. 'That's understandable. I had several girlfriends before I met my wife.'

Hal turned to his dad. 'What you gonna do with the chooks?'

'I'll bury them, later.'

'Could you wait?'

'Why?'

'I'll help.'

Neri thought this was a good idea; it would provide closure to the whole event. 'Indeed,' he said, fiddling with his chin. Then he wrote about it on the paper.

'I suppose it can wait until tomorrow. Tomorrow, was it, Doctor?'

'A day or two.' He had the power, and he intended using it, or at least waving it about like a Coronation flag.

'Could we get a few more chooks?' Hal asked his father.

'If you like.'

Ena was happy with all this. Pills would be taken, Alice would be called, things would settle. She stood, stepped forward and placed a bag on the table. 'These are his things,' she told the doctor.

Hal felt like she was glad to be getting rid of him, to have a few days to herself.

Roland joined them. He squeezed Hal's shoulder and attempted an awkward hug. 'You do what you're told, right.'

'Have I got any choice?'

'No,' Neri said, smiling.

Roland and James walked across the grass with Meryl Bell. She wore black, in memory of Paul. Everything: dress, gloves, stockings. She was a small woman with straight shoulders, and her head drooped in its black hat, although it had been twelve months since he'd died. Since they'd carried him, in his pine casket, across these same lawns. Since they'd laid him on the grass and waited for the young priest with his shaving cuts. Since he'd made some comments about art and artists ('the people who observe, and comment, and give *gravitas* to our lives …'). There'd been a short car ride back to the Bell house and a cup of Lipton's from the kitchen Paul had been too busy to paint.

Standing beside the grave that day, Roland had seen his future. His world was Holden and corned beef, the development of Under-12 muscle bulk, and cheap lino from McLeay's. It hadn't mattered that he hadn't sold a picture for a year, that they were living off money from Ena's inheritance. What mattered was that he was alive, and his hand was steady, and he was able to work. So what if (despite still thinking the stockman was the most important person in the world) art was only good for dentists' waiting rooms.

They dropped back as Meryl approached the grave. She stopped and read his headstone ('Paul Bell, Artist, 1889-1961') and laid her few flowers, cut from her garden. Then she knelt and cleared leaves from the grass that had grown over him. She started to mumble a prayer. They stood back.

'I should go see him,' James said.

'Leave it. He'll be home tomorrow. Maybe we could take him to the pictures?'

Roland had told his friend about the chooks, piled up in the corner of the yard, waiting for their own burial. It hadn't surprised James. There hadn't been one day when Hal was worse than the previous, but when you looked back, you could see it. He said, 'I don't like to think of him in that place.'

'It gives Ena a break. They get him back on his medications, settle him.'

They helped Meryl stand up. She wasn't crying. She didn't seem particularly upset. 'Just as well he never knew,' she said.

'What's that?' Roland asked.

'That Britten fella. Didn't make an effort. Paul gave him lessons for years. You know, half fees, or none. And he didn't come.'

'Maybe he was busy?' James said.

'You were his favourites. Although you, James, he'd be very disappointed.' Turning her back on her husband, she started walking towards the car park. She stumbled on the thick grass and they helped her. She broke free and continued.

'I'll never stop,' James said.

'You gotta stick at it, don't you, Griff?'

'You gotta eat too, I s'pose.'

'That never bothered Paul. And I never made him take a job.' She turned to James. 'What did you say you were doing?'

'Insurance. Assessing claims.'

'See, when do you paint?'

'Nights. Weekends.'

'No, Paul was always in his studio. I read somewhere, some painter's wife, she said that once you got an artist in the family it's all over. I accepted that, early on.'

Roland guessed she was right. Guessed Ena and Sonia and Hal would concur. But they didn't seem to realise there was no choice.

Meryl said, 'Quit yer job, James. Get back to it. That's what Paul would want.'

'He'd want my family to eat.'

'They'll eat. I waited twenty years for a holiday, then it was Cairns, and we stayed in a caravan park. But I didn't care. I knew. Three weeks to change a light bulb, but it didn't matter.'

James guessed Meryl wouldn't understand. How, with people

relying on you, you had to grow up sometime. Make a decision about what you valued most. Love. Maybe what she and Paul had shared was different? Like mistletoe in wattle.

And anyway, what about the dozens of unsold Bell paintings, James wanted to say. He'd seen them, after the funeral, when she'd invited them into his studio. 'Help yerselves, boys. He'd want you to have this stuff. No good to me.' Easels and canvases, hundreds of tubes of paint and gallons of oil.

As they'd packed gear in boxes, James had said, 'It doesn't seem right.' He'd seen his future. 'You take it all, Griff.'

'Why's that?'

'My brother-in-law, he's gonna get me a job.'

And then, six months after Paul's death, the auction. A room full of Streetons and McCubbins, Heysen, two Nolans. Bidding had been healthy. Nothing had been passed in, until the seven lots of Paul Bell. 'Number one, *Morning in Osmond Hill*, what say we start the bidding at twenty-five pounds … twenty? Bell is very collectable. Fifteen … ten?'

Meryl stumbled back into the car park and they helped her again. They loaded her in the car and headed home. As they went, she said, 'Paul often talked about Osmond Hill.'

'He liked it up there,' James said.

'It was nice of you to take him. He was never very social, and he never had many friends … well, none, really. So it meant a lot to him.'

Days sitting on the balcony of the Commercial Hotel – sketching, painting, calling down to Hal (who was playing golf on the main street), 'Back straight, keep your eye on the ball.'

'Hey, Mr Bell, I bet I can get one in the window.'

Meryl said, 'He liked to wander through the old shops. They reminded him of Nyngan. That's where he grew up. He often said he wanted to go back, and I said, "No, what we would do?" But we shoulda.'

'We all shoulda done a lot of things,' James said.

They stopped and bought Meryl an ice cream. She asked about Hal and Roland told her, everything, and she wanted them to take her to Glenside but Roland said, 'They wanna settle him. Maybe after he gets home.'

'He was a good boy,' she said.

'He still is.'

'Paul painted him once. Don't know what happened to that one.' They were sitting on a bench beside the shop. She stopped licking and said, 'I hope he's okay.'

'He'll be fine,' Roland said.

She headed back to the car. 'Hal, you just gotta put a paintbrush in his hand,' she said.

'You reckon?' Roland asked, following.

'Yes. It saved Paul from his moods.' She waited for him to open the car. 'And you, James Bailey, back to work. He'd be turning in his grave.'


Neri had suggested it; shown him what to do. Hal sat on his bed with his legs crossed and breathed in and out. Thoughts jumped into his head, but he ignored them. They returned; he fought them. He found that if you did this for ten minutes the chaos subsided.

He opened his eyes, and he was still in his room. The fat man (and this is the only way he thought about him) was lying on his bed, reading. He was facing the wall, and his arse crack showed. He, they, both wore the bone pants and white shirt each patient was given on admission.

'Who's yer guru?' the fat man asked.

Hal ignored him and tried again. Ten minutes later he was back in the desert, or sky, or wherever it was Neri said you should go. But the voices were still waiting: You can have five minutes, but you gotta return. He knew he had to get out of this room. Like the Poe story he'd read at Dr Bailey's, the walls seemed to be closing in, forcing him towards a deep pit.

'You're moaning,' the fat man said.

'What?'

'I'm trying to read.'

Hal was disgusted by this man. The rolls of fat hanging off his side, his arms, his face; *Peyton Place*; the hair on his back emerging from his collar. 'So what if I fucking moaned?'

'You mind your business, I'll mind mine.'

Tomorrow they'd let him home. He switched off his lamp and lay down, pulled up the sheets, turned against the wall. 'I wanna sleep.'

'I'm reading.'

'How much longer?'

'Long as it takes.'

It was obviously something oppositional. Perhaps he couldn't get along with the old girl; maybe he'd beaten her up. Hal asked, 'What sorta job do you do?'

The fat man read aloud to make his point.

'Sorry for asking.'

'I'm a swimming instructor.'

Hal thought it unlikely. He closed his eyes and continued meditating. Felt relaxed, but not tired. Guessed he wouldn't be able to sleep. Still, he persisted. Drifted. He was with his dad on a tour of a deep limestone cave. The guide was shining his torch around, and he pointed to an opening at the top of the cavern. He explained how, when they'd first discovered the cave, a skeleton plugged this vent. Where a child, hundreds of years before, had crawled down a hole after a wombat, got stuck, and slowly starved to death. Hal remembered thinking this was the worst thing he'd ever heard, or could imagine. Held, with no light, no faces or words, no hope, no love. So bad you might be sent mad as you were forced to see your end. Roland grinned and said, 'You'd have to be pretty bloody unlucky.' And the guide said, 'Or stupid.'

The fat man was asleep at last. A few more hours and he could go home. He'd head to the track and call a few races and they'd give him twenty quid. He'd help his dad bury the chickens, sweep out the shed. He'd help his mum cook tea because Sonia was coming over. He'd apologise to Mr Carey about the stolen carrots.

He looked around, tried to remember. The words. 'The blackness of eternal night', and Dr Bailey standing behind him saying, 'Do you know what happens next?'

'The rats get him?'

'No, something worse.'

'What?'

'Can't say. Keep reading.'

His own cave of white light and a clock: 3:17 am. He lay back, tried to breathe, push back at the world, but couldn't move his arms. A self-imposed claustrophobia of meshed glass and yellow light from the hallway.

So he decided. Stood, quietly opened his wardrobe and pulled on his pants, shirt and shoes. He noticed chook blood on the collar. So he found the fat man's shirt and put it on instead. A hundred sizes too big, but he tucked it in and rolled up the sleeves. He tried his jacket. It was far too big, but in its pockets, a watch and a wallet with five pounds.

It wasn't easy getting out. He lay flat on the ground, kicked the window frame, but it was blocked by a grate. So he found a coin, lifted the glass a few inches, and removed several screws keeping the metal in place. After dropping the grate, he opened the window. Squeezed through and got out. Waited and listened: only the hum of compressors from the kitchen. He followed the wall, all the time looking for one of the nurses, or the guard who patrolled at night. He crawled through the rose garden, to the pepper tree, up the branch that joined earth and fence, over, and (after checking the deserted street) down the other side.

He walked for an hour, half-expecting someone to say, 'Hey,

shouldn't you be in the nuthouse?' Crossing the road, he ran into the Parklands. Towards the city, across paddocks, over irrigation ditches, along paths. He was surprised that he could keep running, but he could. Now he was on the edge of the city. A bakery glowed under sodium lights. Someone had left pallets of bread on the footpath and he took a loaf and kept running. As he went he ate, and then he was thirsty, so he helped himself to milk from a van. The same sort that appeared each morning in Burleigh Avenue, that drew the mums in their dressing gowns to the middle of the street. This took him back again. He felt happy: lying in bed on a hundred mornings, woken by the diesel vapours. Happy.

Soon he was on Torrens Road. He checked the fat man's watch. Five past six. He ran. It might draw attention, but it was the best way. Running always worked: from school, coppers, mothers, roosters (Trevor's idea), shopkeepers, Mr Carey (the carrots), inspectors (who's paid for tickets?).

Stopping, he sat on the ground and waited to get his breath. Thought what to do, where to go. Of course. He found the stop he'd need, waited fifteen minutes and got on an early bus. He paid with the five pound note and the driver said, 'I haven't got change for that.'

'It doesn't matter, you can keep it.' The bus was empty. 'For yourself … I won't tell anyone.'

Soon he was walking down a familiar street of jacarandas and bluestone gutters. Daylight beginning, and viburnum, as he remembered the smell from outside his window. Now this sweet scent *was* childhood. And when he smelt it he was allowed return, if only for a few moments. Sonia's little brother, Griff's boy, John McCabe, the teaser of Shirley, the rider of brontosaur-sized horses. He went through Dr Bailey's front gate, looked up and down the street, walked around the side of the house and fetched the key from the gas box. Again, checking, back to the front porch, and inside through the big door that was so heavy it groaned on its hinges.

'Hello?' he called, although he knew the doctor was still away.

Quiet. Dusty lights in shards from the stained glass that Nan had to polish every fortnight. Don Quixote. Sancho and the donkey and windmill, fields of grain and loaves of bread. Which made him think. To the kitchen, although all he could find was butter and jam, mustard and sarsaparilla. He drank it, searched the drawers where the cereals were kept, filled a bowl with Corn Flakes and tried to eat them dry. There wasn't much point. So he spat out the bolus, washed it down the sink, cleaned up. After all, he had no beef with Dr Bailey.

The stereogram. Mozart. There'd been plenty of Mozart over the years. The operas were best. You could hear the fear and love in people's voices. He just relaxed, a few feet from the bookcase, with the early sun on his face.

*Awake!* Dr Bailey wasn't religious, so why the magazines with Jesus on the front? He opened one, and inside: 'To dear Edmund – I haven't given up on you yet! Your Servant, Charlie Bass'.

He wondered how Charlie had known Dr Bailey. He searched the pile for clues. Every issue, a comment from their zealot neighbour (Roland's words). And September 1960: 'You went a long way to cure me, but it was Him who saved me!'

Hal flipped through a magazine. Predictions about the end of the world; atom bombs would do the work, but it wasn't the Russians or Americans, it was Satan, arranging it all. As he heard Charlie, for the past months, years, sitting under their arbour, opening to Revelations; Mary saying, 'It's funny, isn't it, how people never change?'

'How's that?' Charlie asked her.

'Never get smarter, or wiser, or able to see their own limitations.'

Followed by the usual arguments, Shirley smiling, but covering her mouth, Roland lighting up and explaining how it was nice, wasn't it, when the irises flowered.

Hal was feeling tired. It had been a long night. He went upstairs, laid on Dr Bailey's bed and replayed every moment of the last few days. He'd have to go back. He didn't fancy it. Again. Like the same story told in monthly instalments, the soundtrack of familiar voices pleading with him, soothing him.

There was no hope sleeping, so he went to the window, pulled the curtain across and looked out. A nice little humpty-dumpty sky, stretching out to Darwin, Melville Island, London. A life for the taking, although he felt most of it was just air, little tornadoes of missed opportunity that collapsed in on their own gravity.

He noticed a man staring up at him. He froze. There was no point moving. The man just waited, and eventually called out, 'What are you doing in there?'

*Shit.*

'Dr Bailey never said nothin' …'

Hal couldn't hear the rest. He opened the window and said, 'I'm the new cleaner.'

'He has a lady for that.'

'I'm her grandson, Hal Griffin.' Stopping, cursing himself for saying it.

The man stormed across his garden, along the street, and through Dr Bailey's gate. A moment later there was a knock at the door. Hal ran down the stairs, stopped in the entry he'd learned to polish, and waited for the shadow under the door to go away. But it didn't. Just more knocking. 'Open the door or I'll call the police.'

He wondered what he was afraid of. He'd never done anything wrong. Always tried to be polite, helpful, do the right thing. But it only ever got him in trouble. He moved, knocked the pile of magazines to the floor, tried to catch them but turned awkwardly and disturbed the record. Although Mozart kept playing.

'You still in there?'

'I'm the new cleaner.' Angrily, he opened the door.

'Cleaner, my arse,' the man said.

'Nan Griffin, my Nan, you know her?'

The man stepped forward, grabbed his arm and said, 'You can come with me, and wait for the coppers.' He pulled Hal hard, and it hurt him. And in one action, Hal swung, collected the man on the side of the face, and he fell. Hal watched him lying, almost still, groaning a little, and felt no pity. This is what happened when you didn't give people a chance. The man looked up and said, 'Don't think I won't remember you, Griffin.'

Hal walked through Mary's garden, checked to make sure no one was around, then went in through the back door. Left turn, into Sam's sleep-out.

Sam was sitting on his bed cutting his toenails. Like he was expecting him. 'Did they bring you home?'

'No.'

It dawned on him. 'You didn't?'

'I couldn't stay any longer, Sam.'

'They'll be looking for you.' Sam patted the chair beside his bed and Hal sat down.

'I didn't have much choice, Sam.' Hal feared the old man would say, I've finished with you, Hal. I can't help no more. That would be the worst thing of all.

But Sam said, 'Doesn't matter what's happened. It can all be fixed.'

So Hal told him about his night: Glenside, Dr Bailey's. 'I didn't know what to do, Sam.'

'I know, I know. It's not your fault.' Sam held Hal's hand and stroked it. He realised he hadn't done this for years. Since Hal'd come in, crying, telling him about something horrible his mum had called him.

The back door was ajar. Shirley was standing in a shadow, listening. Her feet were cold on the concrete floor.

Sam was thinking. 'We should tell your mum and dad.'

'No.'

'It can all be fixed.'

Hal stared at him, pleadingly. 'I can't tell 'em.'

'You gotta try.' Sam squeezed his hand tightly. Shirley could see through the crack. She couldn't understand why her uncle was so generous. She repeated this word in her head. *Generous.* Why?

'Haven't I always done the best for you, Hal?'

'Yes.' He started crying.

Sam reached over and half-hugged him. 'Don't start all that. Don't get anxious. Remember?'

Hal said, 'I can't face Dad. Maybe later, if someone explains.'

Shirley couldn't believe it. But she wasn't surprised. She knew Hal could be violent. She knew he liked to get his way. She knew his actions could be loveless.

'Okay,' Sam decided. 'Follow me.'

Shirley ducked back into the kitchen as Sam and Hal emerged from the sleep-out, out the back door and into the shed. Shirley moved forward, into the doorway, and across the concrete, to the shed door. She listened as Sam settled Hal in his old armchair, covered him with a blanket and said, 'Get some sleep.'

Then he came back in. She returned to her room and to bed. She pulled the sheets up under her chin and tried to stop shivering, but her feet were too cold.


Hal had met Alice in the city, bought her a sandwich, taken her to a park; they'd sat down. He'd said, 'I wouldn't say we're partners.'

She'd looked surprised. 'We are, aren't we?'

'Friends.'

'Friends? After all that?'

He'd turned away. 'I don't think anyone would want to be with me.'

She hadn't responded.

'I think, considering, we just go our separate ways.'

Silence, as she held her sandwich in her lap.

He woke with the feeling that he was a bum. Maybe it wasn't too late. He could sneak in, call her, say sorry. She'd take him back. There was no doubt, she always forgave him. Or had.

He remembered watching her shoulders jiggling as she cried and feeling almost nothing, a clinical detachment (like Dr Neri's) as he waited for her to stop blubbering. He couldn't remember why he'd done it. Now he regretted it more than anything. He hadn't enjoyed, or not enjoyed, seeing her cry and plead.

'You won't even tell me why.'

'There's nothing to tell. I'm busy with race calling.'

'Busy? Twice a week?'

He remembered thinking this was a bad excuse, that no excuse would have been better. 'You'll find someone else.'

He felt gutless: the sort of behaviour Mary and his mum talked about over tea, shaking their heads, saying how could people be so awful? All of his *business* had meant nothing to Alice. She'd accepted every bit of it. She knew what it meant when the phone rang. It meant Ena and Roland were having trouble, and could she come over and talk to him.

He heard voices: his mum and dad, and two baritones. He couldn't make out words, but it sounded ominous. He stood, went to the shed door and opened it an inch. He could see beyond the connective tissue of arch. There were two policemen talking to his parents. His mum was standing with her arms crossed, sometimes shaking her head, sometimes asking questions, explaining something (perhaps) before turning to his dad for comfort. He had his arms on his hips. Hal knew what this meant. There was a problem, and they'd fix it.

Then he saw Sam walking down the side of the house. His dad called to him, 'Sam, you got a minute?'

Sam joked, 'I knew they'd get you eventually, Griff.' But went over, listened, acted surprised and made a few comments.

Hal could feel his heart pumping. Wondered whether he should just turn himself in. The only thing stopping him was Ena. He knew she'd overreact. His dad would be okay. He'd listen, argue on his behalf, and try to bring order to the scene. But his mum, she'd just start cursing him.

Sam headed back to his house, under the arch, towards the shed. As he went past he said, 'Close it.'

So Hal slowly closed the door and waited. He stood staring at the old iron, the flaking paint, and felt ill. Then the door opened and Sam came in. He didn't speak. Just looked at Hal, thinking.

'What did they say?' Hal asked.

'The neighbour, from Dr Bailey's ...'

Hal walked back to his chair and sat down. Sam lifted a saddle off another chair and sat opposite him. 'I know this fella, you could go stay with him, while I speak to the police ... sort things out.'

'You reckon?'

'He wouldn't mind. He was one of Trevor's mates.'

'Where's he live?'

Sam didn't respond. He was planning the logistics, weighing it all up. Then, 'I'll lock the shed from the outside. You okay pissing in a bottle?'

'Yes.'

'I'll get you something to eat when I get back.'

'Where are you going?'

'Keep quiet.' He was at the door, then out, then locking it.

Hal was left alone in the dark. He dared not switch on a light.

Sam went into his sleep-out. Mary was inside, making his bed.

'Leave that,' he said to her.

'It's gotta get done.'

'Leave it!' He handed her a tea cup and said, 'Go see Griff and Ena. There's been some trouble with Hal.'

'Again?'

'Go on. Ena's upset.'

She shook her head, took the cup and left.

Sam waited until he heard the click of the Griffins' back door. He moved his bed away from the wall, climbed in behind it and knelt down. Then he removed a loose brick, took out a tin and opened it. The notes had been flattened. He removed them, a few at a time: fifty, a hundred, two hundred. He left fifty and replaced the tin, the brick, his bed. He slid the notes into his wallet, sat down, picked up his form and studied it. He thought about each horse. It wasn't a particularly difficult task. Picking up a pen, he started circling names.

Shirley was still watching: the crack between door and wall.

When he was finished he came out of his sleep-out, looked around, and walked from the yard, down Burleigh Avenue, across Torrens Road into a quieter-than-normal Tuesday race meeting. Shirley followed at a distance. She watched as he took several notes from his wallet, put on bets, collected the stubs, and stood waiting for the broadcast. As he listened, then returned to the bookies, collected money, put on more bets, returned to his spot and waited.

She knew exactly what he was doing. She wondered why he'd never done it before. Mary was always saying how much she'd love to see England. And the roof, that needed replacing. He even let her buy cheap cuts of meat. But for Hal, he'd risk everything. Even his little stash (as he called it). 'Yes, I've got a bit waiting, just in case.'

'What?' they'd asked.

'Remember, the Depression? It'll happen again, and you'll need cash. Anything in the bank will be worthless.'

He'd told them this money was the result of years of saving. 'Enough to keep us comfy, sister, in our old age.'

'So, where is it?'

'Ah, that I can't say.'

Shirley watched and waited. Sam returned to the same bookie, spoke to him, and laughed. Then he handed him all of his money. The man wrote on a slip and gave it to him. Sam leaned on a big iron beam, and waited.

After the race, Sam stood motionless, listening to the correct weights. Then he let his slip drop to the ground; it fluttered, and settled in a sea of stubs.

He walked home. Not dragging his feet, as such, but she knew every thought that was going through his head. Across Torrens Road, down Burleigh Avenue and down the driveway. Unlocking the shed, going in and closing the door, but not enough to keep the voices in.

She heard him say, 'I've still got fifty quid. That's enough for a bus ... you'll have to give him something for board. Wait here, I'll get the money. A few clothes (you're nearly as big as me). Then we'll have to get a bus to town.'

Shirley wasn't happy with this. It was time Hal was made accountable.

When Sam opened the door she was waiting for him. 'You can't give it to him,' she said.

He stopped, realising. 'I gotta.' He walked past her, into his room, and dragged the bed from the wall.

'That's all you got.'

'I got the pension. I gotta help him.'

'He should go to the police.'

'No.' He took out the tin, and the last of the money. He turned, and she was blocking the doorway.

'It's yours ... ours. Running away's not gonna help him.'

Sam glared at her. 'I've been looking out for him his whole life. I'm not gonna give up on him now.'

'What about me? And Mary?'

Sam was standing with the fifty pounds in his hand. He didn't know what to do. All he knew was that Hal couldn't save himself, and he had no intention of seeing him locked away. 'He needs our help, Shirley.'

She knew this was true. A prison would finish him. But she wanted to say, Every time you took him to the track, told him what to say, showed him your badges, squeezed his knee (I saw how you did it, the look on your face), put your arm around him … every time … She turned and Hal was there. 'I'm sorry, Shirley. I think I've fucked up.'

She ran, from the house, the yard, down the street.

Sam handed Hal the money. 'Back in the shed. I better get her.' He went out, letting the door slam.

Hal wondered what to do. Return to the shed, wait, board the bus, arrive in some shithole, lock himself in a room, and every time there was a noise, look to see if they'd come for him? He thought, No more. Running. Listening. Waiting. Thinking things over a hundred thousand times.

He left the house, the yard, and set off.

Three am. Hal sat behind Wisden's fruit shop on a seat they'd left out. The unseasonal rain fell short of his feet, slowly filling a series of puddles full of cabbage leaves and old fruit. A piece of spirit-smelling paper in his lap; a note from the wholesale market explaining that all trucks must be parked in the designated ranks. Hal folded the sheet – halves, quarters, diagonals – until he had a small boat. Aniline purple ran down his wrist, and arm. He examined his boat from several angles, seemed pleased with what he'd done, knelt in front of a long puddle made by the rain from the gutter, and launched the craft. Watched how it floated, but then started filling with rain, becoming heavier, lower in the water.

He could remember his father showing him how to fold a boat. It seemed strange, how you kept looking, but couldn't see where people had gone. But you kept searching the banks and inlets and the shacks people had built and the jungle and its various wild animals.

Hal stood, covered his head with a folded newspaper, and ran out to the street. Then back along Burleigh Avenue, down the familiar drive, through the arch into his second home. He noticed Shirley's light, and knew he could set things right. So he quietly went in the back door, closed it, walked down the hall and knocked.

Nothing.

'Shirley?' He opened the door and looked in. She'd fallen asleep with a magazine in her hands. He knelt beside her. 'Shirley?'

She woke, and realised what was happening. 'Mum!'

'Ssh! I just wanna talk.'

She sat up, covering herself with sheets. 'Get out.'

'I wanted to say sorry.'

She sensed the young, hopeless Hal, before he'd turned. 'For what?'

'I know I did some pretty dumb things, and how you took it, and what you did to yourself that time ...'

'*How I took it?*' The terror gave way to anger. 'You think you can come in and it'll be okay?'

'No.' He tried to make her understand. 'I got out of Glenside, then, at Dr Bailey's ...'

She allowed herself to slide down. 'You gotta go to the police. Now. We'll wake your mum and dad.'

'They're gonna lock me away.'

'For a while, perhaps. But what else are you gonna do?'

'Get away.'

'With Sam's fifty quid? How long will that last?'

'He'll send more.'

'He won't. Now they know he's making bets. He's not meant to do that. He'll be finished. Cos of you, Hal.'

He stood.

'Sam's done everything for you. You know why that is, don't you?'

'Quiet!' Hal said, clenching his fists against his cheeks.

He heard Mary's door open. Turned, ran from the room, and she saw him. 'Hal?' He opened the back door and went out into the rain. Sam came out, calling after him. 'Hal! Get in the shed!'

Now, the rain was heavy. Hal had to work to keep moving. Tripped on a gutter, fell, picked himself up, and wondered what to do. The only light came from Cheltenham. The big spots that lit up the side of the grandstand: NEXT MEETING MAY 3.

The gates were locked so he climbed the lowest of the stone walls and tumbled inside. Then, across the concourse, the saddling yard, the track, up the steps to the starter's box. Where Sam had put binoculars to his eyes and said, 'Watch that mare in the red and black, she's won seven outa eight starts.' Where he'd talked to him, softly, and said, 'No matter what anyone says, believe me, it wasn't no fun.'

'Musta been okay, to kill Germans?'

'No better than you killing your mum and dad. You ever thought about that?'

'They're not Germans.'

'But Germans have got sons, haven't they? And the chances are, they love them.'

This had been the conversation, for years. A fathering, of sorts, while his own dad sat painting leafless trees.

He got to the top and tried the handle but the box was locked. He yanked it, then stood back and kicked it. He felt he must get in. Kicked it again, but the door held firm. Down the steps, across the track and into the grandstand. Up to the back, where he'd first called. He sat in the same spot and tried to remember the names of each horse. Then he started shivering and decided he didn't care.

The rain eased, and stopped.

He spent the next hour walking around the course, remembering. It was nothing without the people he'd grown to know, and like. Mr Graham, the jockey-club president, who'd offered him his first job. 'Two races, every Saturday. You like the country, Hal?'

'Yes.'

'Mount Gordon, first Monday of the month. Then you can drive to St Albans and call the program. Tummaville. That's how all the greats got started, Hal.'

'But I haven't got a licence.'

'So? Can you drive?'

'I guess.'

'So drive. Coppers don't bother about that sorta stuff up there.'

It had been his post-education apprenticeship. Once a month, cheap pubs with names like Fresno's Inn and the Green Anvil. Country-killed lamb and local girls who liked fellas with a bit of oil in their hair, who could talk (and race calling, that was more like a serenade). These were the times he remembered. When the meeting didn't begin until he arrived, studied the form, tightened his tie, strapped on his binoculars and drank a glass of warm barley water.

He came to the stables. Gypsy was watching him. He approached her, and ran his hand across her flank. Then he took off his wet clothes and lay down in the fresh, dry hay.

She sniffed his naked body.

The next morning Mary sat among the sheets in Shirley's bedroom, looking through her daughter's diary. She heard Sam in the kitchen and called, 'I'll be out in a minute.'

It had been a long night. After Hal's visit she'd checked on her daughter, asked what had happened, then Shirley's eyes had rolled and she'd slumped forward.

'Sam!'

He'd come in and said, 'Ambulance. Quick!'

Fifteen minutes later the paramedics had lifted Shirley onto a gurney, covered her with a rug and taken her out to the ambulance. Roland and Ena had been there. Ena had said, 'I'll just pop something on.'

'No, go back to bed,' Mary had replied. 'I'll call. Perhaps come in later.'

Roland, in his pyjamas and dressing gown, rubbing the third day of whiskers on his chin, had said, 'What d'yer reckon brought it on?'

Mary had looked at her brother. He'd said, 'It doesn't take much.'

Mary returned to the diary. Comments about teachers; exam grades; and scribbled in small letters: 'He doesn't have a real interest.

Obsessed with it for his age (not even 16). Why he thought I'd want to see it? Needs help needs help needs help!'

A few pages later: 'Enough to make you decide. Things will be better, ok. Instead of sitting, waiting for him. St Catherine and Theresa showed how'.

Her first thought was to show Roland and Ena. See, proof. She did it to herself because of Hal. But she couldn't do this. That would be the end of everything. Especially now, after a day of searching: Roland driving up and down Torrens Road, fending off more visits from the police.

Sam was at the door. 'Ena says to come in for a cuppa.'

Ten minutes later they were gathered around the Griffins' table. It took another minute until someone spoke. Ena said, 'I've rung his friends.'

'I can't think where he'd go,' Mary said.

'No,' Sam agreed.

Silence, again.

Roland stared into his tea, but didn't want to drink it. 'I walked around the school. Got them to open the sheds, everything.'

And Ena, 'You spoke to Judy and Barry?'

'Yes. John, too.'

'What do you reckon?'

'I reckon he's sitting in someone's shed.' He turned to Sam. 'That race calling … I thought we were onto something, Sam.'

'We are,' he replied. 'It's early days. We'll find him, he'll get looked after. Then he can come with me, and we can keep working.'

Hal listened. He was always listening. This time, in his still damp clothes, standing inside the back door, creeping towards the kitchen.

'He can't stand being locked up, Sam.'

'He'll come home when it's all sorted.'

At last, Roland tried his tea. 'That time we drove to Mount Gordon. He was dressed up in that goddamn suit you bought him, Ena. He was reading the form on the way. Three hour drive. Reading it, the whole way. He said he didn't want to make no mistakes.'

Hal leaned against the door jamb.

'I was sure that'd be it, Sam.'

'It will. I know for a fact, Griff.'

'Then he asked to drive, and I let him, and he was good. Not like that time at Osmond Hill, remember, Ena?'

She tried to smile, but couldn't.

'When we arrived at Mount Gordon he rushed from the car. "First race is in five minutes."' Roland remembered sitting in the stand full of suited farmers, the smell of ale, everywhere, the sound of his son, 'coming up on the inside, half a length …'

To Hal, these were directions on how he should move. Mr Saxby was making it clear: 'Swing your partner round and round and turn your partner upside down …'

Sam said, 'We'll find him today.'

'And then it begins again,' Roland said.

'What?' Ena asked.

Hal knew what he meant. He didn't think he deserved to be locked away. He'd never meant to do any of this. He'd just gone along with what the world had planned. He was sitting in front of the doctor's bookcase, and the number of volumes suggested the size of the world: its every desert and ocean, animal, town and city. He took down a volume and leafed through. The illustrations showed people were made up of sinew and tendon. He could hear Nan calling: 'You're very quiet. Are you behaving yourself?'

He wasn't sure what to say. He thought he was, but you never knew if what you were doing was allowed. So much wasn't; so many things caused problems.

He heard Sam say, 'They're gonna need another caller. It's not something the young ones want to do anymore.'

Hal knew the answers had never been in the shed. You had to look elsewhere: Nan, cleaning the doctor's toilet.

'Yuck,' he said. 'That's a nasty job.'

'Someone's gotta do it.'

'Why can't he clean his own toilet?'

'Cos he's busy fixing people up.' She sat beside him. 'I reckon this is the best job in the world.'

'No?'

'People leave you alone. And you can get lost in your own thoughts.'

He thought he knew what she meant. 'Like books?'

'Exactly. You can get lost in a book. Doesn't mean yer actually lost. Thing is, you gotta find your place in the world, Prince Hal.'

'Where's that?'

'Well, you won't know till you find it, will you?'

He still didn't know; couldn't hear.

'So, when I work it out …?'

'You'll know. But I think you'll be a great man, Hal. I feel it in me bones.'

'Like yer back bone?'

'Yes. You're smart, and caring.' She hugged him. 'Mr Curtin, he's a great man. You could be like him.'

'Dad, isn't he famous too?'

'Yes, you could be like him.'

Hal could hear them talking. About Shirley, and how was she sitting up, asking for a new magazine; the Smith Street shops, you checked them, Griff? He could hear cups in saucers and knew they'd still be drinking tea in twenty years' time. They'd all be talking about small, shitty things that didn't matter, but did, really.

He walked out of the house, into the shed. He knew exactly what he should do. There was a box of ropes and he took the strongest. He kicked the easel out of the way. He threw the rope over the beam and tied it off against the wall; found a chair and climbed it; tied the rope in a loop.

He wanted so much for people to understand, but realised there was no point writing anything. Words would reduce it to a simple problem and solution, like mixing the right amount of paint. He doubted it could ever be fixed. But it was okay. Despite everything (the chooks, the mental ward, the things he shouldn't have said to Shirley), he felt at peace. He loved his mum and dad and Sonia and Sam and Mary and Shirley, all of them, even Charlie Bass, more than anything.

He looked at the half-finished image on his dad's canvas, lying on the ground: the boy in the boat.

George Wallace was saying, 'It takes an old dog for a hard road.'

'What's that mean, Mr Wallace?'

'George, call me George, son. It means that you just keep going. And it's a bloody long road. And it never seems to end.'


Weeks passed: the funeral, the wake of scones and weak tea, neighbours in naphthalene suits and letters sent from friends and relatives who couldn't make it. Dr Neri came, but didn't have much to say. Just, 'I often think about doing something else. You don't want a job that keeps ending like this.' Ena had always thought him arrogant.

Jude Ireland made a stew, and Ena said, 'Thanks, I'll put it with the others.' Showing her a freezer full.

'I remember him mowing our front lawn, Ena. Barry's Victa. One day he went past and watched Barry working and said, "Do you have to push hard?" Barry says, "A bit. Do you want a go?" Next thing, he's doin' the lawn, and Barry's sittin' back watchin', weren't you, Barry?'

'Yes.'

'He was a very decent boy.'

Ena thought it funny how the memories (and you couldn't blame people for trying to soften the blow) were always of Hal-as-child. Children were cuter, funnier, of course, but she wondered if it wasn't something else: Hal-before-the-pills; before the long nights on the cold roof. 'Hi, Mrs Ireland.'

'Hi, Hal. What you doin' up there?'

'Nothin' much.'

John Carey brought bulbs and offered to plant them. Roland said no, thanks. There was no way bulbs could help anything. He knew John was too practical for food, cards, flowers, or even memories.

Anyway, he was sick of memories.

Even now, sitting in his shed, weeks later, looking at his smashed Dodge. He wondered if he'd ever get around to fixing it. What would that matter? Although he'd have a fixed car, he'd still have a dead son. As it was, he had a reminder: of the body (so much dead weight), the rope (which he'd found, curled up, in the boot of the car), the shock that hadn't yet begun to fade.

Backing the car out, waiting on the road, as he drank from the bottle. Driving the streets of Pennington – and then, in a moment of anger-with-the-world, planting his foot on the accelerator, speeding up, flying around corners, wheels lifting, the car taking its own path and hitting a power pole.

Other times it might've been a big deal, but this time he just got out, inspected the damage, got back in and drove home. Wiping the dust from the dash: St Alban's dust (as they'd driven towards another meet), Cloncurry dust (trip three, 1959), Katherine dust (trip two, 1958), Broome dust (trip one, 1956). Thinking, all of this will have to be cleaned off, eventually. In the same way Hal's room would need to be sorted, his clothes given to St Vincent's, his books returned to the lounge room shelves.

Roland was holding his brush, but he didn't want to work. There was a small hole in the top of the canvas where it had fallen. It helped tell the story of the boy. He was eleven (he supposed) and his hair had been shaved (nits). Although his face was tanned the application of light suggested a setting sun, or full moon. Perhaps, he guessed, it was finished. But even if it was, what was to be done with it? Sold (sitting unloved on a cold wall)? Hung in the house? Given away?

He put down his brush and decided he'd had enough.

Hall's Creek (trip one, 1956). He'd been sitting beside a dry creek, capturing it in charcoal, and Hal had said, 'What's it matter?'

'What's what matter?'

'Landscapes. You just paint it all brown, with a little dead tree, so why do you need to sit and sketch it?'

'It's how I work.'

'Better off making it all up. Then we could go do something fun.'

'We do have fun. How many other fathers take their boys on trips around Australia?'

'To sort them out? Cos they've always been too busy painting?'

Roland picked up the canvas, walked across the shed and placed it in the box with the other unsold works. He carried them out to the chookyard and made a pile. Returned to the shed, found turps and matches and went back. He doused his paintings and lit them. The flames ate the oil, the canvas, the frames, especially. It was the same campfire they'd built every night. Hal was still sitting beside it, making toast. 'I reckon Ernie's a few pence short.'

'I wouldn't say that.'

'His hand was always shaking.' And he showed his dad.

'He might have something.'

'Like what?'

'A wasting disease.'

'Like what?'

'There's some bad ones. People just end up in bed, with someone wiping their bum and feeding them like a baby. Promise me, Hal, if I ever get like that ...'

A log had rolled from the fire and Hal had pushed it back with his foot. He'd said, 'You gotta listen, Dad.'

'How's that?'

'Remember that story, about how the little bit got here?' He'd indicated the indent below the nose. 'An angel appeared to some kid, and placed her finger on his lips to make him quiet, and she left a mark.'

'So, angels want quiet?'

'They want us to listen.'

'For what?'

Hal remembered what Nan had told him. 'You never know till you hear it.'

Roland watched the burning canvases, and was glad they were gone. 'Mr Griffin?'

He turned around. 'Alice.'

She stood behind him, smiling. 'I just heard.' She stepped forward and handed him a bunch of carnations. 'I don't know if these are the right sort of flowers.'

He took them. 'Thanks.'

She noticed the paintings. 'Getting rid of a few?'

He only smiled.

'I feel bad I didn't come to the funeral, but I didn't know. I would've.'

'They're not much fun.'

'I thought …'

He felt the heat of the flames. 'I had it all planned. You two were gonna end up together, and you'd have a firm hand (like Ena), and he'd grow out of it.'

'But he never would've?'

He shrugged. 'That was about the worst day, when he told us he'd told you that …'

Ena had called, and apologised on Hal's behalf, and told her they'd talk to him, but neither could understand why he'd done it.

Roland asked, 'I s'pose you've met someone else?'

'Not sure I want to. Sometimes he was just like a little boy … He'd hug you and say, "Do you think I should wear this?" Like that, Mr Griffin. It had nothing to do with … the rest of it. I just wish he woulda let me … but that's how he wanted it.'

Roland thought he should probably invite her in, but didn't

want to. Didn't want to explain Ena, in her nightie, in bed, for the second week straight. Searching for clues. In newspapers, comments scribbled in the columns of books, and in his diary.

But he couldn't avoid it. 'Wanna come in for a cuppa?'

'No, thanks. I don't want to intrude.'

He didn't argue. 'Pop by then, okay?'

'I will.' And she was gone.

He stood beside his fire, and as it burnt down he fed it with the remains of his paintings. He didn't feel bad about it. There were millions of paintings. Now there were a few less.

Then Sonia was at the back door. 'Can you come in and talk to her?' she called.

'Coming.'

Her, sitting propped up with three pillows, trying to read Hal's increasingly jumbled thoughts: *if all of the maths (A × A = B × B) adds up to something (unlikely); if it can be used for something good (unlikely) like pricing raincoats, or ties, or crockary someones sold …*

Or the comments she'd read about Shirley. It seemed obvious what had happened. She wondered if Mary knew. She must've. And if this was the case, perhaps they should talk about it?

He'd written movie reviews (*Key Largo I give this three stars out of five E. Robinson is much better than Bogart*); and a recipe for Lady Alice biscuits (*butter biscuits – sooooo good*).

Sonia came in and sat on the bed. Although she'd returned to her flat, Ena had called her back ('You doin' anything today? I know, but it's so quiet with no one around … Yes, yes, she does, but that's not the same … If you wanna pop over, Dad'll pick you up').

Ena smiled, rubbed her daughter's hand and said, 'Hal and Shirley …'

'What?'

'I think she had a soft spot for him.'

'Rubbish. He made her life hell.'

'And you did too.'

'Well.' Sonia remembered, and guessed this was a good time. 'That time Mr Carey caught me shoplifting?'

'Yes?'

'It wasn't me.'

She explained: Shirley emerging from the shop with the *Photoplay*. Her saying, 'How did you afford that?'

'Can you keep a secret?'

'You didn't!'

Sonia didn't see why there should be any secrets anymore. 'I took it from her and said we gotta give it back, and she argued and said no, and then Mr Carey came out and saw me with it.'

Ena was remembering the day, the shock when they'd been presented with the thief. 'Why didn't you say nothin'?'

'Felt bad.'

'Why?'

'I'd always been a bitch to her.'

Roland walked in, sat on the bed, rubbed Ena's leg and said, 'I'll cook the tea, will I?'

'I'm gettin' up.'

'Stay, stay.'

'I'll do it,' Sonia said, standing.

'Them chops need using up,' Ena said.

Sonia was gone. Ena settled back into her pillow. 'I better get up.'

'You don't have to do nothin'.'

She just said, 'I don't feel I wanna do anything.'

'You will. Alice dropped some flowers.'

Her face lightened. 'You should've asked her in.'

'I did. She said no. She's upset.' He looked out of the room, across the hall, at his son's bed. It had been made with clean sheets, and it was waiting for him.

The following Saturday there were no races. There were several trucks, marked 'J.W. Demolition', loaded with the seats they were stripping from the stands. Several teams of men, unbolting them from the boards and carrying them down. Sam sat on the bottom row. He knew it was only an hour, or less, before they took these.

Governments, he thought. Always looking for something to sell. A hundred and twenty-five acres destined for roads with names like Rosewood and Pine, Curtin and Chifley. In the mid-distance the metal stands from the bookmakers' ring had been crushed and stacked, and the jockey-club offices had been demolished. Now there were gaps full of light, waiting for asphalt. No more Capstan afternoons, or horse shit in your soles.

Roland appeared in what was left of the entrance (every brick taken away for paving). He looked around, across the concourse, and saw Sam. Hands in his pocket, he walked towards him. Sitting, he said, 'Mary told me ...'

Sam didn't look at him. 'I can't see why they need more houses. There are plenty of houses, aren't there?'

'Land this close to the city is valuable. That's what matters.'

'All them new suburbs, plenty of places. But this is all we've got.'

Roland had brought a jar of whisky. He took it out of his coat pocket, unscrewed the lid and drank. 'Not the first time you've been out of a job?' He offered the jar but Sam shook his head.

'The first job I've actually wanted.'

He'd once sold taps, for Nevil Reenen. 'Used to go door-to-door, remember?'

'Yeah.'

'I was shit at that. Never sold nothin'. People kept inviting me in for a cuppa, and an hour later I'd leave empty-handed.'

'He sacked you?'

'He said, "Sam, I'm happy to have you keep trying ... I mean, selling stuff, it takes time ... but you gotta ask yerself: Is this for me?"'

A grader was already levelling the ground in front of the finish line.

'That's what I used to say to Hal: It'll take time. Years, perhaps.'

'And he was comin' along.'

'He was.'

'You were onto something there, Sam.'

Another team was cutting the legs off the starter's box. They watched as it moved, then fell, as the iron crumbled, the legs bent, the box itself shattered to pieces.

'Have I ever said thank you?' Roland asked.

'No, then it'd all be some soap opera.'

Roland looked at Sam, intrigued. After all these years, he still didn't know him.

'If that was the case, I'd be thanking you for all you've done for Mary and Shirley.' Tired of the thought, Sam said, 'I'll have to stop comin' here, eh?'

'You could go to other tracks?'

'No, I couldn't.' He stood, stepped down the few steps, and headed for the gate. Roland followed, and said, 'It's such a pity.'

'What?'

'Losing your interest.'

'I haven't lost that.'

'Your job.'

'That neither.'

Although he had. Weeks earlier. Tim Johnson approaching him and saying, 'I been talking to some of the bookies, Sam.'

'Yeah?'

'I made it clear, years ago, didn't I?'

'You did, Tim.'

'So, I gotta let you go, Sam.'

As they walked, Sam thought of telling Roland, but dared not. One day, he might work it out. Mary or Shirley might let something slip, and they'd know, and that would be the worst thing of all. It would be like he'd killed him, sort of. Like, if he'd said something, and the police had taken Hal, and the doctor had sedated him, it might've been alright.

Roland said, 'I could drive yer, on Saturdays.'

'No. Thing was, the place was here, so you could wander over.' Sam stopped to remember. 'Tulloch. She was probably the best. A hundred years of Cheltenham and she ... hundred thousand at the S.J. Pullman Stakes last year.' He sighed, like even Tulloch didn't matter anymore.

They continued. 'A lot of shouting, and noise, and fellas losing their pay. Better it's all gone.'

'You don't think that.'

'In the grand scheme, Griff, it's nothing. Problem is, if you think about what really matters, you go crazy.'

'Man needs a hobby, Sam.'

'He tried, Griff. And he did fine.'

'He did.'

'Every time I cross that road, and walk through their park, I'll think of him. Every time I piss on their jungle jim.'

They walked slowly. The noise of construction faded behind them. Roland said, 'He fell off one of those when he was a kid.'

'Did he? I can't remember that?'

'Yes. Three stitches ... you don't remember?'

'No. There was that time when he broke his tooth in half ...'

'The fence?'

'That's right. He was trying to balance.'

Hal was walking behind them, at a fair distance. He remembered all these things, and more. He remembered when his dad held him, threw him in the air, caught him. He wanted to say, I would've been out of work too. But they wouldn't hear him. So he stopped, and they walked on without him. He was left alone, on the cold streets of Pennington, with everything he'd ever known: the smell of a roast from Mrs Ireland's place, wet soursobs, the feeling that everything was so right, he could go on living forever.

They walked past Wisden's, and Roland saw it. Screwed up, dried out, but still a boat. A sweet purple colour. He stopped, knelt down and picked it up. Sam asked what it was but he just said, 'Nothing, I guess.' And throwing it in the weeds, continued.

They walked down the drive of number seventeen, and separated at the arch, but it would only be until ten-thirty tomorrow. Roland stood and listened: a mower, there was always a mower somewhere, a voice calling out, piles of chook shit, candied almonds and Mo, still cracking the same gags. He went into his shed, scooped a walnut from the chest, stood at the workbench and cracked it with a hammer. And there, among the jumble of tools, he saw an envelope. An Education Department stamp.

He smiled. Prince Hal had scribbled an explanation. 'Written by Hal Griffin: Father-Son Day 1948. To Sir Roland Griffin (Knighthood for painting pictures), from his son'.

He sat on his chair and opened it, smoothed the letter on his knee. The block print was hard to decipher in the light from the never-washed window. Ignoring, or perhaps savouring the thought of words, he raised his head and breathed deeply. Just the smell of turps, the wood, the almonds.

# Acknowledgements

Many thanks to Michael Bollen, Emily Hart, Margot Lloyd, Michael Deves, Ayesha Aggarwal and the rest of the team at Wakefield Press.

# DATSUNLAND

*Stephen Orr*

*A long-deserted drive-in, waiting for a rerun of the one story that might give it life; a child who discovers his identity in a photograph hidden in his parents' room ...*

Stephen Orr's stories are happy to let you in, but not out. In *Datsunland*, his characters are outsiders peering into worlds they don't recognise, or understand: an Indian doctor arriving in the outback, discovering an uncomfortable truth about the Australian dream; a family trying to have their son's name removed from a Great War cowards' list; a confused teenager with a gun making an ad for an evangelical ministry.

Each story is set in a place where, as Borges described, 'heaven and hell seem out of proportion'. There is no easy escape from the world's most desperate car yard, or the school with a secret that permeates all but one of the fourteen stories in *Datsunland*. Here is a glimpse of inner lives, love, the astonishment of being ourselves.

'When Orr nails it, his writing is piercing, brutal, powerful, both in respect to his unflinching gaze and his wielding of plain English like a weapon. You as a reader will survive, but not without blunt force trauma to show for it.' – Sam Cooney, *Australian*

'[Orr's] stories in this first collection tend to stop very effectively just short of the punchline, leaving the reader testing their own breathtaking interpretation of his implications.'
– Katharine England, *SA Weekend*

'At its best, the writing is insightful and strangely beautiful ... Orr holds the collection together with an impression of force and linguistic brutality.' – Catherine Noske, *Australian Book Review*

*For more information please visit wakefieldpress.com.au*

# HILL OF GRACE

## *Stephen Orr*

1951. Among the coppiced carob trees and arum lilies of the Barossa Valley, old-school Lutheran William Miller lives a quiet life with his wife, Bluma, and son Nathan, making wine and baking bread. But William has a secret. He's been studying the Bible and he's found what a thousand others couldn't: the date of the Apocalypse.

William sets out to convince his neighbours that they need to join him in preparation for the End. The locals of Tanunda become divided. Did William really hear God's voice on the Hill of Grace? Or is he really deluded? The greatest test of all for William is whether Bluma and Nathan will support him. As the seasons pass in the Valley, as the vines flower and fruit and lose their leaves, William himself is forced to question his own beliefs and the price he's willing to pay for them.

The Barossa Valley of the 1950s is beautifully captured in this, Stephen Orr's second novel. His first novel, *Attempts to Draw Jesus*, was a runner up in the 2000 Vogel Award and published by Allen & Unwin.

'His prose lovingly packed with particulars, Orr's characters assume poignant life as modernity and old-time religion go head to head in a wonderful period portrait.' – Cath Kenneally

*For more information please visit wakefieldpress.com.au*

# TIME'S LONG RUIN
## *Stephen Orr*

Nine-year-old Henry Page is a club-footed, deep-thinking loner, spending his summer holidays reading, roaming the melting streets of his suburb, playing with his best friend Janice and her younger brother and sister. Then one day Janice asks Henry to spend the day at the beach with them. He declines, a decision that will stay with him forever.

*Time's Long Ruin* is based loosely on the disappearance of the Beaumont children from Glenelg beach on Australia Day, 1966. It is a novel about friendship, love and loss; a story about those left behind, and how they carry on: the searching, the disappointments, the plans and dreams that are only ever put on hold.

*Winner, Unpublished manuscript award, Adelaide Festival*

*South Australian winner, 2012 National Year of Reading awards*

'In *Time's Long Ruin* [Orr] has conjured up the suburban claustrophobia of the Fifties and added to it streaks of … darker pigments. His Thomas Street, Croydon – particularly on hot days, when no one has enough to do and everyone gets on each other's nerves – is Adelaide's very distinctive version of Winton's *Cloudstreet*, Malouf's *Edmondstone Street* and White's *Sarsaparilla*; but the quality and vividness of Orr's evocation of those stultifying times ensures he can hold his head high in such illustrious company. *Time's Long Ruin* is a compelling page-turner.' – Richard Walsh

*For more information please visit wakefieldpress.com.au*

# DISSONANCE

## *Stephen Orr*

*Dissonance* begins with piano practice. Fifteen-year-old Erwin Hergert is forced to tackle scales and studies for six hours a day by his mother, Madge, who is determined to produce Australia's first great pianist. To help Erwin focus, Madge has exiled her husband, Johann, to the back shed.

Madge takes Erwin to Hamburg to continue his studies. Erwin prospers in Germany with his new teacher until he meets a neighbour, sixteen-year-old Luise, and finds there's more to life than music.

Meanwhile, Germany is moving towards war. Late 1930s Hamburg forms the backdrop to an increasingly difficult love-triangle, as Erwin is torn between the piano, Luise, and the demands of his love and devotion to his mother. Soon the bombs, real and imagined, start falling. Marriage and parenthood give way to death, and tragedy. Before long Erwin and Madge are drawn into the horrors of a war that leaves little time for music.

*Dissonance* is a re-imagining of the 'Frankfurt years' of Rose and Percy Grainger. This is a novel about love in one of its most extreme and destructive forms, and how people attempt to survive the threat of possession.

'Compelling ... an engrossing novel. Orr is a vivid storyteller.' – Stella Clarke, *Weekend Australian*

'Our own Wakefield Press has produced a nicely bound and presented work which ranks as one of the finest pieces of Australian writing I've seen for a long time.' – Peter C. Pugsley, *Indaily*

*For more information please visit wakefieldpress.com.au*

# THE HANDS

## Stephen Orr

*He didn't look like he could jump a bull, but she knew he could. It was all in the hands, he'd often explain. The will. The bloody mindedness.*

On a cattle station that stretches beyond the horizon, seven people are trapped by their history and the need to make a living. Trevor Wilkie, the good father, holds it all together, promising his sons a future he no longer believes in himself. The boys, free to roam the world's biggest backyard, have nowhere to go.

Trevor's father, Murray, is the keeper of stories and the holder of the deed. Murray has no intention of giving up what his forefathers created. But the drought is winning ....

### Longlisted for the 2016 Miles Franklin Literary Award

'Orr's ability to capture characters and the way they interact with each other is truly impressive. … It's pretty darn perfect.' – Sue Terry, *Whispering Gums*

'*The Hands* has the scope of a Greek tragedy – not only in its focus on the violence underlying familial relationships. Ineluctable fate seems to press on a family forced into painful reflection. The encroaching desert is, like the Greek Moirai, remorseless …' – Josephine Taylor, *Australian Book Review*

'The triumphant culmination of a five-book fascination with the dynamics of (family) groups as they function in extreme and often liminal situations ... Orr slides seamlessly in and out of his different characters' heads ... always moving the story efficiently along ... .' – Katharine England, *Advertiser*

*For more information please visit wakefieldpress.com.au*

Wakefield Press is an independent publishing and
distribution company based in Adelaide, South Australia.
We love good stories and publish beautiful books.
To see our full range of books, please visit our website at
wakefieldpress.com.au
where all titles are available for purchase.
To keep up with our latest releases, news and events,
subscribe to our monthly newsletter.


Find us!


Facebook: facebook.com/wakefield.press
Twitter: twitter.com/wakefieldpress
Instagram: instagram.com/wakefieldpress

www.ingramcontent.com/pod-product-compliance
Lightning Source LLC
Chambersburg PA
CBHW020423030726
47495CB00006B/1634